Louisa Heaton lives on Ha[...] with her husband, four child[...] worked in various roles in th[...] recently four years as a Community First Responder, answering 999 calls. When not writing Louisa enjoys other creative pursuits, including reading, quilting and patchwork—usually instead of the things she *ought* to be doing!

Sue MacKay lives with her husband in New Zealand's beautiful Marlborough Sounds, with the water on her doorstep and the birds and the trees at her back door. It is the perfect setting to indulge her passions of entertaining friends by cooking them sumptuous meals, drinking fabulous wine, going for hill walks or kayaking around the bay—and, of course, writing stories.

RISKING HER HEART ON THE TRAUMA DOC

LOUISA HEATON

THE GP'S SECRET BABY WISH

SUE MacKAY

MILLS & BOON

First Published in Great Britain 2020
by Mills & Boon, an imprint of HarperCollins*Publishers*
1 London Bridge Street, London, SE1 9GF

Risking Her Heart on the Trauma Doc © 2020 by Louisa Heaton

The GP's Secret Baby Wish © 2020 by Sue MacKay

ISBN: 978-0-263-28447-8

MIX
Paper from
responsible sources
FSC® C007454

This book is produced from independently certified FSC™ paper
to ensure responsible forest management.
For more information visit www.harpercollins.co.uk/green.

Printed and bound in Spain
by CPI, Barcelona

RISKING HER HEART ON THE TRAUMA DOC

LOUISA HEATON

MILLS & BOON

To Mary, my sister, my friend. xxx

CHAPTER ONE

JESS KNEW SHE'D made the right decision to come back. Standing at the front of the ferry as it chugged its way towards Thorney Island, she felt the cool breeze blowing through her hair, heard the noisy gulls circling overhead.

Thorney Island looked exactly as she remembered. Only smaller. She'd been brought here as a child by her father. Their annual holiday—one week away in a caravan, year after year, without fail. Until she'd got old enough to want something more.

The bustling harbour was filled with boats of all shapes and sizes: trawlers, dredgers, fishing boats and the occasional pleasure cruiser. It was as if she had only left yesterday, and the aroma in the air of brine and fish was just so familiar, so filled with happy memories, that it almost took her breath away.

She'd missed this, and it was something she'd never expected to feel—this *longing*. This *grief*. But of course it would remind her of the happy times she'd had here with her father. She should have expected it. Because remembering that happiness simply served to remind her of what she had lost.

The ferry slowed as it came into port, drifting in on the tide. She heard the harbour master and the others calling to one another in their thick Scottish accents and she smiled before she hurried back to get into her car, ready to drive off when they finally docked.

The waterfront looked the same—as if the island had been trapped in time from the second she'd left to this moment she was in now. She thought briefly about stopping to pop into the Harbour Café, to grab a coffee and a bite to eat, but she knew it would be busy, as it always was, and she was keen to get to the estate agents to pick up the key for her temporary rental property.

She'd have the rest of the day to settle in, and then tomorrow she would start work under her new boss, Dr Jack Campbell, who seemed to be a really nice man.

He'd interviewed her on the telephone and in a video call online, as she'd been unable to make it over to the island. He reminded her of her own father. They'd have been the same generation as each other and, with his silver hair and his twinkling blue eyes and his nice smile, Jack had made her feel very comfortable indeed.

She imagined that working for him at the island's cottage hospital would be interesting and educational, considering how broad the work requirements were. And he'd really liked it that she was already familiar with the island as apparently he'd had trouble trying to fill the post—candidates had been turning it down as there wasn't much opportunity to specialise, and most doctors were looking for their next step up the long ladder of success, rather than a small hospital.

The estate agency she was looking for was a little bit inland from the harbourfront, and she drove away from the waterside and found a small parking area behind the first street of shops. She parked, and pushed open the door of Wainwright's Estate Agency, hearing a bell ringing merrily above her head as she walked in.

There were three desks all in a line, and behind each one sat an agent dressed in a grey suit. Over the left breast pocket of their jackets, they each wore a name tag. Two of the agents were on the phone, so she walked over to the female agent who seemed free and glanced at her badge: *Moira*.

'Good morning, can I help you?' Moira smiled, all white teeth and thick-lashed eyes.

'Hello. I'm Dr Jessica Young and I've rented a flat on Haven Road. I was told I could collect the key here.'

'Okay. Do you know who you were dealing with?'

'Adrian.'

'Ah. He's not here today, but I can certainly help you. Have you brought your documents and ID?'

Jess delved into her bag to bring out all that was needed, and after a few moments of checking, she was passed a key with a label hanging from it.

'There's a map in the documentation, but Haven Road isn't far. I can direct you, if you'd like?'

'That's okay. I think I know where it is. It's that long road that runs towards the hospital, isn't it?'

Moira nodded. 'Aye, it is. Well, I hope you're happy there. Any problems, you'll need to contact your landlord. His details are in the pack.'

'Thanks.'

Jess headed back outside and took a brief moment to suck in the briny sea air just one more time before heading inland.

Fresh air and a fresh start was everything her own doctor had prescribed.

* * *

'You must be Dr Young—Jessica, isn't it?' asked the bespectacled, perfectly coiffed lady.

'Call me Jess.' She reached out her hand for the older woman to shake.

'Call me Judy. I'm Jack's wife. Also his receptionist and assistant extraordinaire.' She smiled. 'Did you have a calm crossing on the ferry?'

'Very calm, thank you.'

Jess liked Judy. She had the look of a stern librarian, with her glasses attached to a colourful chain around her neck.

'I'm afraid Jack has had to go out on a call, so he's not here to meet you as he planned.' Judy came out from behind her desk and indicated that Jess should follow her. 'Can I get you a cup of tea?'

'Oh, I'm fine, thank you.'

Judy escorted her towards a door that bore a plaque stating *Dr Jack W Campbell, Clinical Lead.*

'He's left a few things you'll need today, so let's get those.'

Jess waited as Judy searched Jack's desk, opening drawers and rummaging, and let her eyes scan the room. It was stylishly decorated, and had some added touches that Jess assumed had been made by Dr Campbell's wife. Some beautiful pot plants that she couldn't name. A sofa to one side of the room, beautifully arranged with some modern cushions, a piece of cross-stitch on the wall, of a busy harbourside filled with boats, and a windowsill filled to the brim with family photos in elegant silver frames.

They all seemed to be of the same person. A little boy growing into the man he appeared to be now. Handsome, too. One photo showed him stood in his university gown holding a scroll, a beaming smile upon his face. And to the side was a picture of the same young man kneeling down with a group of kids, all smiling towards the camera as a hot sun beamed down upon them.

Where was that? Egypt? Somewhere in Africa?

Another showed the man standing in the midst of a jungle, his face turned up to the heavens as it rained, his hands stretched out as if he was grateful for the rain.

'Settled in all right?' asked Judy.

'Yes, I have. I must thank your husband for the recommendation. The flat's a good size.'

'In good condition, too. Our son lives in the same building, so he did us all a favour by giving us his landlord's contact details.'

Their son lived in her building? She smiled, suddenly nervous.

'Ah! Found it!' Judy brandished a file full of paperwork and a temporary ID card on a lanyard with her name on it. 'You can use this until we get your photo taken. It's great to meet you at last. Jack had no doubt about you at all during the interview, but it's always better to meet someone in person, don't you think?'

Jess nodded. 'Absolutely.'

'Okay! So, we'll go through a few housekeeping bits and pieces and then we'll get you started. Adam's all ready to get you up and running.'

She frowned. 'Adam?'

'The other Dr Campbell.' She pointed at the framed photos with pride. 'He's been working abroad, but he's been back with us for just over a year now.'

'I thought I'd be working with Jack,' said Jess, her gaze lingering on the most prominent photo.

Adam was exactly the type of good-looking man that she'd be attracted to.

And she didn't need that sort of complication.

CHAPTER TWO

ADAM SAT IN a curtained-off cubicle, attending to a fisherman who'd got a nasty cut on his hand that needed stitching.

John McAllister had caught his hand whilst out on his latest fishing trip, and had bound it with a dirty used tea towel that had been in the boat's galley. Adam had had to clean it out, rinse the wound with saline and give him a tetanus shot, just to be on the safe side. Now he had his suturing kit out.

He had just tied the first stitch when he heard his mother's voice coming down the corridor, and turned to greet her as the curtains behind him swished open.

But Adam's voice caught in his throat when he spied the stunning young woman standing behind his mother. *Wow.* She was incredibly beautiful! And she'd totally taken his breath away. He actually forgot to breathe for a moment, until his burning lungs forced him to snap out of his trance.

He turned back to his patient and snipped the ends off that first stitch, in a state of disbelief that he'd reacted in such a way.

'Adam, sorry to interrupt you whilst you're working,

but this is the new doctor your father was telling you about—Dr Young.'

Adam put down his instruments carefully, trying very hard not to show that his hands weren't in his complete control, and gave his mum his full attention. He liked working for his father. Even though it was different from the way he'd thought it would be and his father didn't let him get away with anything. Not that he tried!

Jack Campbell ran the Thorney Island cottage hospital with a firm hand, ensuring their patients all received top-quality care at every point of contact. Adam didn't get any preferential treatment working for his father, which was what he'd been worried about when he'd first come here, after working abroad for so long with International Health. He'd not wanted the other staff to think that his father treated him differently, and because of that he had been working doubly hard, taking on extra hours and working double shifts whenever it was needed without complaint.

'I'd shake your hand, but...' But he was in the middle of a procedure. He knew she'd understand. Besides, he wasn't sure he wanted to make any physical contact with her.

He tried his hardest not to look at Dr Young again, because she was somehow making him nervous, his body reacting to her in ways he'd not expected.

For such a long time now he'd stopped noticing women in that way, and he'd been totally fine with it. He didn't need complications at work. He certainly didn't need complications in his private life. For a long time women had just been friends and colleagues to him. He liked them, and enjoyed their company, but he had shut off his carefully guarded heart for over a year now and he'd been quite happy that the wall around it was unassailable.

Until now.

This Dr Young—maybe unwittingly—had almost breached his defences. She might not be aware of it, but he certainly was. It was a wobble—and not one he'd been prepared for.

His mother smiled and patted him on the shoulder, as she often did.

'You remember we told you about Dr Young a couple of months ago? You agreed to help show her around the place…work with her until she's up and running and feels confident. Well, I've brought you your apprentice! Not that she's an *actual* apprentice. Dr Young here is perfectly qualified. But she'll benefit from your experience and guidance.'

His mother turned to Dr Young.

'Adam has been working here for just over a year now, but before that he worked overseas in all manner of places! Madagascar, the Congo, Syria, Afghanistan…you name it, he's probably got the fridge magnet.'

She smiled, turning back to him.

'You can teach Dr Young all our procedures, and how we do things—if you could work together for the next few weeks, just until she's got the hang of everything? Your dad would do it himself, but he spends so much time on administration these days I think the only thing Dr Young would learn from him is how bad he is at typing. Is that okay?'

She smiled her motherly smile and Adam knew he couldn't back out of his promise. If he was anything, he was a man of his word.

Adam risked a glance at the new doctor. He couldn't

help it. It was almost as if his brain wanted to confirm that she was, in fact, as devastatingly beautiful as he'd first supposed.

What he saw was a woman who clearly had no idea of her own beauty or her effect on men. Even his previously talkative patient had been struck dumb. Dr Young looked studious behind those black-rimmed glasses, but she also appeared keen to seem amiable. Her smile was broad, and it had the crazy ability to make his heart pound faster than it had ever done before—and he'd been in life-or-death situations more than once.

His body was betraying him. It wasn't meant to do what it was doing. He tried to take in a long, slow breath to calm it down.

'Hello. Nice to meet you,' she said.

She had a very fine accent. English, with a hint of Scottish twang. Very nice.

Fighting to regain some control, he nodded quickly and smiled at his mother. He couldn't show her how he was feeling. He didn't need his mother thinking she was Cupid again. The amount of times she had tried to set him up with someone since he'd returned… He'd had to tell her that he wasn't interested in any of that. Not yet.

His mum had backed off, but he could see that familiar gleam in her eyes. He knew she wanted him to settle down and give her grandchildren to spoil, the way her friends spoilt theirs. But that wasn't on the cards for him. Not any more. Not since Anoush.

He'd thought he'd marry her. That she was his future and they would have a life in Dubai, or somewhere, but then it had all gone terribly wrong.

Now, after that he didn't see that type of future for himself. So this feeling of attraction, or lust, or whatever was happening right now, could damn well disappear—because nothing would ever happen.

'That's fine with me. As long as it's okay with Dr Young?'

She smiled at him, blushed slightly, and he felt as if someone had punched him in the gut.

'Jess.'

Jess.

She gave him a brief nod, and seemed pleased about the situation. He had the idea that the quicker she got used to the place—where everything was and the procedures they followed—the quicker he could work on his own again, get that distance back and rebuild his wall. Which was something he clearly needed to do. With every second he spent with her, he could feel his willpower crumbling away.

'Good. Well, I'll leave you to it then. Adam, you'll meet us for lunch?' his mum asked.

'Aye.'

They both watched Judy walk away, and then Jess pulled across the cubicle's curtain and introduced herself to John McAllister, who shook her hand.

'Nasty cut you've got there,' she said, peering closer.

When she leant in Adam could smell her perfume. It wasn't anything overpowering, but light and fresh, and it did strange things to his senses.

'Aye. Did it this morning, hauling in the latest catch.'

'Crab? Cod?'

'Mackerel. Normally we get a good haul this time of year. Usually come back with a full load. But we had to cut it short today, because of this.'

'Must be nice to be out on the boat... How big is your crew?'

'Just the three of us.'

Adam began to feel like a spare part. How had she managed to make him feel this way? He'd been in complete control of this situation to start with, but now that Jess was there, and his patient was also falling under her spell, he began to feel a little irritated.

Angry with himself—for this was his problem, not hers—he picked up his instruments once again and began suturing as Jess and his patient talked.

Looking on the bright side, perhaps this wouldn't be so bad at all. Jess could talk to the patients whilst he got on with the job at hand and then maybe he could get away with not having to talk to her. Or the patients! The less interaction the better. He could be monosyllabic— or just grunt.

Who are you kidding? You could never be that rude.

Besides, she seemed just as nervous as he was. He could hear it in her voice. In the slight quaver in her throat. Probably just first-day nerves. She'd be fine in a few days.

And so will I. It was just a shock, that's all. My foundations were...challenged.

At least that was what he tried to tell himself, but he could feel that his hands were sweating like mad in the gloves, and he couldn't quite tie the stitches correctly. He kept fumbling, taking deep breaths, trying to steady himself.

He knew what to do—had done this *thousands* of times! He'd sutured with a steady hand under the threat of bullets before. But for some reason—probably because Jess was looking over his shoulder—he was now having difficulties.

When the next stitch failed to tie, he put down his

instruments and stretched out his fingers, as if they were cramped.

'Everything all right?' she asked.

Even though she hadn't said anything derogatory he felt belittled—and embarrassed that he couldn't tie a simple suture. He was a trauma doctor. He should be able to do this blindfold.

'I'm fine!' he replied, a little more aggressively than he liked.

'I'd be happy to take over if you'd like a break. Your mum said you'd done one shift already...'

Adam looked at his patient. He didn't seem to mind who did the stitches as long as it got done. The man had work to do and no doubt wanted to get back to his boat. And Adam didn't want his pride to get in the way.

'No, it's okay. It was just a little cramping, that's all. I can do it. You can observe.' He regretted the suggestion as soon as he'd made it when she stepped closer to him and leaned in and his body reacted keenly to her presence.

What the hell was happening?

He picked up his instruments once again and concentrated so hard anyone would have thought he was a student again, being observed in an OSCE. That was an Objective Structured Clinical Examination, which often used to test clinical skill performances and competencies in medical training. Students would be set a series of tests and be examined by one or two examiners in a real or simulated situation.

He'd always hated that sort of thing—being observed so intently, knowing that the observer was looking for mistakes. And he definitely didn't want to make a mistake in front of Dr Jess Young. It was important to him that she saw him as the confident and knowledgeable doctor that he was.

This time he made the stitch, and the next one, and the next. He slowly let out a pent-up breath and concentrated hard until the suturing was done. He smiled at John as he finished and dressed the wound, then gave him aftercare instructions.

Once he was done, he dismissed him, cleared up his equipment and glanced at Jess. 'Right, I just need to write this up.'

'Okay.' She followed him over to the doctors' computer terminal and sat down beside him. 'I really like your parents.'

He smiled. 'Thanks.'

'Do you find it weird, having your dad as your boss?'

'I did a little, at first. But I find it easy to separate the two. When we're at work we're colleagues and good friends, respectful of each other. When we're at home we're more relaxed and like family.'

'I like your mum, especially. Have your parents always worked together?'

'Mum was a nurse when Dad began here as a doctor. She gave up nursing because of ill health, but sort of took over being Dad's secretary and the hospital receptionist.'

'I hope she's okay now?'

He nodded and glanced at her curiously. He'd known she was beautiful from about a metre away, but up close he saw she had skin like porcelain and brown eyes tinted with flecks of honey-gold. And her mouth, her lips...

I'll probably dream about that mouth...

Her smile lit up her entire face and he could have admired it all day. But then he became aware that he was probably staring a little bit too much and felt self-conscious.

Thankfully, she was the one to break the awkwardness. 'So, what sort of patients do you normally get here? I don't remember the hospital being this small.'

'You've been here before?'

'My father used to bring us to Thorney every year for a week's holiday. I can remember driving past this place and thinking it was huge.' She laughed.

'It's a cottage hospital. We don't do anything overly complicated here. Anything that requires major surgery gets sent to the mainland. We have a midwife here, a gerontologist and a paediatrician, and a primary care clinic. I don't know what you're used to, or if you've worked in a big city. We get scrapes and cuts, the occasional broken bone, one or two urgent resus cases. Typical stuff.'

'You enjoy it after working abroad? That must have been exciting?'

'Very much so. But I enjoy making a difference here.'

Adam typed in his pass code. The screen sprang into life and he began typing in John McAllister's treatment details.

He became acutely aware of how close she was. Normally he would sit here and be just as close to other members of staff and it never mattered. But with Jess it was different. His pulse rate had accelerated and he felt hot and nervous, his fingers skipping over the keys and making mistakes that he had to delete, bashing the delete key with an irritation he didn't want to feel. He could feel her eyes upon him and almost couldn't stand it.

'What about you? Where have you worked before? Will a cottage hospital on a tiny island be enough for you?'

Jess nodded. 'Absolutely. I was working in a big hospital in Nairn, in A&E mostly, but things happen in life that make you reconsider what you're doing with it. After I lost my father I took stock of my life and knew I needed something with a more sedate pace. I remembered this place and when a vacancy came up, I knew I had to fill it.'

But Adam saw something in her eyes as she talked that intrigued him. It was as if she was telling him the truth but keeping out some parts that she didn't want to share with him.

He looked at her, considering her. 'So, you're focused?'

'I am. And ready for what comes next.'

'Well, you'll get a wide variety here. Lots of the staff have multiple roles. It's never boring.'

'That's good. I'm not after boring, and I'm not after easy. I want you to push me hard. Help further my education and understanding.'

'I can do that.'

'What about you? What made you choose to come back here and not stay abroad?'

He shrugged his shoulders and tried to act as if his decision to work here hadn't been a big deal at all. 'It was time to come home. I'd been away for too long and I wanted to work with the people I lived with. I like the continuity of care in the community we have here on the island. There are roughly twenty thousand people on Thorney, and they look after each other. It's close-knit and I like that. It's family.'

'And you needed to be back with family? I get that. It's the most important thing, isn't it?'

She sounded sad. And wistful. It made him wonder what her sadness was. She'd mentioned losing her father, and Adam couldn't imagine losing his. It would rock his world when that terrible day came. Did she know how strong she was, carrying on with that kind of heartache? He admired her.

'Yes. It is,' he said.

And I'm staring again.

He turned away. 'I guess you don't have a GP yet?'

She shook her head. 'No. I'll have to register with someone now that I'm living over here.'

He smiled. 'I can give you a few names of the doctors who still have places on their lists.'

'Thank you. That's very kind of you.'

Was it, though? He felt as if he'd done nothing but judge and assess her since they'd met. She seemed sweet and kind, had been good with the one patient he'd watched her interact with. She was easy to talk to, and clearly intelligent, and it was hardly *her* fault that his body was reacting to her in ways he didn't want or need.

Showing her a little kindness was all he could do.

But when you recognised something in yourself, you could easily see it in others. And he'd seen how she'd looked away from him when she'd spoken about coming here for the job. Something had hurt her apart from the death of her father. It still hurt her. But what business was it of his? She didn't have to tell him anything and nor did he want to know.

Keep her at arm's length.

'I've noticed you have a limp. Can I ask what happened?' Her cheeks flushed as she asked the question, as if she was not sure he would answer her.

'Oh…car accident. It's not a big problem.'

She nodded, smiling, but he could tell she didn't believe him. But she'd done a good thing by asking him that particular question—his walls had gone back up.

He finished off John McAllister's notes and locked

down the computer. There was no one else waiting in the walk-in clinic.

'Don't know about you, but I'm ready for some coffee,' he said.

Perhaps a hit of caffeine would refresh him and knock some sense into his disturbed, newly aware body, which was most definitely feeling way too many feels.

So the photos of Adam in Jack's office had been one thing, but the man himself…

Holy moly.

If she'd been able to fan herself she would have—but, no, she'd had to stand there and try to act normal. Try to act as if she hadn't had her legs swept out from under her—because that was how she'd felt.

Adam was *hot*!

Piercing blue eyes… That just-got-of-bed hair that looked as if a comb had never touched it, but had in fact clearly been carefully styled, flopping over his forehead all too casually… Broad, strong shoulders…the sleeves of his blue checked shirt straining over the size of his biceps… A neat, flat waist…

Definitely a ten out of ten in the looks department.

And he was going to be her mentor.

How on earth am I going to be able to work with him every day?

She'd managed to introduce herself without tripping over her tongue, and she hoped she'd also managed to look capable and interested in his patient.

When he'd stood up to take them both over to the doctors' station she'd been aware he was a good few inches taller than her, and estimated he had to be just over six feet in height. His limp was barely there, but she'd noticed that he favoured his right leg over his left, and that the damaged leg didn't seem to have as much ease of movement as the other.

Nerves had got the best of her. It had been inevitable really. With nothing to do with her hands, she'd started asking him questions. The one about his leg had just popped out and she'd cringed inwardly. It was hardly a first day question, was it? She could have waited until she'd known him for a few weeks.

Had she been rude? Had she pried a little bit too far into something that was none of her business?

He'd brushed her off, saying it had been a car accident as if it was nothing—but she'd worked in A&E, and an accident that had managed to damage his leg up near what looked like his hip flexors had to have been considerable. He'd been hurt. Badly. Yet he was brushing it off.

She liked him for that. Some people couldn't wait to tell you all about their ills and what had happened to them—the fact that Adam hadn't, just boosted her estimation of him. Plus, she understood his not wanting to tell her everything. There was plenty *she* was holding back, and she would continue to do so until she absolutely had to reveal it.

A person's secrets were their own.

Whatever was going on with Adam Campbell was absolutely nothing to do with her.

He was a *colleague*. Nothing more. No matter how stunning he looked. No matter what he did to her insides when he looked at her. No matter how he made her legs feel like jelly.

And she would hardly answer any questions he asked her about *her* health, now, would she?

* * *

Adam led Jess to the small staff room, where there was a kitchenette in the corner.

Her question had caused his barricades to come up again, for which he was grateful. He had spent the last year or so building them. Trying to close the door on a terrible chapter in his life that he didn't want to think about.

He was just a little testy today because Anoush's birthday was coming up soon, and his damned brain kept interrupting his day-to-day life to remind him of that fact and keep him on edge.

That first birthday without her had been the most awful day of his life, and he didn't want to have to go through that agony again. He'd managed to hide his suffering from those who knew him here. He'd even booked the day off. But he wasn't going to do that this year.

Last time he'd allowed himself to wallow in his pity and his grief, and he'd drunk more than he should have to try and numb the pain he'd been feeling. It had been the wrong tactic to employ. So this year he was going to take it as just another day and show up to work. If he kept busy—if he made his focus other people, instead of himself—it just might be bearable.

Jess had asked about his leg, but the injury had happened in the ambush and he didn't want to speak of that ever again. He wanted to put it behind him and use his theory for himself to ignore, ignore, ignore. But something about her asking had instantly niggled, and he'd had to say something.

He wasn't ready to share about what had happened in Afghanistan. If he was going to talk to anyone about that it was going to be a therapist, and seeing as there was no therapist at the cottage hospital on Thorney Island he guessed he would have to go to the mainland for that kind of service.

There was probably a counsellor knocking around the hospital—because he couldn't imagine that a hospital caring for twenty thousand people wouldn't at least have *someone* trained in mental health—but he wasn't going to go looking for them. Not now. And probably, if it was left up to him, he'd never do so. He was coping on his own. He didn't need someone poking about in his mind and he certainly didn't need Jess doing so either.

What was it about her that bothered him so? Was it just physical? The way her brown eyes had met his? He'd felt an instant connection. A connection that shouldn't have happened with a perfect stranger. But it had, and he'd been left feeling winded—as if he'd taken a bullet to the lung. His heart had begun to pound, to race, he'd grown hot, and when she'd smiled nervously at him it had all been too much!

She'd looked at him and asked him that question as if she really *cared*. And that was odd because she hardly knew him. Maybe it was just the doctor in her, or something, but there'd been something about the look in her eyes that had told him he needed to get away. Self-preservation.

He didn't need someone caring about him. He didn't need to make strong connections. That was the whole point of coming back to Thorney Island. He wanted the safety of family. Of a world where there were no complicated relationships. Where nothing ever happened. The point wasn't to get involved with anyone apart from his parents, whom he knew would not be able to stop themselves from caring. He didn't need it from anyone else.

'Coffee? Tea?' he asked.

'Tea, please. White, no sugar.'

'Take a seat.'

He ran his hands through his hair as he walked towards the tea-making facilities and took a deep breath, exhaling slowly. He needed to lose the hair trigger. This was Thorney Island, not Kabul. There were no wars here—no landmines, no ambushes. Just the people he'd grown up with. Fishermen, farmers... Run-of-the-mill people who were just getting on with their lives. Just like those people in Afghanistan until war had come.

He had to stop looking for traps—had to stop second-guessing everything. He had to get a hold of himself and tell himself that Jess was not the enemy. She was a junior doctor, here to learn under his tutelage, and once he'd done that job he could set her free to work under her own steam. The quicker he did that, the better.

But he wished his brain would tell his stomach to calm down. It was churning with nerves, and his mouth was dry, and he felt apprehensive about spending time with her.

Come on, mate. You're hardly going to start a relationship with her, are you? Calm the hell down!

He presented her with her drink and she sat opposite him on the blue sofa, her hands cradling the mug, her large brown eyes looking at him with gratitude.

'This is perfect. Thanks.'

'No problem.'

Inwardly he wondered if she realised what kind of effect she was having on him. With those big brown eyes behind her glasses, her shoulder-length wavy hair with its golden highlights, her wide smile... She wore a wedding ring on a chain around her neck. A big ring. A man's? Her father's?

'You…er…you mentioned that your father had died. Do you have any other family?'

Family was important to Adam. It was what had kept him going when he was abroad, knowing that they were back home, rooting for him. He'd frequently video called them when he'd had the chance and it had always felt good to know that he had a soft place to fall. He hoped she had something similar.

'No. Nobody. My mother died when I was really young. I don't even remember her, to be honest—though I do have photos. I don't have any siblings.'

'Only child?'

She sipped her tea and nodded.

'Me, too,' he said. 'No aunts or uncles?'

'Yes. An aunt—my father's sister. But she lives in Vancouver. I've never met her, and she didn't come over for the funeral. They weren't all that close, apparently.'

'So you're making it in the world all on your own?'

Jess smiled. 'I am.'

'And you decided Thorney Island was the place to do that?'

She tilted her head to one side. 'Yes. I have so many fond memories of Thorney…it made perfect sense for me to come back here. It's where I feel closest to my father.'

He heard a wobble in her voice and realised her father's loss still hurt. But of course it would. She was alone in the world and making her own way. Who was he to judge how she chose to do that?

'Adam, I… I didn't mean to be nosy earlier, asking about your leg. I hope you don't think I was being rude. It kind of popped out, and I want to apologise if I stuck my nose in where it wasn't wanted. I do that... Open my mouth before engaging my brain. Call it my super-power.'

She was babbling, trying to make a joke of it, and he marvelled at her optimism. Even though she'd been through some dark times and was now alone, she wasn't letting it hold her back or colour the way she viewed the world. She seemed determined to be bright and upbeat and perky.

Perhaps he could learn something from that...

He looked at her. 'I wasn't offended. It's just a long story and I try not to think about it.'

'Of course. And you're being very gracious. Thank God you're not one of those evil bosses who lays huge piles of work upon new doctors and consigns them to doing nothing but rectal exams all week!'

She laughed, then looked nervous again, and he couldn't help but laugh, too.

'You never know... I just might.' He smiled back, to show it was just a joke, and for a brief moment he forgot that he was meant to be keeping her at a distance. Forgot that he'd decided to try and have as little interaction with her as possible because of the threat she presented to his emotions.

She brightened up the room and he was enjoying her company. It was a long time since he'd felt that...

But as soon as he realised what was happening he immediately began to bring the shutters back down. He looked down at his drink, suddenly unable to look at her, as if looking at her would somehow make him fall to his doom, or something.

She must have realised he was struggling with something, because she said, 'You've had a long shift. You must be tired, and now you're saddled with me. I'm sorry.'

He gave a small nod. He *was* tired. But not physically. It was emotionally. And she was just so bright and peppy! As if she was full of energy and keen to *do* something—to contribute, to help out.

How many hours had he worked this shift? He couldn't remember. It was often like this. Sometimes he just kept going for hours and hours, and often the days blended into one long shift.

'When did you last eat?' she asked, 'You should try and keep your energy up.'

When *had* he last eaten? He couldn't remember. He had some vague memory of cold pizza?

'Your father left me some paperwork to fill in. It'll take me an hour or two, I should think. Why don't you grab a bite to eat and take a power nap while I do it? I promise I won't deal with any patients without you.'

That did sound good. He was grateful to her. But why was she so nice?

'You wouldn't mind?'

'Course not! Point me in the direction of the hospital cafeteria and I'll bring you back a snack.'

He gave her directions, and a note from his wallet, but by the time she came bounding back to the staff room, armed with a banana, a yoghurt and a chicken salad sandwich he was fast asleep on the sofa, completely ignorant of the way she gently and carefully draped a crocheted blanket over him and stood looking at him, a gentle smile upon her face.

CHAPTER THREE

WHEN ADAM WOKE, he located Jess coming out of the administration offices, clipping her ID card to a lanyard, and told her he'd give her a full tour of Thorney Island cottage hospital. He'd found the food she'd brought him, laid on the coffee table next to him and, feeling ravenous, he'd devoured it in seconds. Now, rejuvenated by the food and the nap, he was raring to go.

They were walking down the long corridor towards the X-ray department when he felt his phone buzz in his pocket with a message. He pulled it out and checked the screen.

Come to dinner tonight. Bring Jess. Mum xxx

He smiled, shaking his head. His mother never stopped trying to set him up.

'Something important?' Jess asked.

He laughed. 'No. It was my mother, inviting you to a family dinner tonight. But of course you don't have to accept. I'm sure you have lots to do and—'

'I'd love to come to dinner. Your parents have been so kind to me, helping me out with everything, it'd be rude to refuse.'

'Right.'

'Unless it's a problem for *you*?'

'No, no, not at all!'

He found himself scrabbling to explain that it didn't matter one iota to him whether or not she came to dinner with his family tonight, but found he couldn't find words at all. Because it did matter. It mattered hugely.

He was trying to keep his interactions with Jess at a minimum, but so far he was failing miserably at the task. He could just imagine what his mother would be like tonight. Making hints. Suggesting he take Jess out and about around the island to show her the sights.

Well, he didn't have to do that, did he? She'd come here as a child. He felt absolutely sure she knew most of them already. Besides, she'd want to settle into her new flat—which was in *his* building, he reminded himself. He'd given his landlord's details to his dad for the new doctor, never expecting for one moment the new doctor would be a woman like Jess.

'No problem at all.' Even to himself, he sounded a little curt. 'I'll text her back and let her know you're coming.'

'Great! I'll look forward to it. I can drive us both home afterwards, can't I? Your mum said we live in the same building.'

Ah. He didn't normally go in cars unless he couldn't help it. He walked, or took buses, or cycled. It only took ten minutes of fast cycling to get from one end of the island to the other.

'You don't have to do that.'

'I'm hardly going to let you *walk* home!'

He grimaced a smile. 'Thanks,' he said, and texted his mother his reply.

Jessica Young was living in the flat above him. How

crazy was that? He didn't know how to feel about that right now—and the more he thought about it, *worried* pretty much summed it up.

He continued to walk towards the X-ray department, knowing she was following as he pointed out the waiting area and the protocols they used. But his brain was going crazy at the thoughts of possibly bumping into Jess in the mornings, or having to ask her to turn her music down or to lend him a cup of sugar.

He needed to distract himself. *Work. Think of work.*

'We have a radiologist, but she only works days. Anyone who comes in with a suspected fracture during the night has to go to the mainland. Though once a week she's on twenty-four-hour call.'

'Doesn't that make life awkward?'

He was used to life being awkward—in many ways.

'Sometimes, but what can we do? Besides, most people here are in bed at night. You've got to remember you're in a quiet backwater now, with eighty percent of the population over sixty-five and in bed by ten. This little island of ours is hardly action central.'

'I'm glad to hear it. It's what I want. A quieter way of life with less stress.'

Okay, so maybe he wouldn't have to tell her to turn her music down. He'd heard the yearning in her voice, the wistfulness, the true desire for a quiet life. He'd seen himself what excitement and stress and horror could bring, so he understood the yearning well enough. Well, she would certainly find what she was looking for here.

'I'll show you the rest.'

And he led her past the X-ray department and into the primary care centre where his father occasionally worked.

It didn't take them long to look around the hospital. Adam pointed out the equipment rooms, the wards, sluices. He pointed out the pharmacy and the small pathology department where they ran blood tests.

Jess seemed quite amazed at how compact and efficient the small hospital was, and how some people doubled up in their skills. But it was a place that Adam had come to love, and he hoped that she could tell how much—how proud he was to work here, to be a part of this place, the beating heart of Thorney Island. It was unique, sure. And that made it special.

He couldn't imagine working anywhere else now. And he couldn't believe he'd ever wanted to leave this place, thinking it was boring and unable to hold his attention. But he'd been a young man when he'd left. Eighteen years old when he'd headed to the mainland for university and his medical degree, and the big, wide world that had beckoned.

He'd thought he would find excitement and adventure—and he had. But he'd also found loss, pain and heartbreak. He'd lost a bit of himself that he would never get back.

'Have you decided on a specialty yet?' Adam asked.

She shook her head. 'No, but I've got plenty of time to choose.'

She did. But in his experience most doctors had *some* idea of where they thought they'd end up.

'But right now, if you had to choose, what would you say?'

He was truly curious. He didn't know much about Jess. Perhaps her choice in specialty would tell him a little more about her? Cardiology or neurosurgery would show the ultimate ambition...

She shrugged, still smiling. 'I don't know...obstetrics?'

'The only specialty where you end up with more patients than you started with?'

Jess laughed. 'You probably think I'm being silly—viewing it as something that generally has happy outcomes. But I'm a realist. I know things don't always end that way. Obstetrics may have some of the best highs, but it has the lowest of the lows, too.'

He stopped to look at her. 'Have you worked in a maternity unit yet?'

She nodded. 'Yes. I did a two-month rotation.'

'Good.' He was glad she wasn't viewing it through rose-tinted spectacles. Most of the maternity cases they saw on the island ended happily, but there'd been one or two that hadn't, and he liked to think she'd be prepared for that.

'You said there's a midwife here, but do you have a dedicated obstetrician for the more complicated cases?'

'No, they have to go to the mainland.'

She smiled. 'So perhaps my choice is a good one, then!'

He watched her walk ahead and then caught up with her. 'Perhaps. But you'll get a broad spectrum of experience here. The work is so varied from one day to the next, and I kind of like that—never quite knowing what I'm going to face each day. Am I going to be in primary care? Am I going to be working in the walk-in clinic? Or am I going to be doing minor surgeries?'

'That's why I came here. Your father promised me variety.'

'You'll get it.'

His phone beeped again with another message and he removed it from his pocket, dreading that it would be another message from his mother, perhaps suggesting he pick up some flowers for Jess, or something. But it wasn't. It was from the nurse who answered the calls from Reception.

Adam read the message and raised his eyebrows. 'Looks like your wish might be coming true. We're needed out in the community. A baby on the way! Are you up for that?'

Jess beamed. 'Absolutely! But doesn't the midwife attend these cases?'

'She's on the mainland at the moment. Having a knee operation. Come on.'

They hurried down the corridor towards a room by the main reception desk, where a bag was kept stocked for emergencies such as this. They grabbed everything they thought they would need.

'Shall we take my car?' asked Jess.

He felt immediately uncomfortable, and let out a heavy sigh. 'Sure.'

He hadn't had to go out in the community for a while, and when he did he cycled, carrying his equipment in panniers over the back wheel. He very often got to places faster than cars could. They were often held back by slow traffic, or lights, or frequent roadworks, whereas he could glide on through by using the cycle paths. But he guessed there was no escaping the drive this time.

Somewhere, a woman was waiting for their help. And he couldn't let his own discomfort and fear stop her from getting that.

'Why don't you get the details of where we need to go? Rachel has them. The nurse with the dark ponytail.'

Jess gave a brief nod and hurried off to complete the task.

Adam quickly opened the bag and gave the contents

a brief scan, checking to make sure that it was fully stocked. He grabbed a few extra pairs of gloves and was putting them inside just as Jess returned with her car keys and a piece of paper with an address scribbled on it.

'Grainger Lane. Number twenty-four. Do you know it?'

He nodded. His adrenaline was pumping now. This was exactly the sort of thing he dreaded. Being trapped in a car. Being trapped in a car with Jess. But he knew she'd be excited. It was the perfect opportunity to show what she could do. And it would be interesting to watch her—see if she really was cut out for this kind of work.

He'd birthed a few babies here on Thorney, and one or two abroad. It was generally a happy thing to do, leaving you on an endorphin high.

Did Jess need any more endorphins? She already seemed happy enough. Upbeat, always ready with a smile and a kind word… But was there something lurking in the dark behind that happiness? Was she trying hard to mask something she didn't want to talk about?

He had a suspicion it was connected to the death of her father. He'd seen it in her eyes. A distant look. Something he couldn't quite name. Yet.

No. And I won't. Jess Young is none of my business.

I've got plenty of time to choose.

That was what she'd said—but that was the thing, wasn't it? She *didn't* have plenty of time. Her clock was ticking. Every day brought the risk that today would be the day that something would go wrong. That she would start experiencing the symptoms that would mark the beginning of her deterioration.

Of course Adam didn't know that, but it was something *she* was very much aware of. It was part of the reason her last relationship had broken up.

She and Eddie had been so happy... They'd even started talking about having a baby!

She remembered the dinner she and Eddie had had with her dad, when she'd told him that they were going to start trying. She'd expected her dad to be happy, to give them both a hug and wish them the best of luck. Only he hadn't. He'd looked away, and before he'd looked away she'd seen something on his face that had looked like horror. And fear.

She hadn't understood it, and when he had gone home she'd snuggled into Eddie and cried, upset that her father didn't want to share their joy. Why didn't he want them to try for a baby? Why was the prospect so horrific to him? He wasn't old-fashioned—wasn't one of those people who thought you needed to be married before starting a family—and she'd known her dad certainly didn't dislike Eddie. They'd both got along so well!

And then... And then her dad had died. Taken his own life and left Jess the note that had shattered her world.

A life-limiting disease. Hereditary. Huntington's.

Eddie had been supportive at first—her absolute rock. Telling her she was fine, but that maybe she ought to get herself tested to see if she would develop it, too. But when the result came back—yes, she did indeed carry the gene, and would suffer from Huntington's too—Eddie had left her, also leaving a note.

The coward couldn't even tell me to my face!

Alone in the world, she'd made a conscious decision that she would not let her diagnosis stop her from being who she wanted to be. She would continue to be a doctor and, although she might not ever get the chance to be an obstetrician, she would enjoy the maternity cases when they came along. That was why she'd been so pleased after talking to Jack. He'd told her that they all mucked in wherever they were needed at the cottage hospital. Primary care, minor surgery...*obstetrics*.

But she'd also known that from then on she would stand on her own. She'd been let down by the two men whom she'd thought loved her as much as she loved them and the disease had destroyed everything. Her relationship with her father, her relationship with Eddie, her future...

She couldn't stand the idea that someone else would get close enough to watch her lose her functionality. Lose her ability to do simple tasks. It wasn't fair to expect someone to be involved with her romantically and then take her on as a responsibility. To become her carer.

Her father had felt the same way. And although she knew that she would not take the escape route that he had, she knew that loved ones left you when it got complicated. That was what she had learned.

She'd had enough darkness. From now on she was determined only to see the light and the love that was in the world. Even if it was never destined to be hers.

Adam was being very quiet. She kept glancing at him and noticed that he seemed agitated, constantly looking out of the window, his gaze shifting rapidly from one side of the car to the other, as if checking their surroundings. What was he looking for? Clearly it was something. Or was he was trying to distract himself from the fact that he was in a car? He'd said he'd damaged his leg in a car accident...perhaps he was worried?

'I'm a good driver, Adam,' she said.

'I'm pleased to hear it. But even good drivers get taken off the road.'

Wow. Okay. 'I'm being very careful.'

'Good. Just keep your eyes on the road and not on me, please.'

She tried not to take offence. He was nervous. Very, very nervous.

His hands rested in his lap—but perhaps 'rested' was the wrong word? His knuckles were white and his hands held on to each other as if they were a lifeline. That was when he wasn't rubbing the sweat from his palms onto his trousers. What had happened in that accident? What didn't she know?

Jess made herself concentrate on the road and the traffic around them, sticking to the speed limit and being very cautious.

Traffic on the island was generally okay. There were one of two roads that could get jammed up during school drop-off times and rush hour, as people headed to work, or to the ferry to catch the boat to the mainland—there were plenty of people who worked off-island. But right now the roads were good. And, even though there was a woman out there about to become a mother, she would not speed. That mother was relying on them arriving safely.

All Jess knew was what the nurse had told her—that the mother was close to delivering and her husband had not been able to get her into the car.

She liked the sound of this call. It hadn't happened at her old job—usually the midwives were called out and they'd hear all about it in the staff room—but she appreciated going outside of the hospital, working in the community, getting hands-on.

Apparently all the doctors at the hospital did it occasionally, when it was required of them. It was part of the service. And it was a service she would enjoy providing, seeing more of this beautiful island that had always made her so happy.

It crossed Jess's mind that if she couldn't be an obstetrician before time passed and her condition got worse, then maybe she could become a doula. That would still allow her to do the work that she wanted to do without the responsibility of being a medic. She could coach women through labour without actually having to deliver the baby.

She hoped that might work. She hoped that once she was unable to carry on being a doctor she would still have options. Because she couldn't picture just sitting at home, hiding away, waiting to die. It wasn't who she was. She liked people…she liked helping…she liked *doing*.

'Are you okay?' Jess asked Adam as they stopped at a traffic light.

'I'm fine,' he answered in a clipped tone.

Jess wanted to say that normally when people said *I'm fine* it meant that they were nothing of the sort. That they were just trying to stop the other person from worrying about them. But she wasn't going to push, so she just turned to look at the lights, waiting for them to turn green, before driving on.

Grainger Road wasn't far now. About two minutes away, according to her car's navigation system. She hoped they would get there in time, but knew that babies went at their own pace and nobody else's. And even if they were late, they could still help, making sure that mum and baby were okay and completing the necessary afterbirth checks before returning to the hospital.

'So, how many babies have you delivered before?'

That had to be a safe question for her to ask him. It was a professional question, not personal. And maybe, just maybe, it might take his mind off whatever was bothering him about being in a car.

'A few here. One in a jungle hut and another at a field hospital in Afghanistan.'

She smiled. This was most definitely safer ground. 'And how did those births go?'

'Both mothers and babies were fine. Though it was touch and go with the first. The baby was too big for a vaginal delivery and we had to perform an episiotomy to get the baby out. It was huge. Ten pounds.'

'Wow. That beats mine. The largest baby I ever delivered was just over nine pounds.'

Jess pulled up in front of the house, and before they'd even got their seat belts off a man who must be the baby's father came running out to greet them.

'Are you the doctors?'

'We are. I'm Dr Young and this is Dr Campbell.' They both showed the ID badges hanging round their necks. 'How's she doing?'

'She wants to push. I've been trying to get her out of the bath, but she says she can't move.'

'And her name is…?'

'Sarah. Sarah Crosby. And I'm Joe. Her husband.'

Adam was already out of the car carrying the kit bag as she followed Joe down the front path towards the house. It was a neat little home, semi-detached, with a climbing jasmine plant creeping over a trellis arch that marked the front door.

'Does Sarah have any medical issues that we need to know about?'

Joe pushed open the front door. 'No, she's healthy as a horse.'

'And is this your first baby?'

Joe grinned. 'Yes. She's this way.'

He led them up the stairs and they could hear a woman's groans and heavy breathing before they even made it to the bathroom.

Jess quickly assessed the situation. Sarah was kneeling over the edge of the bath, in water up to her waist. She was breathing heavily, her brow damp with sweat from her exertions.

Jess knelt down quickly and took Sarah's hands in her own. 'Hey, Sarah. My name's Jess and this is Adam. We're both doctors and we're here to help, okay? Tell me how you're feeling right now.'

Beside her, Adam put down the bag and began to get out the equipment that they might need.

'I need to start pushing. I've been trying not to, but sometimes I can't help it. The contractions are coming thick and fast!' Sarah cried.

'How long are your contractions lasting?'

Behind her, Joe answered. 'They're over a minute long and she seems to have only about thirty seconds between each one.'

Adam took over. 'That sounds about right. I'm just going to wash my hands, put on some gloves, and then I'm going to check on you, Sarah, okay? That means I'm going to have to do an internal examination, just to check your dilation. In the meantime, if you have another contraction, try not to push—just breathe through it. Can you do that for me?'

Jess could feel her heart beginning to pound with the adrenaline coursing through her system. Joe's excitement was in clear evidence too, and Sarah was clearly 'in the zone'.

This could have been me. If it wasn't for the Huntington's...if it wasn't for Eddie leaving...this could have been me.

She tried not to think too hard about that. The loss of her imagined future family was too much to bear. It was much easier to suppress it.

'Oh, God, here comes another one!' Sarah squeezed her eyes shut and began to groan, breathing in fits and starts.

'Try and keep your breathing nice and steady. That's it...in and out, in and out.'

Adam quickly washed his hands in the sink and donned a pair of gloves. The contraction was over by the time he'd finished, and he quickly performed an examination of Sarah's cervix, reaching around her as she knelt in the bathtub.

'Okay, that's perfect. You're ten centimetres, and baby's low, so on the next contraction you can begin to push. When the contraction comes, I want you to take a deep breath and then push out through your bottom. I want you to do that at least three times with each contraction, okay?'

'Yeah, I can do that. Can I have a drink of water?'

Her husband passed her a glass with a straw and she sucked on it hungrily before passing it back.

'Thanks.'

Adam soaked a clean face flannel under the cold tap and rinsed it out before handing it to Joe. 'You might want to use this.' He settled on the floor and looked at Sarah again. 'I think I recognise you.'

Sarah looked at him curiously, tucking her hair behind the ear. 'Adam… Right. I think you were in the year above me at school. You were in that play, weren't you?'

Adam smiled. 'I was in a few.'

'You were a very funny vampire—oh, heck, here comes another!'

Adam coached Sarah through her pushing, telling her when to take another breath and counting out as she pushed. She was pushing well, but this was her first birth and they both knew it might take her a little bit longer than a mother who had given birth before.

Jess looked on anxiously and Adam noticed. 'Put on some gloves and take over coaching Sarah through her breathing for me. I want to use the Doppler to listen in to the baby's heartbeat.'

Jess nodded and grabbed a pair of gloves, smiling nervously at the labouring mother.

When the contraction was over, Sarah grabbed the flannel from Joe, wiping her face and groaning. 'They skip this bit in class. They tell you about dilation, they tell you that you'll push, but they don't tell you how hard, or how long it takes.' She glanced at Jess. 'How long *will* it take?'

'We can't know for sure. Just that every contraction is one less before they stop. And they will stop. Eventually. You're doing well.' She tried to reassure her as best she could.

Sarah laughed. 'I never thought I'd give birth with a vampire in the room.'

Jess glanced at Adam and he looked back, smiling. What would it have been like to have known Adam as a young boy? Asa a vampire in a school play! 'Were you Dracula, or something?'

'For my sins. I wasn't very good.'

Sarah laughed. 'Are you kidding me? You made all the girls fall in love with you. Talent *and* devastating good looks? A potent combination!' She sipped her water again. 'Sorry, Joe, but he took my heart for a little while.' She took her husband's hand in hers. 'For about two weeks. And then I fell in love with you.'

'A school romance? That's sweet,' said Jess.

Sarah smiled. 'Well, I don't think Adam was worried about losing my affections. There were plenty of girls to take my place. Oh, God, here comes another!'

Jess looked uncertainly at Adam. The school heart-throb? Yes, she could most definitely see that. How many hearts had he broken in his time?

She could have spent more time feeling resentful that another good-looking man was the same as Eddie, but Sarah had gone into another contraction and Jess stroked her back as she coached her through breathing and pushing once again. On examination, she could feel the top of the baby's head.

'You're doing really well. The baby is right there. Why don't you reach down and feel it?'

She guided Sarah's hands down and the expectant mum gasped.

'Is that the baby? Does it have hair?'

Jess smiled, trying to hold back her tears. Tears for a happiness that would never be hers. 'It certainly does. Do you know what you're having?'

Sarah shook her head. 'We want it to be a surprise.'

'That's brilliant. Do you want us to tell you what it is when it's born? Or do you want to look for yourself?'

'I'd like Joe to tell me.'

'All right.' Jess smiled at Joe. 'When the baby is born

we will put him or her on your wife's chest and you can take a look. Does that sound like a plan?'

'It certainly does.'

'Okay, here we go. Big deep breath now—and push!'

Sarah pushed and pushed, a mixture of a growl and a yell escaping her with her effort. It wouldn't be long now. The baby was crowning.

I just need to hold it together for a little while longer. I can do this!

'Okay, stop pushing and just breathe it out for me,' she told Sarah. 'Pant... That's it... Adam, can you get the clamps ready?' She knew the clamps would be needed for tying off the umbilical cord.

They waited for Sarah's next contraction, which came about a minute later. Then Jess guided the baby's head and slowly coached Sarah through pushing and breathing until, at just the right moment, the baby slithered out into the water.

It was a moment of sheer joy and sheer terror.

Jess scooped up the baby from the water, and as it broke the surface it let out a lusty cry. The new mum leant back against the bath, holding her baby against her chest as she began to cry with relief and happiness.

Jess had the briefest of moments to glance at Adam, to share the happiness and the joy, and then she had to wipe her eyes and remind herself that she was still there to do a job.

'Joe, do you want to see what it is?'

Joe leaned in and lifted up one of the baby's legs. 'It's a boy!'

'Oh, my God, I can't believe it!' Sarah cried more tears of happiness as Jess draped towels around the baby to keep it warm and then applied the clamps to the umbilical cord and got Joe to cut it with a special pair of scissors.

It seemed to Jess that the tension in the room was gone and that suddenly everyone felt just a little bit of bliss. It was a wonderful moment. Filled with joy and rapture. She knew that at some point she would have to check the baby, and she knew that there was still the delivery of the placenta and checking for bleeding, but for now all that could wait. The baby boy was being soothed by his mother and Joe was kissing his wife, tears wetting his cheeks.

Jess was aware that the envy was back. Envy for what this couple had just been through. Becoming a family, going from a twosome to a threesome. Sarah had got pregnant, carried a baby, given birth. And now she would start many years of watching that child grow into an adult.

It was something that she would never get to experience for herself—because she couldn't allow it and she couldn't take the risk. She could never have a child knowing that she might pass on the disease that doomed her. The people in this room had no idea of just how lucky they were.

Adam touched her wrist. 'You okay?'

Her skin burned at his touch and she pulled her hand away, smiling. 'Of course! Why wouldn't I be?'

She bustled about, clearing up supplies and equipment, occupying her hands in the hope that it would stop the tears releasing themselves from her eyes. This was a *happy* moment. This was *their* moment—Joe and Sarah's—and not one she should spoil.

Jess could think of quite a few things she'd like right now. Someone to hold her tight. To wrap their arms around her and make her feel safe. Kiss her. Reassure her. Comfort her. But none of that was meant to be.

I stand alone.

'We won't need most of this equipment now. Why don't you pack it away and get some fresh towels for when we move Sarah to a bed?' Adam suggested. He turned to Sarah. 'Do you want me to give an injection of oxytocin for the placenta?' he asked. 'It will help speed up the expulsion.'

The new mum nodded. 'Yes, please.'

He checked the drug with Jess and prepared the syringe, before injecting the drug into Sarah's thigh. The oxytocin would help the womb contract so that the placenta would come away from the uterine wall.

It didn't seem to take long to work, and soon Adam had placed the placenta in a clinical waste bag, so that it could be disposed of at the hospital when they returned.

Eventually they all helped Sarah get out of the bath and walked her over to the bed, pulling back the sheets and tucking her in. Joe brought a nappy and some clothes for the baby, and Jess carried out the Apgar tests before the baby was dressed. He did well, scoring nine out of ten and only losing a point because of the colouring of his hands and feet, which was normal for a newborn.

'Have you guys decided on a name?' Jess asked.

Sarah looked up at them, pride on her face. 'Owen. Owen Thomas.'

Jess glanced at Joe, and then back at Sarah. 'That's lovely. Absolutely lovely.'

For a moment, Jess watched the new family as they bonded, her heart aching at what had been so cruelly snatched away from her.

'Jess. We need to go,' Adam said softly.

She sniffed and forced a smile. 'Yeah… Congratulations, guys.'

CHAPTER FOUR

ADAM TRIED TO relax on the drive back to the hospital, but it was difficult. Being in a car made him feel antsy, incredibly confined, and as if he was trapped in one small space. He didn't like the claustrophobic feeling that it engendered, so he did his best to ignore it by looking out of the window and trying to take in the beautiful vista that Thorney Island provided.

The mountains in the distance were a beautiful grey-green, with a hint of purple from the heather that littered the countryside. He even noticed a couple of kestrels high in the sky, hovering perfectly as they gazed down at some item of prey beneath them.

He tried to imagine what it must feel like to be as free as a bird. All that space, all that sky, with nothing to contain you. Humans thought they were free, but the truth was that they were trapped. Trapped by rules and regulations, by jobs and homes. Relationships. Family.

Expectations abounded... It wasn't easy and he often wished that he could disappear to some isolated cabin in the middle of nowhere, where there were no people, no expectations, and he could live the life he wanted to. One that was free of fear and apprehension, anxiety and stress.

He knew his parents loved him, but he felt the weight

of his mother's expectations. He knew she yearned for him to settle down. To find someone to love. To provide her with grandchildren, even though he'd never told her about what had happened with Anoush. They'd known she was his friend, but that was all.

To watch Sarah and Joe begin their family had given him joy, but it was *for them*. He could be happy for others and watch them take the risk with their hearts, but he'd already had to walk through the grief of losing a loved one he'd planned a future with, and he'd lost Anoush in one of the worst ways possible. No one had been through what he'd been through, and he couldn't expect his mother or anyone else to understand just how he felt.

But he'd noticed something at Sarah and Joe's house.

Jess had been tearful. Uncertain and hesitant at times. And the way she'd looked at Sarah and Joe… As if… As if what?

There had been something going on there and he wasn't sure what. She'd said she wanted to specialise in obstetrics—was that it? Had she just been overcome with happiness at getting to do what she wanted to do? Or had it been something more?

Irritated by his own fear at being in the car, he decided to talk to her about it. He might learn something about her *and* take his mind off his phobia.

'Are you okay?' he asked.

Jess nodded and gave him her default *I'm fine!* smile. 'I'm good.'

'You seemed a little…emotional back there.'

Jess laughed. 'I'm not allowed to get emotional at a birth?'

'Of course you are. But…you're a doctor. You have to have some emotional distance.'

Jess seemed to think for a moment. 'You're right. I'm probably just hormonal, or something.'

'You sure? I thought it seemed something more than that. You looked…wistful.'

'Wistful?' She laughed, as if it was the most ridiculous thing in the world.

'Almost envious?'

Jess didn't answer straight away. She seemed to be thinking about her response before replying. 'I didn't realise you were watching me so closely.'

He shrugged. 'I'm your mentor. I'm meant to be watching you.' He stared at her a moment longer, his focus more on her than it was on the traffic.

But then there was a strange noise coming from beneath the car and it jolted slightly.

Adam's stomach almost leapt into his mouth.

Jess cursed quietly as she checked her mirrors and indicated that she was pulling over.

'What's going on?' Now he was the one who was uncertain.

'I think we've got a flat.'

She pulled off the road, parking on a grass verge, and turned off the engine. They both got out and looked at the tyres, and found that the back left tyre had indeed been punctured.

'Dammit!'

'Do you have a spare?'

Jess nodded. 'There's one under the boot space.' She popped open the boot and moved the carpet lining to reveal the spare tyre in its compartment. Alongside it sat a small plastic case containing the tools and the jack that would be needed. 'Have you ever changed a tyre before?'

'Nope. But I guess if we can deliver a baby, we can certainly change a tyre together.'

She smiled at him and nodded. 'Okay, let's do it.'

Thankfully, the weather wasn't too bad. The wind was blowing quite strongly, but the sun was out in full force for the start of spring, and it wasn't cold either.

Jess helped jack up the car and Adam began to loosen the nuts on the tyre. Occasionally other cars drove by, but nobody stopped to help except for one farmer in a big blue tractor, who checked to make sure that they were okay. Adam reassured him that they were, and the farmer continued on after wishing them the best of luck.

At last Adam managed to get the old wheel off and Jess wheeled it to one side, laying it down on the grass for a moment before going back to see if Adam needed assistance in lifting the new tyre onto the axle.

'Thanks,' he said.

He had to admit that Jess was easy to work with. She was calm and organised. Most people would get angry or exasperated at getting a flat tyre, but not Jess. She took it all in her stride, and he admired that about her.

She seemed to be a strong, confident woman. Clearly self-sufficient. But he guessed she'd had to be after losing both parents and having no one else. There was a strength of character in her that ran quite deep, and though he found that attractive, he knew he would never do any-thing about it—no matter how much he wanted to. He wasn't looking for a relationship. He'd had one of those and look what had happened.

He was just fastening the nuts on the new tyre when he heard rifle shots, one after the other, puncturing the air. Something happened within him that caused him to freeze. His breath caught in his throat, his hands stilled, his mouth went dry and his heart began to pound. He stumbled backwards in his urge to hide and take cover, but found that his legs wouldn't move at all.

'Adam?'

He was vaguely aware that Jess was speaking to him, but her voice sounded muffled and far away. His gaze was still fixed on the tyre, but everything around it was beginning to blur and go dark.

'Adam!'

He felt sick, his stomach churning and the trembling worsening, and the rifle shots continued to sound in the air. There were too many, too loud, like an array of fireworks. And even though he tried to tell himself that he was on Thorney Island, not back in Kabul, the logic just did not seem to register in his brain. He was thrown back through time to a desert with hot winds, the smell of cordite and blood, and he began to hyperventilate.

'Anoush...'

He became vaguely aware that someone's hands were on his shoulders and they were trying to get him to look at them, but he couldn't focus on their face. He felt trapped, he felt cornered, and the fear within him was winning.

He tried to scramble further back and fell. He didn't feel the gravel of the road cutting through the palms of his hands. He didn't feel any pain at all. All he felt was fear and terror and the need to flee.

Anoush. What was Anoush? Was that a word in another language? Or a name?

Jess didn't know what to think. One moment they had been changing her tyre, and she'd been thankful that the focus had moved off her reaction to Sarah and Joe hav-

ing their baby, and the next Adam had gone as white as
a sheet and his eyes had glazed over.

She was aware of rifle shots not far from where they
were—was that affecting him? She'd seen this reaction
before.

'Adam? Adam! Look at me. *Look...at...me!*'

But she could see by the look in his eyes that he wasn't
completely present. That in his mind he was somewhere
else completely. She realised the gunshots must have
something to do with it. Adam had been in Afghanistan
with International Health—she knew that. He seemed
traumatised. As if he was suffering from a flashback.
Had he been under fire? Had he been attacked?

She knelt in front of him and tried to get him to focus
on her face. He was breathing too fast, his eyes flicking
from one side to the other as if looking for an escape.
She wasn't sure he was seeing the here and now. He was
going to pass out if he didn't calm down. He was having a panic attack.

'Adam, it's Jess. You're okay. You're completely safe.
I know you can hear gunshots, and I don't know what
they're shooting at, but they're miles away. You're safe.
Can you hear me? Adam?'

She put her hands either side of his face to make him
look at her and somehow her voice must have got through
to him, because suddenly he was staring hard at her, still
breathing heavily.

'That's it...you're doing brilliantly. Just breathe.
Steady your breathing. You're safe. You're okay. I'm
looking after you. Nothing will happen to you. Nothing.'

As she held his face in her hands, staring into his eyes
from only inches away, she realised just how intimate
this was. But she needed to get this right. She needed

to calm him down. How beautiful his blue eyes were—even filled with fear. How close they were right now...

Ideally, she would like to take a step back, because she knew how attracted she was to this man and it felt dangerous to be this close. To be helping him in this manner.

She hoped and prayed that she would get through to him. It was awful to see him like this and she wanted to help. Once he came back to the present, she would step back. Step away. Reluctantly, but she would do it. Because she couldn't get involved with this man. She had nothing to offer him but sadness.

Adam spoke. 'I... I thought that...'

'It's okay. I know what you thought. But you're safe. Okay?'

She stroked his cheek, trying to soothe him with a gentle touch, but suddenly stopped when she realised what she was doing. She pulled her hands away reluctantly, feeling regretful that she had to. But he was getting better. His breathing was more under control. He seemed more present. He was doing well, even though the gunshots were still going on in the distance.

She opened the car door and grabbed a bottle of water and brought it out to him. 'Here—take a drink of this. Just sip it.'

Adam held on to the water bottle, his hands still trembling a little, but he opened it, swallowed some of the water and then tightened the cap and passed it back. 'Thank you. It'll be the clay pigeon shoot at the inn. They do a charity shoot every year. I'd forgotten. I...'

She smiled at him, glad to have been able to help. She had not expected this. It hadn't even occurred to her that Adam might have returned from his travels a little damaged. He seemed so together. And hadn't he been back for over a year? Had he never addressed this with someone?

She had so many questions, but she didn't want to be the person who asked him before he was ready to talk. Because she very much believed that if someone wanted you to know something about them they would tell you, but only when they were ready to. She did not want to push Adam Campbell. Because if she did, he would drag her further and further into his life, and she was trying to keep him at a distance.

'You sit here for a moment. I'll let down the jack and pack everything away.'

She quickly released the jack and managed to lift the punctured tyre into the boot space. It was a struggle, and a little heavier than she'd expected, but she did it. And when she was done Adam was standing up, waiting for her.

'I'm sorry about that. I didn't mean to...'

Jess brushed away some of the dirt from her top. The black rubber tyre had made a mark on her white blouse. 'It's not a problem. Are you...are you speaking to anyone about this?'

Even now the rifle shots were sounding, and she could tell he still wasn't comfortable. He seemed to flinch at every one.

He didn't answer. He didn't seem to be able to look her in the eye. She wondered if he felt a little embarrassed at revealing a weaker side of himself?

She got into the driver's seat and waited for him to get in on the passenger side. He pulled the door shut and began to put on his seatbelt.

'I'd be obliged if you didn't mention this to anyone,' he said.

'Hey, it's none of my business.'

'I know, but… You helped me out and… I'm sorry you had to see that.'

Jess struggled with what she needed to say. There was so much that was crossing her mind, and it was hard to filter out what was most important.

She looked at him. 'Are you getting help for it?'

'Help? I don't need *help*.' He said the word 'help' as if it was ridiculous.

'I think you have PTSD. I could be wrong—I mean, I'm not a psychologist or anything—but that gunfire really set you off.'

Adam looked down and away. 'I don't have PTSD. It was just…something unexpected, that's all.'

'If you say so.'

She didn't agree—not really. To her, it was obvious. Even though she wasn't trained in mental health. Perhaps if she had been she might have spotted that something was wrong with her father before he took his own life.

'But I don't think this is something you should ignore. You should talk to someone about it. I've seen what happens when people don't share their innermost thoughts and feelings and—'

'Jess, I said I'm fine!' he said. Then he must have realised his tone had been sharper than he'd intended, and he looked at her apologetically. Softened his voice. 'Honestly.'

She stared back, not believing him. 'People have said that to me before.'

Jess started the engine and gave him a look. He at least managed to look a little guilty before he turned away and looked out of the window once again. She indicated and checked her mirrors before pulling out.

There was tension in the air. A little awkwardness. And she really didn't like it.

'I'm sorry. I don't want to push you. I'm sure you know if you need counselling.'

He nodded. 'And I know you're just trying to help. I appreciate that—I do.'

'Well, if you ever want to talk, I hope you'll feel that you can talk to me.'

And she meant it. Even though she wanted to keep him at a distance, her need to make sure another human being was safe overrode any personal desires she had right now. Her father hadn't talked to anyone and he had taken his own life. She'd heard of people coming back from war zones suffering so badly they took their own lives because they couldn't deal with their PTSD, or they turned to drugs or alcohol as a coping mechanism. If she could somehow stop that for Adam, just by offering to lend him an ear, then she would do it.

'Thanks.'

The silence was a little more companionable now, as Jess negotiated them through the traffic that had built up around West Thorney and they headed back towards the hospital.

She wanted to push for more. She wanted to say that he should get help, find someone he could talk to about this, because she really didn't think it was something that was going to go away. Surely he knew that, too?

Adam was medically trained. He must have seen PTSD in others, having worked in war zones abroad. He must know this was something that couldn't just be left to heal on its own. The mind needed looking after just as much as the body did.

Maybe she needed to give him the benefit of the doubt.

Give him some time and see how he went. But she knew if she witnessed another event such as this she would insist that he found someone to talk to, because she could not let him carry on untreated. People took their own lives over lesser things.

She parked in one of the doctors' bays and helped Adam carry the equipment back into the hospital. They restocked it before returning it to its designated space, and then disposed of the placenta in the clinical waste.

'Do you want to write up the notes for Sarah?' he asked her.

'Absolutely. Might as well get used to the computer system.'

'Okay. Did Admin set you up with a log-in yet?'

'They said they'd have that done by tomorrow.'

'I'll let you use mine.'

He came around the desk and leant over her to tap in his pass code on the keyboard. She became vitally aware of his closeness and leant back away from him, trying to create some distance.

'What's Anoush?'

Adam stilled. 'What?'

She looked around them to make sure no one was listening. 'Back there, when you… You said "Anoush". What is that?'

He shook his head. 'Nothing you need to worry about.' His fingers flew over the keyboard and she watched each keystroke.

'Chocolate pudding?'

Adam stood up straight as he looked down at her. 'Sorry?'

She smiled. 'Your password is chocolate pudding.'

'You're not meant to look.'

'Yeah, well…sometimes you can't help but see.'

CHAPTER FIVE

ADAM'S MOTHER WELCOMED Jess at the door with a smile that became an unexpected, all-encompassing hug.

At first Jess froze, but then she relaxed into it.

This must be what a mother's love feels like.

Adam was lucky to have both of his parents and not to have experienced loss.

Having never had a mother of her own—not that she could remember anyway—she found Judy's warmth and kindness meant a great deal to her, someone who had been starved of them for so long. And she allowed herself to accept it because surely getting close to Judy wouldn't hurt.

'I'm so pleased you could come tonight.'

'Are you kidding me? I wouldn't have missed it.'

'Good. Come on in! It's getting a bit chilly out there. You too, Adam!'

Jess had decided to walk with him over to his parents' house. She was looking forward to getting to know her boss and his wife better. She might even find out more about Adam, too. Did his parents know of his difficulties? Probably not. Because on the way over Adam had once again sworn her to secrecy about what had happened to him today.

'They don't need to know.'

Considering he was fighting a powerful internal battle, she thought Adam was doing pretty well, presenting himself as an ordinary guy with nothing in his life to worry about. Jess wondered why he hadn't spoken to his parents about what he was going through. But she decided that she wouldn't raise the issue unless he did.

She followed Judy into the house, closing the door behind her. 'Something smells good,' she said.

'I've got some tatties on to go with a stew.'

Jess's stomach rumbled in anticipation. If it tasted half as good as it smelled, then she was in for a treat. And she never made meals like that for herself. Things that took a lot of time to prepare and cook. She was an instant girl. Microwavable meals. Takeout. Something she could grab from the freezer, stick on a baking tray and cook in thirty minutes.

Homely meals made from fresh vegetables that had been peeled and chopped, with meat that had been marinated and stewed, cooked for hours, which would just slide off the bone and melt in her mouth was something she'd never really made. Not since Eddie had left, anyway.

There didn't seem to be much point now she was on her own, and she spent more time at work than anywhere else. Her time off was precious, and she didn't want to stand over a cooker for hours. She didn't have the energy for it.

Maybe I should make the time, if food can smell this good.

'Jess! You're here.'

She instantly turned at the sound of Jack Campbell's voice, a warm smile on her face, and watched as he came out of a room, holding onto a newspaper with one hand and removing his reading glasses with the other.

'Hello, Dr Campbell.'

'Call me Jack.'

She gave him a quick hug.

'How was your first day? Are you overwhelmed with information?'

Jess glanced at Adam. *He'd* overwhelmed her. Very much, and for many different reasons. Looking at him now, she could hardly believe that a few hours ago their faces had been mere inches apart and she'd been staring into his eyes, begging him to come back to her. That kind of thing made them less like strangers.

'A little,' she said.

'Natural. First days are the worst, aren't they?'

'No, it was good. Interesting.'

'Adam showed you everything?'

He showed me more than you'd probably believe.

'Yes, I got the tour.'

'What do you think of the place? Now that you're actually here?'

'It's perfect.'

Jack beamed, clearly proud of what he had built. 'Let me get you a drink. What would you like?'

'Just tea for me.'

'Adam?'

'I'm fine, thanks.'

'How do you take it?' Jack asked.

'White, no sugar,' Adam answered for her, and she smiled at him, thankful for his remembering.

'Why don't you settle yourselves in the living room and I'll call you through when it's ready? It shouldn't be long,' said Judy.

With Judy and Jack gone, she glanced at Adam, who took her jacket and hung it up before leading her into the living room. It was filled with a big squishy sofa, with a ginger cat curled up on one end, and a small fire crackled away in the grate.

'That's Hamish. He's not really a cat. He's a wild animal armed with blades.'

'He looks sweet.'

'He's a con artist. He makes you think he's sweet until you're in range of those claws.'

Jess sat down next to Hamish and the cat opened its eyes and considered her briefly, before standing up, arching his back in a stretch, rubbing up against her, head-bumping her affectionately, and then coiling back into his previous position.

She gave him a stroke. 'He's a big softy.'

'You must have secret powers.'

'Maybe I do!'

Was this flirting? It couldn't be flirting, right? They were just talking, that was all. It didn't matter that he was smiling at her and looking at her as if she was an amazing person, did it? It didn't matter that every time he smiled at her it made her heart begin thumping away, did it? No, it was just normal conversation. Chit-chat. No subtext. No...flirtation. Just colleagues. Just friends. Nothing in it.

So why did she suddenly feel so nervous? Was it because of the situation? It couldn't be anything else. When you dated a guy, he took you to meet his parents at some point, but she and Adam weren't dating. They'd only just met today!

And, boy, what a long day it had turned out to be. Trying to not have feelings towards Adam, helping him through a panic attack, birthing a baby together... Those kinds of things tended to bring people together.

'What are you two talking about?' Judy asked as she came out of the kitchen, looking at them both as if she'd caught naughty schoolchildren scribbling on the walls.

Jess smiled. 'Hamish has accepted me as one of his own.'

'He purred and everything,' Adam added.

Judy beamed with delight. 'Always trust an animal's reaction to a person, I say. It'll tell you heaps. Jack said he knew you were the right doctor to join us and Hamish has confirmed that. What about you, Adam? What do you think to our Jess?'

Our Jess. She noticed that and felt warmed by the words. It spoke of familiarity and belonging—said that she was *one of them*, part of their family already. And, God damn it, if that didn't almost make her tearful!

But she was curious about what Adam would say, having been put on the spot.

'She's good. Aye.'

Judy laughed. 'Very verbose. Don't go overboard, Adam. Come on, you've worked with her all day! Pay the girl a compliment!'

She saw Adam give his mother a stare, as if she was making him do something he didn't want to do, and she almost laughed. It was funny to see him looking so awkward. She didn't *need* him to give her a compliment. She didn't *need* him to say that she was wonderful, or whatever, but it still would be nice.

Adam turned to look at her, a rueful smile on his face. 'She's very kind. Caring. Empathetic.' He turned back to his mother. 'Enough for you?'

'I don't know. Is it enough for *you*, Jess?'

Jess laughed, feeling happier than she had in ages. 'Absolutely. More than enough.' And without thinking she turned back to Adam and gave him a wink.

He tried to suppress a smile, and she liked it that she seemed to be having a secret conversation with him.

Judy checked her watch. 'Right. Dinner-time! Who wants to help me lay the table?'

Jess raised a hand, loving every second of being with Adam and his family. Who knew it could be like this? Family that stuck together and loved one another. That camaraderie, the in jokes, the gentle ribbing of each other.

She'd experienced none of that with her own father. He'd been a distant man in many ways, never one to be over-generous with hugs or praise, and he'd told her once that he was teaching her to be independent and to stand on her own two feet.

How long had he known about his Huntington's? How long had he kept it a secret from her? Had he been preparing her for the day he would leave her? Had he taken his own life thinking that she was settled with Eddie and she wouldn't be alone to get through her grief? Had he thought that Eddie would stay and support her after she'd read his suicide note telling her why he'd done what he had?

He'd been wrong. Eddie had left her, unable to cope with the news that his girlfriend would slowly deteriorate and die sooner rather than later. With the news that their hope to have a family had been destroyed, because Jess would never have a child knowing that she could pass on the disease.

He'd just walked away! Left her a note, just like her father. As if only his grief counted. Had Eddie not realised just how much *she'd* been grieving, too? For the loss of the family she'd been dreaming of. The loss of the future she'd imagined. The loss of her own father and the father of her future children?

I lost this—what I'm seeing today. Lost what it's like to be a family.

She helped get out plates and cutlery with Adam and kept stealing glances at him, her heart warming with every one—especially if he caught her doing it and smiled back. And although she tried to tell herself to stop doing it, that maybe it could be misconstrued, the yearning to be a part of his family, his loving circle, was strong.

I can have it for one night, surely?

What harm would it cause? She was just smiling at him. Appreciating his good looks. The welcome she felt here. It wasn't as if they were on a date. She'd been invited to dinner by her boss and his wife, Adam hadn't asked her to come.

She suspected Judy had hopes that Jess might have feelings for her son. She could see it in her eyes, her smile, and the blatant way she sat Jess directly opposite Adam.

Her stomach rumbled in anticipation as Judy brought the food over in steaming dishes.

'This looks amazing,' Jess said.

'It's just an old stew recipe that my mother used to make.'

'Well, if it's half as delicious as it smells, then I may just want to eat the whole thing myself.'

Judy smiled her thanks at the compliment. 'I heard you two had an exciting day?'

Jess looked at Adam. Had he said something after all? Which bit was she talking about? 'Oh?'

'I heard you two went to Sarah's house and delivered her baby?'

So Adam hadn't mentioned his panic attack. She wasn't surprised at that and, even though this was a family of medical professionals, and Judy obviously knew who Sarah was, she didn't want to share too much. 'Yes, we did.'

'I guess that's a good way to spend your first day at work.'

Adam nodded. 'It was nice to have a happy result.'

'That's all any of us ever want.'

Jess thought about any happy results she'd had in her life and, apart from passing her exams to become a doctor, she couldn't think of anything that had truly made her happy. She'd never really had a mum, her father had taken his own life, she'd been diagnosed with a life-limiting disease, her one relationship hadn't worked out… It wasn't much to cheer about. She was just plodding on, day after day, trying to make the world believe that she was happy and successful and enjoying life, when in reality she was full of doubt and fear.

But she would have liked to know what it felt like to come home to someone she could speak to. Someone who would respond to her with love and kindness, who would envelop her in the kinds of hugs that Judy gave and understand and comfort her, make her feel human again.

Because sometimes—not that she'd told anybody—she felt as if she was a robot. Going through the motions. Just getting through the day, waiting for a malfunction to occur. It would happen one day, and she had the genetic results to prove it.

'I heard it was a little boy.'

Jess had just put a forkful of lamb into her mouth, so she simply smiled at Judy and nodded.

'I know her mother. No doubt I'll see her tomorrow and she'll have loads of pictures to show me. Maybe one day I'll be able to do the same in return. Adam has yet to provide me with any grandchildren!'

'Mother!' Adam growled.

Judy laughed. 'I'm not telling you something you don't already know! What about you, Jess? Do you ever see yourself having children?'

She put down her knife and fork and grabbed her napkin to dab at her mouth and think. Children were totally out of the question for her. She knew there was the possibility of genetic testing if she ever changed her mind and went down that route, but that wasn't the point. Why would she have a child, even if it was healthy and not live to see that child grow up? Have that child lose its mother? She couldn't put a child through that.

But that was too complicated to share with them all. They didn't need to know her problems. 'I'm so busy with work right now I've not really thought about it,' she said, trying to say it nonchalantly.

'Well, I've lived with doctors my entire life, so I know you'll have to think about it soon. Whether to have a child before you specialise or after. If you choose after, you'll probably be in your late thirties, early forties, and time will be ticking! But if you have a family before you specialise you'll have to consider childcare and how much of your child's life you're happy to miss. No matter what you do, your patients will always come first—it's a hard life, being the child of a doctor.'

'I think the decision as to what Jess does with her life is hers to make,' Adam said, sounding irritated.

'I know that, dear. I was just mentioning it.'

All this talk about children and having babies was really getting to Jess. She could hardly swallow her food now, the lump in her throat felt so big. 'Could I use your bathroom?' she managed.

'It's up the stairs, first door on the left,' Adam said.

'Thank you.'

She excused herself and hurried up the stairs as her tears began to fall. Behind her, she heard Adam admonishing his mum about getting too personal.

She ran into the bathroom and closed the door behind her, sinking to the floor and allowing her tears to fall.

How much of your child's life you're happy to miss...

She would miss all of it, because she wouldn't have one.

Jess had thought she'd run out of tears about this. About never having a baby. The grief for something she hadn't even had. The loss of a dream. A future. A baby to hold in her arms.

It was all too much to bear.

CHAPTER SIX

THE NEXT DAY, Jess discovered that she would be working with Adam in the Well Woman Clinic. They had a full morning of appointments—changing or fitting coils, performing cervical smears, inserting implants.

She felt incredibly awkward after last night. She'd emerged from the bathroom after splashing her face with water and giving herself a stern talking-to in the mirror.

You will not dwell on this! You will not! Now, go down those stairs and show them how wonderful a person Jess is!

She was very good at putting on a mask. She'd had years of preparation. Pretending at school that it didn't matter to her that everyone else had a mother and she didn't. Pretending that it didn't matter that her father never gave her hugs or congratulations when she got high marks in class or exams, that his occasional recriminations that she could have done better didn't hurt. Pretending that she was coping at his funeral. Pretending that she was fine about finding out she carried the Huntington's gene. Pretending that she was okay when Eddie left her.

She absolutely refused to show the world that she was hurting, because who the hell cared? No one in her life, anyway, and wallowing in misery led nowhere.

Jess had a goal. A goal to be a great doctor. And she held that goal in front of her at all times, like a carrot on a stick.

She'd been able to tell when she came down from the bathroom that Adam had said something to his parents, because the atmosphere had changed. The conversation had remained light and well away from anything that might be considered personal.

About an hour after they'd finished eating, Jess had felt so uncomfortable that she had been the one who had changed the happy dynamic of the family that she'd pleaded extraordinary tiredness and said that she would be going home.

Adam had profusely apologised.

'It's fine!' she'd said.

'No, it's not! She had no right to ask you those questions!'

'Adam, honestly, forget about it. I'm not upset.'

But she had been. Upset and guilty.

What would Jack and Judy think of her now? What did *Adam* think? He was the one who mattered. He was the one she would be working closely with.

She needed him to see her as a highly competent professional.

She wanted him to like her.

She wanted him to wrap his arms around her and—

Whoa, there. Hang on a second...

That wasn't ever going to happen. She needed to stop thinking of Adam in such a way. Forget he was too attractive for his own damned good.

I am off the market!

She was faulty goods. She should never even have been on the stall in the first place!

I have to remember that the only thing I have to offer Adam is heartbreak and grief.

Adam had spent a restless night. His mind had tormented him with the look in Jess's eyes last night at the dinner table. His mother had asked that indelicate question and although most people would probably have just laughed it off, or given an actual answer, he'd seen the torment and upset in that look.

She'd tried to hide it. He'd seen her internal battle with herself. But he could have sworn that when she'd stood to leave the table her eyes had been glistening with tears.

Well… He wasn't ashamed to say he'd had quite a conversation with his mother before Jess had made it back downstairs.

Adam knew something about grief. He'd been through it and he could see it in others. Jess had lost her father, was all alone in the world, and probably dreaming of the day she would settle down and have children—finally have a family to call her own. His mother, hassling Jess to choose a time to listen to her her biological clock, had been most rude!

And now they had to work together. He wanted her to feel comfortable with him. Not to feel embarrassed about last night. Not to feel as if she had to explain. Because she didn't have to explain anything.

He liked her. Very much. Probably more than he ought to. And, even though he'd told himself many times over the past year that he would not get involved romantically with anyone ever again, he'd tossed and turned last night, trying to fight off images of what it would have been like to wrap his arms around her and hold her close. To protect her. To care for her. What it might be like to spend time with her and learn more about her...to make her laugh.

Her voice, her eyes, her compassion and her kindness all drew him in, despite his logical thoughts to the contrary and his brain screaming at him that getting close to another woman would only bring heartbreak.

It was confusing, but he kept telling himself that he was okay. That it was fine to be with her because he was just instructing her in the ways of the hospital. She was here to learn and would soon be standing on her own two feet anyway.

They set up the clinic so that Adam would sit and do the admin on the computer, speaking to the patients and explaining what was about to be done, checking their preferences for contraception, while Jess would perform smears and coil fittings, with Adam assisting if necessary.

Their first patient was a young woman who had a six-month-old baby. Vicky Collins came into the room, pushing a pram. She was here to have a contraceptive implant for the first time, and once she'd sat down in the chair and got settled Adam began asking her some questions to establish her state of health and previous contraception methods, and how the implant might differ.

'So, can you tell me which arm is your dominant one?'

'I'm right-handed.'

'Okay, so we'll insert the implant in your left arm, on the inner side of the arm just below the skin. What day of your cycle are you on?'

'Day two.'

'That's perfect. So, once it's in, you shouldn't have to use any other type of contraception. I'm assuming that because you have your period right now you're not pregnant?'

Vicky laughed. 'Definitely not.'

'And you understand the benefits and the risks?'

'I do.'

'I'll give you a leaflet to take home anyway—in case you have any queries—but you can always contact us if you're unsure of anything. Do you have any questions now?'

Vicky shook her head.

'Okay, then, we'll get on with it. If you'd like to lie on the examination table, we'll get everything set up.'

Jess had already prepared the equipment trolley. There was a sterile surgical drape, some gloves, antiseptic solution, a syringe prefilled with local anaesthetic, a piece of sterile gauze, an adhesive bandage and a pressure bandage. He would do this first procedure, as Jess hadn't yet been signed off on competency for contraceptive implants.

With Vicky lying on her back, Adam flexed her non-dominant arm and elbow and gave it an external rotation, so that her wrist was level with her ear. He identified the insertion site, which was three or four inches above the medial epicondyle of the humerus bone, and then felt for the groove between the biceps and the triceps muscles, knowing that he needed to avoid going too deep there, as that was where large blood vessels and nerves lay. He needed to insert the implant just underneath the skin.

Using a sterile marker, he made two marks on the arm—one where the implant would be inserted and the second mark a few centimetres proximal to the first. The second mark would serve as a direction guide during insertion. He cleaned the insertion site with the antiseptic solution and then anaesthetised the area before

Jess handed him the disposable implant applicator from its blister pack.

He removed the protective cover from the needle and with his free hand stretched the skin around the insertion site, puncturing the skin with the tip of the needle, sliding it in to its full length. Then he unlocked the slider on the applicator by pushing it down until it stopped, knowing that the implant was then in position. He removed the applicator and verified the presence of the implant in Vicky's arm by palpating the area.

Jess applied a small adhesive bandage over the insertion site after getting Vicky to feel where the implant was, so that she would recognise how it felt.

'Wow, that feels weird.'

'You'll get used to it.' Adam smiled and then applied a pressure bandage with sterile gauze, to minimise any bruising she might experience. 'You can remove this bandage in about a day, but leave the small bandage on for three to five days, okay?'

'That's fine. Are we all done?'

'Absolutely. And the baby slept throughout.'

'He's a good sleeper.'

Adam gave her the information leaflet whilst Jess cleared up the equipment and wiped down the equipment trolley ready for the next procedure. They waved Vicky goodbye, and when she'd left the room Adam supplied the details of the procedure completed to her patient record.

'That went well,' he said.

'It did. It's nice when everything goes smoothly.'

'Unlike last night,' he said.

'I've told you—you don't need to apologise. Your mum's of a different generation—she's used to asking people questions like that.'

'Well, she won't do it again.'

'Honestly, it was fine.'

He knew he wouldn't get her to admit that it hadn't been.

'Fair enough. Next patient is here for a coil removal and replacement. You want to get set up for that and I'll call her in?'

Jess turned to open a cupboard and get out the equipment they would need. Adam watched her work for a moment. She seemed to be an intensely private person, almost introverted, quite content to hide away from life on this little backwater island that was his own sanctuary.

Why had she come here when she could have gone anywhere else and for probably much more pay? Was it simply because this place was where she'd once found happiness with her father? Because being here made her feel closer to him? How alone did she feel?

He was glad that she was here. She'd helped him yesterday through a very difficult moment. He'd not had an attack like that before, and had always downplayed what had happened in Afghanistan and the reasons why he'd decided to finally come home.

Initially, he'd been mortified at the idea of Jess having seen him freak out, but then he'd been very grateful that it had been her and no one else. She'd told him to seek help, and he appreciated her caring about him. That was why he would do the same thing for her. Look out for her. Protect her. Return the favour and keep her secrets.

He opened his mouth to say something, but there was a knock at their door. Their next patient. He bit his lip and called her through.

Later on, Adam found Jess in the hospital cafeteria. It wasn't a big place, but big enough for someone to grab coffee, maybe a slice of cake, or even a hot meal be-tween twelve and two. She was at one of the window tables, with what looked like a cappuccino and a Dan-ish pastry in front of her, and the sunlight shone in her hair. She was reading something on her phone, with a little frown line between her eyebrows to show that she was concentrating.

'Mind if I sit?' He gestured at the chair opposite.

Her face lit up and she put down her phone. 'Please do.'

'Quite a busy morning, wasn't it?'

'I like being kept busy.' She smiled at him.

With a sharp pang in his gut, he once again realised just how beautiful she was, and just how attracted to her he was.

He'd already noticed that, of course—after all, he was a man. The second he'd seen her he'd noticed. He'd just sucked in a deep breath at that moment in time, and told himself that it didn't matter what she looked like because she was here to do a job. There was no way in hell he was going to act on any attraction he felt. Not after what had happened to Anoush.

He looked at her across the table and smiled, feeling his heart and his stomach going all manner of crazy. He couldn't help it. He wanted to fight the feeling and em-brace it, ignore it and explore it. His head was a mess! How was she managing to do this to him?

Anoush had been the love of his life and he'd never thought he could be attracted to anyone ever again—and yet here he was. Trying to fight it.

Was it because Jess knew something about him that no one else did? Had that secret united them?

He didn't know.

All he did know was that something inside him kept on telling him he needed to get to know this beautiful woman more.

CHAPTER SEVEN

'IS JESS OKAY?' asked his dad.

Adam nodded. 'She's fine.'

'Not upset about the other night?'

Adam shrugged.

After Anoush, Adam had told himself that he would never get close to another person again. That he would never feel as strongly for anyone as he had for Anoush. That he would never again feel that rush of feeling in his heart.

And yet something was happening between him and Jess. Something intimate that he didn't yet understand. And because he was feeling sensitive about that, when his father had asked about Jess he'd felt a wave of protection come over him. But he didn't want to upset his parents any more than they already were. He knew they still felt bad about the other night at dinner.

'I guess the two of you are okay working together?' asked his father.

'We are.' Adam wanted to be able to say that they were more than okay. That they were actually working very well together indeed. That he thought she was a very fine addition to their medical team. But he knew if he said anything like that his parents might read more into it than he wanted them to.

He knew how keen they were for him to settle down and meet someone. They'd never known about his romantic involvement with Anoush. He'd kept that back from his stories of being abroad. He'd been going to tell them when he had something to tell, and the day he'd asked Anoush to marry him had been the happiest of his life when she'd said *yes*. He'd planned to video call his parents that night and tell them about the wonderful woman he was going to marry, but he'd never got that chance, because that was the day they'd been ambushed and he'd lost her in a hail of bullets.

Why tell them about his lost fiancée now? Why give them that happiness and then the pain of snatching it away from them? It would be cruel. Bad enough that he had to bear it—but them, too…?

'That's good. I'm glad. After all, you're going to be seeing a lot of each other.'

Adam raised an eyebrow.

'Well, you two are working together and you're living in the same building. I'm assuming she'll give you lifts to and from work?'

Adam relaxed. 'I guess she will.'

But he told himself that if he was going to be spending all this time with Jess then he needed to instil some rules into himself. No more looking into her eyes and imagining how it might feel to touch her face. No telling her that she was beautiful. No more being aware of how, when she blushed, the colour slowly rose into her cheeks and made her eyes glisten. No more letting his heartbeat accelerate when she was near. No more.

He would be strictly professional. Work only. Colleagues. Friends. He'd allowed a shared secret to draw them close, but he knew what happened when he thought everything was going brilliantly. The world had a way of playing with him.

He trusted her to keep his secret. He was depending upon her to do that. And in return he would give her the respect and distance they both deserved.

Jess had come to this island to find happiness and her own little sanctuary, the same way he had when he'd returned home. He would make sure that she got that—because she deserved that small measure of peace exactly the way he did.

The next day Jess was working with Adam in their minor surgery clinic.

These cases weren't anything overly exciting—treating ingrown toenails, excising cysts, removing lumps—but it was a clinic that Adam enjoyed. He could be hands-on, and it gave him a chance to sit and talk to his patients about things other than their ill-health. Most of them wanted to chat, to pass the time of day. It was always pleasant, and at the end of it he usually left work knowing that he had made a difference in someone's life that day.

And that was what it was all about. Making a difference. Making somebody feel better. Making someone smile inside. Because ever since he'd lost Anoush he'd come to realise that it wasn't always about the smiles on the outside—the smiles that you could see.

Those smiles were often a mask, hiding someone's true feelings. It was inner happiness that mattered more than anything else.

He'd found a new way of life for himself back here

on Thorney, even though he was here alone, and he'd come to accept that Anoush would never see the place he called home, where they'd planned to settle down. He'd never be able to bring her back to meet his parents. He was here alone and he accepted that fact. Welcomed it. Used it as a wall.

Everyone had walls. Some were smaller than others, but that didn't mean they weren't as important. Each wall had been built from a pain.

And it might not be considered much, removing a cyst, or a lipoma, or an ingrowing toenail, but if it took away someone's discomfort, took away some of their pain, then that had to be a good thing. And he might be the only person that patient spoke to all day.

'So, who have we got next?' asked Jess.

Adam was at the computer, looking at the appointment list. They had eight patients today in this clinic, and so far he had dealt with a cyst on someone's hand and a chalazion on an eyelid—a blocked oil gland.

'Bruce Moorefield. Aged seventy-two. Lipoma on his back. I think I'll let you do this one.'

Jess lit up at the prospect, and he tried not to feel good because he'd made her feel that way. He simply smiled and nodded and tried to force his feelings back inside the box where they belonged. But all he could think about was that he'd made her happy by suggesting she do a procedure.

Such a simple thing, but it mattered. She'd said she liked to keep busy, so he'd given her the more complex procedure to do because he'd known she would like it.

He liked making her happy.

'He came in to see me a couple of weeks ago,' he told her. 'He'd been wearing a back brace and the lipoma was beginning to become irritated, so I said we would remove it. It's just under the skin, soft and doughy to the touch, and it moves easily with light pressure. About three inches in diameter.'

'Okay. Shall I call him in?'

'Yep. Go ahead.'

He watched her walk to the door, all bright and breezy, and call Bruce in. Jess looked very pretty today, in a blue blouse and dark trousers. She'd swept her hair into a messy up-do and the odd tendril hung down here and there. He wondered what it would be like to take those glasses off her and pull her hair free and watch it swish down...

Stop. It.

He cleared his throat and she looked at him.

'Okay?' she asked.

'Just a wee frog.'

A smile from her—and it was like being punched in the gut. What was wrong with him?

Bruce Moorefield ambled into the room. They both welcomed him in, and Adam bade him sit down, just to go over the basics before the procedure began.

'I know you said it wasn't anything to worry about, Doc, but my daughters are worried that it might be dangerous.'

'They don't need to worry. Lipomas are usually benign. They're just masses of fat cells that have lumped together. We always take a biopsy, just in case, and send it for pathology, but it is extremely rare for one of them to become cancerous.'

'I trust you completely,' said Bruce. 'It's just...you know what family can be like.'

Adam nodded and smiled.

'So, how do we do this?' Bruce asked.

'We mark out where we want to make the incision—it's usually just a small cut in the skin—and then the lipoma can be squeezed out. It's all done under local anaesthetic, so you shouldn't feel a thing. And, like I said, we'll send it off to be checked under the microscope, but that's common procedure.'

'Great. Let's do it.'

Jess smiled. 'Okay, let's get you up on this bed. If you can remove your shirt and lie on your front for me?'

'No problem. But it's a long time since I stripped off in front of a pretty young lady.'

'I'll turn my back.'

Jess smiled and pretended to straighten her equipment. Then she removed the cover from her sterile field and put on her apron and gloves.

Adam was on the opposite side of the bed, placing a drape over the cyst. It had a pre-cut aperture in it, so that Jess could see the lipoma. He used a sterile marker to make a dotted line around the outside edge of the cyst, and then drew a line down the middle, where the incision would be.

'Okay with that?' he asked Jess.

'Yes. That's perfect. Thank you. Okay, Bruce. I'm going to give you some local anaesthetic, but I'm going to need to insert it all around the lipoma. This is the uncomfortable bit and you might feel a little sting here and there. Are you ready for me to go ahead?'

'I'm good. You do what you have to do, Doc,' Bruce said, from his position face-down on the table.

'Okay. But if you need me to stop at any point, then you tell me.'

Adam watched as Jess drew up the anaesthesia into the

syringe and used the lines that Adam had drawn previously as markers. She began injecting the numbing agent. It only took a moment or two.

'So, Bruce,' said Adam. 'The last time we met you told me your daughter was waiting to adopt. How's that going? Has she heard anything?'

'Well, yes, she did hear something. There's the chance that they might be getting a new wee one, but there's so much red tape, we don't know for sure.'

'I think adoption is amazing!' said Jess. 'You get to choose your family.'

'Aye, you do.'

Jess used a pair of tweezers to pinch at various points of Bruce is back. 'Can you feel me touching you?'

'Not a thing.'

'Good. So, I'm going to make a start. If you feel anything—any pain, anything unpleasant—you tell me and I'll stop and give you more anaesthetic, okay?'

'Will do.'

Jess picked up a scalpel and began her initial incision down the line that Adam had drawn. As she worked, Adam used gauze to wipe away the blood that began to build so that she had a clear field to work in. Occasionally he had to use a cautery to stop some of the more determined bleeds.

They worked well together. He didn't get in her way and she didn't get in his. They were like a well-oiled machine. Almost as if they'd worked together for years, rather than days.

'I think I need to make this incision just a little bit bigger,' she muttered, having given the lipoma a squeeze.

'I agree,' said Adam.

She used her fingers to feel inside the incision and

made sure the lipoma was not attached to any of the surrounding structures beneath the skin, and then she began to squeeze the lipoma out. It was quite stubborn to begin with, but eventually, with a bit of manipulation, it began to be exposed.

Jess had started to grab hold of it and fully remove it when her arm suddenly spasmed and her hand contracted.

Bruce flinched. 'Ooh, I felt that!'

Jess stood there in shock, looking down at her arm and hand.

'Is everything all right?' asked Adam.

He'd seen the spasm—the way her whole arm had moved as if of its own accord.

'I...' Jess looked shell-shocked.

Adam frowned, seeing apprehension and fear in Jess's face, watching her cheeks not colouring, but paling. But they had a patient on the table, and he must come first. He would speak to Jess about this later. It had just been a spasm, surely? Everyone had them.

He stepped forward and took the implements from her hands. 'I'll finish up. Why don't you go make a cup of tea? Bruce won't mind—will you, Bruce?'

'No, I don't mind which of you does it. Is it out?'

'Just about,' said Adam.

He nodded his head towards the door, indicating that Jess should go, as suggested. Jess ripped off her gloves and apron, slamming them into the clinical waste bin and hurrying from the room.

He'd never seen her look so terrified. Although it was almost akin to the way she'd looked when his mother had started asking her questions about having children...

He'd never concentrated so hard on a patient, even though all he wanted to do was run after Jess and see if she was all right.

CHAPTER EIGHT

JESS HADN'T THOUGHT it would happen so quickly.

Well, now it had.

She hurried down the corridor, not sure what she was doing or where she was going. Should she tell Jack? Judy? No one?

She needed someone to tell her that it was probably just a spasm, nothing more. But not Adam. Oh, no, not Adam.

Of all of them she wanted him to see her the way she aspired to be—brilliant, able, trusted, strong. One of the team. She couldn't bear the idea of him finding out about this. He was becoming a good friend as well as a colleague, and she really, really liked him. As long as he didn't know about it she could maintain the illusion she'd fought so hard to create—that everything was right in her world. That she was okay.

She didn't need him worrying about her—not when he had his own problems to deal with. Adam was vulnerable, and he cared, and if he found out about this it would change who they were to each other.

Jack wasn't in his office. She asked around but nobody seemed to have seen him. Out of breath, she stopped for a moment and looked down at her hand. It felt weird. As if it didn't belong to her. But was she imagining that because she was fearing the worst? She massaged it, turning it this way and that. It twitched again, and this time she felt the movement in her entire arm, felt both her hands trembling.

Using her good left hand, she held her arm against her body and pressed it tight. What was going on? There was a free computer at the nurses' station and, unable to think of anything else to reassure herself, she sat down at the desk, typed in her newly created password and looked up the word that she'd hoped not to look for for a long time yet.

Chorea.

Chorea. An abnormal involuntary movement disorder. A dyskinesia. Characterised by brief, irregular movements. A hyperkinetic movement disorder. Commonly seen in Huntington's disease, a neurodegenerative disorder.

She'd seen this symptom before, in her father. At the time he'd dismissed it and said it was nothing, and she'd believed him. Why wouldn't she? He was her father and she'd always listened to him, believed him when he said he had some sort of intermittent tremor. But it hadn't been that, and now she knew he'd begun to hide his symptoms, seeing her less and less—until that final dinner when she'd insisted he come to hers and Eddie's so she could make the announcement that they were trying to start a family.

It hadn't ever been a hard choice as to what to do with her life. She'd always thought of becoming a doctor, and the proudest day of her life had been walking across that platform to collect her medical degree. She'd just imagined she'd have a lot longer to practice.

Now she was beginning to understand her father's fear.

She'd been angry with him after she'd read his suicide note. He should have told her! He hadn't needed to keep it a secret! She was a doctor!

In his note, he'd written that taking his own life had been the only thing to do, so that she wouldn't have to care for him as his condition got worse. He'd thought that he was relieving her of a burden. But perhaps he hadn't thought about what effect it would have on her—him leaving her all alone in the world.

He'd left her the house and all his worldly goods, the savings he had in the bank. And she'd thought she'd get through it because she'd had Eddie at her side.

At least until her blood results had come through.

She'd thought hearing the diagnosis was her most terrifying moment in life, but it wasn't. This was.

'Jess?'

She looked towards the voice, saw Adam strolling down the corridor towards her, and instantly used the mouse to close down the screen on the computer, so that he didn't see what she had been looking at.

'Hey.'

'Are you all right? What happened back there?'

'Nothing. I just had a weird spasm, that's all...' She hated lying to him.

Adam frowned, looking as if he didn't quite believe her. 'It happens to the best of us. We're human. But when it happened to you... You looked horrified. Terrified. Like something else was happening.'

She stood up, pushing her chair neatly behind the desk,

smiling as brightly as she possibly could. 'Honestly, it was nothing. Look—I'm fine.'

She held both hands out in front of her, so that he could see that they were once again steady, praying inwardly that her body wouldn't choose this exact moment to go into spasm again.

She got away with it. Her arms and hands remained steady.

But Adam looked at her with question and stepped forward, taking her right hand and arm in his, flexing and straightening the arm, turning her wrist this way and that, palpating her shoulder joint, checking everything.

She tried her hardest not to blush, not to allow heat to suffuse her cheeks at his touch, but it was difficult. She'd spent a lot of time thinking about what it might be like to be close to this man, wanting him to touch her, and now that he was—even though it was in a medical way, and not an erotic one—she couldn't stop her body responding.

She thanked heaven that his fingers were not on her pulse-points measuring her heart-rate!

'You see? I'm fine.' She pulled her hand free and folded her arms, lifting her chin as if in challenge.

'You would tell me if there was something bothering you?' he asked.

'Of course,' she replied, in a lie that came too easily— much to her disgust.

She'd never thought about this moment. Never thought that she would have to lie to him. Keep secrets. She'd hated the fact that her father had done it and now she was doing the same thing!

But I'm trying to protect him.

The way her father had tried to protect her. How easy that kind of behaviour was to slip into. She began to realise just how her father had felt. Lying to protect the person he'd loved.

But had his lies protected her? All those times he'd told her he was fine…all those times he'd told her he was okay. Had she believed him? Yes—naïvely, she had. Because he had been her father and he had loved her, and he'd been all she'd had. Of course she'd believed him. She had trusted him to tell her the truth, because what was love without trust?

She looked up at Adam, fighting the tears that were threatening to spill from her eyes. She could see in his face that he didn't quite believe her and that *hurt*. She didn't want to hurt him, she didn't want to lie to him, but she couldn't think of anything else to do. And she so much wanted to tell him everything, but she couldn't just blurt it out. It wouldn't be right. There was a time and a place for this kind of thing, and this wasn't it.

He stared back—hard. 'I'll find out, you know. If something is wrong… If it's escaped your attention… That's what doctors do—find out what's wrong.'

'I know. But you don't have to look after me, Adam. I'm perfectly fine.'

He shook his head. 'You're not. And you should let me help you.'

It took every ounce of strength she had, not to just tell him everything there and then. The urge to unburden herself was incredibly strong, but she fought it to the bitter end, no matter how hard it was to concentrate when he was holding her hand in such a way.

He frowned and she let out a breath, sinking against the desktop as if she'd just fought an incredible battle. Had she won or lost? She didn't know. But what she did know was that she was exhausted. Fear was exhausting.

She wondered how long she would be able to maintain her lie. He would see through it. Instinctively, she felt that he would somehow know.

'Why should I let you help me? Because you're a doctor? I'm fine, Adam. Please just leave me alone.'

And she walked away, biting her bottom lip to stop herself from crying.

Adam lay in bed, staring at the ceiling. He'd not been able to settle all night and now he lay flat on his back, staring upwards, wondering about the woman in the apartment above who seemed to have every moment of his focus.

Jess.

She was keeping something from him, but he didn't know what. He'd watched her during the procedure earlier on and she'd been happy, smiling, confident—sure of everything she was doing, chatting to the patient, keeping him at ease, and then...

Something.

Something had happened to her arm—a spasm. Brief, no more than a millisecond in length. It happened to doctors around the world every day—after all they were only human, and human bodies twitched on occasion—but Jess had looked down at her hands in such horror, in such disbelief, her cheeks paling.

He hadn't understood what was happening but had known he must quickly reassure their patient. And as Jess had fled the room Adam had looked down at the open incision, trying his hardest to concentrate on what was most important, finding it difficult to do so. All his mind had wanted to settle on was why that spasm had terrified Jess so much. Why she had reacted so strongly to it? They had to be something he didn't know about.

Adam tried to think. Was the spasm part of something bigger? And, if so, what? Muscle spasms could be caused by all sorts of things and all sorts of conditions, from the benign to something more serious. Was it right that her reaction should make him think that something more serious was most definitely going on? Or was he just seeing the worst, because that was what he was used to seeing?

Jess was becoming a friend—a good friend—even though he'd only known her for such a short period of time, and he was used to looking out for his friends. Protecting them, keeping them safe from harm... He'd not been able to keep Anoush safe, but he was damn well sure he would do his best to look out for Jess.

And... I don't know...she's special to me. No matter how much I try for her not to be.

His eyes began to grow heavy and he allowed them to close, looking for the sanctuary of sleep, where worries and concerns had no place.

Screaming the like of which she had never heard before in her entire life woke Jess from her sleep. She jolted awake, heart pounding, semi-upright in bed, looking around her for the source.

Who the hell was screaming?

She quickly realised that it was coming from the flat below her.

Adam's flat.

She threw off her bed covers and grabbed her robe, hurrying to the front door. She quickly unlocked it and hurried down the stairs to the next floor, began banging on Adam's front door.

'Adam! *Adam!*'

The screaming stopped but she kept hammering her

fist on the door until it was finally opened by a half-naked, sweating Adam.

He wore pyjama bottoms and was barefoot and bare-chested, his eyes dull and his hair mussed around his head. At any other time she would have appreciated the sight. He was very built, his muscles defined without being overly so, with a smattering of chest hair. But she shoved to one side her desire to examine him more carefully. He looked so far away, distant, as if he was seeing another place.

She made him make eye contact with her as she had done once before, placing her hands on either side of his face, knowing this would help bring him back to the present.

'What's going on? Are you okay? I heard screaming.'

He gently pulled her hands away, clearly back in reality and obviously not happy to find himself rescued by Jess once again.

'I'm fine. It was just a dream. A bad dream.'

'It sounded like more than that. It sounded like you were being tortured.' She'd never heard a sound like it before and she hoped never to hear it again.

He smiled and wiped the sweat from his brow with his forearm. 'I'm sorry I woke you.'

'I'm sorry you think you have to go through whatever this is alone,' she returned.

He looked away from her, down towards the floor, before looking back up, his eyes challenging. 'I could say the same to you. Something is bothering you, but you won't tell me what it is. You know, you *could* share.'

She stared back. 'So could you.'

They looked at each other in a stalemate for a long

time, until finally Adam backed away. 'I guess you'd better come in.'

She stepped in, pulling her robe tight around her like a shield, and followed him through to his living room.

Adam switched on the light and headed to the kitchen to make them both a drink. 'Tea? Coffee?'

'I'm not sure that's wise if you want to get back to sleep.'

'Don't worry, it's decaf.'

She smiled. 'Nothing for me, thanks.'

He switched off the kettle and leant back against the counter. 'So, are you going to tell me what happened today?'

No. She wouldn't let him make this about her. 'You were the one screaming. Are you going to tell me what's happening with you?'

He sighed. 'I guess I'm not going to win this one, am I?'

'You're not going to get better unless you have some counselling. Adam, I think you've got PTSD—and that's not something that just goes away all by itself. I don't know what happened to you when you were abroad, but I've seen men and women with their lives ruined by trauma—mood swings, fear, night terrors, nightmares. It's not something that can be ignored.'

He nodded. 'I know.'

She leaned forward in earnest. 'Then you must do something about it! Do you want another night like this one? You must have woken the entire building, scream-ing. It was awful—it sounded like someone was hurt-ing you.' She paused. 'I can't bear the thought of you being hurt.'

He smiled his thanks, and for a moment she thought

that he might reach out and take her hand. But whatever internal battle he was fighting stopped him from doing so.

'You're right,' he said. 'I've been like this for a while. I need to make it stop.'

'So, will you get yourself a counsellor? I know of a good therapist in Nairn I can recommend you to.'

'You do, huh? Now, how is it that *you* know a good counsellor?'

She smiled, not allowing herself to give anything away. 'It's my job to know who to recommend people to.'

'Your job?'

Jess nodded. 'Yes, my job. Now, you've got a big day tomorrow—a full clinic. You need to get some sleep.'

'So have you.'

He didn't know about the decision she'd made. The phone call she'd had with Jack, apologising for doing so, but asking to take some time off for 'a health matter'. Jack had been curious, of course, but had readily agreed as long as she kept him informed. She'd told him she would be in the next morning to explain fully. It wasn't a meeting she was going to enjoy.

'I won't be in clinic tomorrow. I'm taking some time off. Something I'd already booked before I started,' she lied.

She just felt that she couldn't work right now. Not until she'd found out if she was safe to practise. And that would mean talking to Jack. That would mean talking to her consultant on the mainland and she wasn't sure she wanted to do that over the phone. She needed to go and see these people—sit down with them face to face. Her consultant would probably want to run some tests.

Since walking out on the procedure with Adam, her

arm had spasmed two more times, and each time it had happened her heart had sunk with dread. If this was the first sign of the Huntington's beginning to affect her, then it was beginning earlier than it had with her father—and that was a scary prospect.

If she could keep this news from Adam, then that was what she would do. No point in telling him if it was something else. No point in worrying him before it was absolutely necessary.

'Oh. I didn't know,' he said.

'Well, you do now. So, let's get you back into bed.'

She blushed, turning away from him so he couldn't see her face. She'd never thought that she'd be leading Adam to his own bedroom. And if she had ever dreamt of it, it wouldn't have been like this.

'Yes, ma'am.'

She pushed open his bedroom door and noticed the tangled sheets on the bed, where he must have thrashed and fought his way out of his bad dream. She stood to one side, feeling awkward, not sure what to do next. She knew she didn't feel right leaving him—because what if it happened again?

Adam looked at her intensely. 'Would you stay? You could lie next to me on the bed. There's plenty of room.'

She looked from Adam to the bed, imagining herself lying next to him, as she often had in her dreams. How could she resist?

'Sure. At least until you fall asleep, if that's what you need.'

'Thanks.' Adam clambered into bed first, pulling the sheets over himself and settling his head on the pillows.

Jess felt awkward as she walked around to the other side of the bed, removing her robe and lying down beneath the sheets, laying her head on the pillow next to his, facing him.

'Do you want to talk until you fall asleep?'

'No. This is good. Just having you here beside me. I feel better.'

She smiled, glad. 'Goodnight, Adam.'

'Goodnight, Jess.'

She liked the way he was looking at her. Loved the way his eyes shone in the darkness of the bedroom. The way the shadows fell across his face. The way it made her feel to lie next to him. She told herself to soak up the moment, because when would she ever have this again? The fact that he'd asked her to stay made her feel...*wanted*. *Needed*.

Adam reached up to stroke her face and her breath hitched in her throat as his fingers stroked delicately across her cheek, down her jawline, his thumb brushing over her bottom lip. He was looking at her mouth so intently!

Her heart was beginning to hammer loudly in her chest. Could he hear it? Could he tell her pulse was racing? Feel the heat in her cheeks? The anticipation of what he might do next was making her body tingle.

His hand slipped beneath her hair at the nape of her neck and he moved closer to press his lips to hers.

Jess closed her eyes in blissful response. She knew she shouldn't be letting this happen. But the fact that she'd told herself that this was forbidden just made it all the more exciting, and she knew she didn't want to stop.

What was one night? What was one connection? Was she going to be a nun for the rest of her life? No! So why not? Why not do this with him?

She liked him. Fancied him. They had a connection

and she knew his secrets. They'd grown close lately and he was starting to mean so much to her. They could be adults about this. And, dammit, if her disease was going to rear its ugly head now, then this might her last chance to enjoy being with a man whilst her body still felt under her own control. And she would take it right now!

Jess reached for his body, pulling him closer, feeling the heat of his skin beneath her fingertips, the hardness of his muscles, the thrilling feel of his arousal against her urging her on, telling her she needed this. She savagely cast aside her doubts and allowed herself to be free of her usual constraints. Free of the tight rules she'd given herself. This was not a time for those. This was a time just for her and Adam.

He manoeuvred himself above her, his hands raking over her body, and she arched towards his touch, revelling in every sensation she could feel. This was how a body was supposed to work. This was what she was meant to have if the world was fair.

He peeled her tee shirt over her head and cast it to one side, his hands enveloping her breasts, squeezing and rubbing her nipples to peaks, and it just felt so damned good!

'Adam…' she breathed, her lips grazing the skin of his neck, his jaw, before they found his mouth again, her tongue meeting his.

She wanted to devour him and to be devoured herself. To lose herself in this. All the tight tension she'd been feeling for such a long time without release was now being freed. She wasn't thinking about her arm, she wasn't thinking about the future, she was just experiencing the *now*.

As his exploring fingers reached down and slipped inside her underwear, finding the sweet spot that had been so long ignored, she gasped and drew him tighter against her, urging him on.

She didn't want this to end.

CHAPTER NINE

ADAM WOKE EARLY to the sound of birdsong outside. He was feeling good, content, safe, and it took him a moment to realise why and remember that he hadn't spent the night alone. He opened his eyes, hoping to see Jess still there, her hair across his pillows, to watch her as she continued to sleep. But he saw with immense disappointment that she had gone.

When had she left him?

How was she feeling after their shared night?

He sank back against the pillows and hoped she was all right. What had driven him to do that last night? To take their friendship and push it in another direction entirely? Had he just been seeking a distraction? Something joyful that felt good after the horror of his nightmare? Had he simply sought consolation in her arms? Did that mean he had *used* her?

He hoped not. He had genuine feelings for her. He was attracted by her compassion, her sensitivity, her caring. Physically, he'd been attracted to her since day one... But he was her mentor, and he had sought a physical release with her without considering what it might do to them as friends.

He felt closer to her, that was for sure, and it had been

so good between them! As if he'd found the yin to his yang. They'd matched each other perfectly.

Guilt almost swallowed him as he thought that last thought. He hadn't been with anyone since Anoush, and now that he had what did that mean? That he was moving on? Forgetting her? Leaving her memory behind?

No. That could never happen.

It had felt good to be holding someone again. He'd never thought that he would, but Jess had felt so right against him. The scent of her, the feel of her…her hair spread over his pillows. The way her face had looked as she'd gasped his name, her lips open as she breathed against him, the heat of her breath against his neck…

Selfishly, he just wanted to put that moment in his mind and treasure it. Keep it. She'd felt so soft and warm and right.

He sat up in bed, swinging his legs so that his feet were on the floor. Should he go and knock on her door? See how she was? Make sure everything was still okay between them before he headed into work? He didn't want there to be any awkwardness between them.

He sat for a moment, trying to figure out how he felt with her gone.

It was funny how a man could change in so short a time. When his father had first asked him to work with her he'd almost been a little bit resentful at being put with such a junior doctor. But then he'd got to know Jess… got close to her.

And now he was finding himself missing her when she was gone. Missing her smile, missing her laugh, missing the way she made him feel when she was around… He missed how wonderful it felt to be close to her.

Something was happening between them, and although he was fighting it, part of him wanted to roll over and give in.

Jess was an amazing person. The way she cared for him, the way she put herself out—as she had last night, coming down to make sure that he was okay, to check on him. Not many people would have done what she had, and he was grateful for her friendship.

He remembered again how it had felt to hold her against him and wondered what it might feel like to hold her properly and know that she was his for ever…

She'd got no sleep at all, lying in Adam's arms for an age, her mind in turmoil, before pulling away and getting dressed as his breathing became steady and she knew he was in a deep sleep.

She'd thought about leaving a note, but hadn't been able to think of what to put. What did you write after you'd just had the most sexually exhilarating night of your life with your work mentor and friend? What would sound casual, as if everything was okay, when in reality her mind was brimming with crazy thoughts and feelings and she simply didn't know how to think?

Allowing herself to get carried away like that…what had she been thinking? It had made all this so much more complicated than it needed to be.

But she had craved his touch last night. She had needed him so badly—had needed to know what it felt like to want so badly she thought she might burst. To be touched as if she had something to give. To be caressed as if she had value and worth—things she'd often felt lacking in since her diagnosis.

She'd thought herself capable only of hurting people if she got involved with them, but it turned out she was

still capable of giving pleasure. Of being a woman underneath the label of her illness.

She had come to work early, knowing that Adam
might try and find her before he left for work, and she
wasn't sure she could face him right now, knowing that
last night had meant more to her than she might ever
have believed, and knowing that in her heart she wanted
more of it and that it would be torture if this was as far
as it could go.

She also knew that Adam would be in the clinic this
morning, so she'd loitered in the female changing rooms,
taking a shower and getting changed before going the
long way round to Jack's office.

She was nervous. Extremely nervous. Because what
he was about to say would change the course of the rest
of her life. If he said that he thought it was the beginning
of Huntington's showing itself then she would have to
rethink what she would do. She'd hoped to be a doctor
for a lot longer than this. She'd hoped that by the time
she started showing symptoms progress might have been
made in Huntington's research.

Only there'd been nothing. Nothing that was useful
to her right now, anyway. There was going to be some
research in the future, screening the entire genome for
new drug targeting, but that would take a heck of a long
time yet.

Ideally, what she needed was for Jack to say that in
his opinion this was just a blip—an intermittent tremor,
perhaps even a trapped nerve. The spasms didn't *have*
to mean it was Huntington's chorea. She needed him to
say that he would support her. Take care of her. Liaise
with her consultant on the mainland.

Judy greeted her with a bright smile and she forced

a smile back. 'I'm just going to have a quick word with Jack. He's expecting me. Does he have anyone with him?'

'Not at the moment. And he's just got off the phone, too. You go right ahead.'

She stood outside Jack's office and stared at his nameplate on the door. Was she making a mistake, telling him about this? He was Adam's father, but he was also her boss, and she knew she should have told him about the Huntington's at her interview, or even on her application. But she'd deliberately left it off, and she knew that made her in breach of the promises she'd made to reveal everything that mattered to her employer.

To go in as a patient, and not as his employee, would be—*was*—frightening.

Jess raised her hand, paused for a moment, then knocked. She sucked in her breath until she heard Jack say, 'Enter.' Then pushed open the door.

'Jack? Is it okay to have that chat with you now?'

He must have seen something etched into her face, heard something in her tremulous voice that told him that this was not just another chat with his favourite new doctor. He looked at her and nodded, then picked up his phone and told Judy that he was not to be disturbed.

Jess closed the door behind her and slipped into the seat opposite him. This room had brought her comfort the first time she'd come here. The pale taupe colour on the walls... The framed certificates... The bookshelves filled with medical books... The windowsill with the family photos...

There was one she hadn't noticed before, of Jack and Judy together, cutting a cake at some party. A wedding anniversary? And on the desk there was a snow globe of the Loch Ness monster that made her smile nervously. It seemed to sit there in expectation, waiting for her to do her thing. To reveal her big secret.

He could fire her, if he wanted to. She'd not been honest. She didn't know how to start this conversation. She didn't know how to voice her greatest fear. To tell him about the thing that could change everything—her life and her future on this island. It could all be over in seconds, and whatever she thought might be happening between her and Adam would be over too, before it had even begun.

Jack stared at her. She could feel his eyes upon her, assessing, wondering. But then he showed her why he was such a great doctor. He leaned forward and asked, in the softest of voices, 'What's wrong?'

She felt the pain of tears prick her eyes, but as her vision became blurry she managed to meet his gaze, nod her head and say, 'There's something I haven't told you.'

Her voice was almost a whisper…

When Adam arrived for work he saw he had a long list of patients for the general practice clinic. He was looking forward to it after having such a good sleep. His best sleep in over a year, because Jess had stayed with him.

His mind kept wandering to ways he could make it happen again, but all of them involved a relationship of some kind and he was too terrified to go down that route.

But he really liked Jess. He was developing feelings for her, he could tell.

I need to keep them under some sort of control!

But how could he when he was so worried about her? She was constantly on his mind and something was clearly bothering her.

Was it him? Did she harbour feelings for him too, but,

because she knew him to be a fragile, broken thing was holding back from him, not sharing with him? Did she think he already had enough going on?

He knew he had a problem, but it was one that he'd managed on his own for over a year now, and he'd thought it was something that only bothered him on occasion so didn't need constant attention.

It was the occasional panic attack. The occasional nightmare. Mostly he didn't have them, and he'd managed to hide them from everyone. Even his parents had no clue. They knew what had happened to him, but they didn't know about the *effects* of it.

Perhaps Jess thought that if he couldn't be honest with himself he wouldn't be honest with her? Was that why she wouldn't share with him whatever it was that was going on with her? Even if she had shared his bed last night.

There was definitely something—something that she wasn't telling him. But he knew it was unfair of him to expect her to reveal all when he was hardly capable of doing the same. They'd bared their bodies, but not their souls.

Imagine what it might be like if we did...

She was there for him. The way she had come to his flat in the middle of the night, concerned for his well-being... It had made him feel a little embarrassed at first—the fact that she had heard him cry out, that she was aware of his bad dreams and how they were making him suffer.

But he knew she was not the one who'd made him feel embarrassed—that was all his own work. The dent to his pride that he felt as a man was stupid—he knew that—but it didn't stop it from being there.

He'd been so used to looking after himself, to standing alone, to *being* alone, that he wasn't sure how to deal with someone who was so intently looking out for *him*. He'd had it working on the frontline, sure, but after the ambush, and the death of his colleagues and Anoush, he'd told himself never to expect that level of support again. Not from people who didn't know him.

He'd known his parents would be there, of course, but not Jess. And yet here she was, caring for him, worrying about him, when clearly she had something going on in her own life. What could it be?

For a brief moment last night they'd both been able to forget the real world and had existed in a simple world of physical pleasure, but he knew that could never be enough. It was fun, yes, but not something that could be sustained with any meaning.

The first patient to come into his clinic was a young girl of nineteen, Cara O'Leary. She was clutching onto her bag as if it were a lifeline, and not quite meeting his eyes as she sat down in the seat opposite him.

He waited for her to settle before speaking. 'Hello, there. I'm Dr Campbell—how can I help you today?'

'I'm…er…pregnant.'

The fact that she wasn't smiling, or beaming with happiness, or doing cartwheels around the room, suggested that maybe this announcement—this situation—was not something that was welcome. However, he often found it was best to wait and let people tell him how they were feeling, rather than making assumptions.

'Okay. How many weeks?'

She shrugged, fiddling with the strap of her bag. 'I'd guess at about five or six. It's early days.'

'And were you trying to get pregnant?' he asked gently.

Cara shook her head. 'No. I wasn't. I can't have children.' She looked down at the floor, biting her lip. 'I'm not meant to.'

Adam passed her a tissue from the box on his desk to help her dry the tears that he could see were about to fall. As she gathered herself, he took the time to have a delve into her medical history. And that was when he realised that poor Cara had congestive heart failure, which meant that if she were to get pregnant the condition would put such a strain on her heart that she most likely would not survive.

'I see. When did they discover your heart issue?'

She sniffed, dabbing her eyes. 'Two years ago. I'd always had problems—my mitral valve was replaced, and I had a significant cardiomyopathy before I went into heart failure. My consultant told me not to get pregnant, that the risk would be too great. The blood volume alone created by pregnancy would put too much strain on my heart.' She sobbed.

Adam sympathised. To be put in such position as this was awful. And she was so young. She'd probably had dreams of having a family one day, only to be told that to do so would put her own life at risk. And now she'd got pregnant by accident and knew that it couldn't continue.

'I understand,' he told her. 'Who's your consultant?'

He looked back at her notes, pulling up a letter from the mainland hospital that had dealt with her cardio condition. The letter was signed by a Mr Porter.

'Do you want me to contact Mr Porter and just double-check with him before we arrange anything?'

She shook her head. 'I know what he'll say. We've been through this so many times. I know what I have to do. Besides, I'm already feeling breathless. It's already affecting me. I have to go through with a termination.'

'Normally I would suggest you talk to someone before making such a big decision. Do you have support from others? The father of the child?'

'Yes, I'm lucky that way, I guess. He's in the waiting room, if you want to speak to him, too. But I need this to be over. The longer I'm pregnant...'

'Of course. Considering your unique situation, I can do that. But the fact that you've mentioned you're breathless already is concerning me—would you mind if I quickly examine you?'

Cara shook her head.

Adam completed a basic examination, spending a lot of time listening to her heart and lungs with his stethoscope. Her blood pressure was a little raised, and her pulse faster than he would have liked it to be—though that could just be from the stress of the situation that she was in. He got her to do a breath test, to check her lung capacity, and the results were not great.

'All right, I'm happy to get you booked in, but I'd like you to be kept under strict observation whilst you have it done. Obviously your heart is already under strain, and the stress of the procedure will add to it. Considering all of this, I'm not sure that we should carry out the procedure here in the hospital. I think, instead, we'll take you over to the mainland and have it done there, where you can be observed properly by a cardiologist. But I'm going to admit you here, straight away, before we arrange the transfer.'

She looked disappointed. 'I thought that might be the case. Okay, let's do it.'

'All right. I'll get you admitted. The request will go over to the mainland today, and because it's urgent I'll ask that they transfer you by this evening. You should get someone to pack you a bag and be ready to go with you, because I want this to happen sooner, rather than later.'

Cara nodded. 'Good.'

'You know, just because this is what you expected, you still need to take some time to process what's happening here. I'd highly recommend some counselling.'

He felt a little disingenuous, suggesting this when he himself had fought against counselling all this time, but in this situation he felt strongly about it. Cara was terminating a pregnancy. She was losing a baby that at any other time and place might have been welcome and loved, cherished and adored. The dreams she might have had for her life had already been changed by her health situation. She might benefit from being able to talk about how this loss had affected her.

After Cara had left the room, closing the door behind her gently, Adam sat for a moment, thinking about her situation as well as his own. He had suggested counselling to his patient, knowing that she would benefit from it, so why was he fighting it for himself?

If he was being honest, he knew that counselling was the right thing. He was suffering from PTSD—he had to admit that. Because until he accepted that he had a problem he couldn't fix it, and Jess had begged him to give it a try. Perhaps if he did, he might just get the perfect night's sleep that he dreamed of achieving. Perhaps it would help him put into perspective exactly what had happened during the ambush and he would be able to accept surviving when others hadn't?

Adam sent through the request for Cara's transfer and procedure first, then looked up the directory of counsellors on the mainland and picked up the phone to make an appointment for himself. He felt nervous doing so, but he also knew that it was the first step in the right direction.

Jess would be proud. He wanted to call her and let her know what he had done. He wanted to hear her voice, wanted to share with her his news. But he knew he had a whole list of other patients to see first.

CHAPTER TEN

JESS FINISHED HER tea and placed the cup and saucer on Jack's desk. 'Thank you for listening. I appreciate you taking time out for me.'

'I will always have time for you, Jess. I'm glad you've told me. I wish you'd told me earlier, so that I could have put some things in place to support you, but...'

'I was worried you wouldn't give me the job, and I wanted to come here so badly.' She felt awful.

'I would never have turned you down because of the Huntington's. But I know now, and we can do something about it.'

She smiled and let out a deep breath. She'd shared her greatest fear with him and he'd been wonderful—had even run a series of physical assessments. The spasms still came, most often when she held her arm in a certain position. And because of this finding Jack had suggested that it might not be the beginning of Huntington's, as she feared, but something completely benign that she shouldn't worry about.

To be on the safe side, and worrying about the safety of her patients, Jess had asked if she could take a week out. That way she could monitor the situation over the next few days, speak to her neurologist, adjust to what was happening and keep an eye on the spasms.

She didn't feel right about practising as a doctor knowing that her arm or hand could spasm at any moment. It would be embarrassing for her, as well as disturbing to any patient who noticed—especially if she was in the middle of a procedure or even the delivery of a baby. What if she dropped the baby? That would be awful! Horrifying! Not to mention downright dangerous. She couldn't justify putting anyone in danger until she knew for herself, for sure, just what was going on.

If this was just an intermittent spasm it was probably caused by tiredness. Or all the nervousness of her attraction to Adam and spending time with him keeping her on edge. Including sharing his bed last night!

She wasn't worried about leaving him in the lurch. He probably wouldn't miss her anyway. Maybe he was even having regrets about last night. Had he woken with a clear head and realised they'd both made a mistake? He'd appreciate the distance, and he'd appreciate not having a shadow reminding him about the need to get help for himself. He probably thought she sounded like an annoying stuck record. Besides, if she was lucky, this could all be nothing and she wouldn't have to tell him anything.

As if Jack could read her thoughts, he leaned forward on his desk. 'Have you told Adam about what is going on?'

Horrified at the idea of telling Adam anything about her Huntington's, she shook her head. 'No. It doesn't feel right to tell him. And what's the point of saying anything unless I know for sure?'

'That seems fair.' Jack sighed. 'I understand you're in a difficult situation. Maybe later? When you know more?'

She looked Jack straight in the eye and nodded. 'Thank you.'

Jack looked uncomfortable. 'I care for you, Jess. My wife cares for you, too. We knew you'd lost your father, and now I know why and how. You're in a difficult position—I appreciate that—but I want you to know just how much you have our support.'

There was a sudden knock at the door just before it swung open and Adam appeared, as if summoned. He looked as if he was about to say something to his father, before he noticed that there was someone in the room with him. He turned to apologise for interrupting the conversation and then obviously realised just who his father was with.

A broad smile broke across his face. 'Jess? I didn't know you were at the hospital today. I thought it was your day off?'

Seeing him standing there, and with his father's wise words ringing in her ears, Jess stood up quickly and gathered her things. 'It is. I was just leaving.'

'Are you all right?'

'Everything is fine!' She glanced at Jack, knowing he would keep her secret.

Everything wasn't fine, and she wanted to tell Adam. But she just wasn't ready yet. Perhaps in a week? After she'd had time to monitor herself, to see if her life was beginning to change in the way it had been predicted.

Jack's empathetic smile made her feel as if she was being complicit in a crime. Standing there in front of Adam and claiming everything was fine.

But news like hers deserved some sort of delicate approach. Soft lighting, relaxing music in the background. It needed to be built up to and gently broken, not just announced in an office doorway before she disappeared for a week. Not right after the wonderful night they'd shared. She wanted to hold on to that memory for a while—not have it ruined by an announcement that she didn't want to make.

'I've got something to tell you,' Adam said, touching her arm to stop her from rushing off.

'Have you?'

She looked at Adam and could see the confusion on his face as he tried to read her nervousness. She so desperately wanted to explain to him what was going on, but until she knew for sure—for herself—there was no point in telling him anything. The thought of telling him was already terrifying, so she was in no hurry to tell him right now.

'I think you'll like it. Let me tell you at dinner tonight.'

Jess glanced at Jack once again. Adam mentioning dinner would make Jack think there was something going on between them. How could she tell him that they were just friends when she knew in her heart that she wanted to be so much more? If she said that out loud—*We're just friends*—it would be like admitting to herself that she was the one thing with Adam that she didn't want to be.

Just friends.

She wanted more. Dreamed of more. Especially after what they'd shared. Being with Adam physically had made her realise all that she was shutting herself off from, and that had hurt. But she couldn't have it.

'I'm sorry, I don't think I'll be able to make dinner.'

She knew she would be disappointing Adam. And she was desperate to know what his news was. But she comforted herself with the fact that she needed to take this week away. After this week, she would know for sure if these spasms were something simple or the start of something she didn't want to even contemplate.

She had to get to the mainland. See her neurologist. Get the facts.

She saw confusion in Adam's eyes—and did she see something else there? Was that *hurt*? It surprised her, startled her, and she looked away as she tried to process it.

'Are you sure?' he asked. 'Because you said last night that—'

She held up her hand to silence him. Whatever would Jack think now? Adam had mentioned that they'd been together *last night*... She didn't dare look at the older Dr Campbell. She could only guess what he was thinking and feeling...

'I'm taking the week off and I'm not sure I'll be at home; I might have to go to the mainland. Now, if you'll just excuse me...?'

She grabbed her things and quickly moved past him, feeling tears prick at the backs of her eyes as she did so.

Why did life have to be so complicated? Why couldn't it be simple, just for once? Why did it have to be so painful?

'You two were together last night?' his father asked curiously.

Adam turned and glared at his father, ignoring his question. 'What was that all about?'

His father looked away purposefully and sat down behind his desk, reaching for some paperwork.

Adam felt his irritation rise. He knew when people were hiding things from him, and he could clearly see that his father knew something that Adam did not.

'What's going on? Is there something wrong with Jess?'

Jack shook his head, refusing to make eye contact until Adam leaned forward over his father's desk.

'If there's something going on, then I need to know about it.'

'There's nothing I can say.'

'Why? Has she told you not to?'

'It's complicated, Adam.'

'Why is it? It seems very simple to me. You know something, and you should share it with me. Jess is my friend and I care about her. If there's something wrong then I should know.'

His father looked back at him, almost imploring him with his eyes not to push the point.

And that was when Adam had a moment of clarity. 'It's not because you don't want to, is it? It's because you *can't*.'

Jack leaned back in his chair and stared at his son regretfully.

'Is it because of some kind of employer/employee confidentiality?'

'That's right.'

'You do realise I could just go straight onto a computer and look up her records right now?'

'You could try—but you won't find anything. There's nothing on the system. You know that the nature of where we live means that I have always protected the confidentiality of my staff. Individual records are kept on *my* computer and my computer alone. They're encrypted and password-protected. You won't find anything on Jess.'

'You must be able to tell me *something*. Is it serious?'

Jack let out a heavy sigh. 'You need to talk to Jess. If

anyone is going to tell you about what is going on, then it needs to be her.'

Adam sank into the chair opposite his father and thought carefully. Something was most definitely going on. Something to do with that spasm. Something that was making her take the week off. What could it be?

His brain raced through all the possibilities he could think of. Medical conditions, other causes of spasms...

Apart from that one moment when her hand had shaken Adam had assumed that Jess was absolutely fine. In good health. Last night she'd been...amazing! He couldn't think of any other symptoms that she might have shown. So what was so scary that she couldn't tell him?

He resolved to find out.

It felt strange not to be going into work. Jess was used to keeping herself busy, helping people out, studying, doing research, working at the hospital, seeing patients...

Suddenly to have free time left her feeling a little bit lost. Logically, she knew that she should use this time productively, to get on with things that she had been putting off. Some reading, maybe enjoying the baking that she used to love so much... Simple things, but things she had put to one side to focus on her work.

She wasn't used to focusing on herself.

But she knew she wouldn't be able to concentrate on anything until she'd got this spasm thing sorted. It could be something simple, but if it wasn't...

More than anything she dreaded it being the start of her disease, but after that her greatest fear was telling Adam.

She really didn't want him to know. Why ruin things for him? She knew he liked her. It was very much mutual, and he'd become a close friend in a short period of time. It was almost as if they'd known each other for ages. But he had enough on his plate. Did she really need to burden him with this, too?

The only way she could get away with not telling him would be to leave the island and go and work somewhere else. Randomly, she brought up a job site for medical personnel and checked out what vacancies there were.

There were plenty. Aberdeen, Edinburgh... Or something further south... London. Dorset. Brighton. She could go anywhere—but who would want her? With Huntington's? She couldn't imagine anyone wanting to take her on, no matter how supportive their occupational health department was.

She narrowed her search to obstetric opportunities and found a part-time position, just Mondays and Fridays, at a hospital in Cardiff. There was another in Northampton. She could go! Leave Adam with nothing but fond memories of her.

Would they take me on even part-time with Huntington's?

But should she take this opportunity now that she'd had this scare? She'd come to the island seeking the happiness she'd experienced here with her father, but what if that had been the wrong thing to do? What if the spasm she'd experienced was a wake-up call? Telling her to do what she wanted to do before she ran out of time? Perhaps she should apply for an obstetrics fellowship? Live her life! Live her dream before it all came crashing down?

And that was when she realised she'd made a huge mistake by coming here to Thorney. She'd headed back into her past, chasing ghosts, when she should have taken a step towards her future!

What have I done?

The 'Apply Now' button glowed a soft blue at her. Enticing her. Prompting her. What did she have to lose? She could have so much to gain. Yes, it would be difficult to say goodbye to Adam, and of course Judy and Jack, but it would probably be a good thing.

She'd allowed Adam and his family to get too close. Had allowed them into her heart. She'd begun to yearn for things. Family, love, affection, Adam's arms wrapped around her... All the things she should not dare to dream of. Not without ripping out their hearts—and she could not do that in good conscience. Adam's parents wanted grandchildren. She couldn't give them that if Adam got more involved with her. She'd not just be ruining his life, but their dreams, too.

Outside, the sun shone brightly. She would go for a walk soon, she thought, but first she would fill out an application. She'd probably never hear back, but what if she did?

Biting her bottom lip, she hit the button and began to fill in the online application form. Her stomach was doing triple somersaults at this turn of events, but she kept telling herself that *if* this had just been a spasm, and *if* she got accepted, she might soon be doing her dream work. Training in obstetrics. Following her passion. Being what she'd always wanted to be!

She worked through it, taking time and care over the personal statement and on 'Extra Information' page. By the time she was done she'd been in her hunched position so long, concentrating so hard, that her back and shoulders hurt.

A walk in the sea air and the coastal breeze would blow away the cobwebs and the feeling of guilt that she'd had since walking away from Adam without an explanation—not just in the middle of the night, but also in his father's office.

She grabbed her keys and a bottle of water and headed down to the coastal path. There was a trail, called the Thistle Walk, that would take you around the entire perimeter of the island—around twenty-three miles in total.

If Jack was right, and this was the start of her Huntington's, then physical tiredness would aggravate the chorea. And hadn't she taken this week off so that she could either confirm or deny the onset of her disease? Jess didn't like uncertainties. That was why she had taken the diagnostic blood test in the first place—so that she would know. So why not do her best to prove it one way or the other?

She set off. She met a few dog walkers along the way, and took the time to kneel down and greet the dogs, scratching them behind the ears and wishing she had one herself.

She'd never had a dog, simply because her working hours meant it wouldn't be fair to keep it cooped up inside. Doctors didn't often finish on time. Their shift might end at seven p.m., but if something was going on with a patient—a complication, or surgery needed—or a baby hadn't yet been born, then they often stayed on until the patient was sorted. That meant sacrificing their free time. The time to rest and recuperate before the next shift.

This week Jess was determined to enjoy her free time and use it wisely. However, as she walked, she found her thoughts often straying to Adam. How would he react if she went back at the end of this week and told him that she'd decided to leave? Or told him that she had Huntington's? Because those were her two choices.

Both would hurt him. Her too. But she had to think of herself right now—not take on someone else's worries. She needed to be selfish. It was the only way she could get through these difficult times. Reel in her emotions and her sympathies, box up her heart once again and steel herself.

She'd got too close to Adam. Had feelings for him. Feelings that were dangerous. She must lock them away.

She had no doubt that he would be kind either way. Understanding. But that kindness, that affection, would be dangerous. Both to him and her. Adam had things of his own going on. Things that she was not yet a party to. And perhaps that was a good thing? Because the more she knew, the more she'd care. The more she'd want to stick around and help. But she didn't need to be dragged into Adam's drama, whatever it was. She had enough problems of her own.

Perhaps we should never have met at all? That would make this whole thing so much easier.

Inwardly, she berated herself for being so open to his friendship, for staying in his bed. But what else could she have done? Walked away? She'd wanted to be with him as much as he had wanted to be with her. He'd been her mentor at the hospital—she'd had to spend time with him—and she'd been so determined to be happy here she'd pushed aside her worry about being attracted to him and just got on with connecting with him.

Because she'd thought she would stay here on Thorney for the rest of her life!

Now she knew that choice had been a mistake. And she had no idea how to rectify it. Perhaps, no matter what, she should leave Thorney anyway? It had been a bad decision to come here—she could see that now.

She could only hope that her Huntington's would remain inactive and that her application would get her an interview. She'd been honest on it. Had told them about her hereditary condition. They couldn't discriminate against her for it, but...

She loved Thorney. She loved the people on it. Maybe she even loved Adam a little. Well, that would have to stop. She needed to be sensible and she needed to take the steps that would set her life back on the path that it should have been on in the first place.

Coming to Thorney, being with Adam, the spasm in her arm—all that had made her see clearly for the first time in years.

He was tired. Exhausted. It had been such a long week, and he'd often found himself looking for Jess, so that he could tell her about a patient he'd seen, or a case that he'd had to deal with, wanting to run it by her, see how she would have reacted. But she hadn't been there, and each time he'd realised that he'd felt an incredible sinking feeling in his gut and his heart and known that his feelings for Jess were running way beyond that of a friend...

The thought had startled him at first. It wasn't something that he'd expected. He'd told himself that she would never be anything more than just a colleague. But something had happened. Something that had started when she'd looked out for him when he'd had that panic attack at hearing the gunshots. The way she'd been concerned about him...the way she'd come rushing down to his flat in the middle of the night when his screaming had woken her...the way she'd felt in his arms...

She'd been there for him in a way that no one else knew he even needed.

He enjoyed her soothing presence. Her proximity seemed to calm him, to help him, but it was more than that. It was a strength of feeling that he'd only felt once before, and that had been with Anoush. He'd used to brighten up when he saw Anoush walk into a room, and he felt the same way when he saw Jess each morning. He liked making Jess laugh, the sound of it warmed his heart, and the smile on her face made him feel so good.

After Anoush's death he'd told himself that he would never fall in love with anyone ever again. It was too painful a loss, watching someone you loved die before your eyes. It was too much for one human to have to go through, to experience, to endure.

He'd thought that the grief would overwhelm him, remain with him for evermore, but as each day had passed he'd learnt that it didn't overwhelm him—it became something that he absorbed. It became a part of him. A part that he chose to not focus upon.

It was always there, gently humming away in the background, ready to poke and prod him with its painful touch on occasion, but being with Jess had made his life better. Happier. And he'd begun to realise that being with her, seeing her smile, hearing her joke and laugh, or focus hard on her work, was something that gave him immense joy. And he was missing that.

It was hard to admit to himself that his life had been without joy since Afghanistan, since before the ambush. That for a long time he had been existing in a world of numbness, just going about his business, trying to get through from sun-up to sundown without anything hurting. Meeting Jess had changed all that and now that he didn't have her by his side it was really affecting him in ways that he'd not expected.

He'd tried knocking on her door a couple of times. Popping round when he thought that she might be in, but she'd never answered. At first, he'd been worried. What if she was sick and had passed out in there? He'd even gone to the landlord who owned the building and asked him to check with the spare key. The landlord had let him in and the relief he'd felt at finding the flat empty was incredible. Clearly she was just out and about.

He'd wanted to linger. Had wanted to absorb everything in her flat to see if it gave him any clues as to what was going on, but there was nothing save for a picture of a man he assumed was her father. He knew her father had died. Knew that he'd been her only family.

Now, Adam closed the door on his own flat and sank into a chair, exhausted. He used to enjoy being on his own, but all of a sudden he was filled with the desire to be around people, people who loved him, and so, even though he was tired, he got back up and headed out through the door.

On arrival at his parents' house he knocked before going in and was happily met by his mother, who was in the kitchen, baking some scones. The kitchen smelt wonderful and he settled in, feeling the comforts of home, the comforts of family, and asked the one question that was at the forefront of his mind.

His father might be bound by employer confidentiality, but his mother wasn't. Because she wasn't Jess's boss. She wasn't Jess's doctor.

'Do you know what's wrong with Jess?'

His mother wiped her hands on her apron and settled down in the chair opposite him at the kitchen table. She smiled sympathetically and laid her hand on his. 'You like her, don't you?'

'You don't have to do your matchmaking thing, you know.'

She laughed gently. 'I'm not. It's just obvious. I've seen the two of you together. The light in your eyes, when you're with her. It's nice. I haven't seen you like that since you came home.'

'I worry about her. Something's sent her running for the hills and now I haven't seen her for days. Her personal files are hidden. And Dad won't tell me. But I really need to know she's all right.'

'I'm sure she's absolutely fine.'

He was really beginning to worry. It all seemed so secretive, and he hated that he was the one in the dark. It worried him greatly. He'd finally found someone to care about again and...

'Hasn't Dad said anything to you?'

His mother shook her head. 'He wouldn't do that even if he wanted to. Speak to Jess when you see her next. I'm sure she will be able to answer all your questions and more. She's a good girl. Open. Honest. Kind.'

'She's never in when I call round.'

'Then perhaps she's busy? Or she's off out enjoying herself. Your father did tell me he'd given her a week off. That she needed it for personal reasons.' She shrugged. 'Perhaps it's something to do with her father? Didn't she say once that it's been nearly two years since his death? Perhaps she's finding the anniversary difficult to deal with. You know how that can be for people.'

He frowned. Maybe his mother was right and he was reading too much into this...

His mother laid her hand on his again. 'When she's back, why don't you invite her round for dinner? Cook her that lasagne you do that's so delicious.'

She stood up again to put on her oven gloves, and opened up the oven to check on her scones. They seemed to be done, nicely golden, and she pulled them out to place them on a cooling tray.

'And if there's anything to tell I'm sure Jess will tell you when she's good and ready.'

'But when will that be?'

'I guess that depends on what's wrong. *If* there's anything wrong.'

She was right. And he knew he did have the capacity to over-worry about things. Perhaps he was blowing all of this out of proportion? Perhaps he was seeing dangers where there weren't any? Perhaps he'd imagined the fear on Jess's face?

Maybe it hadn't been fear, but embarrassment? He was her mentor, he'd been observing her, and she'd probably felt that he was thinking badly about her capabilities, or something.

That has to be it! It can't possibly be anything else, because Jess seems fine!

Adam smiled and thanked his mother. He'd stop worrying and just make sure that he was there for Jess when she came back after her week away. Let her know how pleased he was to have her back.

Because he was missing her.

Missing her so incredibly much.

CHAPTER ELEVEN

JESS'S WEEK WENT QUICKLY. Surprisingly so. And the best part was that she hadn't noticed any tremor since that first day.

No matter how much she pushed herself, and physically tried to tire her body, there wasn't any other evidence of a chorea. Even her neurologist didn't seem too concerned.

It looked as if the spasm that had initially scared her had just been a blip, an unfortunate coincidence—probably brought on by holding her arm in a certain position, trying to remove that lipoma. When she held her arm in the same position to try and re-enact the situation, her arm did, in fact, tremble a little, so it had to be positional.

As the week wore on, she felt more and more delighted by the fact that the spasm did not appear to be the first sign of her Huntington's revealing itself, and she was thrilled when, after her application, she received an invitation to interview for the post as a part-time obstetrics registrar in Cardiff. It made her feel excited about getting back to work, about putting the next stage of her life in motion.

But it would be hard to say goodbye to the island. Heartbreakingly hard. And she couldn't imagine upsetting Adam. The look on his face would be... She simply couldn't imagine it. Would he feel let down? Betrayed? And what would Jack say? And Judy?

But surely she hadn't been here long enough to upset anyone with her departure? And surely they would see that she was simply trying to get the best out of life? Advancing her career in a way that she'd thought she never would?

No. They would have to understand. Coming to Thorney had simply been the wrong direction for her.

She would miss Adam. Incredibly so. And the idea of getting to see him today, being with him, enjoying his company, made her giddy little heart pound away and the butterflies dance in her belly.

It had been so hard to avoid him all week. She'd done the bits and pieces that had needed doing at her flat during the day, when she'd known Adam would be at work. And in the evenings she'd taken herself out to eat, or to watch a play at the local theatre, or to pass the time in a coffee shop, reading a good book. She had not wanted to be at home, knowing that he might knock on her door, because she would have struggled to ignore him.

But, oh, how she had missed him! She couldn't wait to see him again, to work with him, maybe finally have that dinner with him. A goodbye dinner? She owed him that, at least. She'd missed the sound of his voice, the way he smiled, that barely-there dimple in his cheek. She'd missed the glint in his eyes, the way he ran his hands through his hair when he was tired, but most of all she'd missed the way that he made her feel.

She done a lot of thinking in her week off. Thinking about her future and how she could be happy. She'd thought about her past relationships, and what had happened with Eddie, and all that she had learned about herself since.

She might have got a little lost lately, a bit frightened and confused, but she had come out of it with her head clear for the first time in a long time. But at the end of the day it had left her feeling empty and alone, craving a connection, craving a closeness that she had always denied herself. A closeness she had found with Adam. A connection she would have to break.

She and Adam were good together. She really thought they could have something if they tried. But it wasn't worth it. What if Adam fell in love with her and she had to break his heart with her diagnosis? She couldn't make him watch her die. She couldn't make him be her carer. She couldn't bear to deteriorate in front of him day by day.

And her death would not be a quick death. Easy or clean. Her death would be long and drawn out, stretched over weeks, months and years. That was why she couldn't entertain the idea of being with Adam—because she knew what the future would be like, even if he didn't. He would see the future as full of rainbows and sunshine. Getting married, maybe, and definitely wanting to have kids. His mother wanted to be a grandmother so much!

She couldn't offer him that. Ever.

How could she do that to him? Take that happy family future away from him by lumbering him with her useless broken body? How could she put him through that?

She knew that she would have to be honest with him and tell him about her condition. As soon as he knew they would be able to work together without the worry of an unexpected romance. She would effectively take herself off the market so that she could just get on with being his friend for the short time they were together, and it might even make their parting even easier.

Because it was the hiding that she didn't like. The lying. Not telling anyone about her Huntington's had never mattered before, but with Adam it mattered more than anything and she hated keeping it secret.

Adam was at his desk, quietly cursing the computer, which was refusing to let him input the details of his patient's condition, when he heard footsteps behind him. There was something familiar about those footsteps. Light and brisk.

He turned and his face lit up with joy. 'Jess! You're back! How was your week off?'

He tried not to notice how his heart was racing at seeing her again, how his mouth had gone dry, and how his stomach flipped this way and that in his joy. His mind instantly replayed for him the night they'd spent together in his bed. He had to fight the urge to leap up and throw his arms around her and give her a huge squeeze and not let go. At least for a few minutes.

'It was interesting. I did a lot of unexpected soul-searching. How are you?'

'I'm good. But I've been worried about you. I called round a couple of times but you weren't in. Everything okay? We haven't spoken since… Well, you know…'

'I'm more than okay. Actually, I'd like to talk to you later, when you have a moment free. Would that be all right?'

He felt concern fill him. 'Sure. I've got these notes to input for my last patient and then we can see the next together, if you'd like? In about twenty minutes?'

'Okay. I've just got to check in with your father first. Maybe I can grab you for coffee later?'

'Sounds great. I'll page you when I'm done.'

'Perfect.'

'But everything *is* all right?'

He hated it that he had to keep asking. But he *needed* everything to be all right. He couldn't imagine there being something so badly wrong it would hurt her.

She leaned forward and laid her hand on his, smiling. 'Yes, it is. But I'll talk to you later. I need to go and speak to your dad.'

He frowned. 'Problem?'

She shook her head and he saw she was smiling. Happy. As if a huge burden had been lifted from her. 'No. Just one of those return-to-work things. A catch-up.'

He watched her walk away, feeling so happy that she was back. Everything seemed right again, knowing that she was here, walking these corridors.

He'd not realised just how accustomed he had become to seeing her around. How her presence comforted him in ways he'd never expected to feel. He'd missed her terribly, and had found it so hard to give her the space that she'd clearly wanted this past week.

Knowing that she was just in her flat upstairs, knowing that he could just knock on her door, he had held off from doing so after his attempts earlier in the week, when he'd got the landlord to let him in. It had been *so hard*. Especially when he had something to tell her. Something he knew would make her proud of him.

Waiting to tell her his secret was painful. But he was practising patience—just like his next patient. It was just a minor injury, nothing too concerning, but he'd had to make him wait after spending a lot of time with his previous patient, who'd come in with what he'd thought was indigestion but what had turned out to be angina.

He'd run plenty of tests and had finally sent the patient home with some literature and some GTN spray. Now he just needed to finish off his notes and then he would call that patient through.

He was looking forward to it—working with Jess again.

She was back! And the thought of that just made him feel so good.

Jess couldn't help but smile when she saw Adam again, just as he picked up the next patient's file to see what the minor injury was. He looked so wonderful, standing there in dark trousers and a slim-fit shirt. Deliciously attractive. He was a treat for her eyes, brightening her soul after the difficult conversation she'd just had with his father, telling him that she would be leaving to pursue another career path.

He'd taken it quite well, to give him his due, but she guessed he understood her reasoning, knowing that he couldn't offer her the specialism she wanted at his own hospital.

'Maybe you could come back and be our specialist once you're trained?' he'd suggested.

The file said their patient had suffered a burn to his arm, so she went to the waiting room and called him through.

Mr George Harris was a gentleman in his mid-sixties, and he'd been waiting patiently with an ice pack wrapped around his forearm. Jess escorted him to a cubicle where Adam waited.

'Hello, Mr Harris. We're sorry about the wait you've

had. I'm Dr Campbell and this is Dr Young. Why don't you tell us what happened today to bring you in?'

'Two for the price of one, eh? Oh, it was silly. Just something and nothing. But I thought I'd better get it checked out because I have diabetes, and Dr Campbell Senior told me that I have to be careful with injuries in case they don't heal properly.' He turned to look at Adam. 'You look like him. I can see it in your eyes.'

Adam smiled.

Jess guessed that was the thing with living on a small island. Everybody knew everybody.

'And when did you burn your arm?' she asked.

'About six o'clock this morning. I have to get up early to look after my wife. I'm her carer—she's got motor neurone disease and she's in a wheelchair now.'

Jess felt herself stiffen. The poor man! His poor wife! What must that be like? To lose your wife piece by piece, day by day... It was the one thing she dreaded and feared and refused to allow to happen with her own life.

'I see. Go on,' she said, grabbing the overhead light above the bed and positioning it over Mr Harris's arm as she and Adam examined the wound.

'I usually make her some porridge first thing. It's easy for her to eat. And I also take her up a hot water bottle. I'd got the porridge on the stove, and I was just trying to make up the hot water bottle, when something happened with my arm. I'm not sure what...it suddenly didn't seem to have any strength in it. It kind of gave way. I tried not to drop the kettle, but I just seemed to pour the water over my arm. It hurt like a—' He grimaced. 'It hurt a lot. I may have sworn, Doctor. I did what you're supposed to do—I ran it under the cold tap for ten minutes—but the pain was still intense and I could see I'd damaged the skin. I thought I'd better get it checked out.'

'Well, you did the right thing. Who's looking after your wife right now?'

'My next-door neighbours. They're very good in case of emergency. I'm lucky, really. I've got such a broad support network who help me out with Sally.'

'That's good,' said Jess. 'Being a carer, especially to your spouse, can be draining. It's good that you've got people around that you can rely on.'

'I have. But it's not draining at all. I get tired, yes, but I love my wife and I would do anything for her. Knowing that I'm the one who makes her feel better... I'm the one who makes her comfortable... That makes her smile. We have a closeness between us that was never there before. I love her so much... I can't imagine not having her with me. I wouldn't have it any other way. Well, I'd have her healthy, if I could—but that's not to be. It's not the cards you're dealt in life, is it? It's the way you play your hand.'

Jess listened intently to Mr Harris as he spoke, feeling the beginnings of tears at the back of her eyes as he spoke about his wife with so much love. He was a rare man, clearly.

Jess had a lot of respect for carers. For the strength that it must take. The fortitude. It must be a difficult situation, especially looking after those they loved. She couldn't imagine how hard it must be.

Here was a man who was himself getting on in age, who had a medical condition of his own and would probably appreciate an easier life. Enjoying his retirement. Yet here he was, looking after his wife, essentially a full-time job, and still loving her deeply. It would be an honour to treat him and try to make him better.

'Well, let's sort out this burn, shall we?' Adam said, looking at her curiously as she tried to swallow the lump in her throat.

An examination of the skin beneath showed there was some damage to the uppermost layer, but Mr Harris had done the right thing by cooling it beneath cold water for ten minutes. There didn't appear to be any deeper damage, but because of Mr Harris's diabetes they knew they would have to be careful to check for infection.

Adam applied some antibacterial cream and wrapped the wound in a soft bandage, with instructions that he was to have it checked every couple of days by a nurse, and that if he experienced any fever or strange symptoms in the arm he was to come in immediately and not wait.

Mr Harris seemed satisfied, and pleased that he could go home. 'Thank you. I appreciate that.'

'Try not to do any heavy lifting with that arm for a while, if you can. And take care of yourself.'

'I will—don't you worry. Send my regards to your father.'

Adam nodded, and they both watched as their patient left.

Jess cleared away the bits and pieces that they'd used and threw the rubbish in the clinical waste bin.

'Are you all right?' asked Adam.

'Fine!'

'You seemed a little…affected by his story.'

She tried to laugh it off, embarrassed that he had noticed. 'Wouldn't anyone be? All he's doing…looking after his wife…when he should be enjoying retirement and taking it easy.'

Adam shrugged. 'He loves her.'

'But it has to be hard for him! I couldn't do it.'

She grabbed Mr Harris's file to take it back to the doctor's desk and fill it in.

She didn't dare ask Adam if he could.

Now her butterflies had butterflies. She couldn't believe that she was sitting here in the cafeteria, moments away from telling Adam that she was leaving.

She'd told his father at the start of the day, and although Jack had been clearly disappointed he had accepted it and said he would miss her. How would Adam react? After all that they'd been through together? It was a question that had been on her mind ever since she'd made her decision.

She longed to tell him, just so that he would know, so that it would be in the open and she would no longer have to fear getting too close to him.

She'd made a huge mistake by sleeping with him, furthering a connection she now needed to break. But she could let him know just how much she valued his friendship even if she couldn't tell him the rest.

Because she knew the type of man he was. She had no doubt that if she told him the whole truth, once he'd got over the shock, he would want to be there for her, supportive and considerate. His kindness and empathy would trap him.

Her news was not something that was easy to impart to him. It would be different telling someone who wasn't part of the medical profession. Someone who didn't truly understand the ins and outs of what her disease entailed. Someone who didn't care for her. But telling Adam—who was a doctor, who did care, and who would understand exactly what she would be facing—would be a lot harder.

Especially as she suspected that his feelings for her ran deeper than those of a friend—as did her own for him.

She sipped from her coffee cup, wincing at the hotness of the drink. He'd told her that he had news for her, too. She briefly wondered what that might be. He seemed happy, so perhaps it would be best if he shared his news first? That way they would be able to enjoy his news, celebrate it, whatever it might be, without the shadow of her own. And eventually her news would be good news, too. Once he'd thought about it, of course.

She saw him the second he walked into the cafeteria. She perked up, sat up straighter, and smiled as his eyes met hers, lighting up with joy. Not for the first time, she wished that they could be something more than they were.

She had not come here expecting to get so tangled up in the life of Adam Campbell, and yet here she was. When she had allowed herself to imagine what life with him might be like, in no part had there ever been the shadow of a degenerative disease looming over them. There had only been happy scenes in her mind. The two of them taking walks together. Walking along the beach with dogs running around their feet. Walking hand in hand, the wind blowing her hair everywhere, so that when he went to kiss her he would have to tuck her hair behind her ears to see her face, touch her face, and gently press his lips to hers.

How it would feel to be just his? Truly his?

It was an unachievable dream, which just made it hurt even more.

She had to force that image from her mind right now. Because it would never be like that between them. It would never happen.

Once he knew she was leaving, he would stop thinking of how it might be between the two of them, too. And she would content herself with knowing that Adam would one day be happy with someone else, no matter how much it hurt her to imagine that.

Adam was carrying one of the hospital's tablets and he laid it down on the table. 'Can you look after this for me? Just whilst I grab a coffee? Can I get you anything?'

She shook her head. 'No, no. I'm fine. You go ahead.'

He smiled at her and headed back to the self-service area.

She watched him intently, remembering what it had been like to live her life without worrying about the future. Without worrying about the threat of a disease that could attack at any moment and shorten her life. It had been like that once. Before the blood test. But she'd known what she was getting into. And she'd accepted it. But that didn't mean she didn't miss what she'd had before.

Adam arrived back at the table with coffee, a banana and a yoghurt.

She watched as he added a single sugar to his drink, and then some milk, before stirring. 'How are you?' she asked.

He nodded. 'I'm good. Really good. How about you? I haven't seen you since...since we spent the night together. Is everything all right?'

This was it. He'd set up the moment for her to explain everything. He'd got right to the point and she knew he deserved her honesty.

But she was freaking out. Imagining telling him was completely different from actually sitting in front of him, looking at his beaming smile and doing it for real. Best to hear his good news first...

'Everything's fine! But come on—you told me you had some news. Let's hear it.' She leaned forward as if she was really keen, trying to ignore the racing of her heart, the cold lump of dread in her stomach.

'Okay...' He let out a sigh, a heavy breath. 'I did what you suggested. I found myself a counsellor and I saw her last week. A two-hour session.' He smiled. 'No doubt the first of many.'

'You did?'

This was unexpected! She was so relieved! Now she could leave him knowing he was getting his mental health taken care of. That was a major step for him. A major step towards recovery. She knew it was something he needed, having watched his panic attack beside the car when he'd heard those rifle shots, having heard his screams in the night as he'd wrestled with his terrors.

'That's fantastic, Adam!' She was really pleased for him. 'Really good. How did you find it?'

'I was nervous. And I was sceptical at first. I'm not going to lie. I couldn't see how talking about what had happened would help me. But I thought about what you'd said, and I realised that there was no point in trying to ignore the biggest thing in my life and hoping it would go away if I was still going to be plagued by what was happening in my mind. And I think it did. A little, anyway.'

'That's brilliant! I'm so proud of you for taking that step. I know it must have been hard.'

He smiled. 'It was. Especially when it made me realise that speaking about it out loud was kind of cathartic. And...' he suddenly reached for her hand '...and I want to tell you what happened to me.'

Her heart almost stopped. She wanted to know—of course she did. She'd thought about it a lot, what the details might be, and she'd hoped that one day she would find out the real truth. But now…? If he told her—if she knew—she would be drawn further into his life and it would make it harder to leave.

'You don't have to. Not if you don't want to.'

'I need to. You've been there for me and I owe you the truth.'

'Adam, I—'

He laid his hands upon hers and she stopped talking.

'I was working in a medical centre in Kabul. With International Health…'

She decided to listen. To stop interrupting. Clearly he wanted to tell her something huge, and who was she to deny him the privilege of unburdening himself? And, dammit, she wanted to hear what he had to say. She'd be a liar if she said she hadn't wondered often what had happened to him.

'One day I was part of a large convoy of medical trucks assisting the American army. We were relocating to a new field hospital. But we got ambushed just outside the city of Kabul.'

Jess didn't realise that her hands had become fists. 'Ambushed?'

'The first truck in the convoy was hit. It got blown off the road and took out two of my team. Another one was hit by a rocket launcher. The one I was in.'

He was looking her in the eyes but he wasn't seeing her face. She could tell that he was back there, back in that place, replaying the ambush in his head like an awful movie. She'd not expected to hear this. Any of it. She'd assumed he'd remain private. But now he was sharing all this with her.

To hear he'd been in such danger was upsetting to her. 'Adam—'

He held up his hand as if to tell her that he hadn't finished talking. So she said nothing more. Because she knew he had to say this. And she wanted to hear this.

'Then our truck came under fire—bullets from all directions. We knew we couldn't stay in the truck because there were oxygen canisters in there, and if they went off… So we scrambled out, already bleeding. My leg was almost numb. I knew I was hurt, but didn't know to what extent. I knew it wasn't my femoral artery, so for that I was grateful. There were some large boulders near the roadside, and I thought if we could just get there we'd be away from the danger of explosion and would also be able to take some cover from the gunfire.'

She leaned forward. 'You say *we*? The other medics?'

He nodded. 'I was travelling with a nurse. An Afghani children's nurse. You wouldn't think you'd need a children's nurse in a war zone, but unfortunately you do. Anoush had arrived at the camp the same day as me.'

Anoush. Anoush was a person. When he'd been having his panic attack, he'd cried out the word. But she hadn't known what it meant. Hadn't even known it was a name. She'd thought she was prepared for what he might say next, but she wasn't.

'When you work in places like that—away from family, under intense pressure and danger—your colleagues become your friends, your family. Relationships are formed under extreme duress. You get close very quickly…you spend all your spare time together. Anoush and I were very close.'

Adam looked down at the floor for a moment, before looking up again and meeting her eyes.

'I fell in love with her. Whether it was real love or not, I don't know, but at the time it felt real. I didn't tell my parents, because I didn't quite know if what I had there was what it seemed. You're in a bubble—whether that bubble is pleasant or not. The real world…the mundane day-to-day…just doesn't exist for you there. But I couldn't picture my life without her. So I decided to ask her to marry me. I thought if she said yes, then I would contact my parents and let them know.'

Her breath caught in her throat. Adam had fallen in love. With a nurse in Afghanistan. *Of course.* Why wouldn't he? He was a catch, and he'd probably charmed all the nurses there.

She told herself that she had to accept that because she had nothing to offer him. He wasn't hers. He'd never been hers and never would be. But to actually be sitting there, hearing him talk about the woman he'd loved— well, that drove a dagger into her heart that she'd never expected. It left her breathless, her throat painful with the tension caught there, and she fought back the tears that were threatening to spill.

'Go on,' she managed to say, each word choked out.

'Before we left in the convoy she said yes. She would marry me. And when she said that I knew I needed to contact my parents and let them know.'

Jess swallowed the lump in her throat. 'But you didn't?'

'No. I figured we'd get to the new field hospital, get everything set up, and once communications were established I'd be able to call home and let them know.'

'But you never got there,' she said sadly.

'No.'

He looked down, but before he did so she recognised the build-up of tears in his eyes.

'Adam… What happened to Anoush?'

He blinked rapidly, sniffed, and took a sip of his coffee.

'We were pinned against the underside of the vehicle. It was on its side. I knew we needed to make a run for the boulders. I asked her if she could make it, but she was more concerned about me and my leg. It was bleeding quite badly, but to be honest I wasn't feeling it too much at that moment in time. Adrenaline is a great numbing agent. I took hold of her hand and told her that on the count of three we would make a run for it. She looked at me then, and it's a moment I'll always remember—because she looked at me as if it was the last moment she would ever see me. I told her we'd make it. I knew I had to make her believe that. I counted to three and then we ran.'

Jess was on the edge of her seat, not quite believing what she was hearing. That he had been in such a situation was terrifying, and she couldn't be more grateful that he was here, safe with her, and not still back there.

'We made a good start. It was a distance of about ten metres to the boulders and I really thought we'd make it, even though all around us we could hear gunfire. We weren't armed, but some of the soldiers travelling with us were, and they were shooting back. We were running and something happened—I don't know what. I tripped, or maybe my bad leg took me down… I let go of Anoush's hand. I hoped she would carry on running for cover, but she didn't.'

He looked Jess in the eyes and she'd never seen sorrow like it.

'She stopped for *me*. Turned. Waited. And I saw her take a bullet to the chest. Right in the heart. I remember looking at her in total shock, watching as she looked down at me before she dropped to her knees. I scrambled towards her, tried to catch her before she hit the ground. She looked up at me, terrified, for just a moment... And then she died.'

Jess sat listening, open-mouthed, trying to imagine herself in such a situation. What would she have done? How might she have reacted in the same situation? Watching the person she loved gunned down right in front of her face. What if she'd been there? What would she have felt to see Adam take a bullet and drop to his knees right in front of her? What would she have done if he had died in her arms?

She didn't realise that tears were dripping down her face.

'It felt like I held her in my arms for ages, but that can't be right. We were in the middle of a gunfight and right out in the open. One of the soldiers grabbed me by the shoulder and began dragging me across the stones. He was yelling, kept telling me to leave her, that we would come back for her later, and he dragged me over to the cover of the boulders. I don't know how I let go, but I did, and I sat behind a rock, not quite understanding what had happened.'

He looked at her more intensely.

'What if the bullet that killed Anoush was meant for me? If I hadn't tripped, then it would have hit me.'

'You can't think like that. And it doesn't sound to me like that would have happened. You said you tripped, fell. And then you saw her stop and turn around to wait for you. I don't think that bullet was meant for you.'

'But I can't get it out of my head. I feel it was my fault that she died. It was my suggestion to break for cover. I told her when to run and I was the one who tripped. She turned and waited for me. *I'm* responsible for her death.'

Jess took his hands in hers and found that they were icy cold. She rubbed them gently, hoping to warm them, hoping she could show him that she didn't believe he was responsible.

'It wasn't your fault, Adam. You didn't pull the trigger. You didn't start the war. You were trying to save her and she believed in you. She loved you. That's what you need to remember.'

He took her hands in his and turned to look into her eyes. 'You're very kind to say that.'

'It's the truth. Kindness has nothing to do with it. And she died loving you, in your arms.'

He nodded, then seemed to notice that her cheeks were wet. 'You're crying...'

'Am I?' She suddenly felt embarrassed, as if he'd caught her doing something that she should not. 'Sorry, I didn't mean to... Gosh, look at me—I'm ridiculous! I bet I've got panda eyes now.'

'You don't look ridiculous. You look beautiful.'

Jess met his gaze and held it. He thought she was beautiful? She didn't know what to do with that information right now, but she knew she would treasure it in case it was something she never heard from anyone ever again. But to hear it from Adam was...intense. Especially after the night they'd shared.

What was happening here? Was he falling for her? The way she was for him?

Adam reached up and stroked her face, smiling. 'Thank you for listening, Jess. I needed to tell you because you're the one person who's seen through me in all of this. The one person I've allowed to see me.' He smiled. 'You've made me feel like I can begin to move on. Like a weight is being lifted every time I tell the story. I'm even going to tell my parents what happened. I feel… optimistic. And you're a big part of that.'

Her breath caught in her throat. What could she say? All the things she'd wanted to say to him about leaving, about saying goodbye, were impossible to give voice to now. He sat there looking so…so revitalised! So different! The shadow was gone from his eyes. Had he been sleeping better? He said she was responsible for this change in him—how could she tell him she was walking away? Why hurt him when he was finally beginning to heal?

What if he saw this as a step forward for both of them? What if he had expectations of her as more than just a friend? They'd slept together. He'd told her she was beautiful. These were all terrible signs! He would be better off without her, and although it would hurt him in the short run, after a few months he would forget about her.

She pulled her hands free of his. 'I'm glad for you, Adam. And thank you for sharing all that with me. I'm truly honoured.'

'No, thank *you*. Without you, none of this would have been possible—'

'I'm leaving the island.'

She just blurted it out. She couldn't bear to hear him tell her over and over again how important she was to his recovery. She was glad about that, but all it did was taunt her with all the ways she couldn't be important to him. Romantically. Emotionally. Physically. She wanted so much more, but she couldn't have it. She was happy for him, but now it was time to take a step away.

'What? You've only just got here.'

'I made a mistake coming here. I've already spoken to your dad about it. I'm moving back to the mainland to pursue my dream of specialising in obstetrics.'

He looked confused. 'But you'll come back again?'

She shook her head. 'No. I can't do that.'

'But we've got so close!'

Her heart was breaking inside, but she hoped she wasn't showing it. He mustn't know how much he meant to her.

'I know, but we shouldn't have. I'm sorry, Adam. I know it's not what you want to hear. But in the same way that you've made strides forward, so have I. I've done a lot of thinking lately about what I want from life and I can't get it here. It's the wrong place for me.'

'I see. I thought we had something. Maybe I was confused?'

She nodded. Gritting her teeth. Trying not to bawl her eyes out. 'I'm not looking for a relationship. I'm sorry.'

And she slid out of her chair, unable to sit there a moment longer, unable to look at the pain in his face, knowing that she had taken him from happiness to misery in a matter of seconds.

Well, she was doing him a favour.

Better this than a lifetime of misery if he allowed himself to fall in love with her.

She was in turmoil. Her lie—her *life*—was getting more complicated. And at this moment in time she hated her Huntington's diagnosis more than she hated anything in the whole wide world.

CHAPTER TWELVE

ADAM FELT AWFUL. As if his whole world had ended right there and then. How had he gone from feeling so amazing at having Jess back, opening up to her, thinking that it would bring them closer together, only for her to rip out his heart and tell him she was leaving?

This wasn't meant to have happened! He'd imagined sitting there, telling her all his secret as she held his hand, and then once it was over, listening to her as she told him all hers.

It was to have been the ultimate moment of sharing. Of vulnerability. Of openness and honesty. And yet it had all gone terribly wrong.

How had he misjudged this?

Should he go after her? Bring her back? Tell her all over again? Perhaps she'd misheard what he'd had to say? Perhaps she hadn't understood just what he'd been trying to say? Perhaps he'd been wrong in thinking that they were closer than they actually were?

Or maybe she'd sat and listened to him and heard nothing but the ramblings of a broken man? Why would she saddle herself with such a man when he obviously had issues to work through? It was hardly attractive, was it? Plus, she probably felt that he was still in love with Anoush. Still grieving for his lost fiancée.

Yes, he would always feel grief for what he had lost, but he had moved on—and the only reason he had been able to do that was because of her! Had she not heard that part? About how he'd only been able to do all of this *because of her*?

He had tried his *hardest*, his *damnedest*, not to develop feelings for Jess, but he had.

He had even been considering the very real possibility that somehow he had come to *love* her. Which was crazy! But he knew that was what he'd wanted. He'd wanted to take that risk with her.

She had changed his thinking. She had opened his heart to new possibilities, new hopes, a new future, and he'd felt that they were both in a really good place. She was a dedicated doctor and now she'd chosen a specialty that she wanted to focus on. That was good for her. She might need to go to some other hospitals to study, and that would mean moving away from Thorney for a while, but surely he could go with her.

Maybe she thought that he wouldn't want to move away from Thorney because he was getting counselling now? Perhaps all he needed to do was tell her that he could get counselling anywhere? That both of them could find work anywhere?

The week they'd spent apart had been agony, but crucial, because it had given Adam an insight into his feelings for her and he wasn't willing to give those up. Not now that he had them. He'd forgotten how good it could feel, knowing you *had* someone.

No, they hadn't known each other for long, but sometimes you just knew in your soul if someone was right for you. And Jess was.

She'd looked so beautiful this morning. Her eyes bright and shining a honey mahogany behind those silver frames. And the way she'd leaned in to listen to him when he'd first sat down, her face rapt, her joy so clear for him to see, her *love* for him, so blindingly displayed…

He hadn't mistaken that, right?

He had no doubt that she loved him. He just needed to show her that he was okay. That she could depend on him. That he wasn't going to go anywhere.

She'd been left before, hadn't she? By her father. Left alone. Maybe she thought that everyone would do the same? Well, he would prove to her that he was made of sterner stuff.

He needed to talk to her. But maybe not at work.

He wanted to do something nice for her. Something surprising. Something special to mark this day. Perhaps a meal out, somewhere nice? There were a couple of nice seafood restaurants along the harbour. He might ring one of them up and see if he could get a reservation…

He opened up his laptop and looked for the contact details of the restaurant he wanted to try. It had great five-star reviews and the photos looked spectacular.

His mind made up, he rang through to make a reservation.

And then he called a florist.

Jess was finding it hard to concentrate, what with her heart breaking inside her. She'd been so ready to tell Adam everything! She'd built up to the moment, ready for his reaction, ready to tell him that she was all right at the moment and that he wasn't to worry about her, she'd be fine, when he'd hit her with that information about speaking to a counsellor. Told her about what had happened to him in Afghanistan.

He'd watched the woman he loved die right in front of his eyes and it had broken him.

I couldn't put him through that again!

Not when he'd been so happy with his breakthrough moment! That hadn't been the moment to tell him! It wouldn't have been right. He'd done such an amazing thing, admitting he had a problem with PTSD, and she knew how much it took to sit in front of a therapist and open up about your every fear, lay your soul bare.

And now she was expected to work in the primary care clinic for the rest of her shift, and she was finding it hard to remain sympathetic to all the people who came in moaning about a cold, or a sore throat, or a headache, when she had so much more to worry about.

A real disease! With real implications!

Did they not realise how her life was falling apart? No, of course not. That was the role of the doctor—to be human, but not so human that you brought your own problems into the workplace. You were there for your patients, not the other way around. There had to be a professional distance.

She hated herself for being so crabby-minded. Having a cold could make people feel terrible! It could lead to chest infections, or even pneumonia, if they were susceptible. Tonsillitis, laryngitis, bronchiolitis! All that could make someone feel rotten. Stop them from working. Stop them from going to school. And a headache could be any manner of things, so she checked every patient carefully.

It was just...difficult.

But when had anything in her life been easy?

'Mary McMahon?' she called, and smiled when her next patient, a little old lady with silver hair, got up from her chair in the waiting room, clutching a urine sample bottle. Already Jess had some idea of the nature of the presenting complaint, but she tried to not make any assumptions.

Her patient hobbled past her and sat down in the chair, and Jess walked behind her. 'And what's brought you in to see me?'

Mary smiled and placed the urine sample on Jess's desk. 'I've been feeling a little peculiar the last couple of days and I can't stop going for a wee. Pamela, the warden at my building, suggested I come and see you to check for a UTI.'

A urinary tract infection. A common occurrence in the elderly.

'All right. When you say "peculiar", how so?'

'I don't know. I have this constant urge to go to the toilet, even when there's nothing there, and when there is something there it burns so much I break out in a sweat.'

'Okay. It sounds like a UTI. Let's test this sample, then. When did you do it?'

'Just before I came out. About thirty minutes ago.'

Jess dipped the sample with a urine-testing strip, but the results came back absolutely fine. No sign of any infection.

'That's clear. But it doesn't mean you don't have an infection, and because of your symptoms I'm tempted to give you antibiotics. I will send this off to our lab and see if they can grow anything. Would you object to me checking you internally?'

'No, Doctor. You do what you have to do. I'd rather you

got this sorted out. It can't go on like this… I never get through a whole episode of my soaps on the television!'

Jess smiled. If only that could be *her* worry.

She assisted Mary onto the examination table and waited outside the curtain for Mary to undress. Then she went in, washed her hands, gloved up and examined her. Her anatomy was as to be expected in an elderly lady of eighty-one years. Nothing abnormal. Was this some sort of interstitial cystitis?

'We'll treat you with antibiotics, just in case, but I'm going to make a referral to a urologist in case we need it.'

'A urologist?'

'Urologists specialise in this area and they might want to do a more thorough examination if nothing comes back from the urine sample—is that all right?'

Mary nodded and Jess left her to get dressed again, washing her hands and then typing up her notes from the appointment and issuing a prescription for nitrofurantoin.

When Mary came back out from behind the curtain Jess had everything ready to give to her. 'You'll get a letter from the urologist in due course, but I'll ring you when the results come back from the lab and if you don't need the appointment, we can cancel it, okay?'

'Thank you, Doctor. You've been most kind.'

'No problem at all. Take care, Mary.'

'You too, dear.'

And she was gone.

Jess sighed. It was going to be a long day, and it was—

There was a knock at her door.

'Come in.'

Una from Reception came in, carrying a huge bouquet of flowers. 'These just came for you! There's a card, too.'

Jess gasped. The flowers were beautiful! Roses, Scot-

tish thistles, lavender, asters—a real mix of purples and
pinks.

'They must be from a patient,' she said, reaching for
the card that accompanied them and opening the enve-
lope.

When she pulled out the card, she saw the handwrit-
ing and read the message:

> *Dinner at seven tonight? Shrimpton's?*
> *My treat, to celebrate your news!*
> *Love, Adam x*

She couldn't help but smile. How thoughtful he was.
How kind. How wonderful! He would make someone an
amazing husband one day.

He just won't be mine.

The thought filled her with so much sadness, she had
to blink away tears. She'd been so rude, just getting up
and leaving the cafeteria this morning. Dropping her
bombshell about leaving the island and then just rushing away. He could have been angry about that. He could
have been dismissive. But, no, he'd heard what she'd had
to say and, although he must be feeling upset and disappointed, he wanted to show her that what she'd said
mattered and that he was determined to see the best in it.

He was such a good man.

Why can't I have him? Why?

And then she remembered why. And the sadness and
grief hit her all over again.

She couldn't have dinner with him at some posh restaurant. He deserved an explanation. He was trying so
hard to make everything right between them—didn't he

deserve to know the real reason why it could never work between them? He needed to know—simple as that.

And once he did know perhaps it would be easier for him? Because he'd be able to walk away, like Eddie had. He deserved a happy future. He deserved to give his parents the grandchildren they craved. Healthy grandchildren. He deserved to have a long and happy marriage after all he had been through. He'd watched one woman he loved die right in front of him—he wouldn't want to go through that again with another. Once the implications of all the care she'd need in her later years sank in he would realise there couldn't be a future between them.

It was only right that she called a halt to any ideas or aspirations he might have about them. He was being a good friend. Seeing past her abruptness at the café and trying to hold on to the happiness in the decision she'd made to specialise. He was a special man. A good, decent man. Selfless. Caring. Loving.

If you love someone, you set them free.

Who'd said that?

But she couldn't do it in a restaurant. Having such an awkward conversation in the cafeteria had told her she didn't want any public discord.

Jess picked up the phone and called Adam. When he answered, she kept her reply short. 'I can't do Shrimpton's. But I can do dinner at my place…same time. And thank you. For the flowers.'

She hung up and stared at the phone with a rapidly beating heart.

She was going to do it.

She was going to tell him.

If he could be brave enough to take the next step in life, then so could she.

* * *

Feeling nervous about all he hoped to say to Jess, Adam knocked on her front door and waited.

He'd taken a long time to choose what he would wear tonight, when normally that sort of thing barely got a second thought from him. But he hoped tonight would be special. Tonight he would tell Jess how he felt about her, and he figured something like that should be memorable, so it would be better to make it as nice a memory as he could.

He wanted them to be able to look back on it in the future, maybe even with their kids sitting on the floor around them... Wow. That would be crazy. He knew he was racing ahead in what might happen, but he couldn't help himself where she was concerned.

He imagined Jess telling their children that Daddy had turned up wearing a beautiful suit, with a blue silk tie that matched the colour of his eyes, and how impressed she'd been when she'd seen him at her door and had known that the night was going to be a very special one indeed.

He'd never thought of himself as a fanciful person. Or a dreamer. Yet here he was, doing both of those things! Crazy what love could do.

He could hear her moving about inside the flat, and then footsteps as she came to the door and opened it.

She looked stunning! Dressed in a beautiful wrap-around red dress and with bare feet. He'd never seen her in make-up before, and tonight she took his breath away. He really had to remind himself to speak, in case she thought he'd become mute!

'You look amazing!'

'Thanks. So do you. Nice suit.'

'I didn't know what you were cooking, so I brought

red wine and white wine.' He presented her with two expensive bottles.

'We're having fish, so I guess we'll use the white.'

She seemed a little subdued, and he figured it was probably because she felt a little awkward after earlier. He'd not seen her since she'd left him in the cafeteria. Well, he'd done a lot of thinking since then, and he definitely knew what he wanted from life.

Her.

He leaned in to kiss her gently on the cheek and inhaled the scent of her perfume that was like a meadow. 'You smell nice.'

'Thanks. You shouldn't have gone to all this trouble. Buying the wine...dressing up.'

'It's never trouble where you're concerned. Besides, you deserve it. We've both made huge strides forward in the last week and that deserves to be celebrated. You've chosen your specialty! Big step, Jess!'

She gave a small smile and nervously invited him in as she stepped backwards.

He could smell something delicious cooking. Her flat was filled with heavenly aromas that made him salivate. But he was hungry for more than food. He wanted to tell her everything. Wanted to tell her what she meant to him. Wanted to tell her that he saw a future for them both. Together. That he thought they had something really special. Something he thought could be *amazing*.

She seemed incredibly nervous, but he liked it that she was feeling the same way as him. Maybe not for the same reasons, but she had to have realised that tonight was going to be a big night for them both.

He really wanted to put their relationship on an equal footing and make them official. She probably thought that he was going to happily wave her off at the ferry in a few weeks' time, when instead he hoped to suggest that he would go with her! The urge to tell her right now was incredibly powerful, but he wanted to wait until they were dining.

He hadn't been lying when he'd said they'd both taken big steps. He had never predicted this. His feeling about Jess. After Anoush, he'd thought it would be completely impossible for him to fall for someone else. To risk being hurt again. But Jess had made those things possible.

He wasn't going to question it but go with it. See where it took them. He could see a bright future ahead. And that was something else. He was *planning a future*. It seemed possible now, whereas before he'd come home he'd only seen an existence.

'I've got a few things to do in the kitchen. Can I get you a drink?' she asked, holding up the bottle of white.

'Sounds perfect.'

He followed her through to the kitchen, unable to stop himself looking at her gorgeous figure in that wraparound dress, remembering how it had felt to hold her. The softness of her body. The way her back had arched as he'd brought her to orgasm.

He wanted that again—but more than that he wanted to know that she would be his. Wanted to know that she would be sharing his life, making him laugh, making him smile. He wanted them sharing cosy nights in together, watching movies and eating popcorn, snuggled on the couch. He found himself imagining buying a house with her, hunting for the perfect place, settling down, inviting friends over, being a *couple*.

He couldn't imagine a future with anyone else.

* * *

Adam had certainly dressed for a date. The smart clothes, the wine, the way he looked at her...it was almost as if he was trying to court her! But that had to be impossible, right? This was Adam Campbell and she was just Jess. Nobody special. Nobody who could be special to anyone.

It wasn't as if she had anything worth giving him, except friendship. And she'd told him she was leaving the island. Did he think he could come here tonight to change her mind? She hoped not. No matter how much she'd love to stay and be with him, she'd already told him she would be leaving. She didn't want to have to go through such a painful discussion all over again, even if she did owe him an explanation.

That was going to be the hard part.

And yet part of her wanted to enjoy this night. She wanted to wallow in the feelings that being with Adam was engendering. The joy, the easiness, the happiness. Why fight it? Why waste these last happy moments? When else would she get this? This might be her last ever evening with him! Perhaps that in itself was a reason to just take it moment by moment?

She hoped they would make it through to dessert before she told him the truth. At least let the poor man have a decent meal before she ruined everything for him.

'Why don't you take a seat?' she asked him.

'You're sure there's nothing I can do to help out?'

'No. I've got everything under control.' She searched in her kitchen drawer and pulled out the corkscrew. 'Unless you'd like to do this? I'm useless at using these.'

He took it from her gladly, smiling at her, and she had to turn away, grab the oven gloves and check on their main course—something to do to disguise the heat in her cheeks. That way she could blame the oven.

Behind her, she heard the pop of the cork and then the sound of wine being poured into glasses. She turned to accept a glass.

'To new beginnings.' He raised his glass in a toast.

She clinked his glass with hers. 'New beginnings.'

Jess had lit some tealights and floated them in a bowl as a centrepiece for the table. She could see his blue eyes twinkling in the semi-darkness.

Hadn't she wished for this? To be on a date with him? To have one last hurrah? But this was painful. Looking at him right now, knowing that he was hoping for something they couldn't have, knowing that she would ruin any plans he was making for them both... She'd always hated secrets. and she felt terrible at having kept one herself.

'How are your parents?' she asked. A question which was on safe ground.

'They're good. Mum got that twinkle in her eye when I told her I was coming round here for dinner tonight.'

Jess smiled. She could imagine. Judy loved her son intensely, and of course she wanted happiness for him. Wanted to see him settled. With a family of his own. Had Jack told Judy about her Huntington's? She couldn't imagine he'd break that confidentiality. Judy probably still believed her son might have a happy ending with her...

She knew the power of dreams. Of wishing. Of hoping. She'd always imagined her future would hold something else, too. Something like what she had right now. Dinners with a handsome man who cared about her. Loved her. She'd imagined a small house, maybe a cottage. One or two children. A dog. A cat. Chickens in the yard. Growing old with someone. Two grey-haired pensioners still holding hands in the park.

This part right now was painful, knowing it was all just a mirage. This future belonged to someone else. Adam was meant for someone else. Someone who could give him all the things he dreamed of. But he was acting as if he'd already made up his mind. Was this more than a celebratory meal for him? Was he reading something into this relationship of theirs? The thought made her ache inside.

Jess sipped at her wine. She needed to keep a clear head. Besides, she'd never much cared for alcohol. 'I've cooked monkfish. Is that all right?'

'Aye. It's perfect.'

She smiled and put down her glass. 'It should be ready in a moment. A couple more minutes.'

She was nervous. Her belly was filled with butterflies. She almost felt sick. Would she be able to eat? She wasn't sure she'd be able to swallow anything until she'd got this secret out. It was strangling her. She had to do something. Anything.

She grabbed a small knife and stabbed the potatoes to see if they were cooked. They were nice and soft. The food was ready. Thank God! It would give her something to do.

Jess busied herself for a few minutes, draining the potatoes and the baby vegetables and getting the fish out of the oven to rest. She sliced some lemon and began plating up, trying to make the food look pretty—a feast for the eyes. Then she carried the plates over to the table.

'Bon appetit.'

Adam looked up at her. 'This looks and smells delicious. Thank you.'

'No problem.'

She sat down and laid her napkin over her lap, before spearing a piece of broccoli and placing it in her mouth. She wasn't sure where to look. At Adam? Somewhere else in the room? Wouldn't that seem rude?

'This is wonderful. I've not tasted anything better.'

She smiled at the compliment and put down her knife and fork to take another sip of wine. She needed to breathe. Needed to calm herself. Her heart was racing, her mind whizzing at the thought of how he'd react when she finally told him the truth.

He reached across the table to lay his hand over hers, squeezing her fingertips, gently stroking the back of her hand with his thumb.

She almost stopped breathing. She had to stop this. This was too much. It was as if he was reading her mind and doing everything she'd ever imagined him doing. But it couldn't happen. Because Adam didn't know the whole truth.

'Adam...'

If he was going to learn about her condition, then perhaps this was the moment? It would stop him wanting to touch her. Or should she not tell him anything? Could she be a coward and keep her own counsel? Then let him down gently?

It was so hard! She wanted him so much. It was a torture, sitting here like this knowing that as soon as she told him the truth he wouldn't want her. He would pull his hand away, he'd sit back in his chair, and he'd probably just want to get up and leave. What she had to say would be life-changing, for both of them.

Her stomach was churning and she wasn't sure she'd be able to eat anything. However, once she began she realised she could. The food was absolutely delicious, which helped.

Adam started chatting about his father's plans for the cottage hospital and how he wanted to give some of the staff in the Accident and Emergency department more trauma training. She relaxed slightly, glad that he'd taken the conversation on to something easy. Safe. It seemed a good idea and she nodded along, until eventually Adam laughed at himself.

'Listen to me, waffling on. I'm sorry—it's just that I'm nervous.'

'Nervous?' Her stomach did a flip.

'Of you. Of us. Of this. I've been thinking about us a lot just lately, Jess.'

Us. He kept saying *us.* There could never be such a thing!

'Oh?' She heard the tremble in her voice.

'Aye. I have. I really didn't think I could feel this way about another person after what happened with Anoush. I came home to Thorney expecting nothing like this to happen. But it did—it has. And…and I need you to know how special you are to me.'

'Special?'

No. He shouldn't be telling her this! It was agony.

He nodded and reached for her hand once again, unaware that when he did her pulse almost jumped through the roof.

'So special. I… I think I'm falling for you. Falling hard! I can't stop thinking about you, about how you make me feel… And I know you said you're leaving, but… I think you might feel the same way, too. Do you?'

He was looking at her so earnestly. So eager for her answer. And of course she felt the same way. Of course she had fallen hard for him. But it wasn't to be! It couldn't!

'I do care about you, Adam…'

He smiled, relieved.

'But…'

'But what?'

She pulled her hand free of his and tried not to notice the hurt look in his eyes. 'But we can never be together. Not the way I think you want us to be.'

It physically hurt to say the words out loud. To go against everything she actually wanted and sever the ties between them.

There was total confusion in his eyes. 'Why? What's going on, Jess? I thought you felt the same as me. I thought—'

'I'm sorry, Adam. I'm sorry if I made you feel that way. I'm sorry if I made you think that we could be together. Don't get me wrong—I do want that. It's just…'

'Just what?'

She looked into his eyes. Deep into his eyes. He needed to know. He deserved to know the truth. She couldn't hold back any longer. She would tell him and then she would be free, even if it killed her to do so.

'Adam… I have Huntington's disease. My father had it, too. He killed himself because he couldn't bear to make me his carer and let me watch him lose himself day by day—because he couldn't bear to become a victim to this cruel disease. And I can't let that happen to you, either!'

'Jess…'

She couldn't bear it. Couldn't stand the pity in his eyes!

She got to her feet, her chair scraping back loudly

across the kitchen floor. 'I have no future. Not one that you want. That your parents would want for you. There's no marriage or children on the cards for me. I refuse to take the risk of passing it on. I refuse to let you watch me die!'

The look on his face was horrible, and she couldn't bear to see it. The shock...the disbelief.

Jess ran for her bedroom, slamming the door behind her. She didn't know if he would come after her, or if he was still sitting at her dinner table, staring at her empty chair in shock. All she knew was that her heart was hurting and she couldn't stop crying, that the pain in her heart was much too real.

This was what she'd wanted to avoid. This was what she had feared would happen if she got close to someone. And, despite all her attempts to stop it, it had happened anyway. She had got close to Adam. Cared for him. Loved him. And now she'd had to devastate him.

It was like learning about having the disease all over again. Grieving again. How many times could she do this? This was why she had to go. This was why she had to leave Thorney and keep herself to herself. Otherwise how many people would she hurt?

She had hurt Adam, destroying his dreams for the two of them, tearing down their bubble and exposing her life for what it truly was...

At that thought, she heard thunder rumbling in the distance. She closed her eyes to stop the sting of tears and sobbed quietly to herself.

She'd done it. She'd told him. About the Huntington's and what that meant. He was a doctor. He'd understand and, if he had any sense about him, he'd realise how serious it was and respect her decision. He'd just remain her colleague and her friend and keep his distance. Understand her decision to leave. He would realise the truth and let her go.

Only she would truly know how much her heart had broken.

He had given her a glimpse of what it would have like to be with him and now all that had been taken away.

Life wasn't fair.

Love would never be all fluff and kittens and rainbow sparkles for her.

It would be pain and misery and above all loneliness.

It was all she could expect.

CHAPTER THIRTEEN

ADAM WAS STUNNED into silence, into stillness. He'd watched her run from the table to her room and although he'd known he ought to go after her his legs simply hadn't moved. It was as if he'd taken root, her revelation pinning him to the spot.

Huntington's disease... A disorder that caused brain cells to die. An inherited condition that was always fatal. As it progressed it could cause difficulties with memory, depression, clumsiness, jerky movements, problems swallowing, talking or even breathing...

Jerky movements...

His mind flashed back to the lipoma removal and how Jess had reacted. The look of horror on her face.

Now he knew why.

His father must have known. Maybe his mother, too. And no one had thought to tell him. A wave of anger passed over him and he had to let out a slow, steady breath to make himself think about it rationally.

Somehow he managed to stand, his legs now working. He could hear her crying, sobbing, in her room, and the sound of it broke his heart. He needed to talk to her! She was upset...she shouldn't be on her own right now.

His mind was in turmoil. Huntington's! An awful, disabling condition. Poor Jess! And her father had committed suicide! He couldn't imagine the trauma that she had been through, and she had come out of it smiling, bright, happy, determined to bring sunshine into other people's lives, knowing that her own held suffering and upset.

He needed to talk to her. Needed to think. If he let her believe that it was all over for them, then he would lose the second woman he had ever loved. He'd lost Anoush in a hail of bullets, her life snapped out of existence in a second, but Jess?

No future was guaranteed for anyone. Life could be taken at a moment's notice. What mattered was enjoying the time that you did have. Enjoying the present. Because it was a gift. And what was more important than life? Than love? He loved Jess and he couldn't let her be alone, thinking she'd destroyed their chance at happiness, because she *hadn't*.

He slowed as he came to a realisation.

The Huntington's didn't matter.

What mattered was Jess. His love for Jess and the fact that, even though she didn't think so, he believed they had a life to live together. A present. A future. No matter how uncertain. One more day with her—one week, one month, one year—was better than nothing at all.

He knew what it was like to live without love and it was horrible. Now he'd found it again he was damned sure he wasn't going to give it up without a fight.

Jess sat on her bed, utterly numb. She'd run out of tears, but grief still sat like a giant knot in the centre of her gut.

Adam knew everything now and it had not gone the way she had hoped. She'd wanted to tell him in calm, measured tones, to be unemotional, but she'd not factored in just how much she felt for him. She'd not been able to sit there, listening to him declaring that he was falling in love with her, when she knew it was already too late for them!

He'd had to know what he was letting himself in for, and now that he did she had no doubt that he would give her a wide berth romantically. He might knock on her door, whisper in soft tones that he was sorry before leaving, but he wouldn't say anything else. Do anything else. What could he say? He would hardly drop to his knees and propose, would he? Not after that.

Sighing, she got to her feet and stripped off her dress and the constricting underwear she'd put on to make the dress look good on her figure. She got into her comfy pyjamas and bathrobe, used some wet wipes to clean her face of make-up and tearstains. But everything she did was done as if in a trance. Numbly. As if she was having an out-of-body experience and was looking down upon herself, or at someone else in a television show.

He'd not come to her door. Hadn't said anything. Had he gone? She wouldn't blame him.

It was so unfair. She'd dreamed of having Adam Campbell fall in love with her! It had been everything she had ever wanted in life—apart from not having an in-herited disease—and even though he'd practically handed himself to her on a plate she'd had to knock that plate away and let everything crash to the floor. Let the food spill. The wine stain.

She stared at her sad reflection. There was still work tomorrow, and she'd see Adam there. They'd have to get over the initial awkwardness, but once they did that she felt sure—

A knock on her bedroom door.

Adam.

He was still here.

She hesitated for a minute, not sure she could face him, but...

But if I do it now then I won't have to worry about doing it tomorrow. Just get it over and done with. Accept the pity. Accept the sympathy and the apologies. You know what's coming.

She got up on weary feet and went to open the door.

He stood there, looking at her imploringly. 'We need to talk.'

'Do we? What is there to say?' She brushed past him and led him back to the living room, before standing there, arms crossed defensively. 'What do you want?'

He shook his head, as if in amazement. 'What do I *want*? I want to speak to you about what you just said!'

'What is there to say? I have a life-limiting disease and there is no future for you with me. Nothing. Not the kind that your family wants for you. Not the kind that you deserve.'

'Who says?'

'The disease does.'

'Yeah, well, the disease doesn't get to choose what I decide to do with my life and neither do you!'

He'd raised his voice in frustration and, not sure what to say, she just stared at him. She hadn't expected his anger.

'You say you've got Huntington's... Well, so what? It doesn't matter.'

'It *does* matter.'

'No, it doesn't.'

'You watched the woman you loved die right in front of your eyes and it almost broke you! You think I want you watching me do the exact same thing? Only I won't die in seconds, Adam. I'll die slowly, week after week, month after month, losing a bit of me every day as my brain cells *shrink and die*. I won't put you through it.'

Tears came to her eyes, surprising her. She'd thought she was out of those.

'You don't get to choose what I do with my heart, Jess, *I do*! Yes, losing Anoush was tough! Yes, it almost broke me. But it would break anyone! And I wouldn't change one thing about falling in love with Anoush, even though our time together was so brief. The love was worth it! I'd do it again in a heartbeat. But since meeting you, I've realised I was just existing day by day. *You* made me live again. You made me find joy and happiness. You make me complete and I will take you for as many years as I can get with you! I choose to live my life with you in it, no matter how much time you've got left, because one day with you is preferable to years without you in my life at all!'

The tears dripped down her cheeks and jaw. He was saying some lovely things, but he didn't know how hard it would be!

'You think I haven't seen a Huntington's case?' he asked. 'Well, I have. I know what it can do to someone. And I won't let you go through that alone! I love you, Jess. That's what's important. Love! Let's spend the time we have left together, making each other happy.'

'Oh, Adam! I want to do that—I do. But… The idea of you having to look after me…'

'There are thousands of people looking after their partners in this world. You think they hate it? You think they find it off-putting? That somehow it makes them love *less*? That's dedication. That's love. That's in sickness and in health! You don't get to love someone just when they can walk and talk. You love them for who they are, for who they've been—and you, Jessica Young, are the one person who makes me want to be a better man. Who stands by my side when I need help and when I'm broken. So why can't I do the same thing in return? Do you love me, Jess?'

'You know I do…' she whispered, her breath caught in her throat so it hurt to talk.

'Then be brave. Take my hand and my heart and do with them what you will.' He held out his hand to her. 'Just know that if you take them you can't give them back. They're non-returnable.'

She felt the beginnings of a smile wanting to show itself. He'd said some wonderful things. He'd said all the right things. The only question was, was she brave enough to step into the future with him?

He was brave enough. He'd made that quite clear. And there were no secrets any more. He knew what he was getting into and he still wanted to be with her.

How lucky was she? It looked as if she was getting everything she wanted after all.

Slowly, carefully, she reached out to take his hand in hers and squeezed it tight. 'I'm all yours.'

Adam let out a breath as a big smile broke across his face and he pulled her towards him and kissed her gently on the lips. 'And you're mine. Just know that I will never let you go.'

EPILOGUE

JESS BLEW OUT an exhausted breath, remembering just how much she hated unpacking after a holiday.

No… She smiled. Not a holiday. *A honeymoon.*

She and Adam had had a fabulous time in Mauritius, walking on sandy beaches, sipping cocktails and occasionally practising her very bad schoolgirl French on the poor, unsuspecting locals on those days they'd been out and about in the sunshine.

Though there had been other days when they'd spent hours in bed, enjoying each other's bodies, the French doors open to a view of the clear blue sea.

But, as was always the case after going away, you had to go back to reality. Real life. Unpacking everything. *Laundry.*

Adam's arms slipped around her waist from behind and she felt his lips upon her neck.

'Hey, beautiful. I told you I'd give you a hand with this.'

She loved the feel of his body against hers. The way he fitted her just perfectly. As if they'd been cut from the same mould.

'I wanted to make a start. There's so much to do… We haven't fully unpacked from the move yet, either.'

Adam had told her that he would follow her anywhere, and that if she wanted to pursue her dreams of working in obstetrics then that was what she must do. So, after telling his parents the good news about their relationship, they had told them that they'd be moving to Cardiff whilst Jess did her training.

'But then we'll be right back here, Jack. If you'll still have us?'

'Of course I'll have you back! Don't you forget it!'

Jack and Judy had enveloped them both in a large hug, and Jess had got swept up into the arms of the most loving family she had ever known.

Judy had helped her plan the wedding, which had been held on Thorney, and since then they'd been the best in-laws she could ever have. They'd been so good about her condition—even when Jess had sat down privately with Judy, to apologise because she would never give her the grandchildren she wanted.

'Grandchildren are wonderful—of course they are. But the best gift you could have given me was making my son the happiest he has ever been in his entire life.'

Now clothes were everywhere—even hanging on the wardrobe door, ready to be put away, next to the brand-new suit she'd put out for her first day tomorrow as an obstetrics registrar.

Adam touched the sleeve of the suit, drawing her eye to it. 'Are you nervous?' he asked.

'Yes.'

He turned her to face him and kissed her, smiling. 'Don't be. You'll be amazing. It's your dream! Enjoy it. Soak it all up so that when your training is done we can go back to Thorney and establish your practice there.'

'You don't regret it? Moving away? I know it's your home…'

'My home is where you are. And you're right here. Exactly where you're meant to be.'

Jess wrapped her arms around his neck and pulled him in for a kiss. 'I love you, Adam. Have I told you that today?'

'I think you might have done, Mrs Campbell. But it never hurts to hear it again.'

'I love you,' she repeated, smiling, staring deeply into his eyes and feeling the strength of his love flow through her, stronger than she could ever have imagined.

'I love you, too,' he said.

And he pressed his lips to hers.

* * * * *

THE GP'S SECRET
BABY WISH

SUE MacKAY

MILLS & BOON

Dedicated to Lindsay, my rock.

PROLOGUE

Run, Lily. Now. Get away from Max Bryant. Now. Before it's too late. Before your heart's inextricably caught up in his charm…

Her pulse was racing, while at the same time her body warmed to him, and confusion reigned in her head. Max was a playboy who thought women were there for one thing only, namely keeping him happy, and here she was in his bed. She'd used him for her own gain. Except now she wanted more of him. Friendship, sharing and caring. Maybe even a *future*? That wasn't going to happen. He wasn't the settle down kind of guy and she'd already experienced a relationship where her partner had broken all those promises.

Lily shuddered. Just the idea of climbing out of Max's bed for the last time felt as though chains were holding her back from escaping the growing sense that he was getting under her skin and waking her up in ways that wouldn't, or couldn't, work with him. Not long term, and that was the only way ahead for her.

They'd had a spectacular few days, but she had to remember how he gave her grief about being wealthy, almost as though that was more important than anything else about her, like he didn't see her for who she was, so she had to move away, move on. Anyway, it was too soon after Aaron had broken her heart by blatantly cheating.

Short, rapid breaths escaped Lily's mouth. Her throat hurt from trying not to yell her frustration at not just finding Max likable but that he'd shown her a softer side than he ever showed at work. This wasn't meant to have happened. It was supposed to be a fling with no feelings involved, merely a way of boosting her ego and proving to herself that men did find her attractive. That Aaron was wrong to have called her uptight and dull—his excuse for having sex with other women in their bed. She'd needed to gain back some control over relationships, short or long, to fix her heart.

Max was sprawled beside her, legs spread wide and one hand behind his head and one on her thigh as he slept the sleep of the dead after the most amazing sex she'd ever experienced. Apart from the sex they'd shared over the previous two days, that was. 'Shared' being the remarkable feature. Full credit to the man. He gave as much as he took, which probably explained his popularity with the females from work he spent extracurricular time with. She hadn't felt uptight with him, or dull if the sounds emitting from his generous, exciting mouth when she'd ridden him were an indicator.

It would be too easy to roll on top of that muscular body and tease him awake. Lust was pulling at her, heating up fast. Lily began turning towards him. Stopped. No. She mustn't. She wasn't ready to trust another man.

She didn't usually go for casual sex, but with Aaron's words ringing in her ears once too often she'd taken up Max's invitation to join him in bed three days ago after a particularly hectic, adrenalin-fuelled night on duty in the emergency department, despite him being a lady's man with a belt full of notches.

Or was it because of that she'd done this? To show she was just as desirable as those other women? Not that Aaron would notice, and if he did, it was too late. She mightn't be over his hurtful words or the image of what he'd been doing with that nurse in their shower, but she was over him.

Lily began sliding towards the edge of the bed. She needed to get out of there while she had the strength to go. It was one thing to have beyond amazing sex with Max, quite another to think there'd be anything more. His reputation for loving and leaving went before him, and she didn't intend to become a statistic. Better to exit, head high, in control, even if behind her ribs there was a rough pattering going on.

You're on the rebound.

Relief assailed her. Yes, rebound love. No, don't use the L word about this man. Rebound or not, it wasn't love keeping her awake long after he'd rolled off her. Whatever the hell it was, she wasn't waiting around to find out. She was done and dusted with their fling. They'd continue working together and forget all about these few days. It seemed easy, yet doubt fluttered through her mind.

Max's hand tightened, loosened on her thigh.

Squashing that doubt, she waited until his breathing returned to normal. If only her lungs would do the same. Impossible with the heat that hand caused to fill her empty heart. Why should she sneak away? She'd see him at work in five hours. She might as well be open and honest. Lily stood up and snatched up her clothes from the floor, started shoving herself into them.

'Where're you off to?'

So much for thinking he was out for the count. 'Home.' The zip on her jeans caught in the fabric.

'Come back to bed. We've got a few hours left before we have to be on duty.'

'No, Max.' The zip wouldn't budge. Giving up, she tugged her jersey over her head and down below her waist.

The sound of his body sliding up the bed told her he was wide awake. There was a wicked glint in his eyes, reminding her of all he promised her body, which didn't help her determination to get out of there. 'Sure I can't tempt you?'

He could do that, all right. Only he had to get out from under her skin. 'Sorry, but I'm away now.' Tying up the laces of her shoes, she said, 'It's been great, but I'm done.'

His head jerked higher. 'You think?'

'I know.' Slinging her bag over her shoulder, she headed to the door. 'See you tonight. On duty,' she added, to make sure he was understanding her intent.

He was off the bed and standing between her and the door so quickly she gulped. 'Not so fast.'

It was hard to remember why she was in a hurry to leave when she took in the sight before her. Tall, lean, muscular without being too hard, every inch of his body was to die for. Her mouth dried. What was she doing, walking away?

'Why, Lily? And don't tell me you haven't had a blast these past few days.'

'I have. That's what it was all about. Now it's time to move on.' She couldn't look him in the eye. He might see her hesitancy, might recognise he disturbed her on a level she wasn't prepared for, didn't want.

'Move on to what? Another fling?'

Now she did fix her eyes on his face. 'You have a problem with that? With your reputation?' Did he have to be so good looking?

'Yes, I do.'

Got it. 'You can't handle the fact I'm leaving first. I'm supposed to cling to you and beg you to let me stay, not get out of bed and go.'

'Get off your high horse, Lily. I've enjoyed the time we've had together here and thought there was more to come. Seems I was wrong. Should've known you'd exercise your control even over something like this.'

'My control?' she blustered. But he was right in one respect. She was trying to stay in control of herself, but not of him. He could go and do whatever he liked as long as she got him out from under her skin.

'You have everything in hand, never face difficulties.'

He hadn't heard how the surgeon had treated her when the story had been rife on the hospital grapevine? Of course, it'd happened weeks before Max had started working in ED. It probably didn't qualify as a difficulty to this man, who thought relationships were all about sex and not getting involved. 'I'd have thought you'd be thankful I'm going and not hanging on for every look you might send my way.' Another light-bulb moment struck. 'You're not used to being ditched.'

The exaggerated eye roll he did told her she'd hit the nail on the head even before he drawled, 'Naturally.'

Damn, he was full of himself. But she'd known that and had still slept with him for her own needs. She'd had a great time, too. Too great, if that niggling sense of losing control was anything to go by. 'Get over yourself, Max. I've seen the other women you've hurt but I will not be treated like something you've used and tossed aside. I came into this with my eyes wide and knowing it was going to be short-lived. I will not be going around with tears in my eyes and hoping that you'll give me a second chance. Because I don't feel that.'

She swept his body with her gaze, taking in the sight one more time, pretending he was easy to walk away from, and that she hadn't lied, ignoring the thumping of her heart. Stepping around him before she did something stupid like run her finger down his sternum, she muttered, 'See you later.' Hopefully it would be as manic as Thursday and Friday nights had always been so there'd been no time for small talk, or coffee, or drinking in the sight of Max's tight butt in his blue scrubs whenever he bent over a bed to check out a patient.

Tonight was the beginning of the rest of the time they worked together. She just had to remember she was desirable whenever he looked at her with that disbelief blinking at her now. If she wasn't, the sex wouldn't have been so intense and hot, and touching. Max hadn't been making that up. She paused. 'Thank you.'

He turned his back on her.

CHAPTER ONE

LILY SHRANK DEEPER into her warm jacket as the bus pulled
away, and stared up the wide pathway leading to the massive building housing Auckland's Remuera Medical Hub.
'What *am* I doing?'

Preparing to start her dream job was all very well,
but working with Max Bryant again had her head banging with doubts. Could she make it work, or would they
combust the moment they set eyes on each other and
make life awkward at the very least? She shivered—but
not from the cold. It was a risk but one she'd decided to
take in order to have this job. Max had never quite left
her, occasionally popping into her mind to remind her
how she'd walked away from what might possibly have
been something amazing. But she had, and had found
love with another man, or so she'd thought. She'd got
that wrong as well.

Shouting broke through her hesitation and seemed to
be coming from beyond the bus, which was moving on.

'Lily Scott,' a male called. 'Lily, over here.'

Her heart thumped once. Max? Yes. Her mouth dried.
Of course it would be. Straight into the fire without time
to breathe. She looked around, saw the man waving from

further along the busy road. Another, harder, thump. So much for being prepared for this.

Three years and lots of living had passed and amongst all that Max had occasionally sneaked under her skin, reminding her of what they'd shared briefly, of what she'd walked away from because she hadn't trusted him not to hurt her when she'd been vulnerable. Because she hadn't trusted her own strength to remain immune to him.

'One of my patients has fallen. I might need a hand,' he called.

'Coming.' Lily's fingers tingled as she stared at Max while weaving through the rush-hour traffic. He'd caused her to think twice about accepting the position here. She'd thought twice and had taken it anyway because their history was exactly that. History. Yet just hearing his voice brought an image of him calling out to her from his bed, telling her to get under the sheets quick fast. He'd been funny and generous, unlike the ego she'd worked with.

She did regret the awkward way they'd finished their fling. They could have found a way to get along comfortably if nothing else, but instead the barriers she'd raised between them once she'd understood how easily she lost control around him had turned him against her. For the next two long months they had continued working as junior doctors in the emergency department, barely communicating unless it had been about patients.

Someone bumping into her sent her tripping a few steps before she straightened up and blindly pushed through the crowd to the kerb, taking elbows and knocks in her stride, concentrating on getting across the road.

A young woman lay sprawled on the pavement, her left ankle at an odd angle and her hand gripping her left wrist. Kneeling beside her was Max.

Lily gulped, looked at the woman then back at Max. His once straight black hair had become wavy with bright streaks of grey. Lines accentuated the forthright chin and sharpened once soft, come-hither eyes. He no longer looked quite like the man who'd had more notches than leather on his belt. The man she'd slept with three years ago between relationship disasters to boost her confidence. He'd aged. A lot more than to be expected in the time since she'd last seen him, surely? Had something terrible happened? She swallowed the urge to ask and squatted opposite him to focus on the woman cursing ferociously between them and not on him.

'Michelle, what happened?' Max asked, with barely a glance in Lily's direction.

'Some doped-up ass charged off the bus I was getting on,' the woman ground out through the pain contorting her narrow face. 'He shoved me so hard I landed on my wrist and leg on the concrete.'

Lily sucked in a breath through clenched teeth. She couldn't ignore him or he'd think nothing had changed with her. And it had. Another man walking out on her had taught her to be stronger than ever and look out for herself and her own needs, which included getting on-side with this man.

'Hello, Max.' Her tongue was in a knot, belying her resolve to be sensible about him, to work alongside him without rehashing the past. The sizzle that had led to three hot, unforgettable nights was taunting her. She'd walked away from those bewitching sensations with her head high, heart unsteady, and the sensible side of her brain telling her to get out while it was still possible. After all the years in between, Max had her in a pickle within moments? Her hand tightened convulsively.

'Hi, Lily.' His nod was brief, his glance even shorter. 'Not a great way to start a new job, meeting your first patient out here in the cold.'

'She's going to be my patient?'

'Yes, while I'm her sports doctor. Twenty minutes ago she bounced out of my office on her way to catch the bus to training.' He was gently touching Michelle's swollen ankle above her running shoe.

'Yeah, and now look at me,' the woman snapped.

Lily focused on their patient, not on Max and how different he looked and sounded. He seemed more serious, with less ego on display. 'Let me look at your wrist.' Like her ankle, it was already swelling. 'Can you bend it at all?'

Michelle complied by trying to bend it up and down. 'Afraid not.' Neither could she move it sideways. 'You going to take my shoe off, Max?'

He shook his head. 'No, it's best to leave it on to hold everything in place. If there's a fracture I don't want the bones moving.'

That deep, sexy voice brought back memories best forgotten. When accepting the position at one of the city's most reputable medical centres, she'd determined to be friendly towards him while keeping her distance, had hoped to feel only indifference, not have her blood racing and her toes tingling from only a glance. Gulp. When it came to medicine and learning all there was to know, he'd been excellent during his internship and that was all that mattered here, not the brief fling that had led to disappointment in herself for *feeling* something for him. Making a success of this job included getting on with Max.

'How's that wrist, Lily?' he asked, finally looking straight at her for a moment.

'There's little movement because of the swelling. Michelle, how painful is it? One to ten, ten highest.'

'Eight. Ankle's ten.' Despair began pouring out of Michelle's mouth. 'That creep's ruined everything I've worked so hard for. Where is he? He pushed me and now he's run away. The coward.'

Shaking her head to refocus and put aside the flare of interest Max's look had created, Lily reached for Michelle's wrist again. 'I want to check further.' With one finger, she began gently pressing the joints.

'It hurts like hell. I reckon it's broken. And my ankle. How am I going to play with the netball team in England now? Tell me that.'

'We don't know anything for certain.' Max was again gently feeling the tissue above the shoe but quickly stopped when Michelle groaned. 'You need X-rays.'

'Why bother? I felt the ankle crack. The pain's excruciating. I won't be able to train for months. So much for all the hard work I've put in. It's come to nothing because of some idiot who doesn't have the gumption to stay and see if he can do anything to help me.' Tears spewed down Michelle's white face. 'Where is he?' she yelled.

'Take it easy. You're in good physical condition, which is a bonus.' From what little Lily could see, Michelle must work out a lot. 'Let's find out what the damage is first,' she said, her heart squeezing for the woman who was obviously a very fit athlete. There was no denying that she probably wouldn't be playing netball any time soon, though. 'I'm sure Max has ideas on how to get you up and about as fast as possible once we know.'

His head shot up and he stared at her for a moment then replied, 'You bet.' He looked to Michelle and smiled encouragingly.

Lily fought her disappointment. No smile for her. This wasn't how meeting up with Max again for the first time was meant to feel. Awkward, not direct and simple. Not that she'd been silly enough to think it would be quite that easy. But she was home for good and wanted the best out of this career opportunity. As for men, she was done with them. Except for one purpose and that would take a lot of careful thought and good judgement before it came about.

Since becoming single again, a slow, quiet tick-tock had begun deep inside where her heart lay, saying that time was rushing by, that she might never find a man to love her for who she was and to give her the family she longed for. A man who was kind, sensible, generous of spirit and downright decent.

Not Max, then.

She shivered. There was no chance of that with his ego and way of using charm to get everything he wanted. He'd also shown a lack of concern for the women whose hearts he'd broken. Intelligent and clever, he could also be self-centred and egotistical.

He was talking to Michelle, calm and direct. 'You want me to ring your mother and let her know what's happened once we've got you on your way?'

'I guess.' Michelle scrubbed at her face with her un-injured hand, blinking rapidly.

Scrabbling in her bag, Lily found a pocket pack of tissues. 'Here you go.'

'Thanks.'

Max continued talking as though nothing out of the ordinary was happening. 'You need to focus on getting treatment and arranging physio as soon as it's feasible. As I said, you're strong and fit. Those things are on your side in this and will help you back to normal sooner than most people.'

Lily kept watching Michelle while listening to the determination for his patient in Max's voice. It was his way of saying she couldn't fail now. Kindness hidden behind his medical analysis, and that surprised her. If she were ever to consider a man as a father for her child, he would have to be kind.

Just then Max glanced her way, a brief wry smile on those full lips. And something jolted deep inside her. Something warm, and tight with apprehension. It couldn't be. Let's face it. When he'd smiled at her on the final morning she'd woken up in his bed, there'd been no jolting going on. Or so she'd told herself. It had been more remorse for joining Max's statistics and fear she'd let him get to her.

Let it go. Falling for that smile now was not on her agenda. Starting at the medical hub was all about being a doctor and getting on with plans for the future, it had nothing to do with him. But it was impossible to ignore the fluttering in her belly. Soft and continual, as though she was being told to look at Max in a whole new way. It was becoming more obvious every minute how much he'd changed. Concern for his patient was normal, but not the self-deprecating humour he'd briefly shown her. She tightened her stomach to quieten the flutter.

Max had always worked hard and sucked up knowledge like a sponge. That wouldn't have changed. It'd been important for him to do well in his career, which had resonated with her own ambitions, and the only aspect she knew about him that wasn't full of his ego. He'd always accepted when he was wrong if it meant learning something to improve his skills. His patients would no doubt like him a lot.

Something clicked in her brain, solving a pesky riddle that had been hovering in the background since her interview with the partners of the centre. When she'd known him previously Max had been fervent about specialising in surgery.

'Sports doctor?' And GP. What *had* happened in the intervening years?

He told her with a guarded look, 'There's a wheelchair in the room behind Reception. Would you mind getting it?'

'No problem.' Had he deliberately avoided her question? Or was he merely reminding her they were with a patient?

'Door on the left. Avoid Reception and everyone or we'll be waiting out here for ages.'

Where the function she'd been heading to, before Max had called out, was being held. 'On it. What about an ambulance?'

'I'll call when we're inside, out of the cold,' Max replied.

Within minutes she'd returned to the scene with a nifty wheelchair, and locked the brakes in preparation to loading Michelle. 'Here we go.'

Max straightened up. 'Between us we'll lift you onto the chair, Michelle.'

Michelle had other ideas. 'Take a side each and pull me up. I can stand on my good leg.'

'Fine.' Max obviously knew not to argue. She was quickly in the chair and Max was rolling her up the incline to the side door of the medical centre.

Inside, Lily followed them down the hall to an office

that the diplomas on the wall told her was Max's. Again, she wanted to ask about his change in direction but managed to swallow the question. He was affecting her with his focused approach, which was nothing like the vibrant, the-world-is-my-oyster guy she'd known. This quieter, still smiling but in a softer way, man was knocking her long-held beliefs that he was all about himself.

Max held a hand out to her. 'Welcome aboard, Lily.'

She stared at that hand, her skin warming with memories.

'Lily?' He was retracting his welcome gesture.

Quickly sliding her hand into his large one, she gave it a shake. 'Thanks, Max. I'm excited about working here.' *About seeing you.* Jerking free, she stepped back, glancing across to confused eyes. 'I mean it,' she added. *I think.*

'Good.' He turned to the other woman. 'Michelle, Lily Scott's taking over from Sarah in a couple of weeks so technically she's going to be your GP. Lily, Michelle Baxter.'

Lily reached for her hand and shook it. 'Wish I'd met you in better circumstances.'

'So do I.' Michelle's cheeks flushed. 'Sorry, ignore me. I'm acting like a spoilt brat, but it's truly frustrating.'

'You're fine. Anyone would be furious at what's occurred.' But bad things happened to people. There was no avoiding them. She knew that all too well.

Only six months ago she'd arrived home at the Singapore apartment she'd shared with her fiancé, Leo, to find him waiting, bags packed, while a one-way ticket to Scotland and his passport had lain on the table. He was heading back to his home town and she wasn't invited. He'd decided to go back to the girlfriend he'd bro-

ken up with only months before meeting Lily. A woman
Lily had never heard of until that day. Apparently Leo
had been in constant contact with her for months and the
lure of what they'd once had was too strong to ignore.
Stronger than his feelings for Lily. She'd loved him and
it hadn't counted.

Two broken relationships showed how unlucky she
was in love, had proved how unlovable she must be. Two
men had cheated on her. There were only so many heart-
breaks she could survive, and Max wasn't causing her
another. After their fling he'd been cool towards her, suggesting he might've actually been glad she'd stopped it,
and that had added to her sense that she was unlovable
when it came to finding a soul mate. She'd better remember that. It was a strong reason for contemplating having
a baby on her own.

Lily had been as much furious at being duped by Leo
as she had felt hurt. He hadn't wanted children, something he'd failed to mention until he'd been leaving. That
dishonesty had been a bitter pill to swallow, but over
the intervening months it had been dissolving and now
she was almost relieved that relationship was over, as
though Leo hadn't been as much the love of her life as
she'd believed.

Second best because going for the real thing was
too risky, hurt too much when it failed. She just wasn't
good at relationships. Men might let her down, go to
other women for comfort, but she'd be a loving, devoted
mother. No one would take that away from her.

Family meant everything to her, and if she had to
have her own baby in a different way then so be it. No
more hoping for love to come her way, or having her
own thrown back in her face. She'd selflessly love her

child alongside her parents, brothers and sisters-in-law. As her mouth curved upward, her heart slowed. A baby. Her baby. Wow. If she got past the idea of a stranger fathering her infant, it would be amazing.

Max was talking to Michelle. 'Between the three of us, we'll get you back on your feet and beating the hell out of those Poms.'

'You think?' Hope flicked on in their patient's eyes. 'You'd better be right.' The hope disappeared as fast as it had arrived.

Gathering her scattered thoughts, Lily added her bit to Max's encouragement. 'We'll do better than that.' Again an unfamiliar warmth touched Lily's skin. Max had included her in the scenario with Michelle when he could have claimed it was a sports injury and therefore his case. She hadn't expected that. She hugged herself. People did change. She had. She'd faced her demons and found a way to move forward.

'It won't be a walk in the park, but we'll make it happen. You've got to stay positive. That's as important as the rest.' Max locked a formidable gaze on their patient. 'I'll get you some pain relief and phone for an ambulance.'

Michelle nodded. 'The sooner the better for both.'

Through the partially open door laughter reached them. Max glanced over. 'You'd better get in there and start meeting everyone, Lily. I'll look after Michelle and join the fray when she's on her way.'

She couldn't believe the disappointment making itself known in her head at his suggestion. Disappointed she wasn't spending more time with Max? She wasn't admitting that so it must be to do with getting to know her first patient. 'It's Sarah's farewell night. I'll stay with Michelle while you phone for the ambulance.'

'Get on with you. Everyone's wanting to welcome you to the centre. I'm going to stay here until Michelle's on her way.' He held the phone up. 'I've got painkillers in my bag.'

There was no arguing with him. She gave in on a sigh. 'I guess I'd better put in an appearance before they think I'm a no show.'

'You might want to check your face in the mirror,' Max nodded to a cupboard door on the far wall. 'You've got a smear on your cheek.'

She blinked. 'Thanks.'

He grinned. 'No problem.'

Showing her care and understanding was new. Nothing like the guy who'd basically called her a control freak when she'd turned him down after three hot nights together.

Tonight he was presenting an image she'd not seen before. Or had she been so determined to find fault with him to protect herself that she'd missed what had been right before her eyes? He'd tweaked her curiosity with his gentleness in bed, and the heat between them had been a conflagration. He certainly hadn't appeared to find her lacking as a sexual partner, but she hadn't hung around long enough to risk that wearing off and having that sense of something wonderful happening between them expanding to the point she'd be devastated when he moved on. Because he would have without a doubt. It had been his way.

Yet now she wanted to find out more. The unknown made life tricky, increased the possibility of something going wrong. Failure was something she rarely experi-

enced, except with lovers. Growing up with two brothers who had continually goaded her into proving she was
as good as them at any job on the farm had been a constant battle, but she'd always taken up the challenges. Her
brothers had helped her grow a backbone and become resilient, but they had never taught her to protect her heart,
hence she gave it away too easily. Not any more, though,
except to her baby when he or she came about.

Ducking into the bathroom, Lily wiped the smudge
of mascara from under her eye and laughed at herself for
getting excited over Max. He might look and sound different, but Max was Max, end of story. Best keep that in
the forefront of her mind. She'd returned home to get on
with being a doctor in a fabulous centre. Starting now, she
would not let bygone hurts distract her, would put them
behind her and be open to opportunities as they arose.

'There you are.' Devlin, one of the partners, ap-
proached her with a welcoming smile when she entered
the reception area. 'Thought I'd have to send out a search
party.'

'A patient had an accident getting on the bus. Max's
getting her sorted now.' She resisted the urge to hug Devlin in case anyone got the wrong idea. He was her father's lifelong friend, having grown up on a neighbouring
farm, though Devlin had left to become a doctor while
her father had remained on the land. She and Devlin had
agreed to be open about knowing each other well, but
wouldn't flaunt it. She was here on her own merits, not
because of family contacts. 'Being here is great.' Even
with Max in the picture.

Max stood in the doorway, shoulder against the frame,
watching Lily doing the circuit, his hand still tingling

from where her palm had touched his. Shock had flicked in and out of her eyes, a similar shock to the one that had torpedoed his gut. The same sensation he'd known with her three years ago. Apparently not even the gruelling episode he'd suffered since then had fixed that. Being totally at ease with everyone came naturally to her but, then, coming from a wealthy background would boost anyone's confidence, and Lily had an abundance of that.

When they'd worked together in ED, she'd twice appeared on television at her father's side for the national wine awards, dressed in stunning dresses and standing confidently on dangerously high heels, smiling as though she'd won and not her parent. It was something he'd given her a hard time about, and now regretted. There were a few things to do with Lily he regretted, one being how their fling had finished so abruptly. He hadn't taken it well, had been rude to her to hide his hurt. Unbelievably he'd begun to see her as a woman who mattered, who he just might be able to take a chance with.

Lily had been special in bed, generous while not trying to impress, unlike the Lily he'd thought he knew, and unlike other women he'd slept with. Her enthusiasm for life and wanting to share that with him during that short time had touched him in a way he'd not known before. It had been something he'd wanted to explore, to share and give back, which he never did with the women he dated. Yet there'd been a red flag warning him about finding more to her than he could cope with, and failing to let go of her when the fling ran its course.

It had been something he'd wanted to explore, yet had been wary of—worried he might find more to her than he could cope with. A reason for remaining single until he qualified was the oath he'd sworn to himself to avoid getting sidetracked and maybe failing. He'd had to show his father he was worthy of him, that when his mother had left them, taking his sister with her, it hadn't meant he wasn't lovable. The problem with that was that his father didn't do loving and caring, more like demanding and tough. It was only recently that he had realised that for Dad that was being loving.

His eyes were still tracking Lily. She was gorgeous with a capital G.

Michelle was impressed. 'Straightforward and no promises she mightn't be able to keep,' had been her opinion.

Not that he could fault Michelle's decision to take Lily on as her GP. Lily didn't overwork sympathy or try to impress just for the sake of it. She could put on a show when needed, though never when it came to her medical career. He sighed. She had been dedicated to learning all she could. *Huh?* Max jerked upright. He hadn't thought of it before, but he could see it now. That hadn't been about making herself look good. Lily soaking up knowledge and then using it with patients carefully and confidently but quietly, not showing off to anyone. He'd seen her in action and not credited her with what it was worth, too busy following his own path, busy living life to the full, working all hours, and not being impressed when anyone had got in the way or turned him down. He had never stopped to see people for who they were.

Except that time that Lily had said no to another night together. Then he had paused, looking for the Lily others saw. He'd felt a heel as the beautiful, caring woman came to light under his scrutiny. She'd been popular with everyone in the ED and he'd not noticed that before. After their fling, he'd felt there was something more to her that he couldn't quite grasp.

Something that lit a fire in his belly. Something he was afraid to confront in case it got to him in unexpected ways, so he'd quickly moved on to other more willing opportunities. But he'd never forgotten those nights, never accepted she'd pulled the plug on him. It had stung. He'd wanted more and she hadn't.

She'd woken him up to the fact that he had usually been the one walking away, and hadn't been kind in the way he'd gone about it. It was scary how quickly she'd got under his skin when they had become intimate. For the first time ever he'd begun considering other possibilities, such as a real, loving, permanent relationship.

That had made him consider the women he'd bedded and how his love 'em and leave 'em attitude might have hurt them. He hadn't stopped bedding women, but he had become more considerate of their feelings and worked hard at not hurting them by explaining straight up that he wasn't looking for a permanent relationship.

Taking a long, deep breath, he studied the female who'd had his teeth grinding from the moment he'd learned she was joining Remuera Medical Hub. Sparks were flickering in his gut. Her shoulder-length copper-coloured hair gleamed as it always had.

Her one vanity, he'd once heard her say to a nurse and had spluttered into his water bottle, thinking she was nothing but vanity with her stylish hair, perfectly manicured nails, elegant shoes that must've hurt like hell on a hectic day in the department. That hadn't stopped him taking her to bed, though. Hell, he really hadn't been the nice guy he'd thought he was.

Financially he'd struggled through med school and

her attitude had rubbed him up the wrong way. Only once again he'd been wrong. She hadn't pushed people's faces in her good fortune, and really, looking back, she had only been herself, a well-dressed, kind woman who had wanted to help people as much as he did.

Her tall, slim figure had filled out a little now, giving her a more curvaceous shape that suited her—and tightened him uncomfortably. The elegantly simple navy trousers and jacket with a cream blouse added to her appeal. A straightforward, this-is-who-I-am look that had him wanting to get behind it and learn more about why she got him in a tangle. Her face had matured into a beautiful woman's countenance. Why had he sulked when she'd walked away from his bed? Turning him down with no explanation wasn't an excuse to be rude. Quite the opposite. Lily had been the catalyst for him to start putting others before himself.

She turned from talking to Devlin and caught his eye. Her smile slipped then returned; not false as he used to expect but genuine. Now, there was a first, and one he should grab with both hands—if he wasn't adamant about not getting into a relationship. There was no changing his mind now.

The past few years had taught him to make the most of life and the people he met, not to wreck any chances for happiness by being full of himself. Apart from surviving, it was the best to come out of his battle with cancer, and one he held onto tight. It had helped him get through the ghastly, dark days of surgery and chemo, and a new, edgy treatment. It had kept him grounded in unexpected ways—appreciating the honest kindness of the nurses and doctors who had treated him, learning the other side of a medical problem from that of the doctor's perspective, finding he had still been breathing every morning when he'd first opened his eyes to another day of hell.

Oh, yes, it had been a steep learning curve that had taught him things about himself he'd never suspected. He was worthy of giving and accepting love, and giving was way better than taking.

He'd also learned the future came with no guarantees. Hence the reason now for never marrying or having children. It would be selfish to ask a woman to share his uncertainties. Looking at Lily, it made him sad. Not because they now had a chance of getting on like they never had, but because, with her ease and laughter, and love of life and people, she reminded him of those things he did want and had promised himself not to look for in case he caused more pain.

His mother and sister leaving had broken him, and filled him with a belief that women would never give him their hearts completely. Somehow those nights with Lily and the way she had left had made him sit up and take a long hard look at himself and why he'd treated women indifferently. Not any more. Now the rare times he was intimate he hoped he was kind and caring, and made no promises for the future. The past couldn't be undone, but he'd learned and changed, hopefully for the better.

Lily was coming his way. Hell, she'd had him smiling at her with genuine care when they'd been dealing with Michelle's accident. He'd kept his smiles for his patient, though, wary of letting Lily sense he was comfortable and happy to be with her. Their old one-upmanship hadn't resurfaced yet, and hopefully wouldn't. She'd been friendly, at ease in a way he hadn't known with any woman. He liked that. His teeth had finally stopped grinding. He didn't want her even suspecting he'd had a tough time since they'd last seen each other, so, shoving all thoughts of the past and what might be if he had the guts to take risks down deep where no one would see them, he stepped forward, a light smile lifting his mouth. A genuine smile. For Lily. *Careful.* They had to work together. He had to remain neutral around her. The smile slipped.

'Max, shall we start again? How are you?'

'No need to start over.' They'd done well already. But he hadn't changed so much he'd couldn't resist teasing, because that'd keep her a little further away. 'Hello, Lady Lily. How are you?'

She stared at him for a moment, then knock him down if she didn't burst out laughing. 'Probably in better condition than your over-notched belt used to be. You doing okay?'

Ouch. Suppressing a grimace, he took the hand she held out, and shook it, taking longer this time until a flare of heat scorched his palm. Of course there was warmth when two people shook hands, unless they were in the middle of a blizzard, and there was no sign of that here. 'I'm good.' Fingers crossed. It was a regular habit now, hopefully keeping the medical voodoos at bay. And any others. 'We seem to have a knack of getting medical positions at the same place, don't we?'

Lily nodded, not sure where he was headed. She went for neutral. 'I'm looking forward to working alongside you again.' The words tasted false. Then she astonished herself. Was her reaction merely a habit from days gone by? Their aversion for each other had had tense periods but had mostly been a sense of having nothing in common, apart from great fun in bed and that uncanny sense that she had to get away from the attraction those nights had created.

She hadn't liked his easy come, easy go attitude towards women, yet she'd slept with him, had become one of those notches because she'd been desperate to feel attractive and possibly even lovable. It hadn't helped that she'd got in deep quickly. She hadn't understood why she'd gone with him. It had been like an invisible string winding her into Max's web and she'd entered not reluctantly but with a need to gain some self-worth. As if she'd chosen the most difficult man to impress to prove she had triumphed over her failings. Max had been exceptional had and made her feel very attractive. A blush filled her cheeks. She looked away, only to immediately bring her gaze back to him.

Max was staring down at her, a glint she remembered too well in those khaki eyes that said he doubted her sincerity. He spoke in that firm way he'd used with Michelle when she had been more concerned about who'd knocked her off the bus than what he'd been saying. 'Let's not get too carried away, Lily.' It sounded as though he was cautioning them both. Then he gave a small smile, and her caution began to slide. 'It's great to have you on board.' His gaze was steady and clear.

Maybe he meant it. That was something to think about. Again, he struck her as having changed a lot. He'd grown up, and was less jaunty. Although he was just as confident as ever, there were new depths to that confidence and, paradoxically, a few cracks. She was as sure as she had ten toes that something awful had befallen Max. Those eyes held a depth of perception she'd not known previously. A care for others that had nothing to do with what he might want, and no one changed like that over a cup of tea.

Withdrawing her hand from his surprisingly gentle touch a little late, her body pinged as though she'd put her finger into an electric socket. 'Thank you.' They would get on fine, and not just to nod at each other as they passed in the hall. 'I can't wait to get started.' This busy medical hub catered to specialities as well as general practice. She wanted to give it her all, carve out a niche that would go on long into the future and support her and her future child, if and when that happened. *Not now, Lily.* To silence those thoughts, she returned to the topic she'd raised earlier. 'I'm surprised to learn you're a GP, with sports medicine your focus.'

His eyes narrowed.

Quickly she said, 'I'm not having a poke at your choice, Max. I love general practice and understand anyone wanting to be a GP. It's just that you were so determined to become an orthopaedic surgeon.'

An abrupt nod. 'I was, but then I had a change of heart and decided I wanted to see more of my patients than a consultation, followed by a few minutes' talking in Theatre before surgery, a final handshake and goodbye.' His shoulders softened while his focus was entirely on her, making her feel warm and comfortable. Odd. Lovely. Just what she liked in a man. 'Too removed for my liking.'

'I totally agree. Then again, I'm starting over with getting to know patients, so I haven't a lot of experience of following through with families, watching them grow and age and get ill and come out the other end, which is why this is a long-term move.' One that would involve a family of two. Her and a child. No more shocks tipping her off track, no more feeling lost and let down, and in need of a kick up the backside to get up again.

Max's face tightened. 'I hear you worked in Singapore until recently.'

'I worked at an international family medical centre in the city. It's a fascinating country and I enjoyed getting out and about when I wasn't working. As for the street food, it was gorgeous.' She missed that as much as anything.

'What brought you back to Auckland?'

'It was time. I never intended setting up permanently overseas.' After Leo had packed his bags, there had been little reason to stay on. He'd know from what everyone here would have told him about her that she was single. It didn't matter. She wasn't looking for a partner, and Max was not the sort of man she was interested in for the father of her baby.

He may have changed, but she couldn't trust throwing a baby in the mix. It was very possible he'd want to take a part in raising a child that was his, not be content with only donating the DNA. He may treat women in an offhand manner, but there was a fierce determination in those veins to do the right thing that would force him to look out for his kin. 'I missed having my family close enough to see them whenever I want, and to support them when needed.'

'How's your niece? Josie, isn't it?'

He remembered her name after all this time? Incredible. It seemed there was more to Max than she'd ever acknowledged. Apparently he hadn't always been focused on himself. Though thinking back to a frightening time when Josie had rolled her wheelchair over a bank, knocking herself out, and had been flown to their ED, there hadn't been many in the department who hadn't known what had happened and to whom. Still, Max remembering more than just there'd been an accident was something else.

'She's done well. There's no holding her back and she's so strong mentally it can be scary.' She laughed. Then stopped. How strange, talking like this, when they'd never done so in the past. 'In fact, she'll be at the Let's Have Fun camp next week.'

Included in that was the camp she'd established for disabled children with her niece in mind. Josie had been born with spina bifida, and had never ceased to amaze Lily with her tenacity. All kids should have resilience, especially those with tough obstacles to get past. The next intake for disabled kids aged ten to fifteen was all about building resilience to the obstacles life threw their way.

'In Whangaparaoa? You know I'll be there?'

Lily nodded. 'Yes, I do.' Being on the board of the charity organisation running the camp, she knew exactly who signed on to help out every time. 'I heard.' From Devlin, who organised staff rotations. Devlin was her strongest backer, and was always on the lookout for medical people to take a turn helping out. Usually, little serious doctoring was required but it was good to have someone there to discuss aches and pains, and how injuries could be overcome without losing confidence. He understood her need for it not to be known she'd initially funded the whole complex. She had kept that under wraps and only her lawyer—being her best friend—her family and Devlin knew.

If anyone was determined it wouldn't take rocket science to find out she'd created the trust and paid for the land and buildings, but hopefully that would never become public knowledge. She couldn't bear to see her face in the news under a heading like 'Daughter of Wealthy Winemaker Sets Up Trust Fund for Disabled'.

Being asked if it was because of Josie would make her furious and distress her niece. It was bad enough going as her father's support to the wine awards, where her dress got more interest than her father's achievements. Her mother refused to go, not wanting to be talked about for her outfit or hairstyle either. But her dad deserved family backing so she put up with the accompanying nonsense.

'I'm looking forward to it. I've taken the whole week off,' Max was saying.

She didn't encourage anyone to sign up only for a day or two. The kids needed the same people working with them throughout the week, not swapping halfway and getting different ideas on how to manage with their personal problems. 'Hope you're packing your sports gear. You'll be needed to referee and coach as well as deal with sprains and aches.'

Max watched her intently, as though he sensed more behind her words.

She'd got carried away. He'd never been stupid. 'I've gone with Josie before, and I'm on the board.' She knew everything about the camp and what went on, right down to the latest repair job by the plumber for a leaking drain.

'Will you be there next week?'

Damn. Walked into that one. 'I'll be along the road at the family's beach house, available if Josie needs me.' An *aha* light went on in his eyes. 'Naturally I'll drop in on and off to see how she's doing.'

Mention of the beach house would've triggered that look. Her family was wealthy. There was nothing she could do about it, but he'd never got that, had always said

she had it easy when other junior doctors were studying
hard and slogging their guts out, trying to make ends
meet with huge loans to pay back once they qualified.
Little did he know she'd paid in other ways.

Once her father had started the vineyard as part of
the farm there was the annual grape harvest, where all
hands were needed, or meals to be cooked at all hours
for the workers as they slogged day and night to get the
grapes into the vats for her father to begin the wine-
making process.

There was more than one way of being tied to finan-
cial costs and responsibilities and family. Her mother
was the avoider in her family, always becoming chroni-
cally depressed when needed to help out, hence the reason Lily had fought hard to be strong and as good as her
brothers on the farm. 'I want a week chilling out before
starting here. After moving back to Auckland, settling
into my apartment and spending time with the family,
a bit of me time will work wonders on the exhaustion.'

Max's eyes were on her, giving her the once-over.
Making her shiver in anticipation. Of what? No idea. He
asked, 'Exhausted? Doesn't sound like the Lily Scott I
once knew.'

'I'm fine. Moving, packing, getting a new job, a bit of
stress, and, yes, I need time to relax. That's all.'

He stepped back. 'Good. Glad to hear it.' Then he was
looking at her again. 'What stress?'

Let it go. 'Decision-making. I wanted to find the right
GP position, one I could plan a future around.' Then
she'd gone and joined the place where Max worked. *Good
thinking, Lily. That was an amazing decision.* Except she
was starting to feel it might have been and not only for
the work. *It can't. Not at all.*

'Fair enough.' Max was nodding but there was still a question in his expression. Concern? For her?

It looked like it. The angst that had risen too quickly from past memories backed off. If Max could be kind to her, then she owed it to him to be equally pleasant, if not downright friendly. The past was exactly that, and tonight was the beginning of something else. Something she could make into a wonderful experience, and include Max as part of it. As medical colleagues.

A delicate shiver lifted the hairs on the back of her neck. There'd never been nights quite like the ones she'd had with this man, not before or since. She was now a free woman—who did not need a man trying to tell her how to run her life all the time, who didn't accept her for who she was. Would this Max be like that? She looked at him and couldn't find the answer.

'Here, you two. You're the only ones without a glass in your hands and we're about to have some speeches.' Devlin stood beside them, two glasses of red wine in his large hand.

'Tell me that's a Scott Merlot Cabernet,' Max laughed. 'It's my pick of NZ reds any day.'

'What else?' Devlin laughed back.

'Now I work here, you'll get a good deal on any you buy.' Lily smiled. 'That includes anyone who's interested.'

'You might live to regret that.' Max laughed again, a genuine sound with no questions behind it. 'Seriously, thank you.'

'Right, let's get this show happening before people start wandering off for a meal.' Devlin tapped his glass. 'Attention, everyone.' The room went quiet instantly.

'Sarah, come forward and let me wax lyrical about you for a moment.'

Sarah stepped up, a warm smile directed at Devlin. 'That'd be a first.'

As the laughter died down, Devlin continued. 'You've been a wonderful partner in the practice. Kept us all on our toes and created strong relationships with each of us and your patients.'

While he extolled Sarah's talents Lily looked around at the people she'd be soon start working with. Genuine fondness for Sarah showed on all the faces, and she could only hope she'd come close to replacing the GP everyone looked up to.

Drawing a deep breath, she took a sip of wine and felt a moment of insecurity. What if she wasn't up to the position? She'd done a good job in Singapore, and had come home with a superb reference, so why wouldn't she be up to the job? Devlin had head-hunted her when he'd heard from her father that she was returning home. He wouldn't have done that if she didn't have the skills and competence the partners required. But apprehension still knotted deep inside her, and she couldn't understand why. Staring into her glass as though the answer was there, she let her mind roam in search of a clue.

'Hey.' A quiet nudge from her left. Max.

The answer. It was Max shaking her up. Previously, he'd never have quietly brought her back to where she should be focused. He'd have made a joke about her lack of concentration. What else was going to be dissimilar? Working in a different environment from what she'd become used to? She thrived on challenges, but was she up to this one? And did she mean Max or the medical centre's expectations?

'Listen.' Max again, still in a quiet voice no one else would hear.

Glancing around, she found the room's focus on her, and lifted her shoulders into confident mode. Please let no one have seen that moment of worry.

'I'm happy to be handing over to you, Lily. You'll be excellent.' Sarah closed the gap between them and gave her a hug. 'I mean it,' she said quietly.

Lily returned her hug. They'd spent hours together going through their patients and sharing a couple of meals at the restaurant down the road. 'I'll do my absolute best.' To hell with the doubts looming in her head.

Devlin hadn't finished. 'Welcome, Lily. I'm so pleased you're joining us.' Then he raised his glass. 'Okay, let's have a toast to Sarah and Lily, and get on with enjoying the evening.'

As the noise level increased again, Lily stood back to watch, still shaken by her sudden concerns.

Then Max tapped his glass against hers. 'Feel like heading to Capacio's after this for a meal and catch-up?'

Max was asking her out for a meal. Not on a date surely? It would be rude to decline. But suddenly she'd had enough of getting her head around how he'd changed. He'd thrown her preconceived ideas and old memories to the wind and she was struggling. This Max seemed great, but was she rushing her acceptance that he'd changed so much? She needed space to remind herself she was not looking for a man to share her life, and especially not this one. She needed space to quieten the slow drumming in her veins, to douse the warmth filling her.

'Unfortunately I've got to see my sister-in-law, so I'll take a rain-check.' The moment the words were out she regretted them. Why not go along for some fun? It didn't

have to be about Max. But it was too late. There was no
way to undo the words without appearing rude. 'Next
time?'

'Sure.' By the look in his eyes there wouldn't be a
next time.

CHAPTER TWO

MAX ROUNDED THE corner and braked. An SUV with flashing hazard lights was parked in the centre of the secondary road leading to the Let's Have Fun camp at the end of Whangaparaoa Peninsula. Further on, what appeared to be at least one enormous pine tree blocked all hope of further travel.

'Damn. Should've stuck with the main road.' The lure of Lily had tempted him off track, and now he was stopped almost outside her beach house. If he'd been late before this, there was no hope now of making it to the camp before the kids were out and at it. But, then, he wasn't meant to oversee them twenty-four seven, and no one expected him before ten at the earliest.

Even with the windows closed the harsh noise of chainsaws in action was loud. Two people were cutting branches off the tree, while two older men were engrossed in moving the sawn lengths to the side of the road as they came free, ready to be loaded on a trailer attached to a nearby tractor.

Stepping out and tossing his jacket onto his seat, Max shut the car and headed over to the men. Might as well make himself useful. 'Need some help?'

One man straightened up from the growing stack of

timber, sweat streaming down his face despite the chilly winter air. 'Sure do, mate. We can't keep up with those two.'

Max looked over at the people wielding their machines and gaped. A pocket of heat expanded throughout his chilled body. Surely not? Then again, why not? Lily could still surprise him, which shouldn't be a surprise at all. She might be tall enough to lay her head on his shoulder but she was slim and that chainsaw wasn't made for cutting kindling. He couldn't stop looking at the apparition before him. Curvaceous in the right places, no biceps bulging from strain to fill out the sleeves of an oversized plaid work shirt unlike anything he'd seen her wear before.

'Here, put these on.' One man handed him leather work gloves and leaned close to be heard above the din. 'Saves getting splinters in your hands. Name's Archie, and this here's George. That guy over there's Cal. I'm thinking you know Lily by the stunned look on your dial.'

'I do. I'm Max.' He was still gaping at Lily as she attacked a large branch with skill. 'What's she doing, brandishing that lethal equipment?'

'Better not let her hear you say that or you'll likely lose a leg.' Archie laughed. 'She's darned handy with a chainsaw, believe me.'

As he watched, the branch hit the ground with a thud, and Lily straightened, pushed the safety goggles off her face and turned in his direction. And blinked. 'Max?' she mouthed, surprise registering in her steady gaze. A smile appeared on her face.

'Obviously me,' he answered silently, drinking in the sight of her face. How had he never realised how beautiful her smiles were? Because she'd hardly ever smiled at him. Just as well or his gut would have become permanently cramped. Nodding, he moved closer to the destruction to begin lifting logs to carry to the trailer. The muscles in his shoulders tightened as he sensed her watching him. And tightened some more when he realised she'd left her position to come across.

'When did the trees come down?' he asked to prevent saying what was really dominating his mind.

'About five this morning. We waited for sunrise before getting stuck in. How did you manage to come this way? There's supposed to be a warning sign up at the turnoff.' Her breathing was even, despite what that chain-saw must weigh.

'Afraid not. Unless I missed it.' Anything was possible. He'd been dreaming about catching up with Lily again, and fighting the excitement that had brought on. She'd disappointed him when she'd turned down his offer to go for a meal together last Thursday. Once he'd have been irked, but not any more. It seemed those feelings had been replaced with a need to really know Lily, to get on with *her* emotions. Emotions best avoided but already impossible to ignore.

Warmth had flooded him whenever he'd thought about her over the last few days. So had the warning that he wasn't looking for love, even if he wanted it. He had no intention of hurting a woman emotionally to meet his own ends. Hell. Emotion here, there and everywhere. It hadn't used to be in his vocabulary. He blamed Lily. He smiled. Yeah, of course he did.

She smiled back. 'You're out early. Another hour and you'd have got through, no bother.'

'This will be cleared in an hour?' An exaggeration surely?

'We've already cleared another, admittedly smaller

tree further along.' She grinned. 'I'd better get back to
it. Are you okay doing this in those clothes? The pine's
covered in sap. There are overalls in the garage behind
the house if you want.' Her head dipped in the direction
of the stained timber, low-build home with picture windows from end to end and glossy-leafed shrubs placed
strategically around the lawn. Beautiful in its simplicity.

Max sighed. The property was a perfect match for
Lily. 'I've jeans and an old shirt in the car. They'll do.' He
hadn't brought good clothes for the week, preferring casual ones as it often helped kids relax when they wanted
to talk about their problems. He flicked the boot catch
and undid the buckle of his belt—see, no notches, Lily—
and smiled to himself as she hurried back to the fallen
trees. Very prudish looking when she was anything but.
In bed at least. He took a deep intake of air, forced it out.

Those nights together had been a revelation. The ar-
gumentative woman had flipped a switch and been hot
and exciting, giving so much of herself he'd had to wonder if there were two Lilys. Then a third had come to
light afterwards when she had walked away from him
and kept him at a distance with her sharp retorts to anything he'd said.

It had been a wake-up call, forcing him to stop and
wonder what the hell he had been playing at. Finding he
wasn't immune to her, that his heart might want to take
a second look had shocked him silly. Until Lily, playing the field and remaining single had been the only
way to go for him. After that, other women's reactions
towards his easy come, easy go attitude had made him
realise he'd been selfish. He'd got that from his mother,
who'd said girls were easier to raise than boys and that

Max would need his father to keep him on track while he was growing up.

First Lily and then cancer had finally taught him how important kindness and honesty were. All the while Lily had continued niggling away at him, lighting a spark in his body, long after she'd finished working at the department to head offshore. A spark that had been relit across the road outside the medical centre last week.

He'd been his father's son: tough. His mother had been right about that, but it wasn't a strength he was proud of once he'd understood he'd hurt people because of it. And he did love his dad. When he'd been young, his father had dreamed of becoming a doctor but his family had been dirt poor so the day he'd turned fifteen he had left school to find a job. At first Max had wanted to study medicine for his father, but even before he'd started training he'd known there was no other career for him. He'd found a side to himself that involved caring for people without giving away his heart.

The medical scene had absorbed him, made him happy for the first time. He'd found his niche. Only when he'd been ill had his mother admitted being proud of him. Even his father, in his gruff way, had said so. That moment had lifted the cloud that had sat on his heart all his life. *Dad was proud of him.* And his mother.

The females in his family hadn't abandoned him entirely when he'd been young. He'd spent time with them as they'd lived only three streets away, and his step-dad had accepted him as part of his family. But he'd been determined to put on a brave face like his father had done, and not show his hurt over being left behind.

Lily had been the one exception in his life—after the fact. At first she had been no different from any other date, but soon she could have had him eating out of her hand for more of her gentleness and that off-the-scale lovemaking. Yes, lovemaking, the first and only time he'd called sex anything other than sex. For good reason. Sex didn't involve his heart. Lily had knocked on it.

It had been a game-changer. One that had had him raising the barriers to keep her out of his mind and soul. Even now he didn't understand why. More importantly, why had Lily made him feel that when they hadn't been close? He'd sometimes wondered if she too felt abandoned in some way and that he might hold some answers for her needs. Then he'd decide he was being crazy. Lily would never want him other than in the sack. It was payback for the women he'd treated the same over the years. But she'd remained an itch ever since.

The chainsaws roared to life, the sharp sound of blades cutting through wet wood filling the air. Lily and her offsider were careful, keeping distance between themselves and continually checking to see where everyone was. The equipment wasn't something to argue with.

A vivid, gruesome picture came to Max's mind from his first year as an intern in an emergency room. He shuddered. A woodsman working in a pine forest had slipped while felling a tree and the result had not been good, the only thing saving the man from bleeding out being the other woodsmen working the same area with basic first-aid training to their credit. But the real mess had been handed over to Max and his colleagues at the hospital. They'd saved the guy's leg and he'd gone back to work in the forests as soon as he'd been able, saying it couldn't happen twice. Max wasn't so sure. Imagine if anything like that happened to Lily. No, he did not want to conjure up that hideous image. Lily handled her saw with all the confidence she'd use with a dessert spoon, only she was super-vigilant.

'She knows what she's doing.' Archie spoke beside him.

Max shuddered again. 'I'm sure she does, but it's nerve-racking to watch.'

'Learned off her old man and those brothers she pretends are as weak as kittens.' Archie chuckled. 'No one was ever going to hold Lily back. Only had to say bet she couldn't do something and she'd be off to prove them wrong.'

'There's a woman I recognise. Though she never tried to prove anyone wrong in the medical world, only determined not to make mistakes.' Just like him. They'd been more similar than he'd realised. Wonder what else they had in common he didn't know about?

'You've worked with her?'

'While we were training.'

Why hadn't he spent time getting to know her better, instead of overreacting to her confident manner, when she had made it abundantly clear she wanted nothing more to do with him? He'd acted as per normal—distant—but what if he'd wooed her with some finesse? She'd got her own back by popping into his head on and off, except in the bleakest days of his treatment, giving him a nagging sense of a missed opportunity for something wonderful. He'd never know what that was about. Unless... Unless nothing. That'd mean letting her in to get behind the shield keeping his heart safe. How was he going to avoid that *and* get to know her better?

When both chainsaws finally stopped, the silence was overwhelming. Lily swiped her hands on her overalls, highlighting her shapely hips. Max swallowed a groan, squashed the stab of longing hitting him.

'We're done,' Lily called. 'Let's haul the last of this clear of the road and go have a coffee, everyone.'

'Best thing I've heard all morning.' He should head away and find the camp, not hang out with Lily and her old cronies, except the idea of staying on for a bit warmed him. Max lifted a log up onto his shoulder and headed for the trailer.

Looking around, he breathed in the cold air tightening his skin and absorbed the sound of waves crashing onto the shore beyond the road. The air was heavy with salt and above gulls shrieked as they dived and soared while they patrolled the beach. Calm overtook Max. This was a great location for a week away from the madness that was the medical hub. No wonder Lily had come here before starting work.

'I can even run to bacon and eggs if you're lucky, guys.' Lily was speaking to them all but smiling directly at him.

He could return her refusal to join him the other night, show her he wasn't moved by her reappearing in his life, but it wasn't in him to say no.

She'd stung his pride when he'd thought they'd been getting on well, yet there was a warmth tucking around him he hadn't known for a long time, and he was damned if he could shuck it off. It felt good, right, and he wanted more. *Careful.* Damn, but he was tired of being careful. Again, it was Lily upsetting his determination to remain single, to cruise through life without involving, and thereby hurting, someone else. Lily. Gulp. *Lily?* Being careful was so ingrained in him, yet within days—in a blink—of catching sight of Lily again and 'careful' was disappearing from his vocabulary. Dangerous. For her. For him.

The month of isolation to prevent catching anyone's germs when his system had had no resistance due to the new treatment. The weeks after chemo when he hadn't wanted anyone to see him looking so despondent—not to mention bald, though that had been quite funny when the cause didn't tear him apart.

Now that gnawing fear of the cancer returning made him leery of getting involved with someone and having to watch them cope, to pick up the pieces afterwards if the worst happened, of breaking their heart along with his. It wasn't the greatest place to be, keeping a space between himself and everyone else, especially someone who could make all the difference if she was prepared to accept he didn't have a guaranteed future.

Lighten up. You've only just caught up with Lily and you're thinking all this? Get real. Get practical. 'Got mushrooms to go with that?'

One well-styled eyebrow rose. 'The man wants it all.'

Did he ever. Max shrugged, trying to keep that to himself. 'Tomatoes?'

'Thought you knew this woman,' Archie grunted as he dragged a log the length of his body off the road.

'Here, let me take that.' Max leapt after him and took the heavy load from the old man. 'Can't have you falling on your face because Lily didn't cut that in two.'

'My fault, eh? Let me take the other end, Max.' She took hold of the log and headed for the trailer, leaving Max no choice but to follow or drop the wood on his toes.

'It wasn't a challenge,' he muttered, thinking how Archie had said she always took those on.

'No, it's about saving Archie's face. And heart,' she

added quietly as they set their load on the trailer. 'He's got arrhythmia.'

'Which explains the heavy breathing.' He'd wanted to ask Archie about that but had got the evil eye when he'd opened his mouth. 'Tough old guy, isn't he?'

'Yes, which is better than sitting in his rocking chair all day.'

'Can't do that any more,' Archie butted in. 'No newspapers these days.'

'What's wrong with the internet?' Max asked cheekily.

'You have to ask? I remember when we had party lines on our phones. Phones that were stuck to the wall and you couldn't wander around the place yabbering your head off in front of everyone.'

'You've got me on that one.' Max shook his head. 'There's something to be said for modern technology and getting medical test results when they're done, not the next day in the mail. Not to mention keeping in touch with friends when you can't see them.'

Like in hospital in the middle of the night when fear of the future was tracking around your head and there was no way to stop it without talking to someone who knew you.

George had joined them. 'You can keep track of your woman all the time.'

If he had one he'd be in touch, and available, not keeping tabs on her. 'Never. I still believe in privacy.' His gaze went to the tidy shoulders of the woman in front of him. She was a private person. Once he'd mistakenly believed it was snobbery because she didn't blab about herself as some other women did. Watching her work the room during the party the other night, he'd realised he'd got that wrong.

'Ten minutes and we're finished here.' Lily reached for a smaller chunk of pine.

Max picked up a piece. 'I can smell the bacon already.'

'George, Archie, you going to join us?' Lily asked hopefully. 'Cal?'

'Thanks, but I'd better get home and see why Enid hasn't been over with a cuppa like she promised. Probably engrossed in some book and forgotten all about us.' Archie added his load to the trailer. 'There's a fair whack of fire wood here.'

'I'll cut it up over the next few days and bring it across.' Lily nodded.

'You'll split the large rounds?' Max asked. Lily might be tough but she wasn't built like one of those axemen in the wood-chopping contests.

'If there's no one else to do it, I'll cheat and use the chainsaw. It does make a mess but I'm not into body building.'

'Glad to hear it.' Her figure couldn't be faulted. She certainly didn't need muscles on top of muscles filling the sleeves of her shirts. 'You might lose a toe or two.'

'Careful,' Cal growled. 'That's a challenge to Lily.'

He laughed. 'Lily, ignore me.'

'I am.' Her smile was wide and full of fun.

And hit him where he didn't want to be hit. In his heart. He gasped, looked away. Not his heart. More likely in that roped-down centre that kept him on the straight and narrow leading into the future, fuelled by a need to concentrate on those he could help through medicine and not ask for anything back. But he didn't want to be ignored by Lily. Not by anybody. But especially not Lily. Even in jest.

* * *

'Park your car in the driveway, out of the way,' Lily told Max, before climbing onto the tractor and flicking on the engine, drowning out his reply. He'd surprised her by leaping in to help when he'd realised what they were doing. Her family had taught her that—jump in and help, no questions asked. Her back complained when she looked over her shoulder while backing her load around. Tomorrow all her body would ache from the exertion of cutting those trees. The chainsaw was made for heavy work, not weekenders wanting to tidy their yard, and her arms would know about it for days to come, but right now she felt alive and buzzing.

Being physical always hyped her up. *Max hypes you up.* There was no denying that. Strange how any time he was around her blood hummed and hope started rearing its head. But they weren't going to get closer. They couldn't. A sigh trickled over her lips. She wasn't going there. There were only so many knocks a girl could take.

The men strode up the drive, tugging gloves off their hands and pausing to wait for Max to park and step out of his car.

Lily watched him straighten, roll those broad shoulders and look around until he found her and smiled. Sent the blood racing through her veins. Focusing on the job on hand and not Max, she positioned the trailer under the trees for some shelter from any precipitation in the coming days. The forecast was for scattered showers, but around here everyone knew to be prepared for rain any time.

Then, breathing deeply, she feigned nonchalance and

strolled to the back door, calling out, 'I'm putting the kettle on. Archie, try to convince Enid to join us.'

'I'll sling her over my shoulder and bring her across.' Archie headed for the stile over the fence between their properties.

As he unlaced his shoes on the back step, Max asked, 'Can I give you a hand with breakfast?'

Used to getting on with things by herself, Lily hesitated. Max sounded genuine in his offer. This relaxed feeling between them felt right. 'Absolutely. Come on in, guys, and make yourselves comfortable. Bathroom's along there.' She pointed to the hallway on the right for Max's benefit. 'Or there's a hand basin in the laundry.'

Tossing her jacket on a peg inside the back door, she headed to the kitchen. Strong coffee was what she needed more than anything. And for Max to change his mind and get on the road to the camp so she could breathe again. The moment she'd seen him standing by his car her heartbeat had gone haywire and still wasn't settling.

He'd taken the long way round to the camp and had ended up pretty much at her front door. At the family beach-house door, if she was nit-picking. Had he deliberately set out to find her? If so, she wasn't sure how that made her feel.

The restlessness that had gripped her since Leo had left, taking her dream of a family with him, hadn't gone away completely. A need to settle in her own home and have a great job had bought her apartment and got the job of a lifetime, but there was still a hole in her life. Love. A man and a family. After her relationship failures she struggled with getting out there to find a man who might be the love of her life, but having a baby was still as clear as ever.

She'd researched surrogacy, had had an initial consultation at the fertility clinic in Remuera. The next step was as high as a mountain.

Having a baby would be amazing, life-altering in the best way imaginable. Her heart was full of love to give. It was choosing a father that gave her concern. Using a sperm bank was too impersonal for something so special and close. Babies should come not only into love but from love. She'd prefer a man she knew and admired to volunteer, not a number from the fertility bank. It might be a long wait to sort this out, but there was no rush. She wanted to settle into her job first anyway.

A long, sad sigh filled the kitchen. Hers. Startled, she glanced around, relieved to find herself alone. It was time to focus on feeding the men then getting on with the day, including catching up with Josie.

'Where can I start?' Max stepped into the light and airy kitchen dining space and instantly the room felt smaller.

And warmer. Lily hugged herself before turning around. 'Knowing these men, a hot drink will be essential first. You'll find mugs in that cupboard, tea, etcetera over on that shelf.' Clicking the gas on to heat the elements, she removed pans from a drawer under the bench and went to the fridge for eggs and bacon.

'I'll set the table.' George was already opening the cutlery drawer.

Lily loved these men. They'd been a part of her summer holidays most of her life; their children friends to catch up with in summer when everyone had come for Christmas and New Year and to recharge their batteries. 'Cal, this is Max Bryant, a GP and sports doctor at the medical centre I'm starting at next week.'

Max shook the man's hand. 'I've come out to attend the camp and help any poor kid that can't find someone better.'

'Guess you'll have time to split that wood, then.' Cal chuckled.

'Probably.' Max grinned. Then got serious. 'From what I hear, the kids are already resilient and determined to have a lot of fun doing all the activities. I've been told there'll be a few pulled muscles and aches from overdoing some of the challenges, but otherwise nothing major.'

'Don't speak too soon,' Lily warned, ducking around Max in the small space, focused on not bumping into that hot body. 'We've already had a broken leg this year at an earlier camp. An eight-year-old girl with one leg climbed a tree. All good, and to be encouraged to a point, but in this case the branch she was on broke.'

'Along with said leg.' Max shook his head. 'Kids, eh?'

'Exactly. We take a lot of precautions, but we also want them to have fun doing the things their counterparts do, like climb trees and leap over fences and fall in the duck pond. It's normal, and that's what they need more than anything. To be normal.' Lily stopped. 'Sorry, that sounds like I'm lecturing, and I didn't mean to.'

Max nodded. 'It's fine. I get it. It's how you'd have grown up on the farm and how I was in town, always at some park or beach, running riot.' As he added boiling water to the coffee plunger, he said, 'You keep saying "we" when referring to the camp. What's your role in the place?'

That's what happened when she relaxed—she gave too much away. 'Being on the board of directors, I tend to keep an eye on everything.'

'Even when you were living overseas?'

Why had George and Cal chosen this moment to stop talking to each other? She couldn't divert Max to whatever they'd been discussing, though knowing those two it would be about their backaches or stiff knees so wouldn't have been much help. 'I oversaw the set-up and haven't stepped aside since.' The site had been chosen for the rundown motel that stood in the middle of a large area of flat land leading to the beach. An extensive makeover, along with building further accommodation buildings, adding a communal kitchen, dining room and an activities hall had completed the camp. She'd paid for it all.

'Anything to do with Josie?'

He didn't miss a thing.

'Some. She's been luckier than most kids in her situation. Growing up on the farm with my brother for her dad meant she wasn't held back, instead encouraged to get out and do the chores and ride the pony, dig a posthole. I saw what other kids could gain from sampling something similar.'

'It wouldn't only be her dad egging her on. Her aunt's never been one to sit back and feel sorry for herself.'

You don't know a thing, Max. Or nothing that matters. 'I've been known to nudge her along at times.'

Cal roared with laughter. 'Like making Josie fill the trailer with sand for the pétanque court around the side of the house.'

'And did she do a great job?' Lily grinned. She hadn't bullied Josie at all, instead she'd been told she was mean for not letting Josie do the job in the first place.

'She did, and is still proud of herself.'

'Lily, will you come and see Enid?' Archie burst into the kitchen, looking rattled.

'What's up?' Lily moved up to him.

'She's speaking funny and can't move her leg and arm on one side.'

Enid never had a sick day, and adored getting out and about in the garden when she wasn't reading the stack of books by her bedside. 'I'll grab my bag.'

Max flicked off the gas and put aside the pans that had been heating. 'Archie, lead the way while Lily gets her gear.'

'I can't make head or tail of what she's saying.'

Lily bit her lip. *Sounds like a stroke.*

Max's eyes met Lily's over Archie's head, acknowledgement coming her way. They were on the same page.

She dashed to her bedroom for the medical kit and her cellphone.

'We'll get out of the way,' George said.

One look at Enid a few minutes later and Lily was tapping her phone. The left side of her face was contorted and while her lips were moving her speech was gibberish. 'I'm calling the rescue helicopter.'

Max was kneeling by the bed, talking quietly. 'Enid, I'm Max, a doctor and a friend of Lily's. Archie says you were reading when he went out to help with the fallen trees this morning.'

Enid's right eye widened briefly.

'That's a yes?'

Another slight movement in the eyelid.

'How long do you think you've been lying here like this? One hour?'

No movement.

'More?'

No movement.

'That might be good,' Lily muttered. Enid might be in the golden hour. Or she could've been like this for a lot longer. They'd been working on those trees for at least three hours.

'Emergency service. Do you require the ambulance, police or fire service?'

'Ambulance,' Lily answered briskly.

Max asked, 'Archie, what time did you head outside to help Lily and the men?'

'I think it was about six but I can't be sure. What's wrong with Enid? She can hear you. Sort of answers you.'

'It was near six,' Lily said.

'Ambulance service. Please tell me the nature of your call.'

'I'm Lily Scott, a GP. We're on the Whangaparaoa Peninsula and I have a woman who appears to have had a stroke. There's a possibility we're in the golden hour so I suggest sending the rescue helicopter.'

'I need some details, Dr Scott. Bear with me for a moment.'

'There're two doctors here.' It was irritating to go through this when she was a doctor, but she understood the reasons behind the system. Answering the questions quickly and getting information from Max, Lily waited while the woman at the other end put her on hold.

'Archie.' Max looked up at the man. 'We think Enid's had a stroke. Can you tell me if she's got any medical conditions and if she takes any medications?'

'What? A stroke? No, not that. Enid, look at me, tell me you're all right.' He was shaking and gasping for air.

Lily stepped around the bed and wrapped an arm around his shoulders. 'Archie, deep breath in. Let it out. That's it. We're getting Enid urgent help now. Max is checking everything. She's in good hands. I want you to sit down by the bed and hold Enid's other hand. Concentrate on breathing properly. You're no help to her if you get wound up.' She pulled the chair from the dressing table across and gently pushed Bill onto it just as the emergency dispatcher came back on the line.

'Dr Scott, the rescue helicopter is on the way. Is there somewhere safe to land close by?'

'There's an expansive grassed area in front of the houses in this bay. I'll arrange for neighbours to be out there to wave when the helicopter gets here, and to keep the area clear of vehicles and people. There're some wind gusts after last night's storm from the south east.'

'I'll pass on the information. Since Enid has doctors in attendance I won't keep you on the line, but call back if there're any concerns.'

'Just get that rescue team here fast.' She hung up, knowing she hadn't needed to say that, but had been unable to stop herself. This was personal. She and Max were doing all they could but Enid needed to be in hospital. 'Helicopter's on the way, Archie. Max, I need to get George and Cal to head to the reserve and keep it clear.'

'Of course. It's a long shot but you haven't got breathing equipment in the house, by any chance?' Max asked.

She shook her head. 'Sorry.'

That bad, eh? Her heart stuttered for Archie and Enid. *Hang in there, Enid. Help's on its way.*

'I'll be back as quickly as possible.' Max had it covered, but heading outside when this was going on went against all she'd trained for, even though organising people to make it easier for the chopper to land was helping just as much.

'I could do that if you want to stay here,' Max offered.

He understood her need to be there for her neighbours. 'Thank you, but I know where I'm going and I'll be back fast.' She headed outside, leaping the fence and dashing through a back yard to get to George's house. 'George, where are you? We need help.'

As soon as George grasped what she was saying, he insisted on organising everything and sent her back to Enid. She left immediately, needing to be on the spot, not away from Enid and Archie. And Max. 'Really?' she gasped, as she raced through the back yard. Yes, really. This Max was stronger in a kind, caring way.

'How's Enid?' Lily asked the moment she stepped into the bedroom, and immediately wished she'd kept her mouth shut. She knew there'd be no change, definitely not for the better and probably not at all.

'I shouldn't have gone out to shift those trees.' Archie was stricken.

Lily went to hug him. There was nothing she could say. It was natural to blame himself, even when he couldn't have known Enid was in trouble.

Max gave her a tight smile as he continued monitoring Enid's heart and breathing, noting everything down. An eternity seemed to pass before the thumping of helicopter rotors came from directly above the house.

As the machine moved towards the reserve and hovered, Lily was holding her breath, begging them in her mind to hurry while understanding the need for caution. The paramedics would be here as soon as they could. Which was never fast enough. She hugged Archie again, her eyes fixed on Enid, wondering how much she understood.

Suddenly the room was crowded with paramedics and their equipment. Lily and Max were redundant. Outside a stretcher stood ready for loading Enid. Max said, 'It's hard to hand over, isn't it? Even when the paramedics are better equipped, it goes against all I feel about help-ing people.'

'It's difficult,' she agreed.

Max looked at her. 'I'm sorry about your friends.'

She teared up. Slashing her hand across her face, she muttered, 'I know people will say Enid's in her early seventies, it was to be expected something would hap-pen one day. But I've known these two over half my life and Enid still gets around, doing the garden and cook-ing and going to group meetings.' Sniff. 'Am I writing her off already?'

A firm hand settled on her shoulder, pulled her close to that safe chest. 'That's no small stroke she's suffered but, as we both know, there's no telling for sure what's ahead until all the tests have been completed.'

Max was only saying what she knew, but it helped somehow. As did the warmth from his body pervad-ing her senses and taking away the loneliness that had started coming over her. 'Thanks.' She wasn't in a hurry to move away.

One of the paramedics appeared to take the stretcher inside.

'Need a hand?' Max stepped back, leaving her chilled.

'That'd be great. Two of us can carry this and some-one take our gear.'

'Where will you take Enid?' Lily asked as she fol-lowed them.

'North Shore General Hospital. Will someone be driv-ing the husband down?'

'I will.' It was a no-brainer.

Except in the end George and Cal insisted on taking him. 'We're his mates, we go through everything to-gether,' George pointed out.

'I get it,' she agreed. Who else would Archie want in this situation, except those nearest and dearest to him? 'Keep me posted.'

As the chopper rose from the reserve, Lily started back to the beach house. 'I really need that coffee.'

'Mind if I join you?' Max asked.

'I expected you to,' she replied. 'Still on for breakfast?' Her appetite was returning. No surprise there.

'You have to ask?' He smiled.

A smile that touched her, and had her wondering about the warmth returning throughout her. Her wariness was backing off. It wasn't as though they'd have another fling. Definitely not. 'That's a yes, then.' Her next sigh was crisper. Her body was tightening. Good looking, in great physical shape, Max had a way of looking at her that made her toes curl, but they were not getting hooked up again. He'd only hurt her in the end, and anyway she wasn't about to change her mind and start testing the dating waters. Whatever happened, she couldn't get involved with Max.

CHAPTER THREE

MAX GRIMACED. 'MICHELLE'S doing everything possible for her injuries, and more, but the mind games aren't helping.'

'That's to be expected,' Lily said.

'Yes, but she hasn't got this far with her career by feeling sorry for herself.' Lily didn't know Michelle yet. 'There've been times when she's had to toughen up and face reality, whether it was not being chosen for the team earlier or making a mess of a game plan during a match. She works hard, has gone without a social life to be out there keeping up peak fitness levels. Her medical records show a couple of instances when she's overdone things, but there's no mention of feeling down.'

'She might've kept that to herself.' Lily looked at him with determination. 'I've got an idea.'

'Go on,' he answered slowly, already with an inkling of where this was headed, and not sure if it was right for his patient. Their patient, he reminded himself.

'We could suggest she comes to the camp for a day or two to help the kids find their confidence in areas they're uncertain about. Whether it's a different sport or a hobby they might want to learn, she could encourage them with the strength she's used to become successful in netball.'

'You think that would work when she's feeling flat? She might pass on negative thoughts, not encouraging ones.' As he saw Lily's eyes light up, he shrugged, denying the laughter that wanted to escape at her persistence. That was Lily to a T. 'That's what you'd put to her when, in fact, you think the children might help her get her mojo back.'

Lily smiled, and went back to flipping bacon. 'Just a thought. Could work for everyone.'

'It might.' Max weighed the benefits and the negatives, not that he could think of anything against the idea other than Michelle getting more frustrated than ever. Except he didn't think she would. Once she accepted what had happened and began moving forward she'd start looking around to see what her next step was. No wonder he loved his job. He helped people through bad times.

'The kids are usually full of enthusiasm and when the going gets tough they either dig deep or turn for help. That's where she could benefit them, and in turn get something back, watching kids facing long-term difficulties and not losing hope.'

'We'll both talk to her,' Max decided. 'You should put the proposal to her as you're a part of the camp's hierarchy.' Lily started to shake her head. 'Wait. You're new to her medical life and she likes you so she'll listen.'

'You're saying she wouldn't take any notice if you outlined the idea?' The doubt in her voice was strong. 'Come on.'

Lily understood him well. It was unbelievable, and wonderful. He could get too comfortable with this. 'She'd listen, but she might also look at the idea from every way, trying to find what's behind it, whereas coming from you it will be new and intriguing. I've had a lot to do with Michelle's sports side of things in the past year and I think I understand her.' The toaster popped and he placed the toast onto a plate on the table, put two more slices of bread in to toast. 'Anyway, it was your idea.'

'Fine. We'll call her after breakfast and see how she reacts. You'll be better able to read her. If you don't mind,' she added a little tersely.

'Let's get step one out of the way first.' He already knew Michelle would be take on the challenge. 'That being breakfast,' he added, trying to put aside the irritation he felt about Lily's way of seeing straight through him. She did it too easily. Now he had to focus on saving his heart, and while Lily wouldn't want his, he should be safe, but every time he saw her or heard that soft lilting voice, doubt rolled over him, making him wonder if he was more than happy she was back in his life.

How was it he could tell patients to move on to get over what'd devastated them, and not do the same for himself? Other cancer survivors said eventually a lot of the dread backed off and there'd come a time when he'd forget some of the raw fear that had smothered him. It was true to an extent, but he had a way to go.

'You burning that toast?' A sharp nudge in his side stopped his worries head on, replacing them with need for Lily and her soft, warm body.

Banging the cancel button, he snatched the blackened slices and dumped them in a small bucket labelled chook food. 'I'll try again.'

'Where were you?' Lily asked.

'You don't want to know.' Except she might. He didn't want to tell her about his doubts and needs. Though the day would come when he would have to mention the cancer as most of the doctors at the centre knew and he'd prefer Lily to find out from him.

He liked to underline how well he was and how lucky to be able to get on with his life. In other words, he didn't want people feeling sorry for him. He hated it when anyone's face filled with pity. If Lily reacted that way, he'd feel let down. Pity when they'd once taken no prisoners with each other would hurt, make him feel a little unloved, like when his mother had left him. Which was way over the top. The Lily of old would have been more likely to make a sharp retort about moving on and let the subject drop. He wasn't sure about her now.

'Maybe I do.' She served up the bacon and eggs.

He should tell her, get it done with. It wasn't a big deal. He'd been ill, had come out the other side, and was creating a lifestyle and future he was comfortable with, if he ignored his longing for love and family. If he ignored the doubts he couldn't quite get past about the future. Sitting down at the table, he reached for the plate of bacon and eggs. Suddenly he needed to be heading to the camp, away from Lily with all the confusion she brought on, and an intense physical longing that was like an elbow in the ribs.

'Right.'

The only sound was cutlery on plates. The silence between them reminded Max of the post-fling days when they'd spoken only when necessary. But if he tried too hard to get on-side with her, he'd be letting Lily in closer than ever, and that could not happen. He was vulnerable to her. Accepting that, he'd take it on the chin and do his best to ignore the ache in his gut. As soon as he'd rinsed the dishes and placed them in the dishwasher he looked up and found Michelle's number. 'Ready?'

'Yes.'

They listened to the ringing and finally a subdued Michelle answered. 'Hi, Max.'

'Hello. I've got Lily Scott with me and we're on speaker phone. That okay?'

'I suppose.'

Glancing at Lily, he raised one eyebrow.

She nodded back, looking concerned but determined. 'Michelle, I've got an idea to put to you.' She wasn't wasting any time.

Max got in quickly, before their patient could veto things without knowing what this was about. 'Hear Lily out before you make a decision.'

'You're sounding serious.'

'We are. You need to focus on getting well, and I believe Lily's idea will go some way to helping achieve that.'

'I'm all ears.' She sounded anything but.

'Michelle, have you heard of the Let's Have Fun camp for disabled children?'

'Isn't that where Max is working this week? He said something about being away if I needed medical attention.'

'Yes. It's situated on the Whangaparaoa Peninsula and we hold regular camps for kids from around New Zealand. A group aged between ten and fifteen moved in this morning for the coming week. They'll play sports and do other activities to stretch their minds and build confidence.' Lily paused, glanced at him.

He mouthed, 'Go on.'

'I thought that since you're free this week you might like to help out, encourage kids who are struggling. You know what to say or do, and I can't think of a better inspiration for these children than someone who's done so well in her sports career.'

'You're forgetting I can't move without crutches and that I'm no longer going to England with the netball team.'

'Not at all. Those are the reasons I believe you're in a strong position to show that accidents happen and yet you still get up and keep on moving.'

Silence.

Max held his breath. He wanted to add his bit, throw in some encouragement, but Lily had it under control.

Lily stared at the phone as though willing Michelle to give the right answer, her fingers crossed on both hands.

Finally the sound of a long indrawn breath reached them. 'Max? What do you think?'

Lily fixed her eyes on him, daring him to let Michelle off the hook.

'It's an opportunity to help these kids.' Might as well push all the buttons. 'Is there someone who could drive you out here? You can stay a day or all week. Your call.'

'Mum would give me a lift, if I wanted to come.'

'Why wouldn't you?' Lily asked.

Straight for the jugular. Max smiled. There was no backing down when Lily wanted something badly enough. Could she ever be that determined about him? What did she think about him these days?

'I'm not sure I have anything to offer those kids. They're far more used to their situations than I'll ever be,' Michelle came back sharply.

'Maybe, but there're times when they're overwhelmed and need encouragement, and to get that from someone who's working on getting through her own change of circumstances has to be of benefit.' Lily drew a breath.

'My niece has spina bifida and I've watched her achieve so much. She's confident and hates the word "can't" but still has moments of a complete lack of self-reliance.'

Don't we all? Max wondered. His illness had chipped away at his confidence for the future, even when the facts said he was probably better off than others already. The five-year sign-off couldn't come soon enough and yet would he ever be able to let go the fear of cancer returning? Or was this how he'd always be, overreacting to stomach cramps or a headache? 'Give the idea some serious thought, Michelle. I'll call you back later this morning.'

Lily glared at him. That was not how she wanted to approach this. But Michelle always thought things through before acting, never jumped in without looking.

'I'll be there tomorrow morning, bright and early. If I decide to stay over, is there a room I can have?'

Lily gaped at him, shaking her head. Then she relaxed, smiled softly as though he'd given her a present, and answered Michelle. 'The camp's full as some parents are staying too, but we'll find you somewhere to doss down.'

'I've brought the camp up on screen. It looks amazing. Are you staying there, Lily?'

'I'm staying a kilometre away, and will be dropping in often. My niece's attending and I like spending time with her.'

'Cool. Then I guess I'll see you both tomorrow. Bye.'

Max and Lily stared at each other. 'Did that really happen?' he asked.

Lily burst out laughing. 'I think so.' She pumped her fist, then high-fived him. Even briefly her hand felt good against his. 'I can't quite believe it. Thought we'd lost her when you told her to think about it.' Lily crossed to fill the kettle. 'Another coffee?'

He'd love one. And to spend more time with Lily. Especially when she was smiling. Those smiles touched a place inside he'd kept isolated for a long time. Since the day his mother and sister had left. Dangerous. Tempting. Frightening. He stood. 'No, thanks. I'll get along to the camp and make myself known. Hopefully no one will need my medical skills, and require only encouragement and gentle coaxing to push themselves.'

Her smile vanished. 'No problem.'

There was. He stood slowly, reluctant to leave. But his heart was expanding, warming him, softening his ability to remain solitary. His fingers itched with need for her. His foot rose. He shoved it down hard on the tiles. He might feel like getting that close, but there was a lot to consider. Glancing across to the doorway, he had to trust his feet to get him out of there without upsetting Lily. Or himself. Pulling on his don't-mess-with-me face when he was in a right state internally, he said, 'Let me know when you hear how Enid is, will you?'

'Of course.' Lily nodded. 'I'll see you later at the camp.'

Outside goose-bumps rose on his arms as the chilly air struck his feverish skin. Time to get on with what he'd come up here to do, and that wasn't falling for Lily.

'Enid had a stroke.' Archie sounded defeated.

'We thought that would be the diagnosis,' Lily said. 'I'm really sorry, Archie.' Enid was in for a long recuperation, but at least she had that chance. It wouldn't be easy at her age. Enid had often said she never wanted to be reliant on other people for any reason and now she was.

'The doctors say she'll be able to move and talk again, but it'll take time.'

'These things do. She's going to rely on you a lot.'

'I'll be everything I can for her.'

'I know you will. Everyone will be there for you both as well.' Lily chatted until Archie said he had to get back to his wife. 'Talk again.'

Finishing the call, she looked around for something to do that didn't involve a chainsaw because since Max had left so abruptly she had the urge to wreck something. It'd been as though he'd suddenly had enough of her and wanted to get away. He needn't worry. She wouldn't be hanging around the camp, trying to catch his attention. She would see how the kids were faring, and help out when they were playing team games, not follow him around like a besotted puppy, watching his expressions, wondering how being a sports doctor fitted his ambitions better than being a top-notch surgeon.

Max might have walked out of here, but his scent was in the air, his presence lightening an already sunny room. No wonder her body heated and tightened. Being near him, hearing his voice and making him laugh was starting to drive her crazy with longing. So much for being wary of romance. Except she had to keep caution in place. Aaron had left her. Leo had left her. She wasn't good at relationships.

But why was she thinking about Max when their history wasn't great? Why did she even feel like she wanted to be with him? Because she couldn't help herself. On impulse, she checked her file on the week's camp crew, found Max's number and put it in her contacts, then tapped the screen, humming as she waited for him to answer. 'Hi, I've been talking to Archie. Enid did have a stroke.' She gave him the scant details. 'It's going to be a trying time for them.'

'What about family? Will they be around to help?'

'Their son and daughter live on the peninsula. They're a close family.'

'That's a plus.' He paused, and she waited for him to hang up. Instead he said, 'I've already met most of the kids, including Josie. Talk about looking like you. There's a fire in her belly to get on with anything that comes her way, isn't there?' Admiration lightened his voice.

'She's a toughie.' Her stomach softened. Max was unlike the men she'd previously fallen for. Stronger, more reliable, with a knack of making her feel special. Could he be the father for her baby? *Gah.* Where had that come from? They didn't know each other well enough to be thinking that. She shivered. *Getting way ahead of yourself, Lily.*

'You still coming along to the camp today?'

'I'll drop by to see what everyone's up to, and check with Logan that there're no problems.' Logan ran the camp and knew what he was doing, yet she couldn't help staying in touch. Control freak? Her mouth flattened. 'Maybe I should leave him to it,' she gasped. 'It's not as though he hasn't done this often.'

Max laughed. 'He's already asked if I knew when you might make an appearance. When I explained how your morning had panned out he said he'd call you when he had a free moment.'

She soaked up Max's relaxed attitude, relishing the warmth filling her and driving away that need to wreck something. 'So he didn't pull a face and suggest I stay away?'

'Would you?'

'Mostly. Mainly I want to catch up with Josie.' Lily found herself smiling. This happier side had been a long time in hiding, and letting it out for an airing felt so good. *Thanks, Max.* Was it because they were getting on better than before? Or did she feel there was something there she wanted to nurture between them? Was that sense of something deeper she'd experienced during their fling making a comeback? Or was she just getting on with her life and starting to enjoy herself again? Whatever the reason, bring it on. She was ripe for some fun and adventure. Just not of the heart involvement variety. She'd save that for her baby.

'I'd better go and look useful. There's a get-together of everyone after lunch followed by soccer and netball games.'

Sounded about right. 'See you later.' Now what? The kitchen was tidy, she'd talked to Archie and Max, had decided not to go to the camp just yet, and the idea of curling up with her book wasn't appealing. Her nerves had calmed. She no longer felt inclined to create havoc. Under the tree sat the trailer full of pine. Sometime it needed to be cut into firebox lengths and split in half to be left to weather before being stacked under cover. Might as well start on the lengths. Someone else would do the splitting as wielding an axe was not her thing.

'Auntie Lily, where have you been? I've been waiting for you.' Josie threw herself out of the wheelchair at Lily. 'The doctor says he knows you.' She tipped her head back to lock eyes with her. 'He's nice.'

Max could charm any female from two to ninety years old. Including herself, it seemed. 'We worked together before I went to Singapore.' She held Josie against her, breathing in her youthfulness.

'You're going to be at the same medical centre from now on.'

Okay, she could be a rascal, this one. Easing her hold, Lily let Josie stand. There was a cheeky grin on her niece's face that she understood all too well. 'Stop right there, my girl. I don't need you attempting to organise my life. I make a big enough mess of it all by myself.' She grinned. 'What have you been up to?'

'Apart from asking Dr Max lots of questions? I played netball and shot two goals.' Pride brightened her eyes.

'Not bad, huh?' She high-fived Josie's hand. 'What are the other kids like? Anyone you know?'

Crimson colour poured into Josie's cheeks. 'Um, yeah. Ollie from last time's here. I knew he was coming. We text.'

Lifting one eyebrow, Lily grinned again. 'You don't say. I'm going to have to get the chain and padlock from the shed.'

'As of now you're no longer my favourite aunt.' Josie sank back into her chair and chewed her fingernail, before looking up and laughing. 'He looks gorgeous, better than before.'

Great. Should she tell her brother and sister-in-law? Or just keep a covert eye on things and let Josie get on with being a normal teen when it wasn't always so easy for her? Lily sighed. She already knew the answer. Josie was here for a good time, which included normality and fun and learning to be more resilient than most kids their age. Not that her niece wasn't already strong, but there was no such thing as too much resilience to the things life threw at people. 'Take care, that's all I'm asking.'

'Yes, Auntie.' Josie pulled a face then laughed. 'This is me you're talking to. Your super-careful niece, remember?'

'Don't you mean my try-anything, give-it-a-go niece?' Lily retorted, and heard a deep chuckle behind her.

'You two are so alike it's surreal,' Max said.

More than he realised, Lily conceded as she felt her face grow warm. 'Family genes,' she muttered for lack of anything better to say.

'Hey, Dr Max. Lily was telling me...' Josie faltered to a stop as Lily glared at her. 'Um, that I need to go find out what I'm doing tonight.' She wheeled away before Lily could say anything to stop her.

'Little minx,' Lily muttered. 'Except she's not so little or young any more.'

'She's already shown she's a leader in the netball arena,' Max acknowledged. 'The boys can't keep their eyes off her either, and that has nothing to with netball.'

'That's all they'd better be touching her with,' Lily growled, then sighed. 'Listen to me, sounding more like her parents than her fun aunt.'

'Could be you remember what you got up to at that age.'

She loved it when he joked with her. 'Isn't that how parents think? I wonder how I'd cope being a parent. Teenagers can be such trouble.' The good humour bubbled inside her. Babies grew into kids then teenagers. It was part of the deal, and she wanted it all. She'd be fine. Love coped with most things.

'You don't mean that,' Max said with a hint of sadness darkening his features. 'Having children is most people's dream.'

'Max? Why do you sound dejected all of a sudden?'

she asked without thought. She didn't like to see him like this. Didn't want him hurting. Was it a dream of his to have kids that he couldn't meet?

He shook his head abruptly and looked out towards the beach. 'Nothing.'

It wasn't true. His suddenly slumped shoulders backed her conviction she'd touched on something hurtful. Not that they were close and would swap tales of woe but, 'You know where to find me if you ever want to vent. There's always wine to go with that.' *And arms to hold you.*

Slowly he turned to look at her, astonishment quickly replaced with relief. 'Thanks for being understanding.'

'It's not hard. We all get our share of knocks.'

'You, too?'

'Of course. And I'm not being flippant.'

'For once I wish you were. I don't like thinking you've been hurt, Lily.'

Yeah, well. 'It's part of being human. But I'm here, content.' She paused. That was so true it was almost laughable. 'And looking forward to the rest of the week.'

The sadness shadowing Max's eyes lifted. 'Me, too.' Did his intense gaze suggest she take that any way she chose?

Warmth tripped over her skin. Then she did something she couldn't believe. Slipping her arm through his, she said, 'Come on. Logan wants to chat to us both about Michelle's role.' Glancing up for his reaction, Lily smiled. Being this close to Max gave her inexplicable hope. The future was brightening, the darkness fading, just when she'd decided to give men a miss for a while.

Under her hand Max tensed then swiftly relaxed again

and began walking with her towards the office-cum-staffroom. 'Funny, he didn't say anything to me earlier.'

'There's probably a lot going on in his head at the moment. The first day is always crazy busy.'

'I'm beginning to understand just how important this place is to you.' Those intense eyes returned to her.

'Very.' She had no idea why, but she wanted to be open with him. The need to share was grabbing her, no matter what his reaction might be. Unused to telling people deeply personal things, she found this incredibly easy to say. 'I financed it from the start.'

Max nodded slowly and his face opened up in acknowledgement. 'I'm not surprised.'

She was. He used to give her hell about being well off and having it easy. This showed that the awkward areas of their past were wrapped up and not to be aired again. Unless they were to get close enough to slip between the sheets one day, then the airing would be all about the few amazing times they had shared. 'Thank you. Not many people know and I'd prefer it stays that way.'

'I won't be racing off to tell all and sundry,' he assured her.

'Good.' She believed him. Her head felt lighter and she was smiling. Max wasn't the devil she recalled. Had he ever been? Or had she been so focused on keeping him at arm's length she'd been totally wrong about him? But she wasn't good at reading men. Damned hopeless, actually.

Pulling her arm free, she shoved her hands in her jeans pockets and strolled into the building, pretending nonchalance every step of the way.

CHAPTER FOUR

WHAT MORE DO I really want out of life? Lily wondered as she sat before the fire in her lounge later that night. Love. Yes. A child. Yes. Once she'd settled into the Remuera Medical Hub and had created a place amongst other focused medical practitioners she'd follow through on that.

She wanted family, badly. Children were essential to life. Growing up ensconced with loving parents and brothers who gave so much to each other had taught her lots about living and caring. When she and Leo had got engaged, she'd naturally thought he'd want the same. He adored his family, yet when he left he'd said she'd misunderstood, that he wasn't ready to be a father, might never be. Had she ever understood him? Breaking up had hurt, yet her biggest regret was the lost opportunity to have children. Had she done Leo a disservice by accepting his love when it was now obvious she hadn't loved him enough?

A phone ringing cut through the quiet of the house. Max? Why would it be? He wasn't a friend to call for the sake of it. Digging around the armchair cushion, her fingers wrapped around the phone. 'Charlotte, how's things?'

Her friend laughed. 'Nothing out of the usual, I'm afraid. All rather boring really.'

'So you rang me for some entertainment?' Lily's attempt to laugh fell flat.

'I want to hear all about Dr Bryant. I presume you've seen him at the camp.'

In the background Lily could hear Charlotte pouring liquid. 'Wine or tea?' What was she going to say? She usually told her closest friend everything, but... But what? It wasn't as though she had anything to hide.

'Tea. Come on, spill.'

Lily drew a breath. 'I told him my role in the camp.'

'Knew I should've poured a wine.' Then, 'Why? I set up the trust in a way it would be very hard for anyone to find out and you tell the one man sure to give you a hard time, and maybe let it slip to others? As your lawyer I'm saying that was not your brightest move, Lily.'

'And as my friend?' Had she been testing Max to see if he had changed as much as she was beginning to suspect? If so, she'd chosen the wrong subject for that. Lily waited.

'What did he say?' Charlotte asked.

'He wasn't surprised and won't tell others. I believe him on both counts.' He had sounded genuine. 'Max is not the man I once worked with. He doesn't appear to be looking for ways to prove he's better than anyone else, for one.'

'What about the man you slept with?'

No idea. 'No getting away from our past. Anyway, let's drop this. I can't undo what I said, and frankly I doubt there's any need. I feel I can trust Max.' It was in the way he listened to her without rolling his eyes, as if to say, 'Yeah, right', in his ready acceptance of her for who she was now. Not that he knew much about what had gone on over the past years, but that's why she felt he had become a more trustworthy man.

'There's another way of looking at this. Someone, one day, is bound to find out you funded setting up the camp. These things happen, though we have got this one pretty tight. But we're not the only people who know and a slip of the tongue is all it takes.'

Lily pictured her grandmother lying in her hospital bed, smiling as Lily outlined what she wanted to do with her share of her inheritance. In a way it had been an uncomfortable moment as it had underlined what lay ahead for Granny. The pneumonia had taken hold and it had only been a matter of time. Lily had spent many hours at her bedside when work hadn't been taking up her time. Telling Max had reminded her of that day, and the sense of doing the right thing that had gripped her and become a passion that never let up.

'I was clearing the air between us, laying the past to rest. We're going to be working together, and I want a clean slate.'

She also wanted to learn more about him. Like what had happened to his determination to be a top-notch surgeon? What had caused those dark shadows to fill his eyes in the middle of a conversation? Whenever she saw them an urge overtook her to hug him, tell him he'd be fine.

Charlotte broke into her meanderings. 'So, tell, is Max still as good looking as he used to be?'

Lily grinned. 'No. He's better. A hunk, in an older, more subdued way, like he's finally comfortable in his own body. There're shiny silvery grey streaks in his hair, which he doesn't hide, more like wears them as a badge for something he's dealt with.' Charlotte would be loving this. 'He doesn't rush in to be the hero when someone's in need of a doctor. We had an incident this morning when my neighbour had a stroke, and we worked well together.'

'Whoa. Am I really hearing this?' Charlotte teased. 'Seems you're starting to like him. Your voice softens when you say his name. You sure you aren't in the market for a romance?'

'Very certain.' Lily crossed her fingers. Had she just lied? Max was changing her mind about a few things. 'Becoming friends is one thing, falling for him something else.' But unwittingly he had ticked the sincere and kind boxes she needed filled if she were ever to take another chance on romance. What was she thinking? Sure, she wanted to find love, but equally she wasn't going to risk being hurt again.

'She protests too much, methinks,' Charlotte said quietly. 'Be careful, Lily. You might be over Leo, but you're still vulnerable. I know you've got the position you want, and would love nothing more than to be a mother, but take your time, especially over Max.'

It felt good knowing Charlotte had her back. 'Thanks for being there and understanding.'

'As if you don't return the favour,' Charlotte said before hanging up.

Lily unwound herself from the chair and went in search of a can of soup. If only she'd hooked up with a man who understood her and accepted her for who she was, instead of the two she'd known, she might not be on a solo path for a family. An image of Max filled her mind, his eyes sad and body slumped. The new Max, the one she couldn't help but like already.

They'd talked about having kids. Did he want the same things? Was he looking for love? Had he changed so much he no longer did the short flings and walk-away routine? Wait. She sucked a short, sharp breath. Had Max been in love and had his heart broken? It stood to reason that might have happened. Despite his previous playboy rep, if Max had fallen for a woman, it would've been with one hundred percent focus.

The sort of love she'd twice thought she'd found, and given. Only now she understood she hadn't loved either man anywhere nearly as much as she'd believed. Or she had, and now wanted something deeper and stronger, a love that knew no boundaries and didn't falter at the first hurdle.

Only since coming in contact with Max again had this realisation dawned.

She had loved both men, in turn, and hadn't been enough to keep either of them. She might not be the right person to get married and live happily ever after. No, she would not accept that. She *was* loving, cared deeply for the people important to her, and would do anything to make them happy.

As she fully intended to do for her child should she have one.

A text landed in her phone.

Hi, Auntie Lily. I had a great day. Loves ya, J.

Lily's heart melted.

Loves you too. See you tomorrow. xxx

She wasn't expected to turn up at the camp daily, but she'd go and see Josie.

And Max.

* * *

'Catch, Auntie Lily.'

Lily spun around, scanning the space between her and where Josie's shout had come from, and saw an object hurtling towards her. Snatching the basketball out of the air, she hurled it to the boy on the same side of the net as Josie.

A whistle blew. 'Foul.' Max grinned. 'Intervention from the sideline.'

'Yes,' shouted the teens on the opposing side, and one ducked underneath to retrieve the ball rolling their way.

'Spoilsport.' Lily laughed.

Max shook his head, grinning happily. 'You think I want to be nailed to the ground and have this lot riding over me in their wheelchairs?'

'Now, there's an idea,' she retorted. 'What's the score?'

'Five all.'

'Right, come on, guys. Let's whip their backsides,' she called to Josie and her partner.

Josie fist pumped. 'Yeah, let's.'

Max nodded to the other team. 'Come on, give it to them, you two.'

Lily watched the girl balance on her prosthetic leg and swing her fist at the ball. The bravery these children showed melted her heart. Their strength was almost inherent. Her hand rested on her stomach briefly. Children were amazing. Her gaze slipped sideways. Max was engrossed in the game, giving himself over to the kids. *Father material.* Absolutely, but for her child? Unlikely. They were getting on fine but it would be a huge leap, one she was not ready for by any stretch of the imagination. So why did the idea keep popping up?

'Yippee,' Josie yelled. 'Six to us.'

Kids on the sidelines shouted enthusiastically.

'Time to change ends,' Max called.

Lily handed the players water bottles to guzzle from before they started the second half of the match. 'You want one?' She held out a bottle to Max.

'This is hot work.' He laughed, taking the bottle, his fingers brushing hers sending sparks up her arm.

Quickly pulling back, she said, 'You're enjoying it.' Why had she moved away? The tingling in her hand made her feel more alive.

Max fixed his gaze on her mouth as he placed the bottle between his lips and poured water down his throat. Desire filled his eyes.

Tightness clamped her chest. Snatching up the last bottle, she tried to swallow some liquid but her throat was closed. Great. Right in the middle of a conversation she'd gone and lost the gist of what they'd been discussing. Glancing around, she saw children everywhere. Of course. The kids. That's what today, the week, was about. Not Max and herself. But it was ridiculously easy to be sidetracked by those beautiful khaki eyes filled with desire for *her*.

Max seemed to be having similar difficulty remembering where they were. He spun away, staring towards the sea. When he finally spoke, his voice was rough. 'They're all so keen to win and to have a good time while they're at it.' He was onto it. The kids.

'Keener than they'll be when it's time to sit in the classroom and discuss plans for their futures.' Keep talking sensibly and surely the need would die down?

'Some are a little young to be worrying about that yet,' Max noted, still facing away.

'The psychologists don't agree. Something about being

prepared so they can handle setbacks more easily.' This *was* getting easier by the word, but she needed to talk non-stop for ten minutes to be totally heat free.

'What does Josie want to become?'

'A beautician.' Lily saw her niece hobbling to the end of the court. Keep talking, move on. 'It might be a passing fad. She's just discovered make-up in a big way.'

'I noticed the heavy mascara. Right, time to get the game underway again.'

Lily sat on a park bench, watching Max dashing up and down the edge of the sand court, blowing his whistle, shouting encouragement. He was in his element with these teenagers giving their mates cheek, his face was again clear and open, his eyes sparkling with enjoyment.

'Hello, Doctor.' Michelle stood beside her, balancing on crutches. 'What an awesome place.'

'Isn't it? When did you get here?'

'Nearly an hour ago. I've been talking to Logan. He says there's a shortage of beds so even if I chose to stay on I can't.'

'I'll find you somewhere. Don't worry about it.' There were empty bedrooms at the beach house. 'What do you think of the set-up so far?'

'It's amazing. From the main building I saw some boys playing soccer and their sheer determination to score is mind-blowing. I wanted to rush out and join them, help the guy coaching them.'

'Why didn't you? That's the idea of you being here,' Lily told her.

'I was with Logan, getting the rundown on the camp.' Michelle's cheeks were turning pink.

Lily shook her head. Logan and Michelle? Why not? A blinding thought struck. Was romance in the air out here in Whangaparaoa? Did that mean others were going to feel the love this week? Josie and her friend? Her and Max? Lily leapt to her feet. No way. Never. Her gaze went immediately to him as he blew the final whistle. She would not be hurt again. She did want love, but doubted she had the courage to risk her heart once more. Not even with Max.

Look at him. His face had matured to heart-stopping attractiveness. His mouth was kind and soft, and she already knew from the past the sensations those lips created on her feverish skin. Skin that right this moment was prickling. His curls made her fingers restless and her lungs squeeze painfully. Spinning around before he looked over and caught her out, she breathed deep for composure, which wasn't coming. He'd been a wonderful lover. Quivering was going on in her legs. Her head felt light. She swore. She might be in trouble here.

'Hi, Max,' Michelle called across the space, and hobbled across to the courtside.

'You made it. Not that I thought you wouldn't,' he added hurriedly.

'I was up and ready at five this morning. Now I've got something else to focus on other than myself, I want to get cracking.'

Lily dragged her feet over to join them. 'What did Logan suggest you do?'

'Join in the activities.' Michelle waved a crutch between them.

Max laughed. 'You'll go down a treat.' He raised one eyebrow in Lily's direction. 'But we already knew that.'

'We did.' It was still hard to talk sensibly while trying to move past the desire Max evoked in her, but she kept trying. Easier if she focused on Michelle and not Max.

'Not all these guys want to be anything great; most only want to be accepted for who they are.'

'I always feel on the fringe with my friends because I'm driven to get ahead.'

'How long do you think you'll stay?' Max asked Michelle.

'There's the problem. The accommodation is chock full. Lily says she'll sort it, though, so who knows?'

'You can stay at my family's house along the road,' Lily told her.

'Thanks. I'd prefer to be here on the spot so I can chat to anyone any time, but your house is better than heading back to the city,' Michelle said, then shook her head. 'There I go again. Sorry. It was a generous offer and I'm happy to accept.'

Lily managed a brief laugh. 'Don't worry. I like your honesty.'

'If it means a difference in how long you remain at the camp you can have my room, Michelle. I'll bunk down somewhere else.' Max's eyes were on Lily as he said that.

Leaving her with only one thing to say, though it came out slowly and warily. 'You can move into the beach house if you'd like.' Max in the house for meals and showers, and sleeping? Hell, she couldn't remain uninterested when there was a kilometre between them. It would be impossible to remain neutral with him staying between the same four walls as her.

'Talk to you later if there's nowhere else.' Was he saying he wasn't interested in sharing her house? When he'd offered to swap with Michelle? She couldn't blame him for having second thoughts.

'No problem. I'm going to find Josie for a chat.' Not about boys and condoms or being safe, tempting as that was. Though she would keep an eye on the relationship between her niece and the boy who put all that colour in her face and excitement in her eyes. Blimey, was that how *she* looked whenever she thought about Max? Hadn't she just got into a pickle over him? Yes, and still felt at odds with herself. As soon as she'd talked with Josie, she'd head to the house and pull on her running gear. Action was required to quieten the brain.

'Auntie Lily, who's that lady on the crutches?'

'Michelle Baxter. She plays—'

'Netball for the North Shore. She's awesome.' Josie squealed and charged across to her apparent idol. 'Hi, Michelle, I'm Josie. I watch most of your games. You're great.'

Michelle laughed, and said, 'Thanks for that.'

'What have you done to your leg? Is it serious?' Josie didn't stop to think how her questions might be received, but that might be good for Michelle. It was how strangers often treated Josie. But still...

'Some delinquent shoved me out of a bus I was boarding and my ankle's broken. It's lucky my wrist wasn't broken after all.'

'But you're going to England soon.'

Michelle's smile slipped. 'I was.'

About to step in and shut her niece down, Lily opened her mouth but Michelle cut her off. 'It's hugely disappointing, but I'm getting used to the thought of staying behind. It's a block in my career, but not the end. Tell me, what's your favourite sport? I saw you playing netball earlier.'

Lily hesitated, watching Josie talk about how she liked wheelchair basketball the best, and any game that involved using her arms more than her legs were fun.

'They're getting along fine,' Max said quietly beside her.

Her skin prickled. 'They're reacting to each other as I'd hoped they would, only I hadn't specifically factored Josie into the picture.'

'Why would you? It was chance that Josie's the first person to waylay Michelle.' Max sounded thoughtful. 'Seems you might've nailed it. They're both animated and talking non-stop about the situations they're in. Let's leave them to it and grab a coffee and sandwich before the hordes devour all the food I saw being prepared earlier.'

Lily all but bounced up the lawn, wearing a wide smile and humming under her breath.

'So would it be all right if I did doss down at your house?'

Okay, maybe she should quieten the happiness level. But it *would* be good to have him closer on and off; as long as she controlled her hormones and kept her heart from racing and her skin from prickling. 'Wouldn't have offered if it wasn't.' Would she? Was she playing dangerously now?

Stop, Lily. Think this through. You could get hurt again.

Max grinned. 'Think I might be lucky enough to get a meal at your place?'

Too late to stop this. The whole thing was expanding rapidly. First a bed, now meals. What next? Don't go there. 'You haven't asked if I know how to cook.' She wanted to clap her hands in the air and laugh. Max was going to stay with her.

Max turned around. 'Hey, Josie, can your aunt cook a mean dinner?'

Josie's eyes widened with a hint of something Lily

was afraid to interpret. 'Ask her to make beef bourguignon. It's to die for.'

Little wretch. No denying the cheeky smile or the 'I've
got you back for all those times you've teased me' gleam
in Josie's eyes. 'Haven't you got something better to do
than harass your favourite aunt?'

'Nope.'

'Imp.' Lily aimed for the main building.

Max strolled along beside her. 'After I've finished
here I'll drive to the nearest shops to get some wine to
go with that beef.'

'Guess that means I am making the casserole.' Her
mind was going through the fridge for mushrooms and
beef stock. 'Luckily there's beef in the freezer.'

'Text if there's anything you need. I won't head away
before five.'

'Will do.' Outside the building, she paused, not sure
what to say but feeling there was something she needed
to get out.

'Relax, Lily. I appreciate the offer of a room. I won't
make a pest of myself. I'll be here most of the time anyway.' Max touched her lightly on the shoulder, sending sparks right to the tips of her toes. 'We're good. We
haven't argued, and I doubt we will, other than over the
occasional differences that occur at the medical hub.'

At the same time as wishing he didn't sound so serious, his touch did a number on her libido. Obviously it
meant nothing to him. There was a message there she
should abide by. So she should forget the disappointment
sliding through her, act normal. 'You think?' Normal?

His eyes widened. 'I do.' Then doubt crept in, bringing the dark shade into that serious look as he stepped
back. 'Don't tell me I'm wrong. I don't want to return to

the way things were between us.' That elusive sadness filtered through his gaze before disappearing. 'I learned a lot from that time because of you and I hope I've matured and understand people better. You as well.'

What had happened to him? That was a huge admission, and totally out of left field. The more she saw the more she believed something big had occurred, such as a broken heart. They were both like flotsam floating through life, hiding their hurts, in her case aiming for happiness from a new and different perspective from her previous attempts.

What was Max hoping for? Planning on achieving? Who did he wish to spend his life with? She wasn't about to find out while standing here outside the building filling up with hungry teenagers wanting food. It was doubtful she'd ever learn what was behind that sadness. But he had said he'd matured partly because of her, so anything was possible. She gave him a smile. 'Let's grab lunch.' She had a beef bourguignon to prepare, and it was going to be her best effort ever.

Her smile slipped and she stopped. Less than a week ago she had been struggling with the idea of working with Max. Now he was coming to stay in her family home. What was she doing? Romance wasn't on the cards. Max definitely wasn't either. He might be different but how different?

CHAPTER FIVE

So THIS WAS what married life might be like, Max thought. Easy, caring, sharing. Nothing like his parents' relationship even before their bitter divorce. 'Sit down and take a load off,' he instructed Lily after a scrumptious dinner. Another string to her bow. 'Want a hot drink?'

'A hot chocolate wouldn't go amiss.' Lily glanced at him with a cheeky smile. 'I've got a really sweet tooth, which is why I run.'

As if she was overweight. She looked more gorgeous than ever now her curves had filled out a little. 'Not to keep fit, then?' He laughed, trying to ignore the picture filling his head of Lily sprawled across his bed one night a long time ago. She'd been beautiful, and now she was even more so from what little he could see.

'That'd be crazy. The chocolate mix is on the baking shelf in the pantry.'

'You can find it blindfolded?' Having light-hearted fun with Lily was a new concept, and one he liked.

'Naturally.' Her chair balanced on its back legs as she watched him make their drinks.

Yes, he'd join her with hot chocolate. Anything was better than going to bed alone and dreaming about what might be if he let go his determination to remain single.

That determination could be his undoing—or give him something precious. As had happened with medicine. At first he'd been resolute in showing his father how he loved him and wanted the same in return, but what had happened was far better. Medicine was him, and he got so much more from it than he gave. He'd also finally won quiet approval from his father, acknowledged during the cancer battle. What might happen if he could dispel this painful need to remain single?

He might hurt someone else. That's what.

Lily was chattering on, thankfully blind to his pain. 'I started running in Singapore as a way of getting out and about without looking like a lost tourist. I liked getting away from being behind four walls all the time. Usually I followed the smell of street food and cancelled the plus side of running before returning to our apartment.'

He stood straighter, sucked in his gut. 'Our apartment? You weren't on your own?' From what he'd heard when she'd been appointed tó the medical hub, she was now.

'I lived with my fiancé, Leo. We met at the medical centre when I moved to Singapore.'

Lived with. In the past? How far could he go with his curiosity? Why this driving need to know?

Because I like Lily a lot. Possibly more than like.

'It didn't work out?'

Lily's smile flattened, her face closed. 'Not after a while. I came home from work one night to find him all packed up, waiting to tell me he was heading home to Scotland and a woman from his past he'd been in contact with for a few months.'

'I'm sorry to hear that.' She'd been getting over another failed relationship when they'd had their fling. At first he'd wondered if he'd been mad, asking her to his home, but she hadn't brought baggage, and had seemed instead to be happy to spend time with him. It had been beyond wonderful as he had begun to see Lily differently from the woman he'd worked with. Until the morning she'd got up and said that was the end. Talk about a sharp slap in the face. And a dent to his ego. Most of all, he'd felt he'd lost an opportunity for elusive happiness, which had only made him go even harder in locking down his dreams of love.

'You deserve better than that.'

'I do.' She nodded. 'It's behind me and I'm not in a hurry for another relationship.'

It sounded like a warning. About what? But at least he knew. They were on similar pages regarding relationships, though for different reasons. He should be relieved, but instead his stomach sank and his heart was heavy.

Placing a steaming mug in front of her, Max sat opposite, his hands wrapped around his mug. 'I've never been in a long-term relationship.' He gulped. Lily's truthfulness had started him talking. It was long overdue, and not as difficult as he'd have believed.

Surprise lifted her face, widened her eyes. 'I got that wrong,' she said. 'I thought maybe you'd had your heart crushed and that's why you...' She paused. 'Why you stuck to nothing more involved than flings.'

'When I was training I didn't want to get too intense with someone and find myself distracted from achieving my medical degree.'

'You were that determined you gave up other important things to achieve it?'

'I did. My father never had the opportunity to follow his dreams, so I felt driven to make mine come true. It was also a way to show my mother she was wrong to

leave me and take my sister with her when she left Dad.'
Talk about laying his heart on the line. Now she knew
more about him than any woman he'd spent time with.
He should be heading down the hall to the bedroom to get
away—there was a first, getting away from any woman
to go to a bedroom.

He sighed. A load had lifted from his chest by telling
her what lay behind his modus operandi. And to Lily,
strange as it was. Or was it? When she'd been the first
woman to ever have him yearning for something more,
deeper, than his usual short interactions, this felt right.

'Your parents were separated?' Sadness blinked out
of those soft eyes.

'When I was ten. Mum felt I'd be better off raised by
Dad, and not have her and my sister fluffing over me.'
It had always felt like an excuse. No one had asked him
what he might want. 'Mum didn't move far so I visited
often.'

'But it wasn't the same.'

'Visiting your parent? Not at all.'

Her hand covered his for a warm moment then she
gave him a break, trying to lighten the mood. 'I was so
lucky with my family. Growing up on the farm with my
brothers, I was always out to prove I was as good if not
better than them at getting into mischief or doing jobs
around the place. There was no such thing as too heavy
or too hard. I could do it.' Her smile was wistful.

'It was a wonderful childhood, and stood me in good
stead to get through med school. Though there were times
I thought I'd taken on more than I could manage, I never
let anyone know.'

He'd seen that. 'Not once in those two years in ED
did I think you were struggling. Or had you found your

strengths by then?' He couldn't quite believe this conversation with the woman he'd once believed more interested in herself than anyone else. Because she had left him, which was not the usual way flings went with him.

She was strong, tough, but there was a softness to her he'd not seen back then. Because he hadn't wanted to? In case he felt too much for her? Or had he been so intent on getting through what he'd set out to do medically that he hadn't stopped to really see Lily for who she was? What opportunities had he lost? Did he want to try to retrieve them? Or continue on this lonely journey to be safe? His stomach tightened painfully.

Lily cut through his dour thoughts. 'My family's wonderful. We're all close. If I could have I'd have taken up farming too, but it was the one thing my father was adamant I wouldn't do. My dad kept reiterating how I wanted to be a doctor, had done since I was a teenager. He told me it was important to follow my heart and not go into farming to prove to my brothers I could do it as well as them.' She sipped her hot chocolate. 'He had a point. There was a lot of that proving myself again and again in my need to stay on the land.'

'Have you ever regretted your choice?'

'Not once. My dad knows me well.'

'You're lucky.' His father still hurt over his wife leaving him. And for him there hadn't been a lot of sharing dreams and goals or fun times over a beer or going fishing together. He'd always wondered what he'd done wrong to be kept at a distance, but after the cancer he'd come to see that was how his dad coped with everything. But then he could say he owed his father because that's what had made him want to prove he could be worthy of being loved and believed in. Hence the reason he'd become a doctor. What about a husband? A father?

Damn you, Lily. You're causing havoc with my thinking.

'I know. Which is why I've stood by him at the awards ceremonies. The only reason, in fact.' She grinned, obviously unaware of the effect she was having on him. Her striking face became childlike with that grin splitting her mouth wide and her wide eyes glittering like diamonds in the sun.

'Is it too late to apologise for being a prat?' He grinned back, his heart pounding and his toes curling. Being so at ease with her was strange and wonderful all at once. 'I'm serious. I wasn't kind to you back then.'

'If we start apologising we'll be busy all evening, and I can think of better ways to spend the time.'

So can I. The chocolate went down the wrong way, causing him to cough. Quickly on his feet before Lily could pat his back and send his heart rate into dangerous territory, he moved away to take long, slow breaths. And swallow his rising disappointment over not being able to follow up on the longing gripping him. They were not repeating that fling. Not for anything.

He doubted he'd be able to get over it as easily as last time, and there'd been a little hitch then where he'd regretted it, so he was not getting involved with Lily. She was a colleague at the medical centre. She might want a casual relationship after her last one had gone wrong, but he already knew that wasn't all he wanted, and getting into a serious relationship was a no-no.

A warm hand did touch his shoulder, sending heat through his tense muscles. 'You all right?'

'Yes.'

The hand retracted instantly. 'Right.' Lily walked away.

The air cooled but not his body. *Come back. I'll explain.* No. He wouldn't. He wasn't ready. Would he ever be? Could he consider a real relationship with her? Look forward and not let the past darken his thinking? If only he could manage that. Twelve months ago he'd begun moving on a little, had started looking ahead to a bright, happy future. Then he'd had a scare and thought the cancer had returned. That had set him back, strengthened his resolve not to hurt anyone.

Now here was Lily, and he'd started looking forward with a fierce longing that grew every day. Was he being a fool to let the past dictate his future? He could live till he was eighty and regret not marrying and having a family. Or, glancing at Lily's retreating back, he could grab the chance for happiness and run with it. Take the setbacks on the chin, like he'd done with most things all his life before this.

Lily opened her laptop and drank the last of the lukewarm chocolate while waiting for the page to come up. Max had told her more about himself than ever before. They were mostly relaxed in each other's company.

'Max, have you kept in touch with any of the staff we worked with in Auckland ED?'

'We've all mostly lost touch.' He was staring at his feet as he talked. 'Everyone got involved in specialist training and then starting to build their careers, having families, buying homes.'

'You've bought a property in Auckland? Got anyone living with you?'

'I'm on my own, living in a rundown three-bed house I bought in a cul-de-sac along the road from the medical hub, and that's going to keep me busy and happy for years to come. It's enough.'

Something wasn't ringing true but she couldn't put her finger on what it might be. Was he happy? Busy? Was there anyone else in his life? She wasn't prepared to ask more about that. 'What about the sports side of your work? Does it take you to many matches? Rugby? Cricket? League?'

'All of the above. I did a day at the international tennis tournament in January. Most weekends I attend at least one game of some sort, though now I'm officially the team doctor for one of the North Shore franchises I have less time for other games. Which means not a lot is getting done on the house, but...' he shrugged '...it doesn't matter. I'll get there someday.'

Her phone rang. 'It's Josie. Hey, bright spark. What's up?'

'I've been talking with Ollie about his family and stuff. Lily, he's cool. I like him more than last time we were here.'

What was she supposed to say to that?

'He wants me to visit his house and go to the movies with him next week.'

Did kids still do that? 'What's wrong with watching a movie on TV?'

'His parents and sister would be there.'

I get it. You can't hold hands and snog.

'This is something you'll have to sort out with Mum and Dad.' She was passing the buck. Her role didn't include setting the dating rules for a demanding fourteen-year-old.

'They'll like Ollie so it'll be okay.' Josie talked on, barely taking a breath.

Lily sat listening, smiling at her niece's exuberance for life. It was wonderful considering the setbacks she'd had over the years because of the spina bifida and people who couldn't accept she had the same aspirations as everyone else.

'You've got to meet him, Lily. You'll like him. Everyone does. He's so cute.'

Lily tried not to laugh. Had she been like this at fourteen? At fifteen there'd been that boy, Jeff, who'd kissed her at the school disco and she'd thought it was revolting. But then there'd been Johnny and his kisses had shown Jeff to be an amateur. She watched Max reading messages on his phone and smiled. He just did that to her. Made her feel good. Which was unexpected. Or was it? She'd been quick to offer him somewhere to stay. And equally fast to rue the invitation in case she couldn't cope with him in her space. Yet now he was here she was happy spending time with him. Maybe she could take another chance.

Slow down, Lily.

'Auntie, are you listening?'

'Sure. I'll come along during the day to watch your game.' *Concentrate.*

After minutes more of Josie telling her how wonderful Ollie was, Lily finally managed to put her phone down. Dropping her head into her hands, she groaned. 'Josie thinks she's falling in love. At fourteen. Blimey. I need to tell my brother.'

'No, you don't,' Max growled. 'She'd never talk to you again.'

'True. I can't do that. I'm her trusted go-to adult when she has a fall-out with her parents. But love, at her age.'

'Are you saying you didn't think some knobbly-kneed

guy in grey school shorts was to die for when you were that old?'

'Johnny Barstow. He had muscular legs, good knees, and the start of whiskers on his chin.' She began laughing.

'Cassey Jones, long blonde hair and skinny,' Max recounted. 'She danced like a crazed person. Had all the guys lining up for a kiss.' He filled a glass with water. 'Here.'

She hiccupped and took the glass, her fingers brushing his. 'Thanks. This is the closest I've been to parenting, and I'm lucky it's funny. My brother and sister-in-law aren't going to think so.' Neither would she when her turn came.

'Are they very strict?' Max sat opposite her.

'More likely they'll remember themselves at high school. They met when they were sixteen and haven't been apart since.' She downed the water. 'Still get on brilliantly.'

'What about your other brother? He married?'

'Yes, finally. His wife's Italian and they kept seesawing between which country they'd live in if they'd actually tie the knot or stay in their respective places, if he'd give up farming when it was so important to him, if she'd give up the family bakery when there was no one else to take over.' Lily adored Aurora and could sympathise with the decisions she and Toby had had to make.

'Your brother would've given up his share of the farm for her?'

'I believe so. But Aurora understood he'd have struggled living in Florence, and while it wasn't easy to leave her family she has, and to her full credit she's making a real go of being a Kiwi farmer's wife. Her family visit often. There's a baby on the way, too.'

'True love by the sound of it.' Max was looking at her with a smile. 'They're lucky.'

'More than most people I know.'

What about you, Max? Has anyone tempted the heart inside that sexy chest?

What about children? That question kept popping up like she really needed to know.

Max's phone pinged and she left him to it, occasionally glancing across while she did some work for the camp online.

Around ten, Lily yawned and stood up to stretch. 'Think I'll hit the sack.' It was early for her, but her arms and shoulders still ached from the chainsawing effort yesterday. Tomorrow she'd finish stacking the wood that didn't need to be split. 'See you in the morning.'

Max watched her as she stretched, making even more muscles tight. 'Don't get up for me. I can fix my own breakfast.' He stood.

'I don't lie in.'

'See you then.' He waited for her to move past him.

Lily hesitated and lifted her gaze to meet his. 'Never thought I'd say this, but I'm enjoying spending time with you.' Ouch, she shouldn't have said it quite like that. 'I mean...'

'Relax. I know what you meant. It's okay.' His finger under her chin was warm and gentle.

When she looked deeper into his eyes a thrill rolled down her spine. She leaned closer at the same time he did. 'Max,' she whispered.

His mouth was close to hers, his eyes open, watching her. 'Ah, Lily.'

Neither moved, stuck in a warm moment. Move forward and everything changed. Pull back and... She had no idea. What did she want? Right this moment she craved his kiss. Every nerve ending was crying out to be touched, to be woken up in a way she hadn't known since last time they'd been together. Wanting to find love didn't mean getting involved with Max. She stepped back.

Max reached for her hand, raised it to his lips to place a delicate kiss on her palm. 'Goodnight, Lily.' His gruff voice sent tingles of need and heat and happiness spreading through her.

That one step forward would bring her body up to his and the possibility of satisfying this continuous and growing longing he triggered in her. Pulling her hand away, she watched to see if he was upset with her for breaking contact. He didn't appear to be, but neither did he look relieved. Was he in the same messed-up head space she was? She wasn't waiting to find out. She might need him, but she wasn't prepared to accept she might take another chance at love. 'See you tomorrow.'

Charging towards her bedroom, she resisted the urge to turn around and see if he was watching her flight. Damn, damn, damn. She'd just made a mistake. Backing off had been the right thing to do, but being in that situation in the first place had been wrong. It only proved she hadn't quite convinced herself she wasn't going to get close to a man again. Not that she had to avoid the occasional fling to prevent going crazy with unrequited lust. But Max was not the man for that. Sure, he'd fix the lust, while removing the handbrake she'd hauled on to her future.

Closing her door with a thud, she leaned back against it to stare up at the ceiling. He was a great lover, but didn't want a permanent relationship. Or so she'd surmised from the fact he'd never had one. She wouldn't repeat her mistakes but hell. What to do about that sense of something more than sex and attraction that had worried her during their fling and was gnawing away now?

He hadn't laughed at her or said she was a tease. He'd been considerate when she'd backed away just now. And disappointed.

As disappointed as the thudding behind her ribs acknowledged she was.

Lily slid down the door and pulled her knees up to her chin, wound her arms around them and closed her eyes. Max had always managed to disrupt her equilibrium one way or another. Now, when she'd decided to focus on her career and hopefully becoming a mother, he had her wondering if taking another chance on love might be worth it.

Missing pieces to her puzzle were beginning to fall into place in her heart. He understood her, knew her better for their past and wasn't running away. She hadn't told him her dream yet, and that could squash any feelings he might have for her. If any. She sighed. This was probably all wishful thinking.

The sand was hard after the overnight downpour. Max's knees took a pounding as he ran along the beach, but the discomfort was worth it just to be able to breathe fresh air and clear the cobwebs from his head. It had been a restless night, evidenced by the bed cover on the floor and the sheets in a bundle around his legs when he'd woken from what little sleep he'd got. Every time he'd closed his eyes Lily had been there, her face filling his mind, allowing nothing else in. Every breath gave him a repeat of her citrus scent, making his palms tingle and his skin tighten. And more.

By being herself, she'd got to him. In a way no other woman had. She didn't try to flatter him or fawn over him. She accepted him for who he was, or for who he showed he was. It was almost possible to imagine a relationship without instantly bringing up the shutters.

Standing with her, not kissing those full lips, not wrapping his arms around her to pull her length against him, had taken all the self-control he had and then some. He'd wanted her. Badly. His resolve not to touch her would have failed if she hadn't pulled back when she had. Even then he'd wanted to touch her, take her in his arms, and ignore the fact she'd stopped moving towards him. The need hadn't died down in her eyes. She'd found it no easier to walk away than him.

Which made it harder to keep his distance. Two more nights staying in her house was going to turn him into an overheated zombie. He was already tired from lack of sleep. But if he swapped with someone else at the camp Lily mightn't talk to him again. Or she might be relieved.

'Can I run with you?'

Max glanced sideways to the enquiring look coming from the lad who'd caught up to him. 'Certainly.'

They fell into a rhythm and continued down the beach, getting further away from the camp. Max was impressed. The young man had a club foot yet wasn't showing any signs of difficulty or discomfort.

'You're Dr Max, aren't you? I'm Ollie.'

Max nodded. 'You played basketball yesterday.' Josie had been at the court, screaming encouragement at him.

'You know Josie's aunt, don't you?'

'We worked together a few years back, and are about to do so again.' He sensed the lad wanted more than that. 'I'm staying at her family's beach house this week.'

'I really like Josie a lot, and hope her aunt will be okay with us spending time together.'

'I can't see why not.' It depended what they did in that time, Max mused. Not that it was his place to say so. 'Have you met Lily?'

'Josie's going to introduce us today. I want her to like me or Josie might tell me to get lost.'

They'd reached the end of the beach and Max stopped, took some deep breaths and gazed across the bumpy sea. 'From what I've seen, you don't know Josie very well if you believe that.'

Ollie grinned. 'That's what I thought. Thanks for talking to me, Dr Max. It's cool.'

Everyone needed to talk about personal things sometimes, and he was available for these kids this week. 'No problem.' Not that he'd helped solve anything but sometimes all it took was to be a good listener. If only he could download all the stuff in his head as easily. 'Let's go back for a shower and some breakfast.'

He had to get over this. As much as Lily attracted him, keeping his feet on the ground was imperative for his sanity. She had him talking when he never told people his deepest thoughts. It made him feel connected to her in ways he'd not known before. It went beyond the monumental physical attraction to places he wasn't used to sharing. His ribs ached from the continuous pounding going on. Lily was special, and he was afraid. He could hurt them both if he gave in to this yearning for love.

They must not have another fling. She'd had two failed relationships. He wasn't adding to the list.

His pace picked up. His arms pumped, his head pushed forward, as he drove his body to work as hard as possible, trying to outrun the desire filling him, the longing for a normal, happy relationship. With Lily? Yes, damn it, with Lily. He stumbled, righted himself, and continued at the breakneck pace. These feelings slam dunked him again and again. The sense that they could have had more before had bloomed into a roaring awareness of everything about her. The vulnerability he'd felt back then had returned. Larger, more frightening. Had he got more to lose now?

Had he been trying too hard to remain single? But he had to. The five-year clearance from the oncologist was two years away. And when…if he did… No, damn it, when. No more negativity. His results had been all he could want so far. Constantly waiting for the axe to fall was wasting the opportunity to be happy. Okay, so when he got the final all-clear, he still wasn't going to marry and have children. But he could have some fun. If he kept his heart out of the picture.

The path leading up to the camp buildings veered to the left. Max stopped and leaned over, hands on hips, his lungs burning as he dragged in air. So much for a cruisy run to wake himself up. He had been awake all right, just not in cruise mode. Lily Scott had got to him once more. It might not be as the result of a massive argument, or calling off their sexy nights, but her generosity, her smiles, her honesty were even more potent. Far more dangerous. Because he wanted her. All of her. And he couldn't have her. It wouldn't be fair. An expletive tore out of him.

'You okay, Doctor?' Ollie ran up the path, looking in a lot better shape than Max was.

'Fine,' Max croaked through a breath. Fine and dandy.

'See you later.' And the kid was off, making like there was nothing wrong with his foot. Which there wasn't with his great attitude and determination.

'Something I could learn from,' Max conceded. 'Thought I was meant to be helping these guys, not the other way round.'

Resilience was the catchword for the camp. Physical resilience. Peer pressure resilience. Mental fortitude to face what other people threw at them. All these teens seemed to have bags of it and yet there were times each and every one of them suffered doubts or hurt.

Straightening up, Max started walking up the path. He liked to think he was resilient, too. Growing up in his father's house, he'd learned not to complain about his lot, to take life on the chin and get on with whatever was required. Cancer had underlined the lessons in a darker way. Now he had a future to toughen up about. He could not fall in love with Lily. Even if he'd started down the road already, he had to pull back. Now.

He'd start with a shower, breakfast and getting on with the day, making the most of everyone he interacted with, and being friendly but reserved with Lily when she came to the camp. He would not take the coward's way out and find another bed to doss down on. He'd try not to upset Lily, but wouldn't avoid her. They got on well when he relaxed and stopped overthinking everything.

When Lily joined him in the recreation hall for the wheelchair races she asked, looking directly at him, no expectation in her gaze, 'Am I cooking for two tonight?'

He had moved in for the week and not turning up for dinner would be rude. And disappointing for himself. And going against what he'd intended. 'If that's all right?' It seemed when it came to Lily he had no control over his tongue whatsoever.

Surprise filled her big, bright emerald eyes. 'Good.'

His smile seemed to have become a permanent fixture. No wonder he was in trouble. Lily did this to him, no matter how strong his determination to remain aloof.

CHAPTER SIX

HE SHOULD HAVE stayed at the camp, Max sighed. Dinner had been great, delicious food and tasty wine, comfortable company. He'd brought coffee into the lounge while Lily had banked up the fire. As he'd sat drinking the coffee he'd tried not to look too long at her, but how could he not?

Sprawled across the couch, reading something on her phone, she looked stunning in her tight jeans and that navy jersey draped softly over her breasts. Tension started crawling through him, tightening places where he didn't need constriction. Memories returned of the warm softness of those breasts filling his palms, the curves of her backside under his hands as he'd held her close and driven into her, those long legs wound around his waist, holding him to her as if she hadn't wanted him to withdraw.

Max leapt to his feet. 'Think I'll have an early night,' he grunted.

Lily was instantly on her feet before him. 'Are you all right?'

'No.' Dragging his fingers through his hair, he drank in the sight in front of him. The vibrant colour of her eyes added to the vibrancy of the waves of thick hair spilling over her shoulders. Hair that shone in the light and had been silk to his touch last time he'd slid his fingers through it.

'It's early.' Her voice was husky, and as sexy as hell.

'I know.' He couldn't find it in him to lie and say he'd had a big day and wanted some sleep. He needed to get away before she drove him crazy. Crazier. He sure wasn't telling her *that*. Not while he had a glimmer of common sense left in his head.

'Max? What's up?'

Like he was about to answer. He'd put some air between them. But his feet were weights, holding him to the floor as he drank in Lily. She was beautiful with her cute nose, lips full, smooth, pink cheeks. A pulse in her throat rose and fell in time to the rapid thumping going on under his ribs.

Placing his hands on the curves of her shoulders, he gently brought her closer and lowered his head to kiss her. Just one small, soft kiss. He had to, couldn't resist any more.

Lily pressed closer, her mouth opening under his.

The citrus scent filled his head. Those lips blanked all thought. His mouth opened on hers, his tongue slid inside to taste her. His arms were around her, his thighs pressed against her, his reaction pressing into her belly. Oh, Lily.

Her tongue met his, danced between them. On his back her fingers were digging in. She was on her toes, stretching upward, pushing into his chest with her breasts.

He kept on kissing her. He couldn't get enough. He'd wanted this from the day he'd seen her on the pavement outside the clinic with their patient. Her body felt right pressed into his, melding with him, becoming one.

This was what he wanted, needed. And had sworn not to look for.

When he hadn't been looking, Lily had happened, and look where they were. In each other's arms, free to do as they wished. Except, no, he shouldn't. What if he ended up hurting her? He knew little about strong, loving relationships. Relationships that survived no matter what, even cancer. If he screwed up he'd be heartbroken. Yes, he knew that now. He might survive the hurt, though not hurting her. But pulling his mouth away from her, dropping his arms to his sides, stepping back—that was impossible. Drawing in some air, he submitted to his overwhelming need and continued kissing her. Time became immeasurable.

Then slowly Lily drew her mouth away, gasping for air. 'Max?' she whispered. 'What's going on?' A huge question sat in her eyes. Her arms remained around him, holding tight.

'I want you.'

She was watching him with an intensity that didn't bode well.

Did she see his uncertainty about the future? There wasn't any about wanting her. But his promise to himself was rising again, waving a red flag. Lily would see that, even if she didn't understand. Especially how he'd reacted to their kisses. The loving way he held her, the excitement that would be in his face and at the front of his jeans.

'I want you, too.' Now her arms left him, her body pulled back as she dropped back onto her feet. 'There is a but, isn't there?'

She could read him better than he'd expected. With

his fingers, he massaged his scalp. 'Not about taking you to bed and making love. Not at all.'

'Then why are we standing out here?'

'I don't want a repeat of last time.'

Her eyes widened with disbelief. And something more. Surprise? Or understanding? Because she felt the same? What did he tell her? The truth. All of it? Or be selective? Admitting his loving feelings wasn't wise. If she reciprocated in any small way he'd have given hope that he'd then have to shoot down by telling her why he'd never get into a permanent relationship.

Taking Lily's hand, he said, 'Join me on the couch. I've something to tell you.'

'This is serious.'

'Yes, it is.' His heart was thudding, the rhythm rough. If only they hadn't reached this point, had pretended all was okay, he could've continued kissing and sucking up her passion and sexiness and gentleness and... And everything about her.

'Do your kisses usually move in this direction?' A worried smile came his way.

'You'll be the first woman I've talked to about this.' It was too late to pull out. Lily dropped onto the couch and shuffled that cute butt to one end. 'I'm all ears.' No smile of any kind now, but deep concern was coming his way.

The last thing he needed was Lily feeling sorry for him. Sinking down beside her, Max stared at his outstretched feet. 'You asked why I changed specialties. My answer was true, but how that came about is because I loathe being stuck inside buildings and not having a sense of the outside world.' He paused.

Lily briefly rested her palm on his thigh. 'Go on.'

Covering her hand with his, the tension in his gut

lightened. He needed her strength, her resilience. He needed Lily. Which was frightening. He had spent most of his life fighting not to need his parents, or anyone else. So why Lily? But why *not*? She was strong, took none of his nonsense, and could be tender towards him.

'Max?'

'Sorry.' He shook his head. 'Three years ago I had cancer.'

Her hand jerked under his.

'Bowel cancer. I had surgery, chemo, radiotherapy and then a new treatment that's still being trialled.'

'That explains the hair.'

'You didn't think I'm going grey because I work my butt off all the time?' It wasn't hard to smile at her.

'I thought you looked like you've been through something awful. I was right, though not about the reason. Max, your news is shocking. How did you cope? Did you stay in Auckland?'

'I went back to Dunedin, mainly because my family's there, though not all together.' And they had done their best to rally round, but none of them had been used to being so close and talking about serious issues.

'I wanted to get away from everyone I worked with so I didn't have to put up with their sympathy. It didn't take long to realise that'd been a mistake. Most of you would've given me a lot of support in the form of bad jokes and always visiting when I needed to sleep.'

She flicked a grin on and off. 'This happened while I was still in town? Now I think about it, I did hear you'd left the emergency department.'

He nodded. 'You'd just moved to an emergency clinic on the North Shore.'

'Filling in time before going to Singapore.' Shaking

her head, Lily asked, 'Where are you now with the cancer? I'm presuming you're all right and waiting for the all-clear.'

If only it was that simple. *It could be if you let it.* 'Yes. And no.' When she fixed that concern on him again, he hurried on. 'I am healthy, fit and have no symptoms. It isn't easy to let go the fear of cancer returning, though. I've got a little way to go for the all-clear, and I hope when that happens I'll move forward with being positive.'

'You already are. Did you not hear yourself? You said when the all-clear happens. Sounds positive to me.'

Her tender smile pierced his heart when he didn't have a heart to give, despite his growing feelings for Lily. He needed her in his life. Standing up, Max paced across the room, returned to sit down closer. 'I hadn't thought of it like that. Not that it changes a thing. I worry that if I do get ill again I could hurt anyone I become close to.'

'Not even if you hurt someone by walking away when she wanted to be with you?'

Was she talking about herself? Or speaking generally? 'Better sooner than later.'

Suddenly she was staring at him hard. Searching for something. What was the question? He might be able to save her from whatever was causing this. 'Lily? What is it?'

She shook her head. 'No, it doesn't matter.'

'Come on. Spill. I've told you something I never share.'

For minutes he thought she was going to ignore him. Then her chest rose, fell and she faced him. 'You indicated you weren't going to have a family. Does that mean you could if you wanted?'

Where was this going? This wasn't something he'd expected to talk about when he'd started down this track, but he may as well tell her. It couldn't hurt. 'My sperm's in the bank. I didn't want to do it but my oncologist talked me into it by saying best to cover the options, and that a time might come when I'd regret not doing so, and if I didn't nothing was wasted. So I gave in and went ahead.'

'You don't think you will have children, do you?'

'I have no intention of it.'

His own kids? His heart squeezed painfully. It would be super-fantastic to be a dad. But what if he left them without a father? 'I don't want to leave my kids without a dad, and that could happen if the cancer returns.'

'Kids lose their parents for all sorts of reasons. Wives lose their husbands, too. You might live till you're ninety and be as grumpy as hell. That's far more likely than you having a relapse.' Her smile had returned, but it wasn't as straight and happy as before. More as though there was still a question lurking in the background.

'Thanks for your support,' he muttered.

'You're welcome.' She stood up. 'That coffee's not doing me any good. I'm making hot chocolate. Want one?'

Was this the end of the discussion? He wasn't sure whether to be pleased or disappointed. 'I'd love one.' The whole telling Lily thing had gone more smoothly than he'd expected. 'Why did you ask that particular question?'

Lily carefully spooned chocolate granules into mugs while the milk heated in the microwave. Could she tell him? With his fear of the cancer returning, he'd prob-ably be furious if she offered to have his child, say she didn't understand. Which she didn't, quite. But he'd want to be a part of the child's life if she used his sperm. He thought that if he fathered a child it could be left without a dad but she wasn't planning on having a father in the picture anyway. At least she hadn't been until Max had come back into her life.

The romance had been growing on her side, and that had started her thinking they could do this together. Now that romance and his statement of no children reminded her of Leo. They'd supposedly been in love and he hadn't told her he didn't want children.

But Max wasn't Leo. He hadn't held back from telling her anything so far. It was early days, but now she understood he probably never would admit to it if he ever fell for her. He was set on remaining single and not involving children in his life in case the worst happened. For that, she could only admire him and believe in him more than ever. But despite that, the idea of Max as the father of her child was growing stronger every day. As were her feelings for him, and that might make having his child and remaining uninvolved impossible.

Not long ago she'd thought they'd barely be able to tolerate each other and now she was wondering about asking if he'd have a baby with her. If that's what a few heated kisses did then she'd better pull on her wet suit for the duration of his time here. It was hard work getting the tight-fitting suit off at the best of times. A passion-killer for sure.

'I don't like it when you go quiet.' Max half laughed, half growled. He'd shared a lot, and now the doubts over his actions would be setting in.

'Just assimilating everything.' Glancing across to the lounge, she found him watching her far too closely.

'It's a biggie.' He nodded.

'Why you? When you were young and fit? A doctor even. Yes, I get that's irrelevant, but hell.'

'Thank you.' He slumped. 'I thought I was strong, but listen to me whinging like someone stole my ice cream.'

'Come on, Max. You are strong. You took a massive hit, but you're here, getting on with life, if not in the way you might've once envisioned. I haven't been in your shoes, but it seems extreme to not want to try for a happy future that includes your own family. If that's what you want.' It was becoming important that he did for himself, not her.

'You're right.' He turned away.

The microwave stopped and Lily retrieved the milk, poured it into the mugs and stirred vigorously. 'Here you go.' She sat at the table, elbows on top and her chin resting in her hands as she waited for Max to join her. *If* he joined her.

'I saw wives and husbands visiting their terminally ill spouses, kids seeing their parents fading away before their eyes. It was horrific. The brave faces, the downright sad ones, the despair and the hope. I do not want to put anyone I love through that.' He slid onto the opposite chair.

She tentatively sipped the hot drink. 'Who was with you through those months?' Did he have siblings? Parents still alive?

'My sister and her husband were incredibly supportive, my mum stepped up in her own way, making sure I had whatever I needed, which was nice.' He shrugged. 'Dad was a surprise. He dropped in for a few minutes every day, said little or nothing and went away again.'

'A man of few words?'

'Very few, but he did tell me he was proud I'd become

a doctor. At first it hurt he wouldn't talk about the cancer but after he said that I realised he'd never known how to say what was in his heart. It was a relief really, though I still wish he'd been a little more open with me as a child.'

Talk about making up years of silence. 'Go, you.' There was nothing to say that wouldn't sound trite.

Max gaped, then laughed. 'Oh, Lily, I don't think I'll ever fully understand you.'

Sounded like a great arrangement to her. It might help to remember she wasn't looking for love again, only a DNA donor. Which didn't explain why daily that idea was twisting into something new, deeper, and filled with love. 'We see lots of tragedies in our everyday lives as doctors, but facing it personally... Well...' she raised one shoulder, let it fall away '...I haven't a clue how I'd react.'

'That's another reason I wanted to change direction in my career. Surgeons spend little time with their patients while they're conscious. Over time GPs see and hear more about what's behind a patient—family, career or interests, illnesses, mind-sets. I also need a window to look out at the sky and trees and traffic, and that allows the light into the dark corners.' His eyes were haunted. 'I like to use the understanding I've gained to help my patients through whatever they have to face.'

She touched his hand. 'You're incredible. You know that? I bet it still isn't easy.' Lily's stomach tightened. Nothing was. Even if she decided she wanted Max as her sperm donor, she didn't have the right to ask him. He deserved better, to have his own needs recognised and accepted, not wrecked to satisfy hers. She didn't want to hurt Max. 'You've had a lot to contend with.'

'Who doesn't at some point in their lives? Anyway, let's drop this. It's too maudlin, and I prefer being cheerful.'

'Then drink your chocolate. It'll put a smile on your face.' While giving her a moment to move past thinking of Max as a likely prospect for a father. His smile was re-appearing, bringing a storm of need rushing through her. One night wouldn't be enough. One night would lead to trouble, have her wanting to spend more and more time with Max, and then what? As he'd said, the day would come when he'd call it off—if she didn't first to save her heart like last time. Only this time it'd be harder to do. She was beginning to think Max had always been the man for her, that she'd been in denial even when she'd been with Leo.

Max was smiling. 'I feel like a child when I drink this. My mum used to make it for me and my sister some-times.'

Lily's heart lurched. He'd had it hard, growing up, which explained some of the sadness in his eyes when he was far away. Again she laid her hand over his. This sitting around talking to Max was becoming their new norm. Yet as much as she wanted to know all there was about him, she wouldn't return the favour. Not yet. Col-lecting the mugs, she stood and went to rinse them. 'I'm turning in. It's early but I've got a good book on the go.'

Max leaned back in his chair, stretching his legs under the table and tapping the tabletop with his forefinger. 'I'm *that* boring?' he asked through one of those devastating smiles she lusted after.

'Not at all.' But a woman had to do what she could to avoid getting into situations she'd have trouble extricat-ing herself from. Like those kisses. Just thinking about them made her knees weak and her hip press against the bench for support. They'd been moments from heading down the hall to her bed. Max had been hard, pressing against her like he'd never wanted to pull away.

'I thought not.' Max stood up. Came close. Lowered his head so his mouth hovered over hers. 'A goodnight kiss, then?'

Lily swallowed.

'Yes or no?' Max whispered.

'Damn you,' she growled. 'No.'

Liar, shrieked her body. *I want every bit of him.*

But she had to resist. Kissing would lead to making love, and then she'd be in big trouble. She was not ready. Forget the need filling her every moment she was with Max. She could still get hurt. 'Sorry,' she whispered, and turned away.

He opened his eyes wide, studied Lily's tense shoulders, straight back and clenched hands at her sides. 'Why, Lily?'

'Because I am not ready for another relationship.' She turned back to him, confusion puckering her face. 'Wrong. I'm not getting into another at all.'

'I was only thinking of tonight.'

Sadness filled her eyes. 'I guessed as much, and while that fits with what I've just said, I can't do it.'

He reached for her hand, unwound her fingers. 'Come and sit down. I don't want to end tonight on this note.'

She stood staring at him for what seemed a lifetime. Who knew what was whirling around in her mind? But finally she nodded, pulled her hand free and headed for the couch to drop down and grab a cushion, which she held close to her chest.

Slowly sinking down on the chair opposite, Max thought how he was going to talk to her about this without giving too much of himself away. He drew a breath. 'I didn't know I'd missed you until that night of the farewell party. Standing in the doorway to Reception, watching you chat to people like you'd known them for ever, it was as though something solid from the past had returned, giving me hope.'

Now she'd be getting ready to kick him out of the house. He hadn't made any sense at all, except to himself. 'We had our differences. Yet those are what I missed. You didn't care what I thought about your opinions, just kept handing them out. It was refreshing, and I didn't understand that's what I'd enjoyed until you turned up that night.'

Shut up. There's explaining and there's talking far too much.

Her fingers were digging hard into that cushion. 'Yes, that was Max. The Max I once knew intimately.' Then she lifted a finger, doubt lingering in her face. 'But he doesn't *sound* like the man I thought I knew.'

'We didn't know each other. Not really.'

Lily tensed. The sound of waves hitting the beach filled the room. Light gusts of wind stirred the trees in the back yard and then she relaxed. 'You used to infuriate me about many things. No doubt I did the same in return.' Her head tipped back against the couch. 'In the intervening years I've wondered where you were, what you were up to.'

'Snap.'

Her breasts rose and she slowly lowered her head to lock eyes with him. 'I had to finish our fling, Max. We were fantastic in bed, no disagreements, all about giving and taking, but I couldn't see how it could lead to anything but trouble. Our relationship wasn't that great, except for those few nights, and I didn't want us ending up arguing in bed.'

He smiled. He couldn't help himself. 'We would've eventually. It was a given. We both had our own ways of getting through life and they weren't compatible. I was selfish.' He was comfortable with Lily in a way he'd never been. He'd told her about the cancer and how it had affected his hopes for the future when he didn't readily tell anyone. Only his sister and one of his closest friends knew how he'd shut down on wanting a wife and kids. And now Lily did. Who was single and building on her career like there were no other plans for *her* future. Had her ex hurt her that badly? She'd be a great mum if the interactions with Josie he'd seen were anything to go by. 'You ever think about having kids? You'd be great at it.'

Lily stiffened, gripping the cushion even harder, pushing back further into the couch, making a chilly gap between them that did not bode well.

'Lily? It was a compliment.' Were there problems for her around having a baby?

'Thank you,' she muttered.

From what he could see, her face was now devoid of emotion. Which told him a lot was going on in her head. 'Talk to me.'

Silence.

He could manage that, too. He waited, forcing the growing tension to back off, ignoring the questions that kept blinking into his mind. There was no point trying to guess what had upset Lily about his statement. He'd only make matters worse.

Her voice was thick, heavy. 'It's so strange you should say that tonight.'

That he'd paid her a compliment or that she'd make a great mother? He waited for more.

Lily rubbed her palms together, laid her hands on her knees, went back to holding the cushion. 'Please hear me out before you comment.'

The seriousness in her voice and face nearly had him telling her she didn't have to say anything if she didn't want to. The moment she told him what was on her mind he knew there'd be no avoiding a truth he might not want to hear, let alone accept. But this was a new relationship for them, one where he didn't poke fun at her and instead listened and helped if possible. 'Go on,' he answered with as much gravity as he'd heard in her voice.

'I do want to be a mother, have a child of my own.' Her breast rose, held there for a long time. As it fell back into place the words gushed from her mouth. 'On my own. I'm not interested in another relationship. I've had two failures. There's only so much rejection and hurt I can take.'

He should be pleased to hear she wasn't interested in a permanent relationship because he'd always know he was safe if they were to continue what they'd started tonight. But he wasn't pleased. Not one bit. Disappointment rattled him, shocking in its intensity. Why, when he wasn't going for permanency? 'Two mistakes doesn't necessarily mean the next time you fall in love it won't work out.'

'I'm not prepared to risk it. Anyway, you're not meant to be commenting, at least until I've finished what I've got to say.' Another pause. 'This might shock you. I am looking to see if I can find a sperm donor I can agree to. It's freaky, but I so want to be a mum. If I can't have a husband or partner who loves me then I'll go it alone. It won't be easy, especially as I'll continue working, but it's been done before and I'll manage.' She drew another breath.

'You probably think I'm being selfish, that all kids deserve, need two parents, and to an extent you're right. But there're plenty of kids out there with one parent and who are growing up surrounded in love and support. That's my promise to any child I'm lucky enough to have.'

Her eyes hadn't left him throughout the whole time she'd been talking. Looking to see if he flinched, or flattened his lips, or got angry? Then she should be surprised because he felt nothing but admiration. 'You're one gutsy lady.' It would be hard, lonely and difficult to juggle work and a baby, but if anyone could raise a child alone and do it well, then here she was.

One well-shaped eyebrow lifted and her gaze lightened. 'Safe answer?'

'Absolutely.' Max itched to brush the stray strands of hair that had fallen over her face. 'Seriously, it's no surprise about you wanting to take on such a huge project.' He put a finger to her lips when she made to speak. 'That's not being derogatory. This will be a lifelong commitment, more than anything you've undertaken before or probably ever will.' Lily wanted a child, and needed a donor for that to happen.

Was this why he'd given in to the oncologist's suggestion of saving his sperm in case he changed his mind about becoming a father? But even if he got over his hang-ups and offered his sperm he'd be worried about leaving his child behind later. If he wasn't prepared to follow through on his feelings for Lily then he sure as hell wasn't offering to be the genetic father of her baby. 'I take it you've done a lot of thinking and research about this?'

'Loads.' Lily relaxed enough to tuck her legs under her backside. 'You continue to astonish me with your belief in what I do. I only hope you're right.'

Tonight had been an evening of opening their hearts to each other. Strange how much more relaxed about everything that made him feel. The edginess he'd carried since his treatment had quietened. Not disappeared, but it was definitely less apparent. Long may that last. 'You won't let your child down, Lily.'

'My biggest problem is fear of letting myself down.'

'Both those men really did a number on you.' His heart ached for her. How could two men have been so cruel to beautiful Lily? Was he biased, by any chance? Of course he was. The thought of anyone hurting her drove him mad.

'They did, but I'm over them and getting on with what's important to me.'

'You think you're over them when you've altered your dreams for the future because of how they treated you?'

'That's enough, Max. I have told you more than I'd once have thought possible. Don't think it gives you the right to start telling me where I'm going wrong.' She said it with a smile, but there was steel running through the words. Steel best not ignored.

'Okay. Think I'll turn in.' He wouldn't get any sleep, but he couldn't sit here with Lily any longer. She pulled him in, made him hungry. He wanted her beyond reason, yet he also wanted to make her happy, not only in the physical way but in every way possible. That just wasn't going to happen so it was best he give up now while he was ahead. *Ha.* Ahead of what? Already his body craved her and his mind taunted him with what could be if he let go the past. Forget being ahead. He was so far behind it was painful.

CHAPTER SEVEN

Lily's arms were tense from the vibrations coming from the chainsaw as she sized up another tree that had come down during last weekend's storm. This one was at the back of the camp where no one usually went. It could stay there for another time, but she needed something to concentrate on that didn't have anything to do with Max and what she'd told him last night.

Pulling the goggles over her eyes, she chose the first branch to remove and set to work, focusing on the tree and how it was balanced on strong branches and not wobbling as the saw slid effortlessly through her target. The branch fell to the ground. One down. The second one was as easy. A well-sharpened blade made life a lot easier.

She sighed. If only it was as easy to fix the niggling sense of hope for her and Max finding their way to each other. Fix as in get together romantically or get on with their lives separately, not this hovering in between state. They'd come so close to kissing and making love last night that she still couldn't breathe properly. Her head ached with need, her heavy heart thumped with sadness, and she'd berated herself all night for saying no.

To have said yes would've been wonderful, and brought on another headache, only this one filled with worry that she was already on the slippery slide into love and loss and pain. Max was getting to her, and it was getting harder all the time to maintain her resolve not to fall in love again.

But she wasn't here to think about Max. Attacking the next cut too hard, she slowed, drew a breath and continued more carefully.

A while later she paused to study the pile she'd made. Not a bad morning's work. Killing the motor, she put the saw aside, relishing the sudden quiet. Then her skin tightened. She wasn't alone. Spinning around, she relaxed enough to be friendly. 'Max. Hello.'

'Morning.' He sauntered towards her.

She wasn't fooled. There was a wariness in his gaze, in the way he was tightening and loosening his fingers at his sides. He needn't worry. She wasn't raising the subject of last night's conversations. She'd opened her heart about having a child, and he hadn't laughed or thrown it back at her. When they weren't in sexual overdrive they were getting on so well it was amazing. So much so she'd had to get away while it all sank in, and she figured where she was going with this. Yet he'd found her and that made her happy. Damn it all. She wasn't supposed to happy about that. 'Did you have breakfast here?'

'Yep. Thought I'd stay out of your way for a bit. Obviously not for too long, though.' His smile warmed her throughout. 'How're you today?'

Happy. Confused. Worried. Happy. 'Just fine.' It all came down to Max how good she felt. And confused, and worried, and happy. 'Aren't you refereeing a game this morning?'

He shook his head. 'Everyone's inside for talks until eleven. Logan suggested I come over and see if you needed help moving this. Looks like I'm too late. Want a coffee instead?'

When she nodded, he picked up the saw and walked beside her towards the camp kitchen.

Loud shouts of laughter reached her ears. 'Morning break for everyone. Let's move it.' She picked up her pace and Max matched her. Kind of in sync. As they were becoming about a lot of things. They'd been fully in sync when they'd made love. *Sex, Lily. Not making love.* The love word didn't come into anything to do with Max, then or now. Even if she wanted it to, it couldn't. He'd made it clear he wasn't looking for a woman to share his life with. And she'd done exactly the same in different words, for different reasons. Yet it felt as though neither wanted that any more.

He'd make a wonderful father.

She slowed. Yes, he would. *But he wasn't going to be one.* He'd saved his sperm. *He didn't want to use it.* He might change his mind. *He might not.* He could be her donor. *He'd probably say that was too weird.*

Max slowed for her to catch up. 'Where've you gone?'

Wouldn't he like to know? Probably not. It would be too much. 'Dreaming of a hot scone soaked in melted butter.'

Max laughed. 'I hope you're in luck.'

The plates were still half-full of scones, and the coffee pot in the kitchen for the staff had just been refilled. Sinking onto a chair, Lily stretched her legs and rolled her shoulders. A tightness had built up from holding the chainsaw so long.

'Sore?' Max asked.

She hadn't seen or sensed him coming into her space.

SUE MacKAY   127

Slipping, Lily. Though it meant she'd managed to get him out of her mind, however briefly. 'Overworked.'

His smile let him straight back under her guard. If only she had led him down to her bedroom. She jerked. *Stop it, Lily. This is not the time to be reminiscing about last night.* She'd spent the last hour or more ignoring all the hot, exciting sensations Max had woken in her last night. Hell, any time he came near every one of those sensations filled her.

Was she falling for him? She tensed.

'Relax. I'll get you some food.'

Closing her eyes, she drew a calming breath. Was she? Could she? He never left her mind, turned her on with a glance. She felt at ease with him, wanted more time together. But she was afraid to try again, doubted it'd work out this time any better than the previous two times. If she was starting to get serious about Max she was setting her heart up to be hurt again. Anyway, Max was against getting entangled with anyone or having a family. Surely, deep down, he must want to grab life and run with it? Did he need someone to grab his hand and show him the way? If so, was she ready for that?

'Dr Max, Ollie's had an accident.' Josie was shoving her way through people to get to him. 'Come quick.' She spun around. 'Auntie Lily, you come, too.'

Leaping to her feet, Lily banged her mug down and joined Josie as she raced alongside Max. 'What's happened?'

'We were chasing the soccer ball and he got caught in a hole and went down. I think he's twisted his knee.' Tears streaked down Josie's cheeks. 'He's hurting a lot. He says he's all right. Like I believe him.'

Lily reached for her hand. 'Max will take good care of him.'

'What about you, Auntie Lily? You're the best.'

Max tapped Josie on the arm. 'Thanks, pal.'

'She is,' Josie protested. 'When I knocked myself out on the hay bailer, Lily wouldn't let anyone move me until she'd put something round my neck. Then she got me to hospital real fast.'

Lily hugged her as they raced over the lawn towards a group of teenagers. 'Max is very good, too. *And* he's the camp doctor, not me. I promise Ollie's in good hands.' So was she while she sorted herself out. If she committed to Max, fell in love with him, it would be for ever. If he returned that love, she'd be safe. It was a big if, though. He was so doubtful about his future. And to be fair, she wasn't one hundred percent certain of her own, was still wary of handing over her heart only have it squashed again.

'Okay, clear a space, guys,' Max said as he pushed through the onlookers and knelt down. 'Ollie, I hear you put your foot in a hole while running after the ball.'

Ollie groaned. 'It was a rabbit burrow. I heard a pop as I fell. My knee looks odd.'

'It hurts?'

'Yeah, some. My foot's swelling. The shoe's too tight.'

Max said, 'I'll remove it.' As he was doing that, he was appraising the knee in front of him. 'You've sprained your knee. What I'm not sure about is if there's a torn ligament or not. That popping sound suggests there might be.'

It was good how Max was being up front with him, not treating him like a child, which was a tendency with some people when with the physically disabled.

'Josie? You up for bringing me water and food when I need it? And fetching my phone or a jacket?' Ollie teased.

Josie bit her lip, looking worried. Then she giggled. 'Absolutely not. Then you'd be wanting me to wipe your...' She broke off, looking embarrassed when she glanced at Max.

'Trust me, there's nothing wrong with his arms.' Max grinned. 'Okay, Ollie, first we need to get you inside and raid the freezer for ice to pack around your knee. Then I'll phone for an MRI appointment, which might be a couple of days away. In the meantime you should try walking normally, though not too often straight up.'

'So nothing too bad going on?'

'It'll be painful for a while, but more a nuisance than anything.' Max stood up. 'As long as common sense prevails and you don't decide to go for a run.'

'When I need your advice I'll have to crawl to you.'

Lily smiled. The young man had strength and a sense of humour. Josie had done all right first time round. Glancing at her niece, her smile increased. Yes, Josie was smitten. Her eyes were full of love and her face lit up with a full-on smile. She might be lucky and, like her parents, have found her life partner at an early age. No one could predict how these things worked out, especially not her aunt.

Lily's gaze tracked to Max who, with the help of other boys, was getting Ollie up onto his good foot. Max had been straightforward about the injury, hadn't downplayed it, or built it up to reinforce the need to be careful. Ollie could make his own decisions, to a point.

There was a squeezing in her chest. Max was coming up trumps from every angle, making it impossible to deny the burgeoning hope in her heart that she could try for a relationship again. Not only have a baby, but a man in her life. Ducking her head, she wiped her cheek. Could she be so lucky? Max and their baby? Her chest sank as her stomach tightened in on itself.

Could her dreams come true? Why not? *Let go, and see what happens.* Her heart softened as her gaze followed him up the lawn with the boys. Okay, yes, she was falling for him. Wait. Wasn't this a similar feeling to that she'd known when she and Leo had been starting out? It was nothing like it. That time there hadn't been a sense of coming home, of having found exactly what she wanted, required, loved.

Turning to stare out over the grassed field to the quiet sea, Lily contemplated her feelings for Max. Letting *him* down wasn't an option. The first flush of love in both her previous relationships had come with an easy acceptance of everything about the men, no deep thought had gone into it. It had felt right so she'd gone along with the excitement and love. With Max there was history, not all good, but it showed him to be rock solid when it came to giving his all to any person or project he undertook. That gave her confidence he wouldn't change his mind and want out of a relationship, if he ever got over his fears enough to let love reign his heart.

'Auntie Lily, what are you doing? We're going inside.'

'Ollie doesn't need me. Max knows what he's doing so I'm going for a walk.' Wrapping her arms around Josie's thin frame, she kissed the top of her head. 'Go spend time with Ollie. He's being brave but he needs you.'

'You like him?'

'Of course I do.'

'Cool. See you later.' Josie was gone, bounding inside as though afraid of missing a minute with Ollie.

Lily walked to the beach and headed in the direction of the house. The fresh, cool air was good on her face, the increasing silence just what her frazzled mind needed.

Max.

He'd sneaked into her mind, body, everywhere, when she had least expected him. She had to decide whether to get over him for ever or take a chance. She had no idea if he'd join her in that risk, but if she did lay her heart on the line, it would be with everything she had. And it felt as if her heart had already made up its mind.

'There you go,' Max said as he wound the ice bag around his young patient's knee. 'Now, what I said about this not being a major injury is true—to a point. You can wreck it further if you get too exuberant physically. A little often is the way to go.'

'I hear you, Doc.'

'I'll make sure he behaves,' Josie added, sitting as close to Ollie as possible without being on top of him. 'Auntie Lily's gone for a walk along the beach. That way…' She pointed a thumb in the direction of the beach house. 'She wasn't looking happy. I think you should see what's wrong,' she said with a cheeky smile.

Little minx. 'I've got a physio session with some of your pals shortly, so I'll be hanging around here.' What was wrong with Lily? She'd seemed to have got over last night's black moment. Had he said something else to upset her? Nothing came to mind. As far as he knew, they were getting along just fine. More than fine if their intense conversations last night were anything to go by, if the way he couldn't stop thinking about her and them being together a lot more was an indicator. 'I'll leave you two to fill in the rest of the day and see what's happening in the hall.'

First, he'd get some fresh air. Glancing at his watch, he saw he had fifteen minutes to spare so headed down to the beach and began striding out in the opposite direction from the beach house.

Lily. She was so sexy she blew his mind away. He got lost in her just being in the same room. His heart had taken hours to calm after she'd said no to a kiss. Then her revelation about wanting to have a child on her own had been a gut-buster. It underlined her determination not to get involved with another man, yet there was passion oozing out of her when they were together. It wasn't any of his business she was thinking about getting pregnant. He couldn't do that for her.

Pain ripped out of his mouth, roared through the air.

No, he couldn't. Yet he had to. Or take a chance, ask her to take a chance.

An image of them lying naked on his bed three years ago, their bodies intertwined after making love, slammed him. What was it about Lily that these images came as quickly as a blink? With a reaction in his groin that needing satisfying. He couldn't get enough of her body, her sexiness, the gentle touches she gave him, the kisses filled with longing and more. Sharing and caring. And more. Something he refused to identify because then he'd have to face up to facts and he just wasn't ready for that.

Was he ready to give up? Not kiss Lily again? Not to hold her in his arms and soak up the heat she gave him; heat that overtook the cold that had sat in his heart from the day he'd decided never to look for love? Not to sit together over a coffee or a wine while talking about anything and everything? Sharing their hearts? Their dreams?

Max kicked a convenient pebble down to the water. No, damn it, he didn't want to give that up any more. Especially as she'd shared something so personal and dear as wanting to have a baby. He kicked another, larger pebble and grimaced at the sharp pain in his toes.

Lily, Lily, Lily. You always did my head in. Only this time it's for different reasons. You're softer, funnier, more accepting, more compelling. I like you. I love...

Max swore. Wrong. Wrong. Another stone splashed into the sea. They were getting along just fine as they were. *Leave it at that. Don't bring in the heavy emotions. Don't bring in the baby idea.* That would only lead to trouble.

On Thursday, Max's last night before he headed back to the city, Lily placed plates in the oven to warm for dinner, though so far he was a no-show. Not even a text to say he was running late as he had last night. Something must've happened to one of the children. They were all getting a little too exuberant as the week passed.

After pouring a small glass of wine, she added wood to the fire, and sank onto the couch with her legs tucked under her. Tomorrow was Friday. Come Monday she'd be ensconced in the Remuera Medical Hub, getting on with her career where Max would be part of the scene. How much importance had he put on what she'd said about having a baby? He'd better not think she'd been hinting for his involvement.

A shudder ran the length of her spine. She wanted a baby so much, but over the past days the need had begun taking second place to wanting to be with Max. It was still hard to believe she'd pulled away from kissing him. Especially when she'd wanted to so badly. Longed for his kisses, dreamed of them. To have given in would have been to hand herself over to him and trust he wouldn't hurt her when he'd said he wasn't getting into a relationship.

She had to concentrate on having a child, not on losing her heart to a man. She'd love her baby completely and utterly. No doubts whatsoever. Just because there wouldn't be a real, live father on the scene it didn't mean her child would go without love from the males in her family. Try keeping her brothers out of the picture. Impossible. They'd be backed up by their own children too. She sighed. She'd gone through this time after time and always came up with the same certainty. It was fine to have a child as a solo parent. She would be a good mother.

But there was Max. She felt connected to him in a genuine caring and sharing way. There was love there too, though she wasn't admitting how involved her heart was. It was taking over from the ticking biological clock urging her to become a mother. As if she'd come full circle and wanted the man, the romance and then a child would follow from shared love.

Damn, this was difficult. What to do? Max had become important to her future, her plans, herself. She wanted to be the same for him. He had hurdles to overcome if there was ever going to be a happy outcome for him. She wanted that to be with her.

Follow your heart. It was already involved with Max so had little to lose. Lily drained her glass. So much for a small drink. She needed more. Where was he anyway? Dinner would be ruined soon. Opening the oven, she lifted out the plates and a dish of thick creamy sauce and set them on a board. She wasn't waiting any longer.

'That smells delicious.'

She spun around. 'I didn't hear you come in.' How long had he been here? Thud, thud inside her chest. How could she have missed him? Whenever she was near Max her pulse had a way of speeding up. Not tonight apparently. Though it was making up for lost time now.

'I drove up about twenty minutes ago and got waylaid by George wanting to talk about Archie and how he's really in the doldrums about Enid. Thinks it's his fault she's not coming right as he was over here instead of at home.'

'Nothing unusual in that. But I can understand his point. Enid's everything to him, and he'll be lost if she doesn't make it home again.' It was good George had talked to Max. Especially when those men were so stubborn about talking about anything personal.

'I gathered that.' Max opened the fridge to retrieve the wine bottle they hadn't finished on Monday night. 'Top up?'

'A small one.' Now Max was here she'd take it quietly. Spilling her mind was not happening. Since it was the last night he'd be sharing the house she wanted to make the most of it. Who could have known that they would share such intimacy? Not only the physical kind, not the kisses that'd turn her into a riot of heat and need and hope. But talking about hopes and dreams and what had gone wrong in their pasts. She should follow her heart. Get to know everything about him. And if it didn't work out? At least she'd have tried. If it didn't work out, then it didn't. The hurt would be great either way.

Just don't rush Max.

'What's for dinner?' Max asked, then shook his head, looking surprised.

'What?'

'I sound as though this is normal, coming in and asking what we're going to eat.' His lips pressed together as though he needed to stop any more words spilling out. The surprise was being replaced by bewilderment. The wine splashed down the side of the glass he was filling.

By the look on his face, he'd made a blunder and was appalled to have voiced it. That hurt. But this was never going to be easy. Reaching for the glass he handed her, she took a deep sip. Max hadn't meant it to sound like that; it had been a casual reference to sharing the house this week. 'Spaghetti bolognese. Hope you don't mind pasta.'

'When it smells as good as what I'm getting whiffs of, I'll eat anything.' Relief was replacing all the other emotions in his face.

And pouring through her veins. They were getting along far better than she'd ever imagined, and it was good. Better than good. Regardless of the future, colleagues, friends—lovers?—regardless of her indecisions, right now it felt great to be spending an evening with Max, enjoying a wine and meal together. That's what she'd run with and to hell with all those other ideas about love. They could take a hike and leave her to enjoy the night.

Max leaned a hip against the bench to watch Lily talking with Josie on the phone. There was such love in her face as she spoke to her niece. Her child was going to be very lucky to have Lily as her mother. He couldn't explain why he thought the baby would be a girl. 'She' just

kept coming up whenever he thought about the stagger-
ing idea Lily had shared.

He was still absorbing the facts. The more he thought
about it the more he believed it was a great idea. Another
idea had begun lurking at the back of his skull. But he refused to put it into words, even to himself. Then it would
be real, and scary.

She held him in her hand, even if she didn't know it.
He wanted to cherish her, show her not all men were like
those two who'd broken her heart. Unless... No. Don't
even think about it. But... Don't. He could always change
his mind about becoming a father. About being a husband
to the most wonderful woman he'd known.

*Lily wants to do it alone because she no longer trusts
her heart to any man.*

Would he be prepared to help her achieve her dream?
What about the ramifications? It wasn't in him to stand
back and take no part in his child's life. Lily would do
a wonderful job, but it wasn't happening. Wasn't his future planned to be without a child? Without a wife? To
become a respected GP and a part of the community—
on his own? He had friends to spend time with, could
avoid worrying about hurting those nearest and dearest.

That was it, then. No sperm donation. No getting further involved with Lily. His gut ached. Just like that, he
could walk away.

He swore. So much for not voicing the idea.

Lily's head shot up and surprised eyes lit on him.

He must have sworn aloud. Gulping the wine, he muttered, 'Sorry. I didn't mean anything by it.' It showed how
much she got to him. Come on. If the idea of donating
his sperm was alive and bashing around in his skull then

she'd not only got to him, Lily had stormed him body
and soul and he was in deep trouble.

His gut churned. It was one hell of a pickle. One not
so easy to walk away from as others he'd faced. Except
the cancer. That had been a game-changer. Now Lily
had him in a vice and, yes, this was about the future, the
only difference being he held the cards, could choose the
outcome. He could squash these heart-warming emotions sucking the pain and loneliness out of him, or he
could let go and make the most of Lily and all she had
to offer. If she was at all interested in him. His pulse
slowed. Was she?

On Tuesday night she'd pulled back from kissing him,
yet she'd wanted to as badly as he'd wanted to kiss her.
Did she or didn't she want another fling with him? Or was
something deeper and more meaningful on her mind?
Damn all these questions. They spoiled the moment, were
wrecking his last evening with Lily.

Even while she was talking to Josie he was happy to
be in her company. It showed how lonely he must have
been before this week. And, no, he wasn't getting close
to Lily just because he needed someone to spend time
with. If that was all, he had mates to talk to. Admit it.
Again. Lily was special, and it was getting harder by the
day to pretend he wanted to walk away.

They'd got close fast. Heat regularly zapped between
them. So did laughter and enjoyment of the everyday
things. He could feel a new life opening up before him,
a wonderful, happy, exciting one. It made him want to
make love and give her pleasure, to share her bed, and
hold her afterwards as she fell asleep, to wake by her side
in the morning. There was more substance to that than
just having a great time and saying thanks and goodbye.

So he didn't just want a fling, then. He could no longer imagine walking away from Lily. She held him in
her hand, even if she didn't know it. He wanted to cherish her, show her not all men were like those two who'd
broken her heart.

'I think Josie's in love.' Lily tossed her phone on the
couch and unwound that long slim body to stand up.

'Definitely. So's Ollie. Has he talked to you yet about
their...' he flicked his fingers in the air '..."friendship"?'

'Only to say he hoped I was okay with him spending time with Josie.' Her lips tipped up into a smile. 'I
didn't come down like the ogre aunt. Told him it was
fine with me.'

'But watch out for her father as his chainsaw is larger
than yours.'

'Something like that.' She laughed.

He loved it when she laughed. A deep-bellied sound
that slammed into his gut and sent his pulse rate sky-
ward. As did many things about Lily. Things that had
him crossing the room to take her face in his hands and
lean in for a kiss. A kiss for everything she gave him,
for taking away some of his hurt.

A kiss that soon deepened, heated, and became so
much more.

A kiss that led to another and another.

A kiss that Lily finally pulled back from, a wobbly
smile on her swollen lips. 'Max,' she whispered, laying
her hand on his cheek.

Okay, he got it. They had to stop. Frustrating, yet not.
She was putting her own needs out there, and strange but
he didn't mind. Oh, sure, his body was screaming out
for hers, but it was wonderful sharing those kisses without follow-through. As though it was a part of getting to

know her better, and understanding her needs. He wound his arms around her and held her close, listening to her even breathing. He wanted to hold her tighter than ever before, to pull her into himself, be one with her, to become a part of her life, make it their life.

A chill covered his hot skin, cooling him fast.

Wrong, Max. You can't do this. What if you get sick again? You'll hurt Lily. And leave that child she wants so badly without a father.

It wasn't going to have a father if Lily did it her way. But if he were the DNA donor it would, which meant he'd be setting them all up for heartbreak. He couldn't be the means to making Lily achieve her dream. He longed to give his heart and soul to any child of his that came into the world. *And* to the mother of that child. There was only one woman he wanted for that role. He wanted to be the man Lily chose to father her child.

'I have to pinch myself to believe we're together again, and that it's so good,' Lily said quietly.

The chill became colder. He knew what she meant. He'd gone too far. Already he was in deep water and needed to get out fast. What he longed for and what he accepted as possible were at opposite ends of the spectrum. He could not hurt Lily. It might already be too late for himself. 'I shouldn't have kissed you, Lily.'

Leaning back in his arms, she stared up at him. 'Maybe, but I'm glad you did.'

'We can't carry on further.'

She tensed, stepped out of his arms. 'Did I say we would?'

They had to stop. Impossible. Which said he was already screwed. 'I don't know what you think. Hell, I don't know what *I* think any more.' If he leaned forward he could touch her soft skin, but he refrained, understanding the need for the barrier, if not happy with it. He was supposed to be glad she'd stepped away. He wasn't. Damn, his head was all over the place. 'If I'm honest, I'm not sure where we're headed.'

Silence fell between them.

Then she rocked his boat. 'I know I'm not ready to stop spending time with you. I'd like to get to closer to you. I stopped kissing you because I was about to drag you down to my bedroom and I suddenly got cold feet. But they're warming up fast.' Lily had always spoken her mind. Too bluntly sometimes, but he couldn't fault her.

He shouldn't be surprised, yet he was. Probably because he didn't want to believe she might've learned to like him more than they'd once have imagined. 'I'm not so certain about that. I still have things to consider, like my future.' Starting tonight. If this was how Lily felt—not factoring in his own needs—then it was definitely time to quit whatever they had going on. He wanted her. If only he had a crystal ball and knew he wouldn't get sick again. But no one knew that.

'You think?'

Here we go. This was more like the woman he'd once known. 'I told you I'm not getting into a full-time relationship. What if this turns into something deeper? I don't want to hurt you, so I'm calling it quits as of now. I'm sorry I kissed you.' Pain gripped him. His heart was pounding so hard his ribs felt like they were breaking. If only he could take back those words and reach over and haul Lily into his arms, never to let her go. From the moment he'd uttered them he'd known he did not want to finish anything with her. He wanted a future together, no matter what happened. He flung his arms wide, palms up and shrugged. 'I am so, so sorry, Lily.' If he didn't get out of there right now he might never find the strength to go.

CHAPTER EIGHT

MONDAY MORNING AND the sun was shining. No sign of the clouds that had delivered rain throughout the night. The road and paths sparkled, as though they'd had a thorough wash with bubble-bath liquid.

Lily parked at the rear of the medical hub and pushed open the door before she got too comfortable in her maudlin bubble. The three days since she and Max had discussed—disagreed about—how far they were going with getting to know each other had been long and tedious. Chainsawing more trees into firewood hadn't lightened her mood. Neither had Ollie and Josie when they'd stayed over with her in the house, separate bedrooms, funny and sweet as they were.

Those kisses had whacked her around the ears, made her realise she'd fallen for Max and was ready to take a chance with her heart. They'd scared her senseless so she'd stopped in the middle of a soul-warming kiss and said no more. By the time she'd regained her senses and was ready to apologise, Max had changed his mind about caring—for ever. What a mess she'd made of it all. And now she had to start over. She wasn't letting him get away without a fight.

Max had a way about him that spoke of honesty and

kindness and love. She knew he didn't want to hurt her. She also understood the two men who had broken her heart had never held her heart as carefully as Max would if he loved her. And on that she was prepared to take the risk of loving him.

Grabbing her bag off the back seat, Lily locked the car and headed inside. Was Max already here? She needed to get her A-game face in place. Letting him see how devastated she was over what he'd believed were the final words on the subject wasn't an option.

Deep, toe-curling laughter came from the staff meeting room. She had her answer. Her tongue cleaved to the roof of her mouth. Pulling back her shoulders wasn't improving her mood. Max was irresistible. Driving back into the city late last night, she'd headed towards his place to have it out with him, only to turn around at the corner of his street and head home, where she'd realised she'd been scared and that she should have carried on to his house. Well, she'd try again. There was no point arguing. He'd made his mind up. He hadn't changed as much as she'd first thought. That stubbornness had been there in the determined way he'd turned from her and headed for the door and the bedroom next to hers. He believed he would hurt her.

Newsflash, Max, you're already doing that. And I'm not giving up on you.

Yes, she'd gone and fallen for the one man she'd never have believed possible. If he thought he was walking away without a fight, then she had news for him. She'd show him he could live a happy life free of worrying about the pain he might cause her and any children they might have. Of course she'd have a fight on her hands. This was Max. He was worth fighting for, and she was damned if she wasn't going to give it everything she had. It would take time, but she had plenty of that.

Dropping her bag on her new desk, she paused to look around. The walls were bare now that Sarah had removed her diplomas and photos of family, but that wouldn't last. There was a box in the boot of Lily's car filled with her versions of the same things. Warmth finally filled her. She'd made it. Today the next phase of her career was beginning, with Max in the same space. One step towards a joint future achieved without trying. She'd give it a tick for positivity.

In the staffroom she poured a coffee and looked around to say hello to those who'd already arrived. Her gaze immediately landed on Max, looking good in light grey dress trousers and a white shirt. 'You're looking posh.' She grinned, aiming for positivity from the start.

He smiled as he came across. 'Ready to get stuck in?'

'Absolutely.'

'You stay on at the beach house over the weekend?'

'I did. Josie and Ollie stayed Friday night and my brother picked them up on Saturday. He gave Ollie a thorough once-over.'

'How'd that go?' Max sipped coffee and her stomach tightened as she watched those lips she knew so well.

Lips. Kisses. Trails over her feverish skin. Ragged sigh. Slowly, remember, or Max would be bolting for his office and only coming out when he knew she'd left for the day. 'Ollie won the first round just by being himself and not trying too hard to impress.'

'Go, him,' said Max.

'What did you do over the weekend?'

'My sister and her husband were in town for a rock concert so I caught up with them yesterday before they flew back to Dunedin. It was good to see Karen. It's been nearly a year since the last time.' His face had softened and there was a rare relaxation about him. 'She's pregnant for the second time, and absolutely glowing.'

'You miss her?'

He nodded. 'I do. We've always got on, despite the rift between our parents, but it wasn't until I spent time having treatment down there that we became close. She was there for me every single day.' He blinked rapidly. 'I can never repay her for that.'

'You shouldn't have to. You'd do the same for her. For anyone you care about.'

'True, but I'm the older brother. I'm there for her, not the other way round.'

'Excuse me, you're talking to me, the woman with two older, bossy brothers who know how to deal with just about everything, and I'd be there for them any time they needed me, whether they liked it or not.' Her voice rose on the final words, and her throat tightened. Sounded as though she was no different from Max's sister. That had to be a positive for her.

Max locked his steady eyes on her probably less steady ones. 'Easy. I hear you.' Then he smiled again. 'Maybe I shouldn't introduce you and Karen. There'll be no hope for me even if I only wanted an extra piece of cake.'

The tension that had been building backed off. 'Sounds fine to me.' Looking around, she gasped. The room had filled up. 'I'm getting a refill and taking a seat.' First meeting, first day.

'Lily,' Max called quietly. 'Karen will be in town again next month for a work conference. I'll introduce you to her.'

He what? She'd thought they weren't spending time to-

gether away from here. Lily coughed, banged her mug on
the counter harder than intended, nodding slowly. 'Done.'
Maybe she wasn't the only one wanting to make a go of
their relationship. Or was he making up for his abrupt departure from the house on Friday morning? Been doing
some soul-searching? About them, him, or what he'd
said? He'd been heading out the front door with his bag
when she'd gone out to make a coffee at six, unable to
sleep and needing caffeine to get her out of the fog her
head had been in after a sleepless night.

'See you Monday.'

He'd closed the door behind that delectable derriere,
leaving her heart mashing and her head spinning. It had
taken a whole plunger of coffee to get her anywhere near
capable of thinking about the day ahead. Then it had
taken some more and toast before she'd allowed herself
to pick up the chainsaw and head across to George's yard
and the tree trunks he'd towed there from along the beach
over the past couple of days. Hours of heavy work had
finally worn her out enough to fall into her chair and eat
a proper meal.

She'd sat up with the kids until finally she'd been unable to keep her eyes open and had hit her bed to sleep
until dawn, when shrieking gulls had woken her to a
blinding headache. She'd woken with Max in her head,
denying they had a future, and her telling him he was
wrong. She'd also recalled Josie and Ollie on the couch,
sitting close together, holding hands, and guilt had struck
for not making sure they behaved.

When Josie had sauntered out of her room as far as her
crutches would allow and sat at the kitchen bench with
a grin on her face, Lily had felt she'd let the aunt side of
things down, until Josie had laughed and said, 'Relax,

Lily. Nothing happened. Apart from my first kiss.' Her cheeks had turned crimson, and her mouth had crinkled up into a soppy smile. 'It was nice. He's cute.'

Lily had put her hands over her ears and laughed. 'Stop. I don't want to know.' Thank goodness nothing too intimate had gone down. Josie might have fibbed, but she was absolutely hopeless at hiding lies, especially from Lily.

And now this morning Max was friendly and back to their new normal.

She'd run with that. Sitting on the closest vacant chair, she joined in the chatter until Devlin got the meeting underway and she began to learn how this medical centre went about its daily business. Max was a part of this, and for now that was enough. Then she took another look. Under the overhead light, shadows below his eyes had become apparent. Lack of sleep, too?

'How long have you had this sore throat?' Lily asked fifteen-year-old Courtenay Griffith.

'All weekend, and some days before that,' muttered the girl dressed in the uniform from the local high school.

'Are you sure?' Lily asked as she put the thermometer in Courtenay's ear. 'Your throat's raw. What about coughing?'

'No, but my neck hurts, gets stiff sometimes.'

'Your temperature's raised.' Lily clicked the end piece off the thermometer into the hazard bin. 'I'm going to check your neck and throat.' Swelling around Courtenay's neck backed up her diagnosis, along with the high temperature.

'What's wrong with me?'

'I'd say you've got glandular fever.'

'Isn't that called the kissing disease?'

'That is the fastest way to transmit it, yes.' Lily smiled as she locked eyes on her patient. 'Have you been kissing anyone?'

'My boyfriend. But that was last weekend. I was too tired to see him this weekend.'

'Has he got a sore throat?'

'He did, then he got better so it can't be what you're saying.'

Lily sat at her desk and began typing notes into the computer. 'Yes, it can. You probably need to tell him so he can see his doctor.' Filling in a lab form on screen, she pressed 'print', signed the page and handed it to Courtenay. 'I want you to have a blood test to confirm this is glandular fever. In the meantime, no more kissing. You'll need to stay home from school for a couple of weeks. Keep indoors, keep warm and get lots of sleep. Drink plenty of water. I'll give you a prescription for antibiotics and pain relief.'

Loud voices came through the door.

Courtenay jerked her head around. 'That sounds like Mum. What's wrong?'

Lily rushed to open the door, and cries filled the room.

'Someone look at Tommy. He's going blue. Hurry,' a woman holding a small child screamed.

Lily rushed to her side, took the lifeless boy from her arms. 'Follow me.' She headed back into her room, the woman right on her heels. 'Tell me what happened,' she demanded as she sat the lad on the bed. His chest moved slowly, his lips were blue. How long had he been unconscious? Tipping his head back to open his throat, she reached for his wrist. Pulse too slow.

'I don't know,' the boy's mother wailed.

'Mum, what's wrong with Tommy?' Courtenay cried.

'Colleen, take a deep breath and tell us what Tommy was doing when this happened.' Max had arrived.

Lily sighed with relief. 'His pulse is faint, he's barely breathing.'

'Onto it.'

'Playing with his toys.'

'What sort of toys?' Lily asked as she placed Tommy on his back and pulled his top up to his chin to place the stethoscope over his lungs.

Max was feeling the boy's throat, looking in his mouth. They weren't about to discuss who did what, they got on with what had to be done.

It was Courtenay who answered. 'He has small blocks he likes to stick in his mouth.'

'How small?' she demanded, reaching to sit Tommy upright.

Max had it under control with his hands under Tommy's arms and holding him steady. He nodded at Lily. 'Heimlich manoeuvre.'

Nodding, she slapped the small back. And again. And once more. Tommy shuddered and a feeble cough spewed over his lips.

'Again,' Max said.

Another, harder slap.

The boy's cough was stronger.

'Come on,' Lily muttered. Her hand was ready for the next blow.

A small square of plastic shot out of Tommy's mouth. Followed by more coughing and lots of slobber. Then he began crying.

Phew. Lily let out the breath she'd been holding. 'There we go.'

Max was examining the boy's mouth, cleaning away the mess inside. 'You're one lucky little guy, Tommy.'

Lily's heart was racing with relief, and she lifted the boy up and handed him to his crying mother. 'Here you are.'

Courtenay was crying, then Tommy joined in and Lily stepped back for a moment, Max standing beside her. 'That was touch and go,' he muttered.

She nodded, and watched the love pouring from the family. 'Mrs Griffith.' She waited until she had the woman's attention. 'I'm Lily Scott, the GP who's replaced Sarah. Now, you mightn't want to hear this, but those toy blocks are dangerous. You have to get rid of them.'

The woman's face was white as she nodded. 'I know. I'll do it when we get home.'

'No, Mum, I'm getting them out of the car and throwing them in the bin before we leave here.' Courtenay wrapped an arm around her mother's shoulders.

'I'm going to examine Tommy's throat, then I'm going to have him admitted to hospital overnight. There's a strong possibility swelling will occur, which can affect his breathing.'

Max added his endorsement. 'Go there immediately. Courtenay, you're right about getting rid of the blocks, but your brother needs to get to hospital first. I know you won't let him near those toys anyway.'

Lily felt a warm glow engulf her. Max was with her, all the way. Medically anyway. Now she had to make it work personally.

Suddenly her room was empty of everyone but Max. 'Thank you for being here. It's not that I wouldn't have coped, but it's always good to have back-up.' Especially when it was this man.

'You're welcome.' He dropped the softest of kisses on her forehead. 'See you soon.' And he disappeared.

After a few minutes, gathering her breath and steadying her nerves, Lily headed out to get her next patient. 'Michelle? Hello, you're looking a lot better than a week ago.'

Michelle smiled shyly as she hopped along beside Lily on her crutches. 'I'm glad you talked me into going there. It was wonderful helping all those kids. They're so positive despite their physical problems, and taught me a thing or two.'

'That was the idea,' Lily admitted as she closed her door behind Michelle and headed to her desk.

'You set me up?' Michelle laughed. 'I like you, Doc. That was clever. Watching those teens getting on with having fun and being as good as they could made me think about my strengths, and realise one of them is about never giving up. I don't understand why I got down this time, but I'm over it and working hard at getting back on my feet.'

'I'm glad to hear it.' Lily brought up Michelle's records on the screen. 'So what can I do for you today?'

Shyness shone back at her. 'Um, I'd like to go on the Pill.'

To put the woman at ease, Lily asked her questions even though the file had the answers. 'Have you been on it before?'

'Yes, about three years ago. I had no problems so I'd like the same one if possible.'

Lily looked at the file. 'It's a good one and I don't think any of the newer brands would serve you any better so that's a yes if your blood pressure's normal.'

'It might've gone up a bit last week.' Michelle glanced

up at her, her cheeks burning. 'Logan and I… We get along like a house on fire. He's wonderful.'

It really had been a week of romance. Her niece and friend were closer than before. Michelle had found a man she obviously fancied like crazy. And she… Well, she'd started falling in love with Max. It didn't add up when they never used to get on very well apart from the fling days. Self-protection? Had she always held herself back from totally giving herself over to men? If so, there was no apparent reason. Her family was loving and close, never let each down. It was more likely she'd hadn't handed her heart over completely before.

'I take it you're going to keep seeing each other, hence the prescription.' It mightn't be how all doctors talked to their patients, but Michelle seemed open to chatting, might even need someone to talk to.

Lily filled in the prescription form on screen. 'Anything else while you're here?'

'No, I'm good. Max is giving me physio this morning.' She stood up, reached for her crutches. 'Thanks for everything, including the camp. I've talked to Logan about helping out another time. I enjoyed it so much.'

'I'm glad. Thank *you*.'

'How's your morning been?' Max asked Lily as he strode into the tearoom well after midday. He'd barely managed one piece of toast for breakfast so to appease his stomach, which no longer ached, he'd dashed down to the bakery to buy a salmon and cream cheese bagel. Sighting Lily at the table, looking completely at ease, lightened his heavy heart. Did her hands just tighten around her mug? He looked again. Saw her fingers loosen. So he did get to her as easily as she got to him.

'It's been great. I've met some lovely people. Michelle saw me before she came to you for physio. She enjoyed her time at the camp and has asked to do more.'

'She was a hit with all the kids. Not to mention Logan. Apparently they've got a thing going for each other.'

'Quite a week, wasn't it? These camps really do help people get over their disabilities.'

'I agree,' Devlin added from the corner, where he was reading a medical journal. 'Max has been singing the camp's praises all morning.'

'I had an amazing time. My medical skills weren't used much, but showing those teens ways to make moving easier, and giving them exercises to do, well, it was just as good as prescribing treatment for any other malady.' He picked up his bagel. 'I want to put my name down for more, too.' The salmon flavour exploded across his tongue. Food, delicious food. Damn, he was hungry. For Lily. Swallow. Cough. Damn.

'Done,' said Lily and Devlin at the same time.

What's done?

'Devlin's in charge of volunteers.' Lily added, 'In case you weren't aware.'

'I was.' To hell with being hungry. Right now another stronger appetite was winding him up. Need for Lily clawed through him. She looked beautiful sitting there, being herself, not expecting anything from anyone. Heat exploded below his belt. She was gorgeous, and hot, and sweet, and every damned thing he wanted in a woman. *His* woman. His fears for the future annoyed him but were no longer beating him up. It might be unfair to ask Lily to join that ride with him, but hope was rocketing. Lily wanted to have a baby regardless of whether he was in her life or not. *Why not mine?*

He choked. Swallowed. Coughed, swallowed again, and finally downed the food his stomach had been waiting for.

'You all right?' the woman doing his head in asked with concern in her face.

Absolutely wonderful, thanks. 'I'm fine. Lunch went down the wrong way.' He yawned and rubbed his stomach.

Lily was staring at him really hard as though she saw exactly what was going on in his skull. She probably did. The damned woman could read people with her eyes shut. No, she did not know he wanted her to have his baby. She. Did. Not. But he could tell her.

Another choke. This time harder, and painful.

Hands banged him between the shoulder blades, strong fingers dug in. 'Easy. What's going on?'

'Nothing.' Said like a teenager denying the truth. Max tossed the rest of the bagel on top of the bag it had come in. So much for being ravenous. Getting food where it was needed wasn't working. Another need was growing exponentially the longer Lily's hands were on his back. His skin was tightening, heating, and his groin was thickening. As for the rate his blood was pumping around his body, it would burst out of his skin any moment. He held his breath. And waited. Leaping up to get away from that sincere touch would be best, but would probably earn him so many demerit points he'd never see the light of day with Lily this side of Christmas.

At last she withdrew those tender, hot hands, which shouldn't be allowed out, especially at work. 'As long as you're all right.'

'Serves him right for gulping his food.' Devlin laughed on his way out of the room.

She hadn't cared they weren't alone when she'd banged his back, pressed her fingers into his muscles. 'Want a glass of water?' Lily asked.

Did she not have a clue she'd just tipped him on his head? Looking at her, he knew she did. There was a glint of humour in those potent eyes, and the corners of her lush mouth kept lifting. 'Yes, with lots of ice.' He'd probably choke on a cube, but he needed her to look away for a few moments while he gathered some sense and got back to normal.

Except normal with Lily as he'd known it had flown the coop. Picking up his lunch, he tried for a third time to get some of it down where it was needed, and succeeded this time.

'Here.' Lily plonked a brimming glass in front of him and sat down again. 'You have a busy morning?'

He nodded. 'Seems half of Remuera's come down with the flu over the weekend.' Hopefully those patients he'd seen would keep their bugs to themselves. 'It's the last thing I want.'

'Did you have the flu jab?'

Duh. He should have remembered that. 'Yes, I did. It's offered to anyone who's had cancer in the past five years.' Now he was mentioning his illness, something he never did, especially around work. Thank goodness the staffroom was unusually quiet. 'Where is everyone?'

'We're both running late. Also Joanne and Suzie went down to the shops. There's a sale on at Petal's. I'd have joined them if I hadn't been running behind in my schedule.'

'I take it that's a women's clothing store.'

'Not just any store. One of the best.' She grinned. 'My

favourite. Classy, beautiful outfits any woman would give her eye teeth for.'

'Or a small fortune.'

Lily laughed. 'Got you.'

'You'll keep,' he growled. She'd been winding him up. That's exactly what he'd said to her once before, only that time she'd given him a blast about not being ashamed of her comfortable lifestyle. He'd been rude, but she'd seemed to relish not having to worry about how to fund her way through med school. Now he knew better.

That camp at Whangaparaoa would've put a massive hole in her bank account, and no doubt continued to do so. 'Is there an annual fundraising event to put money into the camp coffers?' He hadn't found anything online about how other finances were raised.

Lily glanced around the empty room, as though checking no one had sneaked in while they'd been talking. 'No, and it's not necessary. It may become so in the future, but for now everything's under control.'

'You take donations, though?'

'The board accepts them. I hope we never have to go public on fundraising. There are so many necessary charitable causes out there, I don't want to add to the growing list. There's not enough money to go around as it is.'

'Anyone ever told you that you have a big heart, Lily?' She really did. Sure, she wasn't the only person out there supporting those in need, but he liked it that Lily did. It made her even more special. Made his hands tingle with warmth.

Picking up her sandwich, she took a bite, and chewed thoughtfully. He guessed she wasn't going to answer.

Max followed her example, finally managing to eat his lunch without further discomfort. The silence between them turned comfortable. Until Lily stood up and he got an eyeful of a perfectly curved backside in fitted trousers as she crossed to the sink. At least he'd finished eating. And drinking the ice-cold water. But his heart pounded while his mouth dried. Snatching the paper bag, he screwed it up, threw it at the bin, and stood up. 'I'll see you later.'

He had things to think about before he made a move in any direction. Her need for a baby. His growing need to father one. What would she say if he offered to be the donor? Unless he got over his concerns about the future, she wasn't going to get the opportunity to consider the idea.

He was halfway to his office when he heard her calling after him.

'Max, wait a minute.'

He watched her every step, the gentle, *sexy* swing of her hips, the light shining in her eyes as she focused on him. What was this about?

'Have dinner with me tonight?' she asked as she reached him.

As he drew a breath, he was zapped with a fragrance that was all Lily and nothing like the chemical air of the medical centre. 'I'd li—' No, try again. Be sensible. 'Sorry, but I'm busy. All week.'

Annoyance, even anger sliced through him from those now not so shiny eyes. 'Just because you've pulled the plug on what we started last week, it doesn't mean we can't be friendly and spend some time together.'

'You think that's wise? Given where we were when I…' he flipped his fingers in the air '…pulled the plug? On a few kisses?'

Her throat moved upwards as she swallowed hard. 'I like how we've been getting along on other levels.'

Her disappointment made him feel like a heel for being so blunt. But how could he sit across from her in a restaurant and pretend he didn't want to take her to bed? Or deny he was considering having a baby with her? Or ignore she was giving his heart a damned hard shove in the direction he'd sworn off ever going?

'Lily—' Give her a break. She'd only said what he thought. 'True.' Could he do this? Without going completely bonkers? He gave in. 'I can't have dinner with you tonight, I do genuinely have something on. How about Thursday night? You'll have done four days here and can download on me if you need to. And…' he held his hand up as she started to say something '…we can continue getting to know each other and enjoying ourselves.' There was merit in that. He'd be able to think some more about the baby idea. Why? Lily would be his pick if he wanted someone to have his children. The only question he had to ask himself was if he truly wanted to do this. It meant putting his fears aside, but in reality they'd been lessening since he'd met up with Lily again. 'So, are you available Thursday night?'

The twinkle was back. The smallest of smiles, too. Which meant so was the heat in his aching gut. 'I'll make sure I am.'

Relief swamped his chest. 'Talk more before then.' He turned away before he came up with other reasons to stand talking in the hallway when he had patients waiting.

CHAPTER NINE

'THE VIEW'S STUNNING.' Max was standing with his hands in his pockets on the small deck, looking out towards the Harbour Bridge with all its lights.

Lily stood beside him. 'During the day, seeing the boats in the marina is pretty too. Being on the lower level, I have a back yard as well, which I'm going to make into an outdoor entertaining area.'

'Any trees to cut down?'

She laughed. 'I don't think the neighbours would be very friendly if I started up my saw.' Her elbows dug into her sides and she did a little dance internally. Max was with her, in her home, and it felt right.

He turned just then and placed his hands on her shoulders. 'I know I said no to furthering our relationship, but I'm not doing a great job of staying away from you.' Bright eyes locked on hers. 'I have to kiss you.'

Yes. Up on her toes, she leaned in and placed her lips on his before he could retract his words. *Yes.* Wow. His mouth opened, and his tongue explored hers, tasting her, driving her to the brink so fast her knees were knocking. Wrapping her arms around his waist she held on tight, and kissed him back, again and again.

A sharp, chilly gust of wind slammed into them.

Max lifted his head. 'Inside?'

Lily pulled him and slid the door shut. And returned to his arms, his mouth, pressing up so that her hard peaks ached against his chest.

'Max?' she whispered. They couldn't stop now. Her whole body was rippling with desire, the sparks he brought on with a smile were now burning out of control.

He leaned back, his arms still around her waist. Then he shoved one hand through his hair, staring at her as though he couldn't get enough. He leaned down to kiss her forehead.

He'd changed his mind. He was leaving. This was good-night. She held her breath, begging silently for him to stay.

'Hell.' Swinging her up into his arms, he asked, 'Where's your bedroom?'

Nodding towards the door on the right, she buried her face in his neck, breathing him in, soaking up his heat, absorbing the heat from his hands on her thigh and back. *Yes.* Max was with her. She'd make the most of tonight and wait to see what followed.

It wasn't enough to be held against him. Her lips sought his mouth, tasting, touching, soaking him up. Her body reacted instantly, the heat and desire returning in a flood, softening some places, tightening others. Blinding all reason, drowning any warnings from the sane side of her brain. She wanted Max. Had done so since first seeing him again. It was something she needed to do, to have, to share. But she couldn't bear it if they stopped this time. 'Max?' she squeaked around the rock of need blocking her throat. So much for not getting close.

'Max?' He'd heard his name between their mouths. Drawn out and filled with hunger. Sexy beyond measure. She could not be wanting him to haul on the brakes. But he wouldn't continue if she didn't want to. Lifting his mouth away, feeling the loss instantly, he locked his eyes on those green ones so close. 'Yes?'

'I want you.'

Relief poured through him. Then it stopped. 'Lily, I can't promise anything more.' But he wanted to, more than ever.

Stiffening, she leaned back in his arms. 'I understand, and I say to hell with that. It's one night, Max. One step. Let's see where it leads.'

Those alluring eyes dragged him into her understanding and longing. 'Are you sure?' Because he was falling, falling into her, into the emotions he hadn't had for so long. One night? Was that even possible? But walking away now wasn't either.

'Absolutely.'

In one movement their clothes were torn off. Lily held his hands as she sprawled across the bed, pulling him with her. Covering her with his roused body, his mouth trailed kisses over any skin he could reach. Lily bucked beneath him. Her lips covered one nipple, her tongue flicking back and forth, hot and sharp, driving him to the edge. 'Slow down,' he gasped against her stomach. He wanted to pleasure Lily first, only it had to be fast because he was near breaking point.

'Can't. Don't want to.'

Phew. Reaching between them, he found her throbbing need.

Instantly she was pushing up into him. 'Now. *Max.*'

As she cried out his name he lifted up and entered her heat.

She climaxed immediately, pulling him to join her straightaway.

Her body was his, hers. They were together and he never wanted this to end.

It seemed for ever before he was breathing anywhere near normally. Lying on his back, Lily sprawled along his body, the rate of her breasts rising and falling slowing down, he knew nothing but happiness. It had been fast and amazing. It had been what he'd needed, and had hoped for since coming face to face with Lily for the first time again after all he'd been through. 'I know I've said it before, but I've really missed you.' Staying away from love might be the worst choice to make.

Lily jerked against him. 'What? Did I hear right?'

Did I really say that? He had, and now an explanation was required. If possible. Lily wouldn't let it go. Why did he feel he'd missed her? Because she hadn't bowed to what he'd wanted, had expected to get as good as she got, and while that had bruised his ego it had also made him enjoy her. He'd never forgotten a moment of their fling, whereas other women had come and gone and he struggled to recall very much about them. It wasn't something he was proud of, but there was no getting away from it. 'Nothing wrong with your hearing but, then, we are entwined.'

'Very funny.'

He tugged her sideways and pulled her over his body. His hands slipped under her jersey and found her full, warm breasts. Pushing the jersey up, he covered one nipple with his mouth and tongued her until she writhed with need. For him.

Then Lily's hands caressed, stroking him. Blocking

his mind to everything but her body, her fingers, those lips. Lily.

Together they left talk behind and rose on a wave of passion that shook Max to the core, had him wondering how he was ever going to be able to call a halt to this second fling with the most amazing woman he'd had the luck to get to know in bed. And out of it.

Max laughed as he ran around a gathering of people waiting for the Saturday market to open. The air was crisp and smelled of fruit from the stalls just inside the gate. His head was light, his body bursting with energy, and even his stomach had given the aches a miss. He was happy.

Lily had kicked him out of her bed just after the sun had peeped in around the curtains. She was heading to the farm to spend the day with the family. She would miss the first breakfast because he'd fallen back into bed and tucked her under him to make love again. Making love was so much more special than having sex. Care was involved, love, laughter, sharing.

He'd been utterly bonkers to think he could walk away. There was nothing wrong with a little bit of madness. It added to the fun. Life was good. Lily was his heart's desire. And brought on a whole lot more longing just by standing in front of him or touching his arm with one of those perfectly manicured fingers or smiling mischievously.

Beyond the market he picked up his pace. After last night's time with Lily his body ached in places he'd forgotten were there and he felt good. He loved her. It was hard to believe when he'd stuck to his determination not to get into a relationship for so long. He had sure dropped that fast. Too fast? Would it come back to bite him? If it did, he'd get up again. Lily gave him the confidence to let go the fears that had charted his life for too long. He was strong, had survived a bumpy childhood, and did have love to share.

Could he do this? Really? When he'd always been motivated to save his heart? He could still hurt Lily, be hurt himself. So far he only knew Lily was happy to spend time with him. He had no idea what she felt beyond that. She was always willing to spend time together, had said she wasn't ready to say goodbye, but did that mean she might eventually love him?

Jogging on the spot while waiting for the pedestrian crossing buzzer to go, he shook his head. He'd just have to make the most of the time they had together and see where it led.

He could use the time to think hard about whether to offer her the chance to have the baby she so longed for.

He tripped, straightened, walked across the road and into the park beyond. Sure, the idea had crossed his mind often, but he hadn't really believed he was serious. Was he now? Was this just so Lily could have a child, or was he beginning to accept he could be a parent? If that was the case, he'd want to marry Lily, have a proper family.

I'm getting way ahead of myself.

This needed time to get right. But it was starting to feel perfect, as though he'd found his reason for being, which always came back to Lily.

Lily tried to pay for dinner.

Max refused to let her. 'I like spoiling you and intend to do it often.' His eyes slid to the gorgeous woman walking at his side towards his car, which was parked outside the restaurant. Yes, damn it, he wanted Lily. In his life, at his side; sharing the future, parenthood, *everything*.

She was looking up at him with a cheeky smile and those big eyes sparkling as though the sun was behind them. 'I'm allowed to spoil you, too.'

As he pulled out into the traffic, he said, 'One day I'll let you.' He was having too much fun giving to Lily. Four weeks of time spent together, both in bed and out of it, and he'd done a complete about-face. To the point of falling in love. He loved Lily, no ifs or buts. He completely accepted it. They shared meals at their homes or in restaurants, they talked and laughed, and made love.

'We've just sat through a green,' said the woman screwing with his head. And obviously with his ability to see green when it was right in front of him.

'Thought I heard some tooting.' Speeding away, he tried to laugh. It came out sharp and not at all funny. This was serious. For a moment the old fear of getting too involved popped up. But either he was or he wasn't. Which would it be? Having accepted he loved Lily, it meant there was only one way to go. He had to admit it. He was already on the way to a full-on relationship with her. She appeared just as eager. So when would the questions stop bothering him?

Lily leaned close, scrutinising him. 'Are you all right? You suddenly looked exhausted.'

Right on cue, he yawned. 'I am feeling a bit tired.' Shattered best described the way his aching body struggled to remain upright and his head to think clearly. That might be why he had all those blasted questions trotting around his skull. He'd been fighting exhaustion all day. 'I did nearly suggest another night for dinner, but I didn't want to miss seeing you.'

Lily gasped. 'Did I hear right?' She smiled briefly, before surprising him. 'Max, we are getting on really well, aren't we?'

That sounded like she had some doubts. About her feelings? Or his? 'I think we're doing fine.'

'That's a relief. For a moment there you sounded strained.'

'Probably because I hardly slept a wink last night.' Too busy thinking about Lily.

'As long as you're not coming down with something. That flu's still knocking people over all around the city.'

'It's a nasty one this year. Affecting the elderly the worst, though.' He'd better not be getting it. One, he'd spent enough time being unwell to last for ever. Two, it was busy at work with staff away with the flu. But his head was beginning to pound. 'Don't worry about me. I'm fine.'

Lily gave him one her heart-twisting smiles as he pulled up outside the apartment block. 'You want to come up for a celebratory coffee? Or drink?'

Of course he did. But he wouldn't be much fun. 'I'd love to but I'm going home to take some pills and get some sleep. Do you mind?'

'No.' She smiled. 'It's fine, truly. You look terrible and sleep is probably the best remedy.' She leaned in to kiss him and he turned his head so her lips caressed his cheek. The smile slowly faded. Placing her hand on the door handle, she said, 'I'll see you tomorrow. Sleep well.' And she was out and closing the door behind her.

Damn it. He hadn't wanted to give her whatever was ailing him. He should race after her and explain, but that would take too much energy, and energy seemed to be rapidly disappearing. He'd phone when he got home. He

waited until Lily had let herself in and the front entrance
door clipped shut behind her. Another yawn dragged at
his body as he pulled away from the kerb. There would
be plenty of time for talking later.

In the morning Max groaned as he tried to roll over. The
pain was crippling. Eventually he crawled out of bed and
under the hot shower, his head feeling as though it would
explode any moment. Every muscle in his body ached,
and there was a dull pain in his gut. Near where the tumour had been removed.

Nausea soared. He leapt out of the shower to sit down,
head on his knees, until the feeling passed. No bloody
way. Not now. Now when he was getting his life in order.
Not when he'd decided to love Lily. It couldn't have come
back. There'd been no warning signs. As if there had
been the first time.

He'd been too busy being happy with Lily to notice
any minor health problems. Thinking back over the
weeks, he realised the tiredness wasn't new, had been
growing for some time, and the ache in his gut was real.
It wasn't psychosomatic. Prodding with his fingers he
couldn't find anything out of the ordinary but, then, a
tumour wasn't that easy to find.

Pulling himself upright, he dried off and picked up
the razor to shave for the day, aiming for normality. He
was overreacting. If anything, he had the flu. This was
a hypochondriac's reaction, and he wasn't one of those.
But what if…?

Stop it. Get on with the day.

His hand was shaking, and by the time he'd removed
his whiskers there were two nicks on his chin. If this
was flu he had no right to go into work and spread it

further. Great. He could stay at home and talk himself into any illness he liked. Wrapping himself in the thick, navy bathrobe that had been hanging on the back of the bathroom door, he went into his bedroom and sank down on the bed, all energy gone, and swallowed some more headache pills and half a glass of water, and stared at the floor between his feet. Just a few minutes and the pills would kick in and he could get up and ring Devlin about tests to make sure the cancer hadn't returned. Because his gut was saying it had.

The phone ringing on his bedside table woke Max. The time showed nine ten. As he snatched up the phone he leapt out of bed and slammed his hand against the wall to prevent crashing to the floor. His head was going round and round, his legs barely held him upright. Sinking onto the edge of the bed, he pressed the phone icon. 'Hello, Lily.'

Lily. Darling Lily. He had to call it off with her. This was the wake-up call he needed to make him see sense. He could not get serious with her, couldn't marry her and have children together. Tears streamed down his cheeks and he let them fall onto his chest.

'Max? Are you all right? Where are you? The office tried ringing you, then Devlin. You haven't had an accident, have you?' Lily sounded frantic, full of concern.

Well, she would, wouldn't she? His heart warmed, and for a moment he dared to dream, then his stomach squeezed painfully, shattering the hope. He snapped, 'I'm fine.' Glancing at the phone, he saw what he hadn't noticed before. Three missed phone calls. 'I was asleep.'

'Max, you were tired last night. Have you got the flu

despite having the vaccination? Or something else? Food poisoning from those scampi?'

That possibility had never crossed his mind and the symptoms didn't stack up anyway. 'Not food poisoning. Possibly the flu. I slept all night after downing some pills, and have just taken some more.' Say anything to keep her from asking too many questions. He was going to hurt her but he'd prefer to be on his feet when he did that.

'Stay in bed. Janice is back, Andrew's called in sick. The medical centre's not immune.'

'If I don't come in you'll all be a lot busier.' *Shut up.* There was no way he could stand up for more than a few minutes. Trying to work with patients was definitely out.

'Then we'll be at risk of catching whatever you've got. I'll get you a prescription for the tablets we're all prescribing and drop them off at lunchtime. If you're really nice, I'll bring some lunch to go with them.'

The thought of food didn't do him any favours but there was a remote possibility he might feel a bit better in a few hours. 'The spare key is in the peg basket attached to the washing line around the back.'

'Anything else you need?' Lily asked.

'No. Thanks.'

'Right. I'll see you later. And, Max? Don't spend the morning stressing about what's wrong with you. It doesn't help, and will only prevent you getting much-needed sleep.' She hung up.

'Yes, Doctor.' As he dropped back against the pillows and tugged the duvet up to his chin, he wanted to shout at the world for doing this to him. Not now, not when Lily read him too well, and he liked that. She understood he'd be worried sick about what was ailing him. She wouldn't laugh at him, but she'd sure as hell make sure he didn't spend his time carrying on like a hypochondriac. She also wasn't going to be happy when he told her they really were over this time. Because he had to. For her sake.

Damn it, he was medically trained, knew about symptoms, and understood how some people could overthink their situation until they made themselves ill. Not once had he ever thought he'd be one of those, and yet here he was, acting stupidly. The fear was back, ramping up fast. If only the cancer hadn't returned. That's all he asked. Not when he'd finally decided to make a go of the future, to stop worrying about letting others down. Was the fact he'd taken a step towards a future with Lily putting him in his place for hoping for too much?

Coming back into his life, Lily had tossed all his post-cancer beliefs out the window like they didn't mean a thing. She'd woken him up so that for the first time ever he wanted a permanent relationship, to be married to the woman he loved, and to have a family. He wanted to love and be loved, and he was halfway there, so now all he would've had to do was make her fall in love with him. But not any more. He was backing off.

First he'd ring Devlin. The man was his GP, and a friend, and understood his fears.

'Hey, how're you doing?' Lily leaned against the door-frame of Max's bedroom and took a good, long at him. Dark shadows stained his upper cheeks, while traces of red filled the lower half of his face. His eyes were spewing exhaustion. 'Looks as though you've got yourself a fever.'

'The sheets and pillows are soaked.' He shuffled up the bed to lean back against the headboard, looking everywhere but at her. Like she wasn't welcome.

'She'd ignore that for now. Devlin said Max had called for a prescription, when she'd said she get him what he required. That had stung, but there was no point in making a mountain out of it. 'Don't go getting cold. I'll take your temperature then put the kettle on if you want a hot drink.' She got the thermometer out of the medical bag she carried and moved across to the bed.

Max obliged by turning his head to show his ear. 'This is crazy.'

She managed a laugh. 'It sure is. But it shows you're human. The flu's doing the rounds of the medical centre.' She read the scanner. 'Slightly high. To be expected.'

'You be careful. Don't want you getting sick.' His smile was lopsided, and a little sad.

Punching him lightly in the arm, she shook her head. 'I'm tough. I'll be fine. Right, what do you want to drink? I've brought sandwiches and a sweet muffin for your lunch.'

'Hot water will do. Not sure I want to eat.'

'Too bad.' She got him a large mug of hot water and a plate with two sandwiches. Then she got a mug of coffee and some sandwiches for herself and went to sit on the end of the bed. 'Did you go back to sleep after I rang?'

'Hard not to, exhaustion being the theme of the day.'

Talk about cranky. 'Most patients I've seen with this flu say the same. It takes up to a week to be back on your feet,' she warned.

'Me lying around that long? I don't think so.'

'Get over yourself. This week you're a patient, not a doctor. Now, tell me what other symptoms you're getting, real or not.' She'd known the moment he'd talked to her that morning that he'd been worrying the cancer was back. It had been in his hesitancy and the strain deepening his voice. So unlike the confident Max she knew.

He glared at her.

She laughed back, refusing to show concern for his fears. That would only endorse them, and he didn't need that, though she did sympathise. 'Come on.'

'Lily.' He stopped, swallowed and stared towards the window.

Her heart slowed dangerously. This wasn't about her helping him. This was about them. Deep inside, pain was already growing. Now she recognised the look in his face. Regret. Sorrow. And that damned determination. 'Don't.'

'I have to. I was wrong to think I could have a future without upsetting you. Or me.' Those khaki eyes locked on her. 'I'm sorry. I've let us both down. Please, don't waste your time trying to convince me otherwise. I'd like you to leave now, and only be in contact at work.' His voice cracked, and a lone tear rolled down his cheek. 'I'm doing this for you, Lily.'

Her heart stopped completely. Her hands were wet. Her stomach so tight a golf ball would be large beside it. He couldn't do this without fighting for them. Max was afraid of being hurt, of hurting her. Well, he was already hurting, so was she. But the only way to get through to him was to show him, not tell him. It was going to take time. 'When did you last have a colonoscopy?'

'Don't do this, Lily.'

'Answer the question, will you?' She could do tough if it meant winning him over.

His sigh hung between them. 'Twelve months ago. I was having severe stomach pains. Turned out it was a false alarm.'

Bet he'd panicked then, too. 'You've had your share of medical dramas, Max.'

'I'm not afraid of getting sick or having surgery. It's the unknown I hate, especially when it comes to the people I hold dear.'

Sitting on the edge of the bed, she reached for his hand.

Max pulled away. 'Please, go back to work. I don't need you here.'

Low blow. But she was better than that. 'I get why you're worried, but I truly believe you've got the flu and nothing more. Your stomach could be aching because you're so worried, or because of that dinner you ate last night, or from fear about the future.'

'You might be right. I might be overreacting. But what if I'm right? I don't want you nursing me through it, being stuck with me no matter what. I care deeply for you, Lily, and that's why I have to let you go.'

Her head was shaking from side to side. She couldn't stand, she'd fall flat on her face. Her skin was cold, her heart hot and thumping. He cared deeply? Did that mean he loved her? Then he had just set himself up for a battle, and he was going to lose. 'Right.' Her forehead pulled tight as she arched one eyebrow. 'I hear you. Now I'm out of here.' For now. 'The waiting room opens again in fifteen.'

She'd reached the door when he spoke.

'Lily, I am so sorry.'

Gripping the doorframe to prevent herself rushing over and hugging him tight, she forced herself to smile and said, 'One step at a time, Max. Let's find out what's wrong first, shall we?'

'No, not we. Devlin's helping me. Don't come back

here. I'll see you when I return to work.' His voice broke and he turned to stare at the window.

Which was good because then he didn't see the stream of tears pouring down her face, leaving lines in her make-up. 'Bye, Max.' But not goodbye. She had his key. He needed food, and to be looked out for, and love. And there was plenty of that for him in her heart.

The afternoon dragged. More cases of flu, a referral to a cardiology department, a malaria recurrence, and the removal of sun damage by minor surgery kept Lily busy, and yet the minutes crept by.

'I saw Max at lunchtime,' she told Devlin when they had finally closed the doors and were having a coffee in his office.

'Thought you might've. How is he?'

'Physically or mentally?' If only she could bite her nails to relieve some of the tension holding her in a twist. She loved Max and he'd told her to get out of his life. 'He's a mess. I believe he's got the flu. He doesn't.'

'What about the stomach-ache he's been having?'

'Stress? Exhaustion?' She lifted one shoulder, let it drop. 'I—I don't know.'

'Neither do I, but I think you're right, it's flu.'

Lily waited but when Devlin remained quiet, her tongue got the better of her. 'He's so negative about his future. He doesn't want to love someone and then let them down by getting ill again. He doesn't want to take risks.' Only to Devlin could she talk about this.

He was watching her with something much too like sympathy in his expression.

A look she wasn't grateful for. 'I am going to fight him on this.'

'No surprise there.' Devlin paused, seemed to be collecting his thoughts. 'The problem is that Max is susceptible to overthinking his health when it's not perfect. Something many people who've had cancer go through. You have to wait this out, Lily.'

She lifted her head to look at the man who was like a second father. Her stomach rolled over. *He knew.* Knew she loved Max. Knew how hard she'd fight for him. 'Really?'

'First, he isn't your patient. Second, he's not going to allow you to stand with him while he waits to find out what's going on.' He began tapping at his keyboard.

'You can't tell me anything.' She accepted that. But, 'Are there any times I should be blocking out patient appointments over the coming days because of other commitments?'

'Like I said, I can't tell you anything. Now I think it's time we went home and relaxed after the hectic day we've all had.' He stood up and winked. 'Close my computer down for me, will you? I've got a call to make.'

After Devlin left his office, Lily stepped around his desk and read the screen in front of her. Max had an appointment for a CT scan at seven tomorrow and Declan had also ordered a CRP and a full blood count.

She sighed. The CT scan was the best scan for the condition, and there were nearly twenty-five hours before that was done. She'd have to be patient. But she could help Max in the meantime. He'd need dinner in some form, and there'd been little in his fridge or pantry that would be of any use. She'd hit the supermarket then deliver to his bedside.

He could say what he liked but she wasn't disappearing out of his life yet. If at all.

* * *

'I told you to stay away, Lily,' Max snapped, when he opened his front door to the strident rings that had gone on and on. He'd thought the taxi he'd ordered to take him to the radiology department at Auckland Central Hospital had got the time wrong. Bloody woman. It was hard enough knowing he'd kicked her out of his life, then finding food parcels in his fridge, without having her turning up on his doorstep and waving car keys in his face.

'Stop being a grump. I'm giving you a ride to your appointment, that's all. Nothing out of the ordinary for friends.' Her smile was small but genuine. She wasn't letting him off the hook.

Did he have to get mean and nasty to make what he'd said about their relationship sink in? 'There are taxis in this city. I have one coming in twenty minutes.'

'Then you'll have to cancel it. I'm taking you there and back. It will be quicker and more comfortable.'

How? The temperature outside was freezing. 'Oh, for goodness' sake, come inside.' Max stepped back, holding the door wide, slamming it shut the moment Lily stepped past him. 'This isn't going to get you anywhere, Lily. I meant what I said.'

She shrugged and carried on walking towards his lounge. 'I know you did.'

'So why are you here?'

She sat down on the couch and looked up at him. 'I love you, Max, and I won't give up on you because you are afraid of hurting me. I'm tough, I can take it. I will take it because I believe you care about me, too.'

He swallowed the bile that rose in his mouth. Lily loved him. He'd been hoping for that before the thought of being ill again had recurred. She loved him and he'd hurt her already. 'I...' He stopped. What could he say to make any of this better?

'I mean it. I love you, and that means whatever the outcome of your CT is, I'm here for you. I won't go away just because I'm hurting for you. Hurting for us. I am going to be there when you find out, and I'm going to be here for ever.'

His knees gave out and his butt hit the edge of the chair behind him. Gripping the edges, he pushed back onto it. 'You don't know what you're saying, what you're letting yourself in for.'

'Oh, yes, I do.' Lily stood up, and held out her hand. 'Come on. Let's go find out what's going on.'

CHAPTER TEN

LILY SAT RIGID on the plastic chair in the waiting room, barely daring to breathe.

Max had been gone ages. CTs didn't take this long. What was going on? Had they found a tumour? If that was the case, why hadn't he asked for her to join him while the doctor discussed it? Had he gone out another door to get away from facing up to her with the horrific news?

'Lily?' A pair of familiar, jeans-clad legs appeared in her line of sight.

Deep breath. Her hands clenched.

'Lily, look at me.'

Slowly raising her head, she found Max's gaze on her and a small smile on his lips. 'Tell me.'

'No tumour.'

'Truly?' He wouldn't be smiling if there was.

'Truly.' He reached a hand out. 'Take me home?'

Home. 'Meaning?'

His smile faded.

So did the glimmer of hope that had begun to rise in her heart. 'I see.' Ignoring his hand, she pushed off the chair and headed for the door. 'Come on.'

It was a silent trip home. Silent and tense. When she

pulled up in his driveway she said, 'I'm coming in for a coffee.'

'Don't do this to yourself, Lily.'

She shoved her door open and got out, waited impatiently for Max to do the same before pinging the lock.

Once inside she put the coffee on as though it was her place to do so. 'Sit down before you fall down.' He mightn't have cancer, but that flu was punishing him. And *she* hadn't started on him yet.

When the coffee was ready and they were sitting at the table with a mug each, Lily drew a deep breath and reminded herself why she wasn't giving up. She loved Max and would do anything for him. As well as making him get over the past and move on, even if it didn't include her. 'You are letting yourself down, Max.'

'You think so?'

'Come on. Haven't we been great together these past weeks? Think about the times we've spent talking and laughing, enjoying meals, being a couple.'

'I have thought of exactly the same things.'

'You were happy with me? You did start looking forward to a future you'd hidden from yourself?'

'Ye-es.'

'Then think about the camp. About those kids and how each and every one of them got up after being knocked down physically or mentally to carry on. How they wouldn't let anything keep them from trying for what they want.' Her hands shook too much to lift the mug so she gripped them together in her lap. 'Didn't they show you anything?'

Max reached across to touch her arm. 'Hope. Strength. Love for life.'

'Where's yours, Max?'

'Lily, you don't understand how it hurts me to hurt you.'

'You're saying you love me?' Thump, thump. Please mean that. Please.

'I'm saying we're over.'

Lily sagged forward. *Here I go again. What's so wrong with me that men don't stay around?*

Pain bashed at her. She loved him. So much so she'd begun to feel he might just be starting to reciprocate her feelings. And he'd pulled the plug. Did that mean he didn't care for her? Or that he did and was afraid to follow through? Wasn't that idea just her being overly hopeful? When she'd already been here and knew the outcome? No, not this time. She wasn't accepting this. Not yet. Not so quickly or easily. But first she had to get away, think it through, not react blindly to a past pain. Not let this man walk away without a fight because others had done that.

Her face had blanched. Her eyes were dark with sadness and, yes, anger.

Max felt sick to his toes. But how else did he get through to her?

Silence stretched between them.

Finally he had to fill it. 'You've got nothing to say, have you?' Pain lashed at his heart. He did not want Lily to walk away, yet she had to.

'Until you start accepting you have a rosy future if you're brave enough to grab it with both hands and make the most of it, you are going to be unhappy.' With that, she walked out of his house, quietly snicking the lock shut behind her.

Leaving him aching to hold her, desperate for them to be together, sharing the night in his bed. His lonely bed, where he now headed after swallowing a handful of painkillers.

The house creaked, highlighting his aloneness. No, damn it. Loneliness. For the first time in his adult life he missed the company of someone in his house as they went about everyday things. While he lay in bed and then got up to eat and return to the warmth of his duvet. There were the days Lily had arrived with prepared meals, talked with him, laughed over stupid stories of his or her past, discussed what they both hoped for in their futures at the medical hub. It had been real and fun, honest and hopeful.

Now she'd walked out without kissing him, without a speech about drinking lots of water and taking his pills.

He mustn't forget this was Lily Scott. She'd changed, but there was no denying she was still that strong, independent woman who always followed her own heart, looking out for others along the way. Like Josie. Putting her niece's needs before her own. He'd seen her do the same with patients, years ago and recently.

Lily had put him first since he'd come down with the flu. She'd seen through his fear and basically, kindly, told him to get over it. He'd been given a second chance and he was wasting it. His words, her meaning.

His heart thumped once, hard and painfully. Lily Scott. Since his first day on duty as a junior doctor in Auckland Central Hospital's emergency department she'd been a thorn in his side. Annoying, frustrating, aloof, sexy and tormenting. And a hundred other things. He'd thought he'd forgotten her when she'd left the department, but in reality he never had. She'd been there, under the surface, leaping up into his consciousness the moment he'd heard her name and realised they were going to work at the same clinic. With that came the memories. Bad, great and everything in between.

Lily was in his psyche. Like it or not. Like? Try love. Yeah, he'd gone and fallen head over feet in love with Lily. He had a choice to make. He'd done it earlier then backed off in a flaming hurry. This time he had to be one hundred percent certain. Did he take a chance on the future he'd been handed by the specialists and his own determination to survive, and declare his love to her, ask for a life together, share the raising of their child, children even? Or...his chest rose then fell...move away out of her life and that of her baby that she'd have and adore for ever?

A sour taste came to his mouth. He couldn't do that. Not without trying to convince her he was worthy of her, and would stick with her through whatever the future threw at them. The good and the not so good. Even if... Another long breath. Even if the cancer returned and wreaked havoc on him. Them. They were both strong, together they'd be resilient. They'd have a rock-solid, loving relationship.

Was he ready to commit to life with Lily? Regardless of how she felt about him, he had to be certain this love was for real, for ever, before he did anything about it.

'Make an appointment to see me in a week's time,' Max told his patient. 'I want to see how you're coping with the new diet regime.' The middle-aged woman had a fasting glucose of ten mmol/L.

'I started the day you phoned to say my blood result was indicative of diabetes. I'm walking every day.'

'That's good, Meryl, but I'd like to keep an eye on you until you're used to the new routine. Any time you're uncertain about anything you can talk to our nurses, too. I've seen patients start out well then falter after the tedium sets in. This is a life-changer, not something you do for a few weeks.'

'I understand. I have been reading about diabetes and how other people manage. It's a bit scary.' She stood up and headed for the door. 'I'll make an appointment when I pay for today.'

Max headed out to the waiting room. 'Bill, come in.' He watched as his sixty-five-year-old patient limped across the room. 'That hip's getting worse. I'm going to refer you to an orthopaedic surgeon,' he said as Bill settled onto a chair by his desk.

'It's still good enough. I get around fine. I only came for a repeat prescription of the anti-inflammatory.'

Max shook his head. Stubborn old guy. 'Get up on the bed so I can check that hip out thoroughly.'

Bill dropped his jeans, hobbled over to the bed and hauled himself onto it to lie down. 'I'm still mowing the lawns, going to the gym and riding my cycle to work.'

'From one to ten, ten being the highest, what's the pain level now?'

'Five…six.'

Max didn't believe him. Pain had reflected out of his eyes as he'd stood up from the chair. 'When you ride to work?'

Bill sighed. 'Eight. On a good day.'

'Lie on your good side, please.' Max lifted Bill's leg with the damaged hip and watched Bill's face for a reaction. He didn't move it far. 'Now I'm going to rotate your leg gently. Tell me if it's too painful.'

'You can stop before you start,' Bill grunted. 'You win. How long do I have to wait for an op?'

'That'll be up to the surgeon and whether you go private or public.'

'I've got health insurance so I won't have to hang about on the public list.'

'Good. You can get up.' He wasn't going to inflict any more discomfort on him. Bill knew as well as he did that hip needed to be replaced sooner rather than later. 'I'll refer you to one of the surgeons next door, unless you have a preference.'

'You know best, Max.' Bill gasped as he shoved his bad leg into his jeans.

'That's settled, then. I'll write a prescription, too. Anything else you need to talk about?' Max brought up the correct screen.

'No, I'm good to go. You've given me enough of a shock already.'

'You really weren't thinking the time for surgery was close?'

'I was hoping it wasn't. I get around all right. There are people far worse off than me who aren't getting their hips done.' Bill looked baffled.

'I can't answer for them, though I know you seriously need to have this done. You won't know yourself afterwards and will wonder why you waited so long.' Scrawling his signature on the prescription printout, he handed it to his patient. 'I'll get that referral away today. And go easy on the bike. It wouldn't help to fall off and damage that hip any further.'

Bill ignored that, pocketed his script and headed for the door. 'Thanks, Max. I'll be seeing you.'

Leaning back in his chair, Max flicked a pen back and forth between his fingers. Bill had been his last patient for the day. For the week. Damn, he was tired. The flu had done its number on him, but this past week had been more about lack of sleep. About thinking about Lily and how impossible it would be to carry on without her in his life, at his side. In other words, he was a fool to deny himself love and a happy future. Lily made him happy, made him look at his choices differently and want to change them so he could have that future—with her. He did love her, every little and big thing about her. The future looked bleak without her in it. *Would she have him now?* The big question that kept him awake too much. There was only one way to find out.

'You staying there, daydreaming, all night?' Devlin asked from the doorway. 'Or are you joining the rest of us for a drink?'

'Neither. I'm heading home. There are things I need to do.'

'Like talk to Lily.'

Max's head snapped up and he stared at Devlin. 'Lily?'

'Yes, the woman you've been doing your best to avoid and when you can't avoid her have been friendly with in an offhand manner.'

'I was that obvious?' What did Lily think after all she'd done for him when he'd been ill?

'I've known Lily most of her life. I can read her well and she's confused about you.'

Ouch. That hurt. 'I see.'

'Do you?' Devlin was sounding like a father figure, not the medical hub's boss. 'If so, then fix what's holding you both back from being happy.'

Pushing up from his chair, Max picked up his jacket and bag. 'I intend to.'

Lily wasn't at her apartment when Max got there. She wasn't there an hour later when he tried again, driving through a torrential downpour that had flooded roads, with his windscreen wipers unable to cope. When he finally made it back home she wasn't answering her phone either. She could be anywhere, but he suspected he knew exactly where she'd gone.

It was too dangerous to drive far at the moment. He could only hope that Lily had reached Whangaparaoa before the weather bomb hit. Or it had given that area a miss. He'd take to the road at first light.

The weather had played havoc with the roads and maintenance crews were out in force, causing traffic delays that had Max's blood fizzing with frustration.

The first sound he heard on opening the car door was a chainsaw. 'What else?' He grinned and followed the sound across the road to look along the beach.

There Lily was, brandishing the saw, slicing trunks as though they were butter before throwing them out of the way to attack the next section of tree. She looked wonderful. In her element. In control. Being physical. Being useful. Helping the men who were loading a trailer with the results of her efforts.

Max's heart fluttered. He loved her with all his being. This was the woman he wanted to love for ever, to marry, to have a family with. To take chances with and come out the other side stronger and happier than ever. 'I love you, Lily Scott.'

Back at the car, he replaced his shoes with work boots and tossed his jacket onto the seat before striding along to help out, receiving a surprised but heart-warming smile from Lily as he reached for the first log.

After nearly an hour Lily stopped the saw for the final

time. 'Job done.' She high fived the other men, and finally him.

'Thanks for that, Lily,' George said. 'I reckon we've all got enough firewood to last next winter as well.'

'How've you been?' Archie asked Max.

'I'm good. How's Enid getting on?'

'She's fighting. The progress is slow but she's started heading in the right direction. Still be some time before she comes home, though.'

'Glad to hear things are working out.'

Lily stood beside him. 'You coming to my place?'

It was why he was there. 'Yes.' He picked up the chainsaw in one hand and took her hand in the other. 'I have something to tell you.'

Her eyes widened. 'Something good, I hope.'

'Yes.'

Nothing more was said until they'd removed boots, washed hands and walked into the kitchen–cum-family room and stood by the warm fire box.

'Coffee?' Lily asked.

Coffee took time to make. He couldn't wait another minute. 'I've been an idiot, Lily.'

One eyebrow rose and she laughed sadly. 'You're telling me?'

'I love you.'

The laughter died, the eyebrow returned to its usual place. Questions filled her eyes. She stared at him, not moving closer or further away.

Not the response he'd hoped for. His blood flow slowed. His heart was heavy. Dread crept in where there'd been happiness. He'd told the truth. He needed her to know that. He wouldn't repeat himself. That would sound pathetic. He waited.

'I love you, too, Max,' she said quietly, softly, her voice filled with longing. 'Right from the day we saw each other again after those long years. I wasn't certain, but it felt like love. Love so different from what I've known before. Love for you. It came as a shock to find I might've always felt something for you and had been denying it all along.'

He reached for her and bent close. 'You talk too much.' His mouth took hers, and he kissed her, deeply and filled with what was in his heart. With what he couldn't put into words.

And she kissed him back with what she had managed to say. Love. Her arms wound around him, holding him tight against her.

He melted into her. His love. The one woman who'd got to him, who'd shown him he didn't have to be alone. He did believe in a future with her. Pulling back just enough to look into her eyes, he asked, 'Will you marry me?'

Her smile lit up her eyes. 'Yes.'

His heart picked up its pace. 'Will we raise babies together?'

'Yes.'

'Be together for ever?' He could believe in for ever if Lily was at his side.

'Absolutely.' She stretched up and returned to kissing him.

Kissing wasn't enough. By a long way. Sweeping Lily up into his arms, he headed down the hall to make love. Make love, not have sex. A permanent relationship, not a fling. He'd found his love, his future, his happiness. Now all he had to do was make sure Lily never tired of him, starting by showing her how important she was. 'I love you, Lily Scott. So much my heart is singing.'

'That the noise I can hear?' She smiled up at him, her hand on his cheek. 'I've been wanting to tell you how much I love you and now, well, now you know. This is perfect.'

And it was. Max only got out of bed during the next couple of hours to get a bottle of champagne to celebrate. 'To us.'

'To us.' Lily tapped her glass against his. 'To for ever.'

EPILOGUE

Six months later

TEARS POURED DOWN Lily's cheeks. To heck with the make-up. The look of amazement and wonder on Max's face scrunched her stomach, tore at her heart and lifted her mouth into the biggest smile. 'We've done it,' she whispered. 'We're having a daughter in June.'

Max's cheeks were equally wet as he gazed down at the slight bump at the front of her gown. 'We have, Lily, darling, we have.' He was squeezing her hand, and smiling as if he'd got everything he wanted in life.

They had. Together. As warmth from the sun touched her shoulders, Lily looked up at the blue expanse high above, dotted with gulls dive-bombing the sea beyond her family beach house. 'A perfect day.'

'Not a chainsaw to be heard.' Max leaned in and kissed her cheek. 'You look beautiful.'

Brushing a hand down the front of her cream wedding dress with the full skirt and fitted bodice that accentuated her breasts, she smiled. She had to be the luckiest woman in the world.

'Shall we do this?' Charlotte appeared before them.

'Absolutely,' Lily and Max said in unison, then laughed.

Charlotte had a license to be a marriage celebrant as well as her other qualifications. Now she held up an empty wine glass and tapped it with a silver rod. 'Listen up, everyone. We're about to get underway with the reason you're all here.' She paused to allow everyone to quieten.

Lily looked around at the rows of white fabric-covered chairs with peonies tied to the corners, and felt her heart swelling. Her family and Max's, including his father, just about everyone from the medical hub, friends, and of course Josie and Ollie were here to share their special day. Logan and Michelle stood holding hands at the edge of the group. There was something about the air in Whangaparaoa—romance seemed to take over, putting people together.

Another tapping of silver on glass, and Lily's breasts rose on an intake of that magical air.

Charlotte grinned at her. 'Let's do it.' She handed Lily the sheet of paper with her vows, but Lily knew them by heart.

'Max.' She reached for his free hand. 'We didn't make it easy for ourselves, but it has been a journey I'll never forget or regret. Along the way I saw your strength, care and kindness, your big heart and most of all your love. I have found my soul mate. I love you with all my heart. Thank you for what you've given me.' She stretched up and kissed him, a salty kiss that was gentle and full of all she had to give him.

'Thanks, sweetheart,' he whispered against her lips, before straightening up and taking his vows from Charlotte. 'Lily Scott, I love you. You've turned my life around, and for that I give you everything. I can't promise to be perfect, but I'll do my best, and I will always love you. And our daughter, and any brothers or sisters she may have in the future.' He got down on one knee. 'Thank you for accepting me into your life.'

Bending down, she kissed him again, then held his hand as he stood up.

Charlotte was wiping a hand across her eyes. 'That's enough.'

Behind them everyone laughed.

'Now you can swap wedding rings.'

Max dug into his pocket and withdrew a box from which he withdrew a gold band. 'Lily, with this ring I pledge to love and cherish you, to care for and protect you for ever as my wife.' The ring slid onto her finger without a hitch.

She stared at it. It felt so right. Perfect. Charlotte was handing her a similar box. Taking out the ring, she reached for Max's hand. 'Max, I pledge to honour and care for you for ever.' She locked her eyes on his, and saw he knew she meant for ever, no getting sick. 'I love you, as my friend, my lover, my fiancé and about-to-be husband.' She had to push the ring hard to get it over his knuckle.

Charlotte grinned. 'I am so happy to say this. I now declare Lily and Max husband and wife. I give you Mr and Mrs Bryant.'

Loud cheers burst out and they were surrounded by everyone, hugging and rejoicing. Until Josie interrupted with a loud call. 'Uncle Max.'

Lily laughed. 'Uncle Max.'

Josie had abandoned her wheelchair for crutches today. She came up to stand in front of her new uncle. 'Welcome to the family.'

Just as Max started to smile, she added, 'Auntie Lily is special. Don't ever hurt her or there'll be trouble from me.'

Max gaped, then roared with laughter. 'I wouldn't dare.' He pulled her into a long hug as all around them laughter filled the air.

Locking his eyes on Lily, he smiled. 'We've done it. I love you.'

* * * * *

MILLS & BOON

Coming next month

A PUP TO RESCUE THEIR HEARTS
Alison Roberts

'Off the sofa, Lucky,' he commanded. 'We've talked about this before, haven't we?'

Lucky jumping down was enough to break that stillness for Stevie. She was moving further away from him – towards the fireplace.

'This mantlepiece...' She stepped onto the flagstone hearth to reach up and touch the massive beam of wood that was embedded in the wall. 'It looks like a whole tree trunk. It's incredible. How old *is* your house?'

'Dates to about mid-eighteenth century I believe. The wood burner doesn't look too out of place, though, does it?'

'It's gorgeous. And I love how you can stack the logs on either side like that. Did the flue from the log burner just go inside the original chimney?'

She was leaning in, to peer up into the space and Josh didn't think to warn her not to touch the inside of the chimney. It hadn't occurred to him that there could still be some ancient soot clinging to stonework until Stevie straightened and pushed that curl back off her face, leaving a huge, black streak in its place.

'Oh, no...'

'What? Have I got something on my face?' Stevie was touching her nose now, and then her cheek and then she saw her fingers and laughed.

'Don't move...' Josh walked past the fireplace to where the living room led into his kitchen. He grabbed a clean tea towel, ran it under the tap and went back to Stevie who used it to wipe her hands and then her face.

'Have I got it all?'

'Almost.'

Without thinking, Josh reached out and used the pad of his thumb to wipe a remnant of smudge from her cheek. Close to her mouth. So close, he could feel the corners of her lips. And how incredibly soft her skin was... It was his turn to stop in his tracks, suddenly overwhelmed with what he could feel. And see. The way Stevie's gaze was locked on his, the way those gloriously tawny eyes darkened and...oh, man... the way her lips had parted again. And this time, he just knew that she *was* waiting to be kissed.

That she *wanted* to be kissed.

Continue reading
A PUP TO RESCUE THEIR HEARTS
Alison Roberts

Available next month
www.millsandboon.co.uk

COMING SOON!

We really hope you enjoyed reading this book.
If you're looking for more romance, be sure to
head to the shops when new books are
available on

Thursday 21st January

To see which titles are coming soon, please visit

millsandboon.co.uk/nextmonth

WE'RE LOOKING FOR NEW AUTHORS FOR THE MILLS & BOON MEDICAL SERIES!

Whether you're a published author or an aspiring one, our editors would love to read your story.

You can submit the synopsis and first three chapters of your novel online, and find out more about the series, at **harlequin.submittable.com/submit**

We read all submissions and you do not need to have an agent to submit.

IF YOU'RE INTERESTED, WHY NOT HAVE A GO?

Submit your story at:
harlequin.submittable.com/submit

MILLS & BOON

LET'S TALK
Romance

For exclusive extracts, competitions
and special offers, find us online:

- facebook.com/millsandboon
- @MillsandBoon
- @MillsandBoonUK

Get in touch on 01413 063232

For all the latest titles coming soon, visit
millsandboon.co.uk/nextmonth

MILLS & BOON

THE HEART OF ROMANCE

A ROMANCE FOR EVERY KIND OF READER

MODERN

Prepare to be swept off your feet by sophisticated, sexy and seductive heroes, in some of the world's most glamourous and romantic locations, where power and passion collide.
8 stories per month.

HISTORICAL

Escape with historical heroes from time gone by. Whether your passion is for wicked Regency Rakes, muscled Vikings or rugged Highlanders, awaken the romance of the past.
6 stories per month.

MEDICAL

Set your pulse racing with dedicated, delectable doctors in the high-pressure world of medicine, where emotions run high and passion, comfort and love are the best medicine.
6 stories per month.

True Love

Celebrate true love with tender stories of heartfelt romance, from the rush of falling in love to the joy a new baby can bring, and a focus on the emotional heart of a relationship.
8 stories per month.

Desire

Indulge in secrets and scandal, intense drama and plenty of sizzling hot action with powerful and passionate heroes who have it all: wealth, status, good looks…everything but the right woman.
6 stories per month.

HEROES

Experience all the excitement of a gripping thriller, with an intense romance at its heart. Resourceful, true-to-life women and strong, fearless men face danger and desire - a killer combination!
8 stories per month.

DARE

Sensual love stories featuring smart, sassy heroines you'd want as a best friend, and compelling intense heroes who are worthy of them.
4 stories per month.

To see which titles are coming soon, please visit

millsandboon.co.uk/nextmonth